Sofia's Secret

Sofia's Secret

SHARLENE MacLAREN

WHITAKER
HOUSE

Publisher's Note:

This novel is a work of fiction. References to real events, organizations, or places are used in a fictional context. Any resemblances to actual persons, living or dead, are entirely coincidental.

Unless otherwise indicated, all Scripture quotations are taken from the King James Version of the Holy Bible. The Scripture quotations on pages 172, 173, and 175 are from the American Standard Edition of the Revised Version of the Holy Bible.

SOFIA'S SECRET

Book Three in the River of Hope Series

Sharlene MacLaren
www.sharlenemaclaren.com

ISBN: 978-1-60374-214-6
Printed in the United States of America
© 2012 by Sharlene MacLaren

Whitaker House
1030 Hunt Valley Circle
New Kensington, PA 15068
www.whitakerhouse.com

Library of Congress Cataloging-in-Publication Data (Pending)

1 2 3 4 5 6 7 8 9 10   LU   18 17 16 15 14 13 12

Dedication

To Mason Jax Tisdel.
When you came to us on October 22, 2011, this
grandma could not get the smile off of her face for days.
You are a heart stealer, you handsome little man.

Chapter One

June 1930
Wabash, Indiana

The sacrifices of God are a broken spirit:
a broken and a contrite heart, O God,
thou wilt not despise.
—Psalm 51:17

The blazing sun ducked behind a cloud, granting a smidgeon of relief to Sofia Rogers as she compressed the pedal to stop her bike in front of Murphy's Market and, in a most inelegant manner, slid off the seat, taking care not to catch the hem of her loose-fitting dress in the bicycle chain. She scanned the street in both directions, hoping not to run into anyone she knew, then parked the rusting yellow bike next to a Ford truck. These days, she dreaded coming into town, but she couldn't very well put off the chore much longer if she wanted to keep food on the table.

Her younger brother, Andy, had won the race to their destination. His equally corroded bike leaned against the building, and he stood next to it, his arms crossed, a burlap sack slung across one shoulder. As she approached, a smug grin etched his freckled face. "Didn't I t-tell you I'd b-beat you?"

"That's because you had a full minute head start on me, you rascal." Sofie might have added that her present condition did not permit the speed and agility she'd once had, but she wasn't about to make that excuse. "Just you wait. I'll win on the way back home."

"N-not if I can help it."

She pressed the back of her hand to her hot, damp face and stepped up to the sidewalk. "We'll see about that, Mr. Know-It-All."

Andy pointed at her and laughed. "Now your face is all d-dirty."

She looked at her hands, still soiled from working in the garden that morning, and frowned. "I guess I should have lathered them a little better when I washed up." She bent over and used the hem of her skirt to wipe her cheek before straightening. "There. Is that better?"

He tilted his face and angled her a crooked grin. "Sort of."

"Oh, who cares?" She tousled his rust-colored hair. "Come on, let's get started checking those items off my shopping list."

They headed for the door, but a screeching horn drew their attention to the street, where a battered jalopy slowed at the curb. Several teenage boys, their heads poking out through the windows, whistled and hollered. "Hey, sister! Hear you like to have a good time!"

At their crudeness, Sofie felt a suffocating pressure in her chest. With a hand on her brother's shoulder, she watched the car round the bend, as the boys' whoops faded into the distance.

"Who were those guys?"

"Nobody important."

As if the baby inside her fully agreed, she got a strong push to the rib cage that jarred her and made her stumble.

"You alright?" Andy grabbed her elbow, looking mature beyond his eleven years.

She paused to take a deep breath and then let it out slowly, touching a hand to her abdomen. Even in her seventh month, she could scarcely fathom carrying a tiny human in her womb, let alone accept all of the kicks and punches he or she had started doling out on a daily basis. She'd read several books to know what to expect as she progressed, but none of them had come close to explaining why she already felt so deeply in love with the tiny life inside of her. Considering that she hadn't consented to the act committed against her, she should have resented the little life, but how could she hold an innocent baby accountable? "I'm fine," she finally assured her brother. "Let's go inside, shall we?"

Inside Murphy's Market, a few people ambled up and down the two narrow aisles, toting cloth bags or shopping baskets. Sofie kept her left hand out of view as much as possible, in hopes of avoiding the condemnation of anyone who noticed the absence of a wedding band on her left ring finger. Not that she particularly cared what other folks thought, but she'd grown weary of the condescending stares. Several women had tried to talk her into giving the infant up for adoption, including Margie Grant, an old friend who had served as a mother figure to her and Andy ever since their parents had perished in a train wreck in 1924. "The little one growing inside you is the result of an insidious attack, darling. I shouldn't think you'd want much to do with it once it's born," Margie had said. "I happen to know more than a few childless couples right here in Wabash who would be thrilled to take it off your hands. You should really consider adoption."

Because Margie had long been a loyal friend, Sofie had confided in her about the assault, including when and where it had occurred. As for going to the authorities and demanding an investigation—never! Margie had begged her to go straight to Sheriff Morris, but she had refused, and then had made Margie swear on the Bible not to go herself.

"That is a hard promise to make, dearest," Margie had conceded with wrinkled brow, "but I will promise to keep my lips buttoned. As for adoption, if you gave the baby to a nice couple in town, you would have the opportunity to watch it grow up. That would bring you comfort, I should think, especially if you selected a well-deserving Christian couple."

"I can't imagine giving my baby away to someone in my hometown, Christian or not."

"Well then, we'll go to one of the neighboring towns," the woman had persisted. "Think about it, sweetheart. You don't have the means to raise a child. Why, you and Andy are barely making ends meet as it is. Who's going to take care of it while you're at work?"

"I can't think about that right now, Margie. And, please, don't refer to my child as an 'it.'"

The woman's face had softened then, and she'd enfolded Sofie in her arms. "Well, of course, I know your baby's not an 'it,' honey. But, until he or she is born, I have no notion what to call it—I mean, him or her."

"'The baby' will do fine."

Margie had given her a little squeeze, then dropped her hands to her sides and shot her a pleading gaze. "I sure wish you'd tell me who did this to you. It's a crime, you know, what he did."

Yes, it had been a crime—the most reprehensible sort. And it was both a blessing and a curse that Sofie couldn't remember the details. The last thing she could remember was drinking her habitual cup of coffee at Spic-and-Span Cleaning Service before starting her evening rounds. She'd thought it tasted unusually bitter, but she'd shrugged it off at the time. Half an hour later—at the site of her job that night, at the law offices of Baker & Baker—she'd been overcome by dizziness and collapsed. She'd teetered in and out of consciousness, with only a vague notion of what was going on. When she'd awakened, it had been daylight, and she was sore all over. Fortunately, it had been a Saturday, and the offices were closed; no one had discovered her lying there, nauseous and trembling, her dress torn, her hair disheveled. A particular ache had given her a clue as to what had gone on while she'd been unconscious. As the sickening reality had set in, she'd found beside her the note that had haunted her ever since.

*Breathe one word about this and you can
say bye-bye to your brother.*

It had been typed on the official letterhead of the sheriff's office, making her even less inclined to go to the authorities. Whoever had assaulted her had connections to the law, and she wasn't about to risk her brother's life to find out his identity. Plus, without a name, and with no visual or auditory recollection, she had nothing to offer that would aid an investigation.

By the time she realized she'd gotten pregnant, two months had passed—too late to go crying to the authorities. Not that she'd planned to. Her attacker's threat had been enough to keep her quiet. She could bear the scorn and the shame, as long as he left her alone. And the only way of ensuring that was to comply with his demands. No, she couldn't say anything more about it to Margie.

"Margie, we've been over this. It's better left unsaid, believe me."

"But, don't you know people are going to talk? Who knows what they'll think or say when you start to show? If they learned the truth, perhaps they'd go a little easier on you."

"No! I can't. No one must know—not even you. I'm sorry, Margie."

Margie had rubbed the back of her neck as if trying to work out a kink. A loud breath had blown past her lips and whistled across Sofie's cheek. "You know I love you, and so I will honor your wishes...for now." Then, her index finger had shot up in the air, nearly poking Sofie in the nose. "But if he so much as comes within an inch of you again, I want you to tell me right away, you hear? I can't abide thinking that he'll come knocking at your door. You must promise me, Sofia Mae Rogers!"

Sofie had hidden the shiver that had rustled through her veins at the mere thought of crossing paths with her attacker again. Why, every time she went to work, she couldn't get the awful pounding in her chest to slow its pace until she was home again. She'd stopped drinking and eating at work—anywhere other than at home, really.

"Show me your list, Sofie." Andy's voice drew her out of her fretful thoughts. She reached inside her pocket and handed over the paper. When he set off down an aisle, she idly followed after, her mind drifting back into its musings.

❦

Dr. Elijah Trent parked his grandfather's 1928 Ford Model A in the lot beside Murphy's Market. As he climbed out, he was careful not to allow his door to collide with a bicycle standing nearby. Another battered bike leaned against the building. It looked as if it could use some serious repair work. He closed his door and took a deep breath of hot June air, then cast a glance overhead at the row of birds roosting on a clothesline that stretched between two apartment buildings across the street.

When he pulled open the whiny screen door, an array of aromas teased his nostrils, from freshly ground coffee beans to roasted peanuts in a barrel. As he stepped inside, a floorboard shrieked beneath his feet, as if to substantiate its long-term use.

"Afternoon," said the shopkeeper, who glanced up from the cash register, where he stood, ringing up an order for a young pregnant woman. Beside her, a boy dutifully stuffed each item into a cloth bag. The young woman raised her head and glanced briefly at Eli, who sensed a certain tenseness in her chestnut-colored eyes. Then, she shifted her gaze back to the clerk.

"Say, ain't you Doc Trent's grandson?" the man asked.

"That I am, sir. Elijah Trent. But most people call me Eli."

The clerk stopped ringing items for a moment and gave him an up-and-down glance. "Heard you're takin' over the old fellow's practice. That's mighty fine o' you. I understand you graduated with honors from the University of Michigan, an' you worked at a Detroit hospital for two years, but you were itchin' for small-town livin'. Timing's good, since Doc's retirin'. S'pose you two been plannin' this for quite a while now, eh? Hate to see Wilson Trent retire, but most folks seem to think it'll be good to get in some new blood. Get it? Blood?" He gave a hearty chortle, causing his rotund chest to jiggle up and down.

Eli smiled at the friendly man. "It sounds like Grandfather's been keeping everyone well-informed."

"He sure has. Plus, the *Plain Dealer* wrote up that article 'bout you."

"Yes, I heard that."

The woman shifted her narrow frame and fingered one of her short, brown curls, but she kept her eyes focused on the counter. Beside her, the freckle-faced youngster poked his head around the back of her and met Elijah's gaze. They stared at each other for all of three seconds, but when Eli smiled, the boy quickly looked forward again.

As the clerk resumed ringing up their order, Eli reached inside his hip pocket and grabbed the short list his grandfather had scrawled in his somewhat shaky handwriting. In Detroit, he'd taken most of his meals at the hospital. Helping his grandfather in the kitchen would be an entirely new experience. At least it would be only temporary, until Grandfather's housekeeper of twenty-odd years, Winifred Carmichael, returned from her two-week vacation out West.

"You lookin' for anythin' in particular?" the clerk asked.

"Nothing I can't find on my own, sir."

"Pick up one o' them baskets by the door for stashin' what you need. Name's Harold, by the way. Harold Murphy. I've owned this place goin' on thirty years now."

Eli bent to pick up a basket. He hadn't thought to bring along a sack in which to carry the items home. The store he had occasioned in Detroit had offered brown paper bags, but the trend didn't seem to have caught on in Wabash just yet. "Yes, I recall coming here with my grandmother as a kid."

"And I remember you, as well, with that sandy hair o' yours and that there dimple in your chin."

"Is that so? You have a good memory, Mr. Murphy."

A pleased expression settled on the clerk's face. "You used to ogle my candy jars and tug at your grandmother's arm. 'Course, she'd always give in. She couldn't resist your pleadin'. Seems to me you always managed to wrangle some chewin' gum out o' her before I finished ringin' her order."

"It's amazing you remember that."

"Well, some things just stick in my memory for no particular reason." He glanced across the counter at the freckle-faced boy. "Young Andy, here, he's the Hershey's chocolate bar type. Ain't that right, Andy?"

The lad's head jerked up, and he looked from Mr. Murphy to the woman beside him. "Yes, sir. C-c-can I g-get one today, Sofie?"

Her slender shoulders lifted and drooped with a labored sigh. "I suppose, but don't expect any other treats today."

"I won't."

The brief tête-à-tête allowed Eli the chance to disappear down an aisle in search of the first item on his list: sugar. He found it about the same time the screen door whined open once more, with the exit of the young woman and the boy. Next, Eli spotted the bread at the end of the aisle. He picked up a loaf and nestled it in the basket, next to the box of sugar.

"Well, I think it's plain disgraceful, her coming into town and flaunting herself like that. My stars, has she not an ounce of decency? And what, pray tell, is she teaching that brother of hers by not keeping herself concealed?"

"I must agree, it's quite appalling," said another.

Eli's ears perked up at the sound of female scoffs coming from the other side of the shelving unit at the back of the store. He stilled, slanted his head, and leaned forward. If he could push a few cans and boxed goods to the side without creating a commotion, he might manage a partial view of the gossips.

"I always did wonder about her and that pitiable little brother of hers, living all alone on the far edge of town. No telling what sort of man put her in a motherly way. Why, if I were in her place, I'd have gone off to stay with some relative in another state. One would think she'd have somewhere she could go. She could have birthed the child, given it to some worthy family, and come back to Wabash, and no one would've been the wiser."

The other gossip cleared her throat. "Perchance her 'lover' won't hear of her leaving, and she doesn't dare defy him. She always did come off as rather defenseless, wouldn't you say?"

"Yes, yes, and very reclusive. Never was one to join any charity groups or ladies' circles. Why, she doesn't even attend church, to my knowledge. As I said before, the whole thing is disgraceful."

Eli shuffled around the corner and stopped at the end of the next row, where he picked up a couple of cans of beans, even though they weren't on Grandfather's list, and dropped them into his basket with a clatter. The chattering twosome immediately fell silent. Eli cast a casual glance in their direction, and he almost laughed at their poses of feigned nonchalance. One was studying the label on a box, while the other merely stared at a lower shelf, her index finger pressed to her chin.

When Eli started down the aisle, both of them looked up, so he nodded. "Afternoon, ladies."

The more buxom of the two batted her eyelashes and plumped her graying hair, then nearly blinded him with a fulsome smile. "Well, good afternoon to you." She put a hand to her throat. "My goodness. You're Doc Trent's grandson?"

"Yes, ma'am."

"Well, I'll be. I overheard you talking with Harold, but I didn't lay eyes on you until now." She perused him up and down. "You sure are a handsome devil."

"Oh, for mercy's sake, Bessie, mind your manners." The second woman bore a blush of embarrassment. "Don't pay her any heed, Doctor. She's such a tease." She extended a hand. "I'm Clara Morris, the sheriff's wife, and this is Bessie Lloyd. Her husband owns Lloyd's Shoe Store, over on Market Street. Welcome to Wabash, Dr. Trent. We read about your impending arrival in the newspaper. I hope you find yourself feeling right at home here."

"I'm sure I will." Eli shifted his shopping basket and extended a hand first to Mrs. Morris, then to the annoying Mrs. Lloyd. He would have liked to remind them that two upstanding women in the community ought to put a lock on their lips, lest they tarnish their own reputations, but he hadn't come to Wabash with the intention of making instant enemies, so he restrained himself. "Nice meeting you ladies. You have a good day, now."

He glanced to his left and, seeing a shelf with maple syrup, snatched a can and tossed it into his basket. Casting the women one last smile, he headed down the aisle in search of the remaining items.

"My, my," he heard Mrs. Lloyd mutter. "I think it may be time for me to switch physicians."

"But you've been seeing Dr. Stewart for years," Mrs. Morris said. "What about your bad knee?"

"Pfff, never mind that. I'd much rather look into that young man's blue eyes and handsome face than Dr. Stewart's haggard mug. Why, if I were younger...."

Eli picked up his pace and made it out of earshot before she finished her statement.

Several minutes later, he'd rounded up everything on his list, so he made his way to the cash register. As he did, the voices of the two gabby women carried across the store. Evidently, they'd found a new topic of conversation. "I went to McNarney Brothers yesterday," Mrs. Lloyd was saying, "and would you believe they raised the price of beef by five cents a pound? Don't they know times are tight? Before you know it, folks won't be able to afford to eat."

"She could afford to go a few days without eatin'," Harold Murphy muttered. His eyes never strayed from his task, as he keyed in the amount of each item before placing it back in the basket.

Eli covered his mouth with the back of his hand until his grin faded. He decided it was best to keep quiet on the matter. Something else bothered him, though, and he couldn't resist inquiring. He leaned in, taking care to keep his voice down. "That girl...er, that woman, who left a bit ago, who is expecting...."

"Ah, Sofia Rogers? She was here with her little brother, Andy." Mr. Murphy rang up the final item, the loaf of bread, and placed it gently atop the other goods. Then, he scratched the back of his head as his thin lips formed a frown. "It's a shame, them two...well, them three, I guess you could say." He glanced both ways, then lowered his head and whispered, "Don't know who got her in that way, and I don't rightly care. When she comes here, I just talk to her like nothin's different. Figure it ain't really my concern. I know there's been talk about her bein' loose, an' all, but I can't accept it. Never seen her with anybody but that little boy. She takes mighty fine care o' him, too."

"She's his guardian, then?"

"Sure enough, ever since...oh, let's see here... summer of twenty-four, it was. They lost their ma and pa in a terrible train wreck. They'd left Andy home with Sofie for a few days, whilst they went to a family funeral somewhere out West, little knowing their own funeral would be three days later." The man shook his balding head.

The news got Eli's gut to roiling. Even after all those years of medical school, which should have calloused him to pain and suffering, his heartstrings were wound as taut as ever. He needed to learn to toughen up. Needed to accept that, thanks to Adam and Eve's fateful decision in the garden, bad things happened to innocent people; that he lived in an imperfect world in which evil often won.

"Where do they live, if you don't mind my asking?"

"Somewheres out on the southwest edge o' town. River Road, I believe, just off o' Mill Creek Pike."

Eli didn't know Wabash well, but his grandfather certainly did, having driven virtually every street within the town limits to make house calls. But what was he thinking? He ought to bop himself on the noggin.

He knew next to nothing about this woman, and the last thing he needed upon taking over Wilson Trent's medical practice was a reputation for sticking his nose where it didn't belong.

Eli paid the shopkeeper and took up the basket. He had a good feeling about Harold Murphy. "Nice to see you again, sir. I'll bring this basket back next time I come in…or shall I return it to you tonight?"

Harold flicked his wrist. "Naw, you bring it back whenever it's convenient. You give ol' Doc a hearty hello from me."

"I'll do that." Eli turned and proceeded to the door, shoving it open with his shoulder. The first thing he noticed when he stepped outside was the absence of the two bikes, and it occurred to him then that Sofia and Andy Rogers had ridden to and from Murphy's Market on those rickety contraptions. A woman in what looked to be her seventh month of pregnancy, riding a bike clear to the edge of town? In a dress? And in this heat?

This time, he did bop himself on the head.

Chapter Two

Teach me thy way, O LORD; I will walk in thy
truth: unite my heart to fear thy name.
—Psalm 86:11

Sofie wiped her brow with her shirtsleeve and tried to ignore her unusually sore muscles and upset stomach. She stepped back from the stove, where she'd been cooking supper, and reached up to open the cabinet where she kept a small bottle of Bayer Aspirin. Rarely did she resort to painkillers; years of hard work had built up her tolerance for most bodily aches. But her sore joints, coupled with the dull headache she'd acquired earlier in the day, now clutched her body like a cold, hard fist. She unscrewed the aluminum cap and extracted a couple of small tablets.

At the sink, she ran the spigot and filled a glass with water, then chased the pills down her throat with a few good gulps. Waiting for them to settle, she rubbed her rounded belly and stood at the window, watching Andy pull weeds from the garden—a chore that never failed to elicit his complaints.

The baby gave her a good kick, reminding her for the thousandth time that day of the vile act she'd fallen victim to nearly eight months ago. Whoever the father was, he'd never experience the sensation of the baby moving inside him, and that gave her a measure of satisfaction, however minute.

But then, she might never again experience the comfort and confidence she'd enjoyed before the attack. Just two months ago, when news of her protruding abdomen had started to spread, she'd received another note—a threat to reinforce the one she'd discovered upon waking up that frightening morning. It had said, in effect, that if she breathed a word to anyone that she'd gotten pregnant against her consent, she could kiss her brother and her dog good-bye, never to be found, because their bodies would have been cut into a thousand tiny pieces.

Whoever he was, she didn't for a second doubt his capability of harming Andy, and the realization had only cemented her decision to keep the truth a secret. Forever.

The aromas of meatloaf and fried potatoes called her back to the present, and she shuffled back to the stove to finish preparing their Saturday evening meal.

"This is good, sis. I was hungrier than a bear," Andy said later as he shoveled food into his mouth, his forehead still dotted with beads of perspiration from his work in the yard.

"Wipe your face, would you, Andy? I don't think you used soap when you washed up."

"O' course I did, but you didn't tell me to wash all over." He did a clean sweep down his face with his napkin, then laid the cloth next to his plate in a wrinkled heap. "Why aren't you eatin'?"

"I'm not feeling so well tonight." The Aspirin had worked to ease her aches within an hour, but her diminished appetite and developing cough had her picking at her food rather than eating.

"Oh. Sorry. Is it the baby again?"

"No, I'm just feeling under the weather. I'll be fine by tomorrow."

Andy had never asked how she'd gotten pregnant, and she'd never volunteered the information. However, she did wonder what sort of ruminations stirred in his young mind. Had school still been in session, he surely would have gotten an earful, what with all of the rumors floating around town. The bigger boys probably would have liked nothing better than to take him to some secluded corner of the schoolyard and fill his mind with all manner of sordid speculations.

"Oh. Well, it's probably 'cause it's so h-hot today," he said, wolfing down more potatoes like some famished pup. "I don't f-feel so good m-myself after all that weed pullin' on the hottest d-day of the year."

"Poor thing! And here I'd thought you were hungrier than a bear. If you're not feeling well, I guess you'll want to skip the peanut butter fudge I made for dessert."

His green eyes popped. "P-peanut butter f-fudge? I think I just got b-better."

She laughed in spite of her returning headache. "You can share a piece with Georgie when he comes over later."

Eight-year-old Georgie Walters lived down the road from them with his parents, Bruce and Tildi, and two brothers. He came over almost every day to play with Andy. Despite the three years separating them, the boys enjoyed each other's company. Sofie cherished her friendship with Tildi but knew that she must wonder, along with everyone else, about the identity of her baby's father. Mercifully, she'd never probed. And Sofie hadn't felt compelled to offer any details. She hated being tight-lipped toward those she was closest to, but her fear of her attacker gave her no choice but to keep her secret tightly bound.

While Andy played outside with Georgie, Sofie lay on the couch, trying to sleep off her discomfort. Soon, though, the Aspirin's effectiveness faded, and her symptoms now included a sore throat, a throbbing head, and a feverish warmth.

Andy came inside at dusk, out of breath and sweaty from running through the neighborhood. His grin disappeared when he saw Sofie. "You don't look so good."

"Gee, thanks," she muttered.

"You w-want some water or s-somethin'?"

"Water would be nice."

He went to the sink and filled two glasses to the rims, gulping his down by the time he'd crossed the room. He settled down on the floor beside the couch, setting both glasses on the coffee table. "I should've come in sooner to keep you company."

"It's alright." She tried to sit up, but a wave of dizziness forced her to plop back down. "Good gravy," she groused. "Being sick is such a bother."

Andy helped her up to a sitting position, then handed her the full tumbler of water.

With trembling hands, she gripped the cool glass and managed a couple of swallows before her queasy stomach signaled to stop. Exhausted, she collapsed in a heap and started shivering. "Will you bring me a blanket, please?"

"A b-blanket?" Andy stood up. "It's durned hot in here."

"Well, I'm durned chilled—and hot—at the same time."

Andy returned with a wool blanket and spread it over her. Their dog, Buster, a medium-sized brown mutt who'd wandered into their yard three years ago and never wandered out again, seemed to understand her misery. He rose on his haunches from where he'd been lying under the table, stretched his lean frame, meandered across the room, and plunked himself back down on the floor next to Sofie.

"Good thing it's S-Saturday and you d-don't have to go to work tonight," Andy said.

Sofie sighed heavily as she tucked the blanket under her chin, then cut loose a coughing spasm that delayed her reply. "I'd never have made it to work on my bike, let alone had the gumption to clean offices." Her job at Spic-and-Span Cleaning Service meant working nights Monday through Friday while Andy slept. She generally tucked him in and then locked everything up tight before riding off to work. It wasn't an ideal arrangement, but the cleaning had to be done at night, when the offices were closed, and Spic-and-Span had always been good to her.

Now, with jobs so scarce, after last year's stock market crash, she counted herself blessed to hold any job. Without her income, there would be no way of putting food on the table, besides what they harvested from their garden and either ate right away or canned for the long winter months. And when the baby came, Sofie could only imagine how much harder it would be to keep everyone fed.

"Just trust in the Lord," her mother would have told her. But her faith in God had lost a lot of its substance recently. In fact, she'd been lax about attending church, and so Andy had been riding to and from services with Bruce and Tildi and their boys. It pained

Sofie to think of the terrible example she was setting for Andy, but she could hardly bear the looks she got from folks when she went out, even to the tight-knit community church she'd attended all her life.

Sofie spent the remainder of the evening on the sofa, watching Andy work on the jigsaw puzzle they'd been piecing together for the past week. When he finally tired of the activity, he went to bed, and she retired to her own room shortly after.

No sooner had she drifted off to sleep than she awoke with a terrible urge to vomit. Throwing off her blankets, she leaped out of bed and made for the bathroom, where she emptied her stomach into the commode. Sprawled on the floor in a state of utter wretchedness, she gathered what strength she could muster and headed back to her bedroom. Just inside the doorway, dizziness overtook her, so that she zigzagged across the room, bumped against a table, stubbed her toe on a chair leg, and then fainted into black oblivion.

꧁꧂

Elijah awoke to a loud clamor of the doorbell ringing, the brass knocker banging against the oak door, and panicked shouting.

He jumped out of bed, shimmied into the trousers he'd draped over the footboard, and then slipped on a cotton shirt while hurrying barefoot down the stairs.

In the entryway, he nearly collided with his spry, seventy-eight-year-old grandfather, whose bedroom was on the main level. He was dressed in a nightshirt and a belted cotton robe, and his white hair stood at attention on one side of his scalp.

Eli flung open the door and immediately recognized the wide-eyed lad standing there as the one he'd seen shopping with his sister at Murphy's Market several days ago.

"C-c-c-come quick. M-my sister, she-she-she—something h-h-happened, and she's real s-sick."

"Slow down, young man," Eli said, pulling him inside and closing the door to keep the mosquitoes outside where they belonged.

Grandfather rested a wrinkled hand on the boy's shoulder. "Andrew, try to calm yourself, now, and tell us what's happened." He never seemed to get his feathers ruffled, a trait Eli had yet to acquire.

"Sofie f-fainted d-dead away on the f-f-floor. I f-finally g-got her to wake up long enough to g-get her to the c-couch, but she's burnin' up with f-f-fever."

Grandfather cast Eli a solicitous glance, then steered the boy to a chair. "Alright, Andrew. Sit down and wait while Dr. Elijah and I finish getting dressed and fetch our bags."

A rush of adrenaline pulsed through Eli's veins. This would be his first official house call in Wabash. Yet his exhilaration didn't quell the wave of anxiety that swept through him. He hoped that the young woman hadn't harmed her unborn baby when she'd fallen. But there was no point jumping to diagnostic conclusions prior to seeing the patient.

Grandfather instructed the boy to throw his bike in the trundle seat of the car, and then the three of them piled inside. Elijah drove, with Grandfather directing him.

In just under ten minutes, they reached the house—a little box of a place that couldn't have been more than seven hundred square feet. There was a tiny front stoop outside the door, illumined by a dilapidated outdoor lamp.

When Elijah cut the engine, the boy opened his door, jumped out, and bounded toward the house.

Elijah's mind swam with questions, but he stored them away in his memory. He would bring them up again later, when he had a few minutes alone with Grandfather.

Inside, they found the boy kneeling by the couch, where his sister lay on her side. Eli scanned the room and saw no blood, an encouraging sign in regard to the health of her baby. He held back to allow his grandfather to pass. The older gentleman touched Sofie's forehead. "Not feeling well, are we? Andrew, here, tells us you fainted on the floor."

"I feel so queasy, Doc. I...I had to...empty my stomach. Andy, you shouldn't have left the house like that. It's not safe."

"He did the right thing in coming for us, Sofia," Grandfather said. He glanced at Eli. "This is my grandson, Dr. Elijah Trent."

She gave him a droopy-eyed smile.

"We've met, sort of...the other day, at Murphy's Market," Eli told him, his eyes not wavering from the flushed-faced girl. "It wasn't what you'd call a formal introduction. Sorry you're not feeling well, miss." For a fleeting moment, he thought about the father of her child. Had he stayed involved in her life? Did they love each other? Would he want to be notified that she wasn't well?

Grandfather dragged a chair close to the sofa and sat. "Why don't you take her vitals, Elijah?" He turned to Sofia. "Is that alright?"

Wincing, she nodded.

"And, young man?" He turned to the boy. "Would you bring us a cold, damp cloth?"

"Y-yes, sir." Andy dashed out of the room.

Eli unzipped his leather satchel and selected various implements as he listened to Sofia's heart, checked her pulse, and measured her blood pressure. He stuck a thermometer under her tongue, and then, as he awaited a temperature reading, he turned his attention to her protruding belly, pushing, prodding, and listening to the rapid *thump-thump* of the baby's heartbeat. All signs pointed to a healthy fetus, and he heaved a sigh of relief.

Next, he pressed her left side, then her right. "Are you experiencing any pain at either of these sites?"

She closed her eyes and shook her head.

His trained fingers walked gently across her abdomen, feeling for unusual swelling, lumps, or hot spots. "How about here? Or here?"

She winced but continued shaking her head.

He removed the thermometer and read the temperature. Nearly 103 degrees. "She has a pretty high fever."

Eli handed the instrument to his grandfather, who screwed up his mouth and cocked his head to the side, an old habit denoting deep thought. Then, he ran a hand down his weathered, bearded face. "We'd best take her to the hospital, to run a couple of tests and pump some fluids into those veins."

"I agree."

"What did you say?" Sofie's formerly droopy eyes were now wide with alarm. She tried to sit up but quickly abandoned her efforts, moaning as she slumped against a pillow. "I'm not going to any hospital." Her protest was punctuated by a coughing spasm.

Andy returned with a cloth, which he pressed against his sister's forehead. "Sofie's goin' to th-th-the hospital?"

Sofia's emphatic "No!" coincided with Eli's calm "Yes."

"Have you been consulting another doctor for prenatal care, Sofia?" Grandfather's tone was quiet yet straightforward.

She stared straight ahead. "You know you're the only doctor I see."

"I thought perhaps you had consulted someone more...objective."

"She won't g-go. All she's b-been doin' is readin' books from the library about...well...you know."

"Having babies?" his grandfather coached.

The boy's face flushed to a rosy hue. "Yep."

"Well, it's high time we gave you a thorough examination, Sofia." Grandfather set his hands on his knees and stood up. "And what better place to do it than in the hospital, where we can keep a watchful eye on you? A high fever and a cough, not to mention fainting, are never good signs when you are expecting."

"But I—can't afford—"

"We'll discuss the money later."

"But...what about Andy? He can't—"

"Andy can stay with us. We have more than enough room in that big old house."

"We don't cotton to charity, sir."

"And I don't fancy it myself, Sofia. So, we'll consider this a loan from the hospital, which you will repay in small increments. How does that sound?"

"Can B-Buster come, t-t-too?" Andy wanted to know.

"Buster?" Grandfather looked about the room, as if expecting someone to emerge from the shadows.

"He's p-prowlin' around outside right now, but he's no t-t-trouble, you'll see."

Grandfather frowned. "Is Buster a cat?"

"A dog. He ain't—isn't—that big, n-neither."

"Buster can stay with Tildi," Sofie put in with a shaky voice.

At least she'd acquiesced to the idea of going to the hospital. Eli couldn't help but steal a glance at her fine, porcelainlike features: the diminutive nose, high cheekbones, pink lips, and sculpted, slightly arched eyebrows and lashes, which matched the deep brown of her eyes and also of her cropped curly hair.

He averted his gaze, giving himself a mental scolding. He had no business looking at her in any way other than professionally, as his patient.

"But Mrs. Walters doesn't know the first thing about takin' care of him."

"Andy...." A frail-sounding sigh came out of her.

Grandfather cleared his throat. "The dog will come with us, too." He turned to the boy. "Can you go round him up, Andrew?"

"Y-yes, sir!"

In two shakes, the dog was curled up in the back-seat of the car. Andy moved hastily through the house, gathering up enough items for a stay of several days, as well as turning off lights, double-checking faucets, and locking the kitchen door.

"Do you think you can walk, Sofia?" Eli asked. A dubious expression furrowed his brow.

"Of course." Sofia sat up—too fast, evidently, for she turned as white as paste and slumped back.

Andy gawked, his mouth hanging open. "Sofie never gets sick. Is she gonna be alright?"

Grandfather smiled. "She'll be fine, son. A couple of days in the hospital should do wonders for her constitution."

Sofia gazed up at them, a hint of defiance in her eyes. "One night, that's all. One night, and I'll be good as new."

Chapter Three

We may boldly say,
"The Lord is my helper, and I will not fear
what man shall do unto me."
—Hebrews 13:6

*H*ow you f-feelin', Sofie?"

Did her brother even need to ask? Dressed in a horrid gown of coarse, stiff fabric, Sofie lay on a hard mattress in the hospital ward, where curt nurses with starched white uniforms and matching caps bustled in and out, barking orders at the various patients.

Four beds over, someone coughed so hard that Sofie feared the poor soul might just burst a lung. Across the room, a woman moaned in agony.

Andy stood next to her, nearly squeezing the life out of her hand, no doubt in an effort to avoid panicking.

"I'll be fine," she managed. "Everything will be fine." If only her stomach would stop roiling and her body quit its quivering.

Carrying out the instructions of the younger Dr. Trent's orders, nurses jabbed her with needles, drew her blood, and hooked her up to some newfangled contraption that dripped fluid through her veins, all of them oblivious to her pain, in spite of her wincing.

All she wanted to do was go home. Even if they did allow her to leave, she doubted she'd be able to find her way out, as she'd been pushed by wheelchair into the hospital and onto the elevator that had conveyed her to the second floor. Moreover, she wasn't sure she'd have the strength to walk. At home, she'd faltered at the door, and the young doctor had whisked her into his arms and carried her to the car, as effortlessly as if she weighed no more than a box of cotton balls. Her cheeks had burned—with mortification, rather than from fever—like tomatoes under a roasting sun.

On the way to the hospital, Doc Trent and his grandson had talked continuously about her prognosis and the procedures they would follow at the hospital. Sofie had sat huddled in the back, wrapped in a blanket but still shivering, Buster nestled at her side.

"Why's she sh-sh-shakin' so much?" Andy had scooted as far forward as he could, apparently trying to catch the doctors' every word.

The younger Dr. Trent had taken his eyes off the road for an instant and given Andy a reassuring smile. "It's the fever. We'll get some Aspirin in her at the hospital, and that should help."

"Sh-she's not gonna die, is she?"

"No, Andrew, we'll see to that," Doc Trent had reassured him in his familiar, comforting tone. Wilson Trent had been the family's doctor for as long as Sofie could recall, and it pained her to think of him retiring, even though she'd avoided him over the past seven months. "We're going to take good care of your sister. In her condition, it's wise to go to the hospital for observation."

"You okay with that?" the younger doctor had asked. Sofie appreciated how kind he'd been with

Andy, how he'd treated him no differently than he would someone who didn't stammer. But Dr. Elijah Trent's pleasant demeanor, gentle ministrations, and engaging smile had no bearing on her whatsoever, and she would do well to remind herself continually of that fact.

A mature-looking nurse approached and stuck a thermometer under her tongue. "I'll be back in five minutes to take that out." She flashed a smile, the first show of compassion Sofie had received from the hospital staff. "We're very busy tonight, but we won't forget about you."

Sofie watched the nurse scurry away to tend to another patient, and that's when she noticed the younger Dr. Trent approaching, a folder tucked under his arm. The dimple in his chin was concealed only slightly by the sprinkling of sand-colored whiskers on his face, and his hair, the same color as his shadow of a beard, formed a cowlick at the peak of his forehead. She hadn't noticed it before. A good cut would fix it, but something told her he didn't much care about the state of his hair in the middle of the night. It looked pretty disheveled. "How are you feeling?"

"Peachy," she said around the thermometer.

He gave a low chuckle and pressed a cool hand to her forehead, making her wish he could keep it there. Somehow, she didn't seem to mind his gentle touch. "I'll have one of the nurses bring you a damp cloth. That should help while we wait for that Aspirin to take effect. And when we've finished taking your temperature, you can try sipping some cold water." He took out his stethoscope and listened to her heartbeat. She hoped he didn't notice how it skipped when he touched her. After a moment, he tucked the thing around his neck and, all business, jotted something on her chart. "At breakfast time, we'll have you try a piece of dry toast and maybe some hot tea."

She might have laughed if she hadn't felt so rotten. "I can hardly wait." Sliding the thermometer to the side of her mouth, she said, "There're a lot of sick people in here. When can I go home?"

"When you've regained some strength and you're feeling better."

"If that's the criteria, I'm feeling just fine. Hand me my clothes, please, and then kindly leave so I may dress."

He tossed his head back and laughed, revealing a nice smile with a perfect set of teeth. "I must say, your sense of humor is an encouraging sign."

"Sh-she m-makes me laugh a lot," Andy chimed in.

The man's patient blue eyes registered on Andy, then moved back to Sofie. "Laughter is medicine for the soul."

"'Course, she orders m-me around a lot, too. Makes me work like a h-horse."

Dr. Trent chuckled. "Ah. Maybe you'd just as soon agree to extending her hospital stay to give yourself time to rest up."

As the two bantered back and forth, Sofie felt the makings of a smile on her lips, even though it never materialized. At least the man had helped to dissolve some of the worry she'd seen on Andy's face.

Doc Trent came on the scene. "How's our patient?"

"She says she's p-peachy," Andy offered.

White eyebrows arched over twinkling eyes. "Well then, I imagine she won't mind if I examine her. Elijah, would you take Andrew down the hall for a few minutes?"

"I'd be happy to." He set her chart at the foot of the bed, then pulled the starched white curtain until it fully encircled her wrought-iron bed, leaving her alone with his grandfather.

Doc Trent removed the thermometer from her mouth and squinted at it. "Hmm. These things are so blamed hard to read."

The curtain opened a crack, and Sofie recognized the nurse who'd promised to return. "I'll take that."

Without argument, he handed it over. "Good luck."

"I don't need luck. *You* need a stronger prescription for your spectacles." She winked, then held the instrument several inches away from her face. After she'd recorded something on the chart, she tucked the clipboard under her arm and raised an eyebrow at the doctor. "I thought you were retiring."

He chortled. "You aren't trying to get rid of me, are you, Eva?"

"Humph. You know how hard of a time this hospital will have without you." She smiled and bumped against him playfully, and Sofie wondered how long they'd worked together, to have developed such a close camaraderie. "Of course, that grandson of yours will follow straight in your footsteps."

He grunted. "I hope he'll carve his own path. He's brilliant enough."

"Handsome enough, too. Maybe a tad more than you."

"Eva!" He chortled. "I thought you'd reached an age that blinded you to such things."

"Ha! I may be getting up there, but my eyesight is just fine, thank you." She glanced at Sofie. "Speaking of my eyesight, her temperature is a hundred and one point four."

"Good. It's dropped some."

"Does that mean I can go home?" Sofie asked, knowing the answer before he gave it.

Doc Trent's eyes crinkled in the corners. "Not so fast, my dear. You'll stay put until we're confident that your baby is fine and you're ready to resume normal activity."

She sucked in a long breath, too weak to argue.

With the nurse present, he pulled his stethoscope from inside a deep pocket and gave her heart a listen, then moved it down to her abdomen. Next, he performed the usual tests, looking in her ears, up her nostrils, and down her throat. "How is your stomach feeling at the moment?"

She gave a wry smile. "Big."

He chuckled. "That's not exactly what I meant. Is it still queasy?"

"Yes, but not like before."

"Good. The IV drip is probably helping. I'd like to do a quick internal exam, if you don't mind...you know, to see if all is well with the little one. Eva, here, will hold your hand."

Her stomach pitched at the mere thought of the intrusion. What if she fainted or, worse, screamed? She didn't know if she could endure a man touching her in that area, even a well-intentioned doctor, without suffering visibly.

As if Doc Trent had read her tortured mind, he held up a hand. "I won't do it if it'll make you uncomfortable, Sofie. But, if you think you can handle it, I'd like to make sure your little one is fine, maybe get an idea of his size. Or hers. You can always tell me to stop if it bothers you."

She supposed she could try, for the sake of her baby. "Can you make it quick?"

His smile was grandfatherly. "I'll do my best. And Eva will do her best to keep you distracted."

Sofie didn't have it in her to object further, so she sighed and gave a slow nod, then took the nurse's hand and squeezed. As the doctor started his examination, she closed her eyes and returned to the dark place in her mind.

True to his word, he finished the exam within minutes, then politely asked Eva to give them some privacy.

With an encouraging pat to Sofie's arm, Eva turned and disappeared through the curtain.

Doc Trent found a stool on casters and rolled it up close to her bed. "I helped your mother bring you and Andrew into the world, Sofia, so I feel I know you pretty well, but I had no idea you had a boyfriend. Are you going to tell me who he is?"

If only she knew. "I don't have a...a boyfriend."

His left brow arched. "Then, just how did you find yourself in this state?"

"I can't discuss it. Please, you have to understand."

He sniffed and ran one hand down the back of his head. "I see. He left you, did he?"

"I said I can't discuss it."

"Can't? Or won't?"

She gazed over his shoulder, avoiding his penetrating eyes. "Both."

He studied her for a moment, but she refused to look at him, even when he spoke again: "At least tell me this. Do you love this baby's father?"

Her stomach lurched and swirled, and she pursed her lips in a tight line, giving a brisk shake of her head. Fresh tears threatened to fall. Were it not for the tube shooting fluid through her veins, she would turn over to avoid his scrutiny.

He laid a hand on her shoulder. "Alright, Sofia, I'll let you rest, for now. But, at some point, you'll have to talk about it. You have some important decisions to make."

She closed her eyes to block out the light. "I want to keep my baby, if at all possible."

The lecture she expected never came. Instead, she felt a pat on her shoulder. "Either Elijah or I will pop in to see you tomorrow. Don't worry about Andy. Buster, either. We'll take good care of them."

At that, she raised her eyelids. "Thank you, Doctor. It was so generous of you to offer them a place to stay."

His smile made her almost believe everything would be okay. "Of course. Try to get some sleep, now."

After he left, she lay there in total misery, her head aching, her body chilled and weak, and her stomach still queasy. All she wanted was her own bed.

Elijah pored over several patients' records stored in a file cabinet in a back room behind the nurses' station. He hadn't intended to stay the night, but since Sofia Rogers had been admitted to the hospital, he'd deemed it a good idea. This way, he could keep an eye on her, get familiar with the hospital routine, and maybe even look in on a few other patients, whether his grandfather's or not. If he didn't get any sleep tonight, so be it. He'd accustomed himself to surviving on little sleep while working the overnight shift at the hospital in Detroit.

"You finding everything you need, Dr. Trent? You know Dr. Stewart is on duty tonight, so it's not necessary for you to stay."

He glanced up from the chart in his hand and smiled at Eva Abernathy, the head nurse he'd met earlier. "I know, but I've much to learn, so I decided to hang around—look through some files of former patients; see what sorts of diseases, ailments, and injuries you've dealt with in the past."

She crossed her arms and leaned against the door frame, her starched white cap tilted enough to one side to reveal a crop of short white hair. "It's a small hospital, probably much smaller than what you're used to. It shouldn't take you long to learn the ropes."

He closed the file on Frederick Peterson and slid it back where he'd found it, in between Dorothy Perry and Arthur Phelps. "If the Detroit hospital is a watermelon, Wabash is a seed."

She smiled. "You must miss all the activity."

"Not on your life. I'm a small-town boy at heart."

"Where do you hail from?"

"Lindsey, Ohio. I don't think it even warrants a spot on the map. It's a few miles northwest of Fremont, a bigger town."

"I'm familiar with the area. I had an aunt who lived in Woodville. So, if you're an Ohioan, how did you wind up at the University of Michigan?"

"Grandfather attended there, and my dad moved the family to Michigan before I started tenth grade, already planning for me to follow in his own dad's footsteps. Dad took a supervisory job at an automobile production company in Detroit. By then, my two older sisters had both graduated from high school and either had jobs or were attending college, so they didn't come, but eventually, when they both married and started having kids, they moved to Michigan to be near my parents. Interestingly, they all live within a half hour of each other, in the Grosse Pointe Park area."

She lifted two white brows, and her eyes were bright with mischief. "Sounds like a tight-knit family, and you have your grandparents to thank for that. You do know Doc Trent wears some pretty big shoes around here."

"You're not the first to tell me that. Good thing he'll be nearby to lend me his wisdom."

She scoffed. "Be careful what you wish for. He may not grant you a second's peace. I can hear him now. 'How's Mrs. Featherstone's gout?' 'Is Herb Castle coming in for his biannual checkups?' 'What's the status on old Mr. Weaver's ticker? Is it still operating?'"

He chuckled at her prediction.

"What's your assessment of the Rogers girl?" she asked.

"She'll be fine in a couple of days. Grandfather mainly wanted to make sure the baby was healthy. It's good that her brother had the sense to seek help."

"Yes, that was quick thinking on his part."

"Do you know much about them?"

Eva gave a slow shake of her head. "Afraid not. Just that Sofia's been raising her brother ever since their parents were killed in a train wreck a few years back. To my recollection, an express passenger train went through an open switch and plowed headlong into an oil tank at the rear of a stationary freight train. Of course, it made big news here in Wabash, since it killed two of our own. I didn't know the Rogerses— they were a good bit younger than me—but I understand they were good people."

Eli nodded, remembering that Harold Murphy had given him a similar report. How terrible to lose one's parents so violently and so suddenly. Sofia and Andrew had endured a difficult life, and adding a baby to the equation certainly wouldn't make things any easier.

He had enough on his plate without fretting over some young woman and her little brother, but he couldn't shove aside his inbred keenness of heart for other people's welfare. Attribute it to his genes or his love for God, he cared deeply for the downtrodden, which was the primary reason he'd pursued the medical profession.

"Thanks, Mrs. Abernathy. I think I'll go peek in on her now, see if she's resting comfortably."

The nurse stepped aside and pointed behind her. "Her chart's on the desk right there. And it's Eva."

He grinned. "Thank you, Eva."

When he pulled back the curtain surrounding Sofia's bed, he found her lying there with her eyes closed, her breathing steady. He pulled the lightweight blanket up to her chin and then yanked the cord overhead to extinguish the beam of light reflecting off of her face. Considering the feistiness she'd exhibited in her sickly state, he couldn't help wondering what she might be like when fully well.

When he was about to go, she muttered weakly, "You know, I'd be much better off at home. It's hard to get any sleep around here." She didn't open her eyes.

A smile crept across his face. "You were faking it, eh?" He lowered himself into the chair at the foot of her bed. He supposed she was right, though, about having trouble sleeping. Across the ward, someone had broken out in a coughing fit, and the drone of the whirring ceiling fans along the corridor was almost deafening. "You'll go home soon enough, as long as we manage to keep that fever at bay. You still need to rest for a couple of days."

Her eyelids fluttered open. "I can't rest that long. I need to work on Monday."

"What sort of work do you do?"

She shifted in the bed. "I clean offices at night."

"That sounds a bit strenuous. It would be best if you could take off for a few days."

Her chin jutted out. "Somebody would have to double her work."

"You don't expect me to believe you've never helped out another employee in a pinch, do you?"

She stared at the ceiling, evidently unwilling to affirm his supposition.

He folded his arms, her chart tucked in between them. "How much longer do you expect to work at this cleaning job?"

She gave a short-lived smile that lacked spark. "Forever."

"And your baby...."

"Is none of your concern."

"It is, actually, since I'm your physician now, by default."

She snorted. "I can switch doctors if you get too nosy."

Good grief! She was a testy little thing. "Any doctor would ask you the same question. 'Nosiness' is part of our profession, I'm afraid."

"Maybe so. But having the title of 'Doctor' in front of your name doesn't make you an expert on everything."

"Well, you have me there." He would get nowhere arguing with an ailing pregnant woman at two thirty in the morning. Shoot, he reckoned he'd be hard-pressed to win any kind of argument with this fireball, no matter the circumstances.

He drew his right foot up over his left knee and clasped his ankle. "How long has your brother had a stuttering problem?"

She narrowed her eyes. "What does that have to do with my illness?"

"Nothing. I'm only interested."

She reached for the water glass on the bedside stand, but the various tubes attached to her arms hampered her efforts. Eli dropped his foot to the floor, stood up, and seized the glass. Then, he helped her sit up to take a few sips. When she nodded, he set the glass back down. She sighed and fell back against the thin pillow, tiny beads of perspiration dotting her forehead, which was framed with ringlets of short dark hair. "Right when he started talking, my parents noticed his stammer. But it got a lot worse after they died. Dr. Trent has always been of a mind that he'll have to learn to live with it."

Eli returned to the chair at the foot of the bed. "He could very well be right. Have you noticed any patterns in his stuttering? For example, are there times when he hardly stutters at all?"

She looked thoughtful for a moment, then nodded. "He seems to stutter a lot less at home than in public. And I know he stammers more when he gets excited." She knit her brows into a frown. "When the school year starts up, it gets worse. I've always blamed it on the big boys who poke fun at him."

Eli adjusted his position, crossing his legs again. "My roommate at university wrote his thesis on stuttering and other speech impediments. He and I had many a long conversation in the midst of all his research. I found it fascinating, especially when I found out there are studies refuting the belief that there's nothing to be done for stutterers. The world of medicine is changing fast. There are scientists working right now to develop antibodies to cure some of the gravest bacterial diseases and infections."

"Hmm. Wouldn't it be fine to live in a world without"—she gave a long, wide yawn—"disease?"

He smiled and stood. "I'll let you get some rest."

"While you're at it, would you tell the nurses to stop sticking that thermometer in my mouth?"

He chuckled. "They're just doing their job."

"There are people here a lot sicker than I am. Tell them to worry about them, instead."

Her last words faded fast, so he tiptoed away. When he glanced back, she'd closed her eyes again, though he didn't think she faked her sleep this time.

Chapter Four

*The LORD is my light and my salvation; whom
shall I fear? the LORD is the strength of my
life; of whom shall I be afraid?*
—Psalm 27:1

Sofie's fever returned on Sunday morning but then
dissipated altogether. However, her nagging cough
persisted, and the doctors insisted she remain in the
hospital for two additional nights, to monitor the potential onset of pneumonia. When it was determined
that the dread disease would not take hold, they allowed her to return home, on the condition that she
promise to get plenty of rest.

The sickness, as well as the recovery process, had
robbed her of a great deal of energy. When it was time
for her first shift back at work, on Thursday night, she
wondered how she would ever make it through. "Lord,
give me strength," she uttered feebly, almost sheepishly, as she slipped into her uniform. Her shift started at
10:00 p.m., but she always liked to arrive well ahead
of schedule. She doubted that would happen tonight,
though, as she would be pedaling slower than usual
to get there.

Before heading out, she went to check on Andy.
He lay sleeping in bed with an open book, *Buff: A Collie*

and Other Dog Stories, spread across his chest. Near his feet, a slumbering Buster snored contentedly.

Sofie tiptoed into the room, picked up the book, and closed it, setting it on the bedside stand. Then, she planted a light kiss on Andy's cheek. He made a snuffling noise and rolled over on his side. Buster opened his eyes and raised his head.

"You protect him, you hear?" she whispered.

Buster blinked at her, then settled back down again, resting his chin on Andy's leg. Sofie smiled and reached over to pat his downy-soft head.

Outside, Sofie retrieved her bicycle, which she'd left leaning against the house in the side yard several days ago. She'd long been in need of a new bike—one that wasn't rusty and prone to veer to the left. Right now, however, too many other expenses took precedence—a baby crib for one, not to mention other items essential for a newborn: blankets, bottles, clothes, diapers...the list went on. Mercy, she had so many things needing repair or replacement around her house, including the roof, as it leaked something fierce in a bad rain. She wondered how she'd even scrounge the money for a *used* crib. "Overwhelmed" seemed insufficient to describe her state of mind.

"You should really consider adoption." Margie's advice shot through her like a blazing bullet, jolting her body before lodging in the center of her chest. And not for the first time. Margie's words had haunted her ever since she'd first heard them. *"I happen to know more than a few childless couples right here in Wabash who would be thrilled to take it off your hands."*

She studied her bike in the light of the moon as she wheeled it out toward the street. How did she expect to cart a baby around with her on such a rickety thing? And what would she do with the baby while she was working? Take him along? She doubted her boss would approve. She could hire someone—Tildi, maybe—to look after the baby, but the thought of parting with even a small portion of her meager income made her stomach churn. Margie had been correct in pointing out that they were barely making ends meet as it was, without adding a baby to the equation. She'd thought of having Andy do it, but there were days when he didn't remember to feed Buster. How, then, could she trust him with a brand-new baby?

Sofie heard a rustling noise nearby, and her fingers froze to the handlebar grips. She looked all around, meanwhile telling herself she'd only imagined the sound, or that, at worst, it'd been a nocturnal creature of some sort. With a gulp of air, she held her breath and listened, her tense body motionless. After a few moments, she exhaled, shuddering slightly, and started pushing the bike toward the road. At the sight of a car parked out front, she gasped, dropping the bike.

∿

Eli rested a hand on the hood of the car and watched Sofie emerge from the darkness, pushing her decrepit bicycle. The starlit sky illumined her face just enough for him to see her expression of shock when she noticed him. "What are you doing here?" There was a breathless quality to her voice, as if she'd just run a few laps around her house, and her big, brown eyes went as round as basketballs. He figured her body hadn't fully recovered from that bout with the flu. She would be better off waiting to return to work until next week, but he already knew the uselessness of making that argument.

"Well, it's a long story, but my grandfather and I have been talking, and we don't think you should be riding your bike in your...condition. We came up with a plan, of sorts, and I immediately jumped in the car and drove over. I'm glad I caught you before you took off. I was afraid you might have left already."

"You needn't have bothered coming. I'm used to riding my bike." She sniffed, raised a baggy pant leg over the bike's bar, and rested her right foot on the pedal, making it clear she intended to leave before hearing him out.

He advanced on her before she had the chance, stepping in front of her bike and grabbing the handlebars. Their gazes met and held.

She was a pretty little thing, but he had no business noticing, considering she carried the child of another man. Yet Eli wondered how close she really was to the father of her child. To his knowledge, Sofia hadn't had a single male visitor, aside from Andy, during the three days she'd spent in the hospital. The only people who'd come to see her had been a neighbor lady named Tildi and an older woman by the name of Margie. According to Eva Abernathy, Margie had made arrangements to cover the hospital bill—and requested that Sofia not be informed. Eli had been touched by her generosity.

"I know you're used to riding. But the more you progress in your pregnancy, the greater the risk it poses to your baby. One spill on this thing, and...well, you could very well lose the baby, to put it bluntly." He cleared his throat. "Let me drive you to work. Grandfather's already agreed to pick you up in the morning."

She shook her head. "I will not impose on either of you in that way. Now, kindly release my bike." She wriggled the handlebars impatiently.

Eli held them tight. "No need to be so stubborn about this. It isn't an inconvenience for either of us. And preventing unnecessary risks is part of our job as physicians."

"What do you mean, it isn't an inconvenience? Of course, it's a problem. You both have important jobs. This is just plain silly, but please tell Doc Trent I appreciate the offer. Now, please let me go. I don't want to be late on my first night back to work."

"You won't be late, because I'm driving you."

She released a loud sigh. "You don't owe me anything, and I don't want to be beholden to you. I don't have money to pay you for gasoline, or for your trouble, for that matter."

He scowled at her. "Who said anything about money? This is just something my grandfather and I would like to do." He lowered his face and stared intently into her eyes. "And I will not take no for an answer."

"But...but...." She turned fully around to look at the house, then faced him again. "It seems like such an extravagance, riding in a car to work. Like being chauffeured, or something." He saw the minutest gleam of delight in her eye, but it vanished in an instant. "I wouldn't feel right."

"Please, Miss Rogers. A woman in your condition deserves a little chauffeuring."

Her expression contorted with emotion—regret? sorrow? grief? He couldn't tell. "I don't deserve any special treatment just because I'm—"

"Sure you do. And I would think the father would—"

Her head shot up. "The father is none of your business, Dr. Trent. And I will thank you not to mention him again."

He tilted his head and matched her stare. "Fine. Now, go put your bike away, and I'll take you to work." He hadn't intended to sound so curt, but he was irked by her outburst at his mention of the father.

She was right, though; it was none of his business.

The trip to Spic-and-Span Cleaning Service took no more than eight minutes. Eli drove where Sofia directed him, down a series of dark roads and dimly lit streets that brightened the closer they came to town, where streetlights were more commonplace. They had set out in pitch darkness, and Eli couldn't imagine trying to find his way without the help of headlights. Sofia must have memorized every bump and crack; otherwise, travel by bike would be almost impossible.

"I do appreciate this," she said for about the tenth time. "But, truly, I don't want to make a habit of it."

Eli pulled the car into a parking space in front of the building Sofia identified as Spic-and-Span Cleaning Service. The one-story structure was nestled between two taller buildings: an abandoned warehouse and a manufacturing company of some sort.

Eli shifted the car into neutral. The engine chugged and whirred, making him picture a cat purring contentedly. Grandfather had always been fond of automobiles and had kept all of his cars in perfect working order, not to mention as shiny as polished apples. At present, there were four vehicles parked in the oversized garage situated behind his rambling, two-story brick house.

A lamp glowed from inside the front window of Spic-and-Span, and Eli could see a man seated at a desk, thumbing through a stack of papers. Two women wearing aprons emerged from a back room. "Your colleagues, I presume?"

Sofia nodded. "That's my boss, Mr. VanDyke, and two other ladies on the cleaning crew."

"Do you all work together as a team, or do you go to your job sites alone?"

"It depends on the size of the job. If it's a small office, then only one of us goes, but if there are multiple rooms or floors, we usually work in pairs. Mr. VanDyke drives us to our destinations."

"And leaves you there?"

"Of course. If the job is close by, we walk." She gave a tiny shiver and shifted in her seat.

"Seems that VanDyke fellow ought not to be sending women out alone at night."

She didn't respond but tapped her toe impatiently on the floorboard. "Well, I should be getting inside. My shift's about to start." She clutched the door handle. "Thank you again for the lift. But, please, don't feel obligated to come back. Or to send Doc Trent in the morning. I'm perfectly capable of—"

"I know. But I don't. Feel obligated, that is. I'll be by to pick you up tomorrow night. Maybe I'll come a little earlier and visit with Andy. He and I had some good conversations while you were laid up in bed. You don't mind, do you?"

"I guess not, but...I don't want to make this a habit. I mean—"

"What time should I tell my grandfather to swing by in the morning?"

She blew out a loud sigh that made her cheeks puff out like two pumpkins. "Did anyone ever tell you you're stubborn?"

"I could ask you the same thing."

She gazed ahead while he waited for her response. "I'm usually done by six."

"Good. I'll let Grandfather know."

"I hate to make him come at such an early hour."

"He's usually up by four. Starts every day sitting at the kitchen table with his coffee, reading his Bible."

"He's always been a fine Christian man."

"The best I know, generous and kind."

"He attends that little white clapboard church in town."

"Yep, the Wesleyan Methodist church. I've been going there myself. The people are wonderful. So warm and friendly. Where do you go?"

So warm and friendly. She doubted they'd remain that way if she darkened their door. "My neighbors have been taking Andy along to the Presbyterian church over on West Hill Street."

"That didn't exactly answer my question."

She glanced out the window toward the office. "Oh! Mr. VanDyke is looking out the window. I best go in." She opened her door and stepped outside, then leaned in to add, "Thank you again. I...I really don't know what else to say."

"How about, 'See you tomorrow night'?"

Her mouth did a slight upturn at the corners.

"You have a nice smile when you decide to show it." *And you're just about the prettiest thing I've ever clapped eyes on.*

She let her smile grow a little.

"You'd better get in there. Otherwise, it looks like that VanDyke fellow may come out here and haul you inside himself."

"Good night, Doctor. And thanks again."

"You can call me Eli, you know."

"'Doctor' will suffice." She closed the door and strode to the building without so much as a backward glance.

Chapter Five

He that worketh deceit shall not dwell
within my house: he that telleth lies
shall not tarry in my sight.
—Psalm 101:7

*O*wen Morris climbed the front steps of his parents' house and crept stealthily across the front porch. He opened the screen door, paused when it squeaked, and then cringed at the sound of his father's scolds booming from the second-story bedroom he shared with his wife. The windows were wide open, so his voice carried around the entire neighborhood. Across the street, old Grady Martin sat on his porch smoking a stogie and probably soaking up every earful. Beat any radio show when it came to drama.

Owen shook his head. He needed to find a decent paying job so he could bust out of this house for good. Spending his high school years at a boys' school in a remote corner of the State of Oklahoma had nearly scrubbed his name off of the Wabash records. When he'd returned last year, most folks had greeted him with an odd look that seemed to say, "Oh! I'd forgotten you existed." Better that than pepper him with questions about Peterford, which his dad had led folks to believe was an exclusive prep school. Nobody knew it was a reform institution for "wayward and troubled" boys—a prison, more like it.

"I'm sick of you spendin' all our cash," his father barked, "goin' shoppin' near every day."

"I shop but once a week with Bessie Lloyd," came his mother's retort, "and most of my money goes to groceries, anyway. I work a job, so I should be allowed to treat myself every once in a while. Lord knows I don't have any fun with you."

"Sittin' at a desk all day—you call that 'work'? The only reason you got that job is because I gave it to you. I could hire most anybody else, and they'd work circles around you. All you do is yak at everybody who walks through the door, from the county commissioner all the way down to the guy who washes the windows."

"I do a lot more than that, Buford, and you know it. But go ahead—try to replace me. Few other women would put up with your demands, not to mention your grizzly bear personality."

Owen crept past the living room and into the kitchen, not wanting to announce his arrival, but the stinking floorboards groaned with just about every step. At least his parents' yelling had them distracted. In the kitchen, their conversation grew muffled, which suited him fine. He got plain sick of their hateful words. He snagged a glass from the cupboard and opened the icebox, hoping to find some bootleg whiskey. But, after he'd rifled through the contents and found no sign of the bottle, he realized his lousy father must have drunk the last drop.

"What are you doing home so late?"

He swiveled around to face his fifteen-year-old sister, Carolee. She'd need a lot of luck to land a guy, poor thing, given her pudgy figure, pimply cheeks, and mousy brown hair. She had a couple of cute friends, though, and Owen enjoyed gawking at them on occasion.

"None of your business. I keep my own hours."

"You shouldn't be drinking, you know. It's against the law."

"Ha! Tell that to Daddy. He's the lawman around here."

"You get in any more trouble, he'll send you away again, and the next time, it won't be to Peterford."

"Shut up, dinglehead. What do you know?" He bent over the icebox, trying to decide what to drink. Finally, he settled on lemonade. He hauled out the long-necked bottle, set a glass on the counter, and filled it to the rim. Perspiration beaded his brow. This had to be the hottest summer on record. To make matters worse, his nerves had been on end ever since seeing that car pull up to Sofie Rogers' house.

"Don't think I don't know what you've been doing. If you don't watch out, Daddy's going to send you off to who-knows-where. Maybe jail."

Without a second's consideration, he plunked down the glass, whirled around, and nabbed her by the wrist until she squealed. "What sort of trouble are you talking about?" he hissed. Surely, she hadn't made a connection between him and Sofia Rogers. She couldn't have.

Carolee slapped his hand, hard, and twisted her arm till he lost his grip on her. Upstairs, their parents continued going at it, oblivious to their own kids doing the same. "That hurt, you snake." Carolee rubbed the red spot on her wrist and whined. "What's wrong with you?"

"What did you mean about knowing what I've been doing?"

"I know you're hanging around those no-goods Lester White, Marvin Duran, and...some other jokester. Those boys got caught breaking windows last year and went to jail for a month."

"Yeah, so? They did their time."

"But did they learn their lesson?"

He turned and picked up his lemonade, gulping the whole thing down in a single swig. Then, he slammed the empty glass on the counter and glared at his sister. "I couldn't care less if they did or didn't. I ain't them."

She sniffed and lifted her chin a notch. "Well, you should steer clear of those troublemakers."

"Quit lecturing. You don't know anything."

"What are you two arguing about?" Their father stood in the doorway, taking up most of the space. Carolee whirled around and jolted.

"No arguments here," Owen protested. "We're having a discussion, and she's being her normal nosy self."

He grumbled something under his breath, shuffled past them, and opened the icebox. "Yeah, well, you were discussing loud."

"No louder than you and Ma." There had once been a time when he was afraid of his father, but now he merely despised him. The fact that he'd grown to almost the same stature gave him added confidence.

"What you doing eavesdropping on your ma and me?"

"That's really funny, Dad. Old Mr. Martin heard you clear across the street. You guys put on a better performance than *Fibber McGee and Molly*."

"Pfff." His dad bent over, one arm slung over the icebox door, the other reaching inside, shifting items around. "Where's my—?"

"You must've finished it."

"I didn't drink it all. You been getting into my brew, have you?"

"Lately, I get my own."

"Oh, yeah? Where from?"

"I've got my contacts."

"You better be watchin' yourself, boy."

"Didn't I tell you, Owen?" his sister squawked.

Owen could have hit her on the spot. "Shut up, Carolee!" He glared at her, ready to pounce if she opened her mouth again. "I can't stand the way she's always butting into my affairs. She loves making trouble."

"Do not!"

Their father puffed out his big chest and stared both of them down. "Go to bed, Carolee. No need for you to be payin' your brother any mind. What he does is his business—and mine. Isn't that right, son?"

He rolled his eyes. "Whatever you say."

Owen knew better than to take his dad seriously. He was vigilant at upholding the law, for the most part—except when it came to booze. He imbibed as much as anyone, and, like everybody else in violation of Prohibition, he had to bend the law to get his liquor. Owen had picked up on his methods, and he liked to think that the two of them were in cahoots, even if they were opposed in every other regard.

After a long sigh, Carolee left.

Owen's father nudged him in the side. "You find someone else makin' hooch?"

Owen shrugged.

"Who?"

"Can't give you any names."

His dad chortled with mock indifference. "I'm not really interested, anyway. If he's a beginner, he's small-time. Stuff probably tastes like dog gut."

The laugh they shared was devoid of geniality, as always, and just barely concealed the uneasy tension that was ever between them.

With the back of his big hand, his father wiped away the spittle that had gathered at the corners of his mouth. "You best be keepin' out of trouble, boy. Anybody files a complaint or finds you in the act of somethin' questionable, I'll have no choice but to take the necessary measures. It's an election year, and I won't let anything stand in the way of my getting' re-elected. You get my drift?"

"Yeah, yeah, but bear in mind I got me some good ammunition I could just as well use on you. You get *my* drift?"

The veins in the man's thick neck bulged, and his face went bloodred with fury. It was such fun putting Buford Morris in his place.

"'Night, Daddy," he sassed. "You have sweet dreams, now."

Owen snickered all the way up the stairs and past his parents' room, where he caught a glimpse of his mother reclined in bed, reading a book. She didn't bother to glance up.

※

The next morning, Sofie exited Spic-and-Span to find Doc Trent waiting for her in his car. The sight of him was a welcome relief, exhausted as she was from her first night back to work after her bout with the flu, and she was glad he'd insisted on driving her. She couldn't imagine pedaling the two-mile trek back home. And having an escort was nice, considering how troubled her stomach felt at the notion of being ambushed.

When she opened the passenger door, Doc Trent grinned up at her. "Well, good morning, young lady. How was your shift?" His chipper mood served to ease her jitters a smidgeon.

"Long." She slid inside and couldn't help slumping back against the seat.

"I figured you'd be tired. It's hard enough working such long hours in your condition. Add to that a weakened body, and you're prone to collapse from exhaustion. It's straight to bed with you when you get home."

"That was my plan. Thank you for picking me up."

He backed out of the parking lot, then started up the street. "Why don't you send Andy over to my house for the day? That way, you can get plenty of rest without interruptions."

"Oh, I wouldn't even think of it."

"Why not? He can even bring that furry creature along, if he'd like. It's no trouble. Now that Elijah's taken over my practice, I find myself wondering what to do with myself. I could use a checkers partner."

Sofie smiled. "I'm sure Andy would love that. He hasn't stopped talking about the three days he spent with you while I was in the hospital, especially how much he enjoyed playing games at your 'mile-long' dining room table. In truth, I think he was disappointed when he had to come home to our tiny abode."

Doc Trent chuckled. "He's welcome anytime. As are you."

"That's very kind of you, sir."

"It's not just me, my dear. My grandson's already taken quite a liking to Andy. He seems to have a knack for drawing that boy right out of his shell."

Her nerves jangled at the mention of Dr. Elijah. She didn't like admitting to herself that his good looks made her heart jump in peculiar ways. It wasn't as if a handsome doctor like him would ever pay attention to a scraggly pauper like her—especially a pregnant one. And, even if he were to notice her, she was hardly ready to entertain a man's affections. In fact, she wasn't sure she'd ever be ready for anything beyond friendship, considering how she usually flinched at the thought of a man touching her.

"I'd guess Andy's not even up and dressed yet," Doc Trent said as he stopped the car in front of her house. "Why don't I pick him up around nine?"

"Oh, I couldn't ask you make another trip out here. He's perfectly capable of riding his bike there and back."

"I don't mind. It will give us more time to visit."

Perhaps that would be the best plan. There were the threats against Andy to consider. "Well, if you wouldn't mind...."

"Not at all. Tell Andy I'll see him at nine. You have yourself a good day's rest. Your eyes are looking a little droopy."

She opened the door, slid over on the smooth leather seat, and climbed out. "Thank you again for the ride, sir, but I don't want to burden you further. I'll ride my bike tonight."

"Sofia." His soft voice stopped her from shutting the door. "Elijah and I agree that it isn't safe for you to be riding that bike to work, especially late at night. We insist on picking you up for work and then taking you back home again. In fact, both of us have been independently convicted by the Lord to do this. You wouldn't want to prevent us from following His instructions, now, would you?"

She choked down a sob. "I don't deserve such kindness."

"Nonsense, my dear. You've endured very difficult circumstances, and it's time someone stepped in and offered a helping hand. Now, get some rest. I'll see you again bright and early tomorrow morning." His tender gaze caused her heart to ache. With no other recourse, she closed the door, then shuffled along the walkway and up the creaky steps. On the porch, she turned and waved. Doc Trent honked his horn and pulled away, stirring up a cloud of dust in his wake.

Later that afternoon, Sofie awoke to Andy speaking in low tones to someone at the door. She threw on her robe and peeked into the living room just in time to see a casserole dish pass from someone's hands into Andy's. He turned around and met Sofie's gaze. "Oh, you're awake. Mrs. Grant brought us dinner. Nice, huh?"

"Margie!" She tied her wrap more snugly as she hastened toward the door. "Please, come in."

"No, no, I can't stay." Margie smiled at her from the stoop. "Howard's waiting in the car. We have to get home again, as we're expecting some company most anytime now. Howard's cousin and his wife are driving down from Mt. Pleasant, Michigan, to spend a few days with us." She gave Sofie a motherly perusal. "Sofie, dear, your face looks thinner. A couple of helpings of my creamy chicken and vegetable casserole ought to help. And there's a small ice cream cake in your ice compartment. Make sure you slice yourself a big piece after dinner." She looked at Andy. "You'll see to it that your sister eats good, won't you, Andy?"

"Yes, ma'am."

She smiled, then turned back to Sofie. "You're to be drinking plenty of milk and water, too."

Sofie giggled at her friend's maternal concern. "Isn't it enough that the doctors nag me?"

Margie didn't crack a smile. "I'll be back in a few days to check on you again."

"Good grief! One would think I'd had a brush with death."

"You haven't gone back to work yet, have you?" Margie had never been one to let things go.

"I did…last night," Sofie admitted with reluctance.

"Dr. Trent, the younger one, c-came and picked her up." Of course, Andy had thought to announce that tidbit. "And Doc Trent brought her h-home again this m-morning."

Margie arched her eyebrows as her gaze shifted from Andy to Sofie. "Is that so? I've heard nothing but good things about that young doctor since his arrival in Wabash. So, he took you to work?"

"They don't want her riding her bike to work anymore, cause of her…um…condition. It ain't safe."

"*Isn't* safe," Sofie corrected him gently. "It seems a little silly to me. I've been riding my bike for years."

"Well, I think it's a fine idea. I should have offered to take you myself. Where's my head? They're right— you shouldn't be riding that clunky bike down those dark streets. So, back to this young doctor.…"

Sofie looked at the car idling by the curb. "Don't you think Howard's getting anxious to leave?"

Margie flicked her wrist. "Oh, pooh. He's used to waiting on me. Just give me the short version."

"The short version of what?"

"Of your first impression of Dr. Trent, of course! What he's like, the color of his eyes, whether he—"

"His eyes? Margie Grant, I haven't the foggiest notion."

"Of course, you do."

Of course, she did. They were the loveliest shade she'd ever seen. Bluer than a mountain sky. "Don't be silly. You should get going, before your husband decides to beep the horn." She moved to close the door. "Thank you for the casserole. It smells wonderful."

"Thanks, Mrs. Grant!" Andy echoed.

With obvious reluctance, Margie turned and made her way down the steps to her husband's fancy roadster. Times were tough, but Howard's farm was still flourishing; it had yet to be affected by last year's market crash and the ensuing bank failures. "Folks need to eat," Margie had once told her, "and if the day comes when they can't afford to buy food, then we'll feed them. The Lord has blessed us with much, and we are prepared to give much, as the need arises." Sofie knew no one more kindhearted and generous than Margie Grant.

Margie paused outside the car and waved a finger in Sofie's direction. "Next time I see you, I'll want a more thorough report!"

Sofie groaned. She also knew no one as nosy.

Chapter Six

*Behold, what manner of love the Father hath
bestowed upon us, that we should be called
the sons of God.*
—1 John 3:1

*E*li finished up the last chart of the day after seeing patient number thirteen. Most of his appointments
were scheduled at half-hour increments, with a couple
of breaks, including an hour for lunch. But he routine-
ly found himself spending more than the allotted time
period with certain patients and then having to rush
through other appointments in an effort to get back on
schedule. In the future, he would need to find a better
system. His grandfather's housekeeper, Winifred Carmichael, had assisted with various office duties when
the need arose, but Eli wanted to hire a full-time secretary—someone to file reports, set up appointments,
handle the billings, and so forth. Most folks came in
with no intention of paying for his services; they said
that Doc had always sent them a bill. Although Grandfather had worked alongside him immediately following his arrival, he'd since sort of pushed him out of the
nest and told him to try flying on his own.

It was quite the clinic. When Grandfather had
designed his rambling house, one wing on the ground

floor had been designated as doctor's quarters, with a separate entrance on Sinclair Street. The partition included two examination rooms, an office, an apothecary, and a waiting room. In the waiting room, chairs lined all four walls, and there was a reception desk with a leather chair on casters. Three tall file cabinets were situated just behind the desk On the windowless wall was a framed painting of a scene from the English countryside, and on either side hung an ornamental brass candle sconce. In the center of the carpeted room stood a wooden coffee table stacked with dog-eared magazines, a few children's books, and the latest Sears and Roebuck catalog.

Leaning back in his leather chair in his office and propping his feet atop the big maple desk, marred from years of use, Eli closed his eyes, clasped his hands behind his neck, and relived the day. He'd treated everything from sore throats to broken bones to shoulder displacements, and if the appointment book his grandfather had handed him earlier that week was right, he'd face many more patients tomorrow. His body ached with fatigue, and he probably would have taken a quick nap, if not for his fear of falling out of his chair in a heap.

The door hinges creaked, and he opened his eyes and dropped his feet to the floor. His grandfather chuckled, pushed the door the rest of the way open, and plunked himself into the chair closest the door. "Busy day?"

"You really need to ask?" Eli chuckled. "How did you do it all those years?"

"What do you mean?" Grandfather crossed his legs and folded his arms over his broad chest.

"Your system seems a bit...well, antiquated. Don't you have a bookkeeper?"

"Winnie's always handled everything. She's a very capable woman." A wistful expression passed over his grandfather's face. "Unfortunately for you, she plans to retire."

Eli lifted his eyebrows. "I wish she wouldn't. How am I going to manage without her?"

Grandfather grinned beneath his white mustache. "I guess you'd better get the word out that you're accepting applications for a secretary."

"The last time I hired someone was in seventh grade, when I chose Grady Belk to take over my paper route."

Grandfather chuckled. "Well, you'll need to find someone with organizational skills and office experience, not to mention business sense."

"You think Winnie will agree to train the new hire?"

"I'm certain she'll be happy to." The old fellow's eyes brightened like a kid's on Christmas morning, and he craned his neck to look at the calendar on the wall. "She'll be home in four days."

"You must miss her cooking."

"I sure do. That, and, well, something else altogether." The fellow trained his gaze on Eli and smiled, his muttonchop sideburns rising a notch. "I've been meaning to tell you ever since you arrived in Wabash."

His mind swam in various directions. "What?" he prodded.

"I've asked Winifred Carmichael to marry me." He clasped his hands, his thumbs circling each other. "And she's said yes."

As if a pail of ice water had been poured over him, Eli lurched in shock. "Grandfather! Are you kidding?"

"Go ahead, say it: you think I've lost my marbles."

"What? No! I wasn't going to say that. I think... well, I think it's great, if...if you really love her."

He seemed to breathe a little easier. "I do. Deeply."

Eli settled back in his chair and grinned at his grandfather. "Well, I'll be a red-nosed toad. You old scalawag! You're really getting married again."

"It's not so crazy, you know. Love can strike at any age."

"I'm not refuting that. It's just...she's been your housekeeper for as long as I can remember."

"Yes, she has. And it didn't happen overnight, I assure you. Our attraction was gradual, and we both denied it at first, but...oh, this is rather embarrassing." He rose, both his knees creaking.

Eli stood, as well, coming around the front of the desk to wrap him in a big hug. "No need to be embarrassed. I'm happy for you." He stepped back and held him by the shoulders, which still had a good deal of bulk to them. "Winnie's always been like one of the family. I remember you telling us how she tended to Grandmother right up to the end, sitting at her bedside and reading the Bible until she drifted off to sleep."

Grandfather's eyes brimmed with wetness. "She certainly did. I don't know what your grandmother would say to my marrying Winnie, though."

"Are you kidding? She and Winnie were like sisters. She'd be overjoyed."

"Our engagement isn't official yet, but it will be soon. Winnie's telling her family this week. When she returns, I plan to call your parents. I hope they'll take the news well."

"They'll be elated. Everyone has always loved Winnie. When's the big day?"

"We haven't set a date yet, but I don't think we'll wait long. Old folks like us don't have a lot of time to waste. Winnie wants to do some traveling."

"Traveling? You've always been a homebody."

"Well, we don't plan to travel the world. I might take her to...I don't know. Maybe Chicago. I hear there's a lot to see there."

"Chicago's nice." He couldn't get the grin off his face. "So, there was a specific reason you wanted me to come to Wabash."

"You know there was never a question whether I wanted you to take over my practice. That's been a dream come true."

"I feel exactly the same."

"As for this house...."

"I'm planning to move; don't worry. I could stay another month, if that would be alright, until I get my feet on the ground, and then—"

Grandfather shushed him with a gentle pat on the arm. "You're staying right here."

"No, I'd want you and Winnie to have the place to yourselves."

"She has a nice house, and I fully intend to move in with her. In fact, it was her idea. This house has become too much for her to handle, what with the stairs and that monstrous kitchen."

"Well, it's too big for me, as well."

"That may be...for now." Grandfather winked. "But it's the perfect place to raise a family."

Eli recalled with great joy coming here as a youngster. It had been the gathering place for his parents, his aunts and uncles, and all the cousins. Strangely, he'd been the only one of the lot who'd followed in his grandfather's steps.

"I can't give it to you, but I can sure sell it to you for a song."

"I wouldn't even think of it. Besides, one of your children might want it."

"No, I've talked to each of them, your father included, and none of them is interested, but they would love to see it stay in the family. They all said that since the medical practice is right here, it only makes sense for you to buy it, provided you want to."

Just moments ago, he'd been too exhausted to think, but now his pulse quickened with new life, his mind shooting in several directions. "I don't even know what to say, much less think."

"Well, why don't you pray about it? You don't need to decide overnight." He grasped the doorknob, then whipped his head around. "You're doing a fine job in the office, son. I'm proud of you."

"Thanks, Grandfather. So far, so good."

"Aside from running the show alone, have you run into any major problems?"

"None to speak of, unless you count the issue of payment. Every patient sings the same tune: 'Doc never makes me pay the same day. He just sends a bill!'"

Grandfather gave a hearty laugh. "Winnie has always billed them, but you can use whatever method works best for you. I'd say, for the most part, the monthly billing statements work well."

"What do you mean, 'for the most part'?"

"Well, some don't pay in a timely fashion, if at all. Given the state of the economy, folks who need medical attention get it, whether they can afford it or not. I don't let anyone take advantage, mind you, but, in time, you'll learn which ones can and can't afford to part with even a cent. It's up to you, of course, to handle that matter as you see fit. Since the stock market crash, you never know what could happen. So far, Wabash has reaped its share of blessings, but every day you hear about another small-town bank going under. Nobody's safe these days."

Eli nodded soberly. "I'll see to it that folks get the care they need, whether they can afford it or not."

Grandfather gave a knowing nod. "I thought as much. You and I are alike in many ways."

Before he left, Eli thought to bring up another matter. "Speaking of folks with little, how do you suppose Sofia Rogers is going to support herself once that baby comes?"

"I've wondered the same. She's a determined young woman, but I think you've already figured that out. I think adoption would be a wise solution, but she doesn't seem to be sold on the idea. I can't imagine what other option she has, though. And then, there's Andy to think of. He spent the morning with me, by the way. We played checkers and tinkered around in the garage. I got plain used to his presence while Sofie was laid up in the hospital. Mighty fine young man. Too bad about that stutter."

"I know," Eli said. "I wrote to my friend from university and asked for a copy of his thesis. After a vast amount of research on various speech impediments, he concluded that there is hope for stutterers, with effective speech therapy and plenty of encouragement. I'd like to read up on his findings. Stammering places an unforgiving stigma on people. I'd like to do what I can to erase that ridiculous belief."

"Well, good for you. If nothing else, interacting with another male role model will be good for him."

"Got any notion as to who fathered Sofia's baby?"

A frown crossed Grandfather's face. "None what-soever. As you know, Sofia is a stubborn little mite. I can't get anything out of her."

Eli brushed a hand through his already mussed hair. "I think I've picked up on that trait."

"Don't know if someone jilted her, or if...well... something far worse transpired."

"You don't think...?"

"It's been known to happen, even in Wabash. There are some characters around town that I don't trust much further than I can stick out my tongue. I'm not saying they're capable of committing that horren-dous a crime, but one can't be too careful these days, another reason I'm glad we both agreed to drive that young lady to and from work."

"I agree. She may be stubborn and independent, but she's also vulnerable, living alone with only her brother and their dog for protection. No telling what—"

The door buzzer sounded. Grandfather raised a finger. "That would be our supper."

"Our supper?"

Mischievous eyes flickered back at him. "I ran into Debbie Stinehart at the post office this afternoon and mentioned that Winnie's been away, and she said it was a crime for us to have to fend for ourselves in the kitch-en. She insisted on bringing over a kettle of beef stew, along with one of her famous peach pies. With the left-overs, it might even hold us over till Winnie gets back."

"Why, you manipulative rascal!"

"Yes, and mighty proud of it."

❧

That night, Sofia made sure to pull all the drapes tight so that not so much as a crack to the outside showed. Her skin crawled just thinking that her attacker might be keeping watch. Thankfully, the temperature had dropped enough that they would still be comfortable with the drapes down.

Sofie glanced at Andy, sprawled on his stomach on the living room floor, his chin in his hands, listening to a radio show.

"Don't open any windows tonight, okay, Andy?"

Andy gave a vague nod. "'Kay."

"Did you hear what I just said?"

"W-what?"

"I told you not to open any windows tonight."

"I know. Why not?"

With a sigh of frustration, she went to the radio box and turned down the volume. "I don't want you catching a chill."

"Alright, b-but what if it g-gets hot?"

"Use the electric fan, but keep the windows closed, you hear me? In fact, from now on, we're going to lock them up tight every night before I leave." Her tone was testier than she wanted it to be, but she couldn't bear to think of anyone with evil intentions coming in through an open window.

"Fine. Would you turn that back up? It was just gettin' good."

She turned the volume knob to its original position, then walked back to the kitchen, her nerves a jumble. At least she felt stronger tonight, even after baking bread, mopping the floors, and scrubbing the kitchen cabinet doors. The short rests she'd taken in between chores must have rejuvenated her. She still had a lingering cough, but even that had started to dissipate.

Around eight thirty, she started growing restless thinking about going to work. It wasn't just the thought of leaving Andy alone that put her nerves on edge, but also that she'd have to take that two-mile ride with the young Dr. Trent. His good looks disarmed her, and she hated the idea of putting him out. A light shone through her drapes, indicating the arrival of a car. She ran to the window to peer outside and clutched her chest at the sight of him opening his door and climbing out. Yes, he'd said he would arrive a little early to spend some time with Andy, but this was beyond early.

"Who's here?" Andy emerged from the washroom in his pajamas, a towel in hand and his face scrubbed clean. "Is it the doctor already?"

Sofie dried her damp palms on her shirt. "Yes, he came early."

"Hot dog!" Andy raced to the door and yanked it open wide. "H-hi, Dr. Trent! C-come on in. I th-think it's m-mighty nice of you, t-takin' S-Sofie to work."

"Hey there, Andy. Good to see you again." His low, mellow voice wrapped her in warmth.

Andy stepped aside to allow for his entry, and the first thing she thought was that his presence filled her tiny house and made her heart skitter faster than usual. He granted her a pleasant smile. "Is it alright that I came early? I thought Andy and I could visit while you got ready, at your leisure. You start at ten?"

"Yes, but I like to get there in plenty of time."

"How about we leave at nine forty?"

"That sounds good. Thank you for driving me."

His smile lengthened. "You don't have to keep thanking me, Sofie. It's my pleasure, really."

He had a way of taking the wind right out of her sails, making it hard to argue. Eli put his hand on Andy's shoulder. "I see you're getting yourself ready for bed. What's this?" He gestured to the card table in the living room, where a half-finished jigsaw puzzle was displayed. "Looks like you've been busy."

"It's a t-tough one." Andy picked up the puzzle box to reveal the completed scene. "We w-work on it most n-n-nights, ain't—I mean, *isn't* that right, sis?"

Sofia nodded.

Eli scratched the back of his head, bent over the table to eye the pieces, and immediately fitted one into a spot.

Andy dropped his jaw. "Hey! Th-that was fast." Lighthearted laughter spilled out of him, the sound touching a chord of warmth in Sofie's barred-up heart.

Eli cast her a glance over his shoulder. "He stays home alone all night while you work?"

"He always has. And he's always managed just fine, Dr. Trent."

His mouth registered a tiny grin. "I don't doubt it for a second." There he went again, stealing her wind.

He turned to Andy. "May I help you with this puzzle? I think I found another piece." He reached across the table and situated a piece in just the right place.

The two kept up a quiet conversation while Sofie finished putting away the supper dishes and wiping the countertops. Not wanting to sit with them, yet wanting to remain close by, she busied herself with sweeping the linoleum floor—which bore nary a crumb, having been thoroughly mopped that very afternoon. Every so often, she felt Elijah Trent's eyes on her, and it was all she could do not to meet his gaze as she eavesdropped. Her brother's stutter persisted, but the moments of shared laughter indicated the beginnings of a friendship, and, for the life of her, Sofie could not figure out how to feel about that.

Some thirty minutes later, Sofie tucked Andy into bed, repeating her orders that he wasn't to open any windows.

"I won't, sis. Gosh! Why are you s-so fired up about that all of a s-sudden?"

She straightened and crossed her arms, tipping her face to the side. "No reason in particular. It's just that one can never be too careful. Bad things happen."

"You mean, like how you got that b-baby in your belly?"

"What?" Her eyes darted to the door. She was relieved not to see any sign of the doctor. "Don't talk like that." Regretting that she'd snapped at him, she lowered herself to the edge of the bed and reached down, gently pushing a few stray strands of reddish hair off of his forehead. "We'll talk about it more later, okay? It's just that now is not a good time."

"I know. You don't really have to tell me, anyway. I already know how it got there."

Her jaw dropped, nearly reaching her top button. "What on earth do you mean?"

"I'm not some dummy, Sofie. I am eleven, you know."

"Yes, but...who told you...I mean, what exactly...?" She had no idea how to continue.

"I heard some of the bigger boys talking after school one d-day last year. One of 'em said that a boy and a girl—"

"Stop right there. First, you should not have been listening to their conversation. Second, I don't want you thinking the things you overheard were appropriate. You're far too young...."

He pulled a sheet over his face so that his next words came out muffled. "Don't worry, I'm not plannin' on kissing any girls. Yuck! And you shouldn't've kissed a boy, either. Just look where it got you." Ever so slowly, he drew the blanket back to reveal one green eye. "Can we stop talking about this now?"

She almost laughed out loud. Andy thought she'd ended up in this condition by kissing a boy? She didn't know whether to be relieved or alarmed. "Absolutely," she replied, then bent over to give him one last light peck on the cheek.

He squirmed. "You c-can start just giving me hugs, not kisses. Even though I know bad things only h-h-happen from kissin' on the l-lips, I think I'm gettin' too big for you to b-be kissing me g-good night."

She was taken aback by his words, but she shrugged them off. "I can respect that, I guess. But don't for one second think I'm going to stop hugging you anytime soon."

"Fine." His eyes roved to the door. "You better go now. Eli's waiting. I'll see you in the m-morning."

"Eli?"

"He tol' m-me to start c-calling him that instead of 'Dr. Trent,' so's we don't get mixed up b-between him and his grandpa. He s-said me an' him are goin' to be g-g-good friends. Isn't that good news? Who d-doesn't want a new f-friend?"

Yes, who? *She* didn't, for starters. What gave this new doctor in town the right to barge in on the life she'd built with her brother? They'd come up with a decent arrangement, if she did say so, and hardly needed his assistance. Sure, things were about to get very complicated after her baby came, but she'd done well without his interfering. She had no reason to think she wouldn't continue to find sufficient means for her little family to survive—no matter that the country had entered into a staggering depression and things in Wabash might worsen. She thought about asking Mr. VanDyke if she could add an extra hour to her shift. That would at least bring in a little extra money each week. But it would also mean spending less time with Andy. And then, there was the baby—always the baby—to think about.

"You should really consider adoption."

Land sakes, there came that dread idea again. She pushed it aside and quietly slipped out of the room.

Chapter Seven

How excellent is thy lovingkindness, O God!
therefore the children of men put their trust
under the shadow of thy wings.
—Psalm 36:7

If Sofia Rogers ever meant to give in to the idea of Eli driving her to work, she sure didn't let on. If anything, she'd become even more brusque, presenting him with quite a challenge whenever he tried to strike up a conversation. "She is a spirited little thing," he told his grandfather over supper one night. "If it weren't for my budding friendship with her brother, I think I'd offer to pay somebody else to do the honors of driving her."

"Hmm. She's been downright pleasant to me," Grandfather reflected, "always asking how my evening went, and thanking me profusely for going to the trouble of driving her home."

"Gee, thanks. Now I feel much better," Eli groused. "'Thank you, Dr. Trent' is about all I ever get out of her. That, and 'It's really not necessary your driving me. I've been riding my bike to and from work for years.' I tell her, 'Yes, but have you been pregnant for years?'"

Grandfather chuckled. "Maybe you should stop reminding her of her circumstances. She's got a lot on her mind."

"The baby, you mean."

"Yes. As I said, I've asked her to consider adoption, but she closes up tight as a clam at the mention of it. I've no idea how she plans to get around with that baby in tow. Maybe fashion some kind of carrier she can strap on her back, tote the baby around like a papoose."

"A car would solve a lot of her problems."

"That girl can't afford a car, let alone another mouth to feed." Grandfather pressed his napkin to his bearded chin. They were nearly sick of eating bologna sandwiches and chicken noodle soup, but Debbie Stinehart's beef stew had fed them for only two meals. Winnie Carmichael would receive an equally warm welcome from Grandfather and Eli tomorrow, no matter the difference in reasons.

"I guess you're right about the car. Besides, someone would have to teach her to drive, and you know I won't be volunteering."

"That's because you intimidate her." Grandfather scooted his chair away from the table, stood, and brought his dishes to the sink.

Eli furrowed his brow. "What makes you say that?" He picked up his own plate and carried it to the counter. "I'm hardly an ogre." He turned the faucet on to let the water run then stood and waited for it to heat up.

Grandfather's chuckle was low and resonant. "Like many women, Sofie is shy around men, especially nice-looking ones like you."

Eli put a stopper in the drain and then poured some Ivory dish flakes into the sink, working up a few bubbles by swishing his hand in the water. "Apparently, she's not too shy, to have gotten herself in a motherly way."

Grandfather sobered. "As we discussed the other day, we don't know the whole story. She could have been the victim of some insidious act."

The mere notion made Eli cringe. "Wouldn't she have reported it to the authorities?"

"Could be she did, and there's an investigation going on that we don't even know about."

"Maybe we should report our suspicions, just in case."

"We're physicians, Eli, not detectives or law enforcement officers. In order to report something, we'd need grounds for suspicion. Right now, all we've got is a pregnant woman who, for reasons unknown to us, refuses to share any information. But you can't fault her for that."

Eli lowered several dishes into the sink of warm, bubbly water. "Andy stays at home alone every night while she works. Did you know that?"

"Of course. Ever since she assumed care of him, she's done things her way, and, as far as I know, nobody's been able to argue with the job she's done. She's a smart girl with a level head."

"Not sure her pregnancy qualifies her as having a level head."

"Can't you give her the benefit of the doubt? At least learn her story first."

"I'd like to, believe me. Do you suppose Andy knows anything?"

"I doubt it, given how protective she's always been of him." Grandfather picked up a dripping plate and started wiping it dry with a dishtowel.

"Well, it's high time she came out with the truth. I'm half tempted to go straight to the sheriff myself."

Grandfather shook his head. "You have to let people live their lives, Eli. Honestly, the moment I first

laid eyes on you, lying in that frilly bassinet and wearing that little white bonnet, you were already making
plans to save the world."

A smile teased the corners of Eli's mouth as he
stared down at the water, watching several bubbles
pop and disintegrate. "I guess God planted some big
dreams in my head that somehow wound up in my
heart."

"That, my boy, is the definition of passion. You
knew early on that you wanted to be a doctor, ever
since you started bringing sickly critters home and
nursing them back to health. When I told your mother
that I'd done the same thing as a youngster, she said, 'I
guess that settles it, then. Time to start putting money
aside for medical school.'"

That stirred up a number of memories. "Dad and
Mom sure sacrificed a lot for us kids. They weren't
rich, by any means, unless you count the love they
dished out to all of us."

"You have good parents, Elijah, I'll grant you
that."

He affectionately bumped against the old fellow.
"And my granddad ain't too bad, either." His grandfather finished drying the final dish while Eli let out
the water. "Are you as anxious as I am for Winnie's
return?"

His grandfather's head jerked up and his eyes lit
like two street lamps. "What do you think?"

Eli laughed. "I think I'm going to squeeze the
stuffing out of her and tell her what a lousy cook you
are. Then, I'll gladly hand her over to you."

Grandfather chuckled. "I think I'll be the first one
to hug her."

"Won't she be embarrassed with me looking on?"

"Who said anything about you looking on? I intend to pick her up at the train station...alone. And I expect you to behave yourself when you greet her. I don't want her having any regrets about agreeing to marry me."

Laughing, Eli wrung out the dishcloth and draped it over the edge of the sink. "I'll try to be on my best behavior."

❧

A pan crashed to the floor, followed by a scamper of feet, waking Sofie with a terrible start. She leaped out of bed on instinct, only to fall backward on the mattress from sheer dizziness. "Andy?" she called feebly. "Are you okay?"

He appeared in her bedroom doorway, holding a large pot by the handle. "Sorry, sis. I was t-trying to get the kettle down, and I lost my grip."

She dropped her arm across her face and moaned. "What were you planning to do?"

"B-boil up some taters. Go back to sleep."

She looked at her bulging belly, which seemed to have grown overnight. Lying on her back, she couldn't see her toes over the top of the bump. "Too late," she groaned. "I'm awake now." She rose, slowly, and shrugged into her cotton robe, which she could no longer button around the middle. "What time is it?" she asked, too tired to focus her pupils on the clock across the room.

"Ten to twelve."

"Twelve noon? Why did you let me sleep so long?"

"I figured you were t-tired, and you need plenty of sleep. That's what Eli said."

Eli, Eli, Eli. That's all Andy had been talking about for days. "Eli said this," "Eli said that." And now, Eli had the nerve to talk about her? "He did, did he?"

"Yep. He said I need to help you as m-much as I can, so you won't tire yourself out."

"Oh, good gracious. I'm not an invalid." Andy turned and walked toward the kitchen, and she followed him. Why should the young doctor care about how much sleep she got? She needed to find a tactful way of telling him to mind his own business. However, now that it was customary for him to drive her to work each night, she knew she needed to hold her temper at bay. She appreciated the car rides more and more, especially as the baby grew.

As Andy filled the kettle with water from the kitchen faucet, Sofie leaned against the doorframe and studied him, struck by how much he'd grown, by the way he looked more and more like their daddy every day. A wave of pride rushed over her to think of what a fine young man he was turning out to be.

She moseyed up beside him at the old white stove, where he'd set the kettle over the flaming burner and now dropped potato after potato into the pot. "I hope that you scrubbed those potatoes, Andy. And just why are you boiling so many?"

"'C-course I washed 'em. I thought you might like to make up a batch of p-potato s-salad. There's still some ham in the icebox, so we can m-make sandwiches."

"Hmm. Sounds like you have the lunch menu all planned out."

"I do. A-actually, I thought we c-could go down to the river for a pic-picnic."

"That sounds nice."

"Eli's goin' to come, too."

"Eli? No, I don't care for that idea."

"Well, t-too bad, 'cause I already invited him."

"You what? Why did you do that? More impor-tant, when?"

"This mornin', when I was over at the Trents'."

"Why would you do that? Invite Dr. Eli, I mean. He's a busy man. You shouldn't have bothered him on a Saturday."

"You don't like him v-very much, do you?"

She whisked both hands through her short curls and grimaced, staring down at the kettle as he plopped the last potato into the water. "It's not that I don't like him. I suppose he's nice enough. I just don't think…I don't know. You shouldn't have invited him without consulting me. I'm sure there are a million things he'd rather do today than go on a picnic with us. You prob-ably made it hard for him to say no. Oh, Andrew." A panicky sensation rolled through her belly.

"N-no, he said it'd be f-fun. He said he's been wan-tin' to spend some time at the river, 'cause he hasn't relaxed much since he moved here. Oh! I almost forgot. Mrs. Carmichael p-promised to bake us a p-pie."

"Mrs. Carmichael?"

"Yeah. The lady who cleans Doc Trent's house."

"I didn't realize she worked there, too. I know her as the secretary at Doc's office."

Andy shrugged one shoulder. "Don't ask me. All I know is, w-we get pie."

"Oh, Andy, I don't know about this. I feel…awk-ward, I guess."

He gazed at her, his green eyes hangdog. "Don't worry, Sofie. It'll b-be okay. Just make the p-potato salad. Please?"

"Oh, fine. Goodness gracious!" She rolled up her sleeves. "When is this picnic supposed to take place?"

"Eli's c-coming over at two."

"Two o'clock? That hardly gives me time to complete all the chores I had on my list for the day."

"You c-can do 'em later. I'll even help."

"Oh, you stinker." She rolled her eyes and ruffled his red hair. "What am I going to do with you?"

※

Eli pulled his grandfather's car alongside the curb in front of the Rogerses' and gazed about the neat little yard. The house itself looked rather run-down, with its peeling shingles and sagging shutters. The needed repairs were certainly too expensive for Sofia to have fixed, as meager as her wages were sure to be. But she'd almost made up for the tumbledown appearance by planting greenery and flowers of every color along the front walkway. Besides that, there were flower boxes under every window and a big pot of red geraniums on the front stoop. Clearly, Sofie had a skill for gardening, proven further by the large vegetable patch he'd noticed the other night.

The beginnings of a smile tugged at his mouth as he imagined her bending down in the baking sun to pull weeds and tend the plants, with that bulging belly getting in the way. He hoped she wouldn't mind that he'd stopped by to take Andy down to the river. Andy had promised she wouldn't. Eli knew Sofie considered him a pest, but he'd begun to build a friendship with the boy, and he wanted it to continue. Besides, visiting Andy also allowed him to keep an eye on his sister. The closer she came to her due date, the more she needed watchful attention, as adamantly as she might deny it. If she had a boyfriend—doubtful, it seemed—he kept himself well hidden.

Eli opened the door and held it a moment with his foot, pausing to breathe in the fragrant air and to thank God for the gift of a perfect summer day. A warm breeze whistled gently through the trees, and a crow swooped past, landing on the peak of Sofie's roof with a screeching caw.

The front door opened, and Andy skipped down the steps. "Eli, you came!"

He noticed the lack of a stutter in the boy's excitement and grinned. "Well, of course I came!" he called back, climbing out of the car. "Did you doubt me?"

The lad was out of breath when he reached the car. "Nah. I figured you were g-good for your word."

Just then, he spotted Sofie standing on the tiny porch, plaid skirt billowing and wide-brimmed straw hat covering her expression, the handle of a wicker basket looped over her arm. It struck him that he'd be hard put to count on one hand the number of natural wonders much prettier than Sofia Rogers.

"Is it okay if Sofie c-comes, too?"

Eli kept his eyes trained on her. "Yes, of course it's okay, but I'm surprised she'd want to come, considering she doesn't seem to have much use for me."

"Aww, she's got use for you. She just don't sh-show it very good. Anyways, she's real excited about goin' on the picnic."

"Is she, now?"

"Well, she did say she had ch-chores to do, but she thought a p-picnic sounded nice."

"Why do I get the sense that you neglected to tell me on purpose?"

Andy squinted up at him. "Huh?" He wore an innocent face. "D-did you b-bring the pie?"

Clever boy, changing the subject quicker than green grass grows a goat. Eli chuckled low in his throat. "Sure did. Mrs. Carmichael's apple supreme. It's on the backseat." He nodded toward the car.

"Sofie made p-potato salad and ham sandwiches. Sh-sh-she also dug out a big blanket from the chest, so's we'd have something to spread out on. Do you like grasshopper huntin'?"

"Grasshopper hunting?" The boy sure could hop from one topic to the next. "Can't say I've ever tried my hand at it." He glanced up at the porch, but Sofie must have gone back inside. He put a hand on Andy's shoulder and nudged him forward. "But I'm pretty sure I'm about to learn."

"S-Sofie taught me, back when I was a little kid. She'd probably be h-happy to teach you, too."

"Is that so?" On the way to the house, he decided he'd been hoodwinked good, and he found he didn't mind it one bit.

Chapter Eight

The heart is deceitful above all things, and
desperately wicked....
—Jeremiah 17:9

Owen stewed with anger as he watched Sofie, her dopey kid brother, and that new doctor head north on River Road in that swanky sedan—a 1929 Packard, if he wasn't mistaken. They probably had plans for driving down to the riverbank, which most folks did when they headed north, since the street dead-ended at the river. He'd seen them hauling a few things out to the car—the makings of a picnic, from the looks of it. Sofie had better not spill the beans about what had happened to her. But the doctor was probably pretty smart. If he got too close, it was only a matter of time before he figured out how she'd found herself in a motherly way. He could kill Sofie, of course, but he didn't want to harm his kid. He'd wait until she gave birth to do away with her.

In the meantime, Owen started thinking up ways to do away with the good doctor. He would make it look like an accident, of course. Old Doc Trent had more cars than anybody had a right to own, and it wouldn't be all that hard to finagle a car wreck. Cut the brake line or something. Any of the local back roads could become treacherous when one got going too fast.

Yes, indeed. A tragic auto accident could solve a multitude of potential problems.

When the car disappeared in a dusty cloud, Owen yanked his pack of cigarettes from his pocket, stuck one in his mouth, and struck a match to light it. He inhaled slowly, then exhaled smoke in practiced rings, for a few minutes. Next, he adjusted the gearshift of the rusty, rattletrap truck his father had been letting him use to drive to Godfrey's Garage, where he worked for a pittance, then pulled out onto Mill Creek Pike and drove due west. He was supposed to meet up with Elmer Bacon, Lester White, and Marvin Duran at the deserted Chester farm, and he didn't want to be late. They'd probably end up doing the usual—getting wasted on booze and brainstorming ways to make some extra bucks for buying hooch, even if it meant pulling off a couple of minor heists. Owen had absorbed a lot of knowledge at reform school—and not the kind of book learning his daddy had bargained for. He'd sent him away with the assumption that an environment of rigid rules would "fix" him. What a joke. It must not have dawned on him that reform schools were full of kids just like Owen—spoiled brats who had a bone to pick with the world and were more than happy to share their knowledge and learn from their peers about how to fight the system and come out on top.

He wasn't sure how he could have been expected to turn out any differently. His dad had climbed the ladder of local prestige, serving on countless city boards and vying for various county positions until finally landing his dream job as sheriff, meanwhile treating his family like road dirt. He'd demanded the respect he never could have earned, knocking them around when they failed to follow orders. Of course,

Carolee had been exempt, as Daddy's pride and joy.
But not Owen. One broken rule, and he'd been tossed
aside and spurned by the man whose reputation was
ever at stake. Once, he'd overheard his dad say he
wished Owen had never been born, that life would be
a lot easier without him. And Owen had been happy
to oblige, diving headlong into all kinds of things that
would either tarnish his dad's perfect record or get
him kicked out and sent far, far away.

The lot of them were hypocrites, as far as he
was concerned, attending mass on Saturday night or
Sunday morning then living strictly for themselves the
rest of the week—his mother gossiping, his dad breaking the very laws he was meant to uphold by drinking
himself into oblivion on Orville Dotson's homemade
brew, and his sister bossing him around as if she ruled
the kingdom with Alfred the Great. In the course of
his fourteen years before being shipped off to Peterford
School for Boys, Owen had fallen victim to more beatings by his father than Indiana had corn, and it would
be a cold day in the Sahara before he ever felt one ounce
of affection for the bully. Truth was, he hated his guts,
and nothing pleased him more than when he got his ire
up. To his advantage, he'd grown more than a foot at
Peterford, and, since his return, his dad hadn't seemed
inclined to mess with him. Owen had the upper hand,
for a change, and he found he liked his new position
of power in the family. His own mother steered clear of
him, having given up on him years ago, and his sister
was nothing but a big fat nuisance. The lot of them
could go to the furthest regions of Hades, as far as he
was concerned, and it wouldn't bother him one bit.

He took a long drag off his cigarette. A white
cat with black markings darted across the road, and

he turned the wheel, hoping to turn the fluffy fe-
line into vulture food. When he missed it by a hair's
breadth, he slammed his fist on the steering wheel in
disappointment.

The other guys were waiting for him at the end
of a long two-track where the rickety old barn stood,
the only structure remaining of the Chester farm. The
area was overgrown with tall grasses and sassafras,
fairly concealing Elmer's car, parked in the shade of
a sprawling oak. Owen drove his truck through the
remains of the big barn doors and then cut the engine,
climbed out, and tossed his cigarette on the dirt floor,
grinding it out with the toe of his boot. He couldn't say
he really liked his friends, but they provided him with
sufficient entertainment, and so he didn't mind whil-
ing away his hours with them on the days he didn't
have to work. Tonight, when he got bored, he'd go back
out to Sofie's house and check on things. Make sure
she wasn't getting too cozy with the doctor.

"You bring any suds?" Lester White, an over-
weight, pockmarked brute sauntered up to him, his
hands tucked in his pockets.

"I managed to buy two jars off old John Sauter
yesterday after work, but he wouldn't part with more
than that. Said if I reported him, he'd make me pay
big time. I says, 'Yeah, yeah, I'm so scared I might wet
myself.' The codger's so hard of hearing, he made me
repeat myself. He's got a good stash in his back shed,
by the way. I saw it. Shelves and shelves. Bet we could
break in there and get us a good year's supply. And
what's he gonna do, report it to my half-stewed dad
who's got his own secret stockpile?"

They all cackled. "Why don't you steal from your
dad's supply?"

"No way. He counts his bottles every day, and if any came up missing, he'd suspect me right off. Oh, he knows I take from the icebox, but there isn't much he can do about that. Right now, my folks are my bread and butter, and I've got to watch my step so they don't kick me out. Not that I like living there, but at least it's free. Anyway, what did you fellas come up with in the way of booze?"

"I found me a couple bottles over at my grand-dad's house," Marvin supplied. "He keeps a stash in his closet. He's pretty blind, though, so I don't think he'll miss 'em."

"Any new girlie magazines to feast our eyes on?" Owen asked.

Lester's eyes lit up. "Yeah, I got a heap of 'em. Pa keeps 'em hid in the chicken coop, where Ma won't find 'em. They kind of smell, but you get used to it."

"I don't mind the smell," Owen said. "My kid sister probably smells worse."

The comment brought on a round of snickers from the group. So far, this promised to be a good time, maybe even better than usual.

※

Glorious sunshine shone down on their picnic spot, warming Sofie's shoulders almost to the point of discomfort. Her cheeks burned, as well, but she didn't know whether to blame the heat or her sheer lack of composure in the doctor's presence. She doubted a finer-looking gentleman resided in all of Wabash. It downright pained her to be so large around the middle, not to mention uneducated beyond high school.

The picnic turned out to be one of the most awkward events ever, and if Andy had still been young enough to be spanked, Sofie would have turned him over her knee first thing upon arriving back home. The little rogue had arranged the three-person outing without Dr. Trent's knowledge. She couldn't imagine what he had up his sleeve, but she intended to find out later and quickly put a stop to it. She did not need her kid brother orchestrating her love life. For now, though, she did her best to cover up her mortification by making small talk and watching the waterfowl skim the rippling waters of the Wabash. Andy was wading knee-deep in the river, a long stick in his hand.

"Your potato salad hit the spot," Eli remarked. "I'd even say it rivals my mother's recipe." He lay on his back, hands clasped behind his head, legs crossed at the ankles, on the blanket they'd spread on a nice, soft patch of grass. He seemed to be studying the array of puffy clouds overhead. "I think I ate the equivalent of a horse," he mused. "Good idea Andy had, putting this picnic together."

Sofie fingered the handle of the picnic basket, where they'd already repacked the lunch dishes after rinsing them off in the river. "I ate far more than usual, myself," she admitted. "And, yes, Andy and his ideas."

He lifted his head slightly, angling her a grin, his blue eyes twinkling. "You didn't know I was coming?"

"Oh, I knew you were coming, but he made it sound like you knew I'd be along, as well. I'm sorry he tricked you. I feel like I'm intruding on one of your usual get-togethers."

"No, don't feel like that. I'm glad you came." His gaze went to her belly, just as the baby gave her a good jab in the side, provoking a wince.

"You alright?" He reached over and touched her arm, which made her jerk to life.

"Yes, of course. It's just that the baby's been very active lately."

He rose to a sitting position, his long legs stretched out before him, and leaned back on his palms. "The bigger he grows, the less he'll move around. It'll get too crowded in there."

"Humph. I don't know how I feel about that. I'm not looking forward to delivering a big baby."

He chuckled. "You'll do fine. You're young, strong, and healthy."

She didn't know why it should surprise her that his words brought such comfort, but they did.

"You should come to my office so I can weigh you and check your vitals."

"I don't see what that would accomplish. You just said I'm young, strong, and healthy."

"But it never hurts to have a check-up."

"I can't afford it."

"The office call will be on me."

"I don't accept charity."

She heard his soft sigh and dared not look at his sea-blue eyes, for she knew she'd catch a glimpse of frustration in them. She decided to turn her attention to Andy, who was still wading in the river. "Don't go out too far," she called to him. Then, she muttered to Eli, "I don't know what he intends to do with that stick. Spear something, perhaps."

Eli's gaze followed hers. "Boys and sticks just go together."

"Hmm. I guess you're right."

"He's a great kid, you know. You're doing an excellent job raising him."

"My parents were wonderful people, and they still have a big influence on us. Andy's a lot like my father;

he has a kind soul, he loves nature, and he enjoys tearing things apart and trying to put them back together. Daddy was a fine mechanic."

"It must have been awfully hard for you when they died so suddenly, and then to find yourself assuming the role of parent at—what? Fifteen? Sixteen? Didn't any relatives or friends offer to take you in?"

"I was fifteen at the time, and, yes, we had an aunt and uncle in Kansas who wanted us to come live with them, but I didn't think it would be good to uproot Andy. He didn't need another major change in his life. And, quite frankly, neither did I. Friends of ours insisted we stay with them, and we did, for a couple of weeks. But, once I got control of my emotions, we moved back home again. It seemed like the best thing to do, and we felt closer to our parents there. We've managed, for the most part."

"You're a brave woman, you know that?"

"Not brave. Just practical. I've always been of the opinion that nothing good ever came from moping around and fussing over things that are out of my control. Life goes on, and all we can do is try our best to get by."

"Hmm. And where does God fit into that picture?"

Unnerved by the abrupt question, she smoothed down her blue and yellow plaid skirt with her palms, stopping at her knees, then brushed her hands together and gazed out at the river. How to answer him? "We grew up going to that little community church in the center of town, but I haven't been there in some time. I started to feel...I don't know. Out of place, I guess. I think I told you that Andy goes to church with the Walters family most Sundays."

"You don't think it's important for you to go together?"

Her head snapped up. Startled by something, a flock of geese took wing and honked as they followed the river's path west, toward Potter Island. She yanked a tall blade of grass out of the soil and fingered its featherlike smoothness as she pondered his question. "I think it's important, yes. But, given my...condition, it doesn't seem like a good idea right now." She smoothed the front of her dress again with one hand. "I don't particularly enjoy having people stare at me."

"Is that the only reason you don't go? You don't strike me as the type who would be concerned about what people think." He gave her arm a gentle nudge. "You sure do have a mind of your own. You ever feel like God doesn't care about you, so why should you care about Him?"

She jolted to life again. He had pegged her so accurately, it was unnerving. "Something along those lines," she conceded. "I mean, if God is love, why would He leave us to fend for ourselves? Mother and Daddy were so devoted to us, and we depended on them for our needs."

He, too, pulled a long, thick blade of grass from the ground, then separated it from top to bottom. "Maybe God wants you to learn to depend on Him a little more now."

"Perhaps." She tossed the grass down and swatted at a couple of flies eager to get at the remainder of food packed away under the basket lid. "I do know the Lord as my Savior, mind you. I asked Him into my heart when I was in second grade. I remember the moment to this day. My mother had been reading me a Bible story, as she always did before tucking me into bed, and I just looked up at her and said, 'I want to ask Jesus into my heart.' She prayed with me right

there." Such a tender memory, and one she'd long forgotten. What had caused her to drift so far from her
heavenly Father? Was it indeed that she hadn't seen
any evidence of Him working in her life? And whose
fault could that be? Had she grown so self-sufficient as
to think she didn't need His provision, strength, and
sustenance?

Like a flash in the dark, a passage from the book
of Luke came to mind. She'd committed it to memory
some years ago.

> *And I say unto you, Ask, and it shall be given
> you; seek, and ye shall find; knock, and it
> shall be opened unto you. For every one that
> asketh receiveth; and he that seeketh findeth;
> and to him that knocketh it shall be opened.*

It came to her that God never pushed His way
into a life, but instead He patiently waited. She'd asked
Him into her life, yes, but what had she done with that
decision in the following years? Only left it to simmer
over low heat. Didn't the Scripture say that she should
ask, and it would be given? She supposed if she never
asked, she couldn't expect God to give.

Eli had refrained from speaking, as if to offer her
time to mull over her own words. It was Sofie who finally broke the silence. "I assume you've known the
Lord forever."

A round of soft laughter rolled out of him. "Not
quite forever. I grew up in a Christian home, so I sort
of knew God from afar, but it wasn't till my teenage
years that I came to know Him in a personal way.
I'd been going to church regularly and living a decent, clean life, but, deep down, I'd always known I
couldn't get into heaven by hanging on my parents'

shirttails. I had to decide for myself. I think too many people are of the opinion that good living, attending church, growing up around other Christians, and throwing the occasional dollar bill into the offering bucket will secure them a spot in heaven for all eternity. I'd heard enough sermons to know I would one day reach a climactic point when I'd have to decide— God's way or my own. That came at a camp meeting one hot summer day, after an especially convicting fire-and-brimstone sermon. I was the ripe age of sixteen, about to begin my senior year of high school. I thought my pounding heart would burst right out of me if I didn't respond to God's voice that day, so I beat a path down the sawdust trail, and I've never been the same since."

"How so?"

"Well, for one thing, allowing God to direct my decisions has made a world of difference in my life. Not that I'm any expert on discerning God's voice, but I've sensed it from time to time, sort of like a gentle nudge."

The notion of that gentle nudge intrigued her, and she tried to imagine what it would be like to actually sense God's voice. "Is that what brought you to Wabash, then? A gentle nudge from God?"

"You could say that. I'd been offered a position in Detroit to head up the emergency department. At thirty-two, it would have been a great career opportunity."

So, now she knew his age. She brushed a few breadcrumbs into a neat little pile at her side and tried to remain aloof. Still, she did love listening to him talk. A warm breeze kicked up a few stray leaves that came to rest on a corner of the blanket. "But you obviously didn't take the job. Is that because Wabash seemed a much more exciting place to you than Detroit?"

In one fluid move, he lay down again, this time reclining on his side, facing her, and propping his chin upon his left palm. She thought him quite an appealing sight, lazing there with his sandy hair all mussed and the shadow of a beard darkening his jaw, and she rebuked herself for noticing.

"Something like that," he said. "Actually, Grandfather called me just two days before I was supposed to give the hospital board my decision and asked me to take over his practice, said he'd decided to retire. For years, we'd talked about my taking over his practice when he retired, but it always seemed more like a dream. I just couldn't picture him ever relinquishing his post. He built it from the ground up, and now he was offering it to me. It seemed almost surreal."

"But clearly a dream come true, or you wouldn't be here."

He smiled. "True enough. The hospital job would've put me in high standing with my colleagues and provided me with the assurance of future advancement, but I quickly realized I would have found it unfulfilling. I like getting to know my patients on a personal level, and it's nearly impossible to do that as an administrator. Here in Wabash, I can build relationships, make a difference in people's lives. The timing was perfect, so that's where the gentle nudge came into play. Grandfather's calling me just two days before the hospital board expected a decision confirmed to me exactly what I was supposed to do. I turned them down and came to Wabash." He craned his head back around to peer at Andy, crouched by the river's edge, poking at something with that stick. "I wouldn't have met your little brother had I taken that hospital promotion." Then, his gaze landed on her. "Or you."

Her baby kicked again, and she automatically rubbed small circles into the spot. "That would not have been any great loss," she answered. "Not meeting me."

"Now, that's where you're wrong." He met her gaze, his expression serious. "You should think a little more highly of yourself, Sofia."

The meaning behind his words wasn't entirely clear, but the whispery way he spoke her name, and the flickering warmth in his eyes, set her heart aflutter. Mercy! His gaze was intense, yet absent of any malicious intent. Right now, she could scarcely look away. What was it about his regard that captivated her so? Was it a show of heartfelt sympathy for her plight? Or a hint of attraction?

She surely didn't want any sympathy, from him or anyone else. As for the latter possibility, she dismissed it altogether. She couldn't afford to get her hopes up, especially when she knew, deep within her, that she would never be able to fully trust a man again. She especially didn't relish the thought of growing dependent on anyone else. Gracious, she hadn't even learned how to lean on God, let alone some guy.

But when Eli rolled onto his back again and closed his eyes, his face illumined by a ray of sunlight peeking through the tree branches overhead, she scolded herself for being so presumptuous. What a preposterous notion—that a man of such high Christian character, and with a degree in medicine, no less, would have eyes for a pregnant pauper. She gave her head a couple of stern shakes and welcomed the silence between them.

※

The rest of the afternoon moved at a slow, comfortable pace, with the three of them sipping lemonade, snacking on the leftovers from their midday meal, and enjoying companionable banter. As much as he fought it, Eli couldn't deny his attraction to Sofia Rogers. It didn't make any sense; she didn't fit the formula. Of all the girls he'd dated, probably the closest to being a good match had been a pretty nurse named Nancy Parsons. She'd had a pleasant personality, a quick wit, and a compassionate nature; plus, she'd loved the Lord. They'd had a lot in common, above and beyond a medical background, and they would have made a great team, if it hadn't been for one problem: the absence of sparks. In time, they'd parted ways as friends.

There'd been other women who'd turned his head, some of whom he'd even dated for short periods, but none had truly captivated him. In many cases, it had been those women who had pursued Eli rather than the other way around.

So, what was different about Sofia Rogers? Here was a woman wrong for him in every way possible. Why should he give her as much as a second glance? True, hers was a rare beauty, with her porcelain complexion, fine features, and chocolate eyes. Nothing hard about gazing into them, that was certain. And, yes, he'd noted those shapely calves in more than one instance; he'd gotten a particularly nice view of them when she'd lifted her skirt to climb into the car. But she carried another man's baby, for crying out loud! Plus, she'd as much as admitted her lack of zeal for God. No, she most definitely should not appeal to him. And yet she did.

She is My beloved, and she requires much care. Shower her with affection and tenderness.

He had no idea where the voice came from, but it startled him. Often, the Holy Spirit spoke in gentle nudges and whispers, but surely he'd misinterpreted the cue. Shower her with affection and tenderness— this pregnant, unmarried woman?

Later, after Eli had been running races up and down the riverbank with Andy, he'd decided to sit a spell to catch his breath and mop his sweaty brow. Sofie had joined her brother by the river, trying to capture grasshoppers in a big Mason jar, and as Eli lay there on the blanket, watching, something tugged at him like a magnet to metal. He smiled at the twosome, Sofie pointing at something in the tall river grasses, Andy sneaking up on his victim and then diving for it, coming up empty after almost every attempt. Sofie's soft laughter, carried to him on the gentle breeze, settled in the deepest corner of his heart. At one point, she glanced over her shoulder at him, and when their eyes met, she jerked her attentions back to Andy. Her reaction did strange things to his innards.

Lord, what am I doing even looking at her? She's got a mountain of troubles to deal with, and I'd be a fool to get myself involved.

A small flock of red-winged blackbirds soared across the expanse, then swooped down and vanished behind a clump of weeds upriver, probably searching for an early supper. Eli glanced at his watch, which read almost a quarter to five. He wished that time would stand still, but the blinding sun kept its course, marching steadily in a slow arc across a Wedgwood-blue sky. All too soon, he would return Sofie and her brother to their home, not knowing the next time he'd see them.

You could invite them to church tomorrow. The idea took him by surprise, even coming as it did from his own subconscious brainstorm. *Or maybe not,* he argued with himself. *What would people think if the three of you walked in together? You don't want to jeopardize the reputation of Grandfather's practice.*

He supposed he could ask Grandfather and Winnie to walk them inside, even sit with them during the service. That way, it would appear as if they'd been the ones doing the inviting. Surely, no one would look down on the well-respected doctor and his wife-to-be. But hadn't Sofie made it clear she didn't want to go to church? What made him think she'd even accept an invitation?

You should invite them, anyway. The last thing he wanted was to allow his tangled emotions to hinder his pragmatic way of thinking. Perhaps the Lord would give him some sort of sign, so he could know beyond a doubt that his inclination to invite them was the right thing to do.

They stayed another hour, each nibbling on another slice of Winnie's delicious apple supreme pie and finishing off the last drops of lemonade.

"That was a fun day. Thanks for comin' with us," Andy said, with no trace of a stutter.

"You're welcome, buddy. I enjoyed it, as well."

Sofie folded the blanket and hugged it to her chest. Her cheeks had tanned to a golden hue, as the hat she'd started out wearing had spent most of the day on the blanket rather than perched atop her curly head. "Yes, it was lovely. I'm glad you thought of it, Andy." She avoided Eli's gaze, he noticed, just as she had for a good share of the afternoon. He was inclined to suspect she merely wanted it to appear as if she didn't fancy him, and the notion made him smile to himself. Still, he wondered how he could possibly expect her to accept an invitation to church if she wouldn't spare him even a second's glance.

In the car, they jounced along River Road with the windows down, dust clouds billowing behind them. Andy leaned forward in the seat and stuck his head out the window, his hair ruffled by the cool air. When they pulled up to the house, Buster emerged from beneath the front steps. "Why didn't you bring your dog along?" Eli asked. "He would have been welcome."

"Sofie said I c-couldn't," Andy said as he pushed open his door. "She said he might get fur on your uh-uh-upholstery. Plus, he needs a b-bath."

"Well, he's ridden in the car before, and I don't recall Grandfather complaining about any fur. We'll take him with us next time."

"Next time?" Andy bounced in the seat. "Are we gonna have a-a-another p-picnic? W-when? How 'bout n-next Saturday?"

"Andy!" Sofie scolded him. "Dr. Trent does not want to spend all his Saturdays—"

"Next Saturday would be great," he hastened to say. "But what if we did something different?"

"Like what?" Andy leaned forward, his chin resting on the back of the front seat. Eli turned around and met his green eyes, which were as round as cake pans.

Sofie opened the passenger door. "I don't think... that is, Saturdays are usually spent completing the majority of our chores. We'll be busy in the garden, and if you'll remember, Andy, I told you all of the windows need washing. And then, there's that rotted front step to work on, and a couple of shutters coming loose.... So, thank you, Dr. Trent, but I'm afraid we'll have too much to do."

"Aww," Andy whined.

Eli looked thoughtful for a moment. "Why don't I come over and help?"

"Hot dog!" Andy leaped up from his seat and whooped, bumping his head on the ceiling in his gusto. Buster grew so excited at the commotion that he leaped into the backseat and started licking Andy's face.

Judging by Sofie's expression, she didn't share her brother's enthusiasm. Her dark brows knitted into a tense little frown. "That's really not necessary, Doc—"

"Eli," he quickly inserted. He turned his gaze on her and leaned closer, his mouth itching to grin, his hand itching even more to reach up and tweak her pert little chin. "Is that okay, Sofie?"

Her lips formed a tiny frown.

"Wipe that worried look off your face."

"Who said I was worried?"

"I can tell you are. You think that accepting a little help from somebody is going to undermine your independence, make you appear weak in some way. I know you're very capable of replacing your own porch step, reaffixing those loose shutters, pulling weeds or whatever it is that you do in that garden, and washing every last window, inside and out. But I'm offering to help, and I can't see the sense in turning me down." He swiveled in his seat. "Does it make any sense to you, Andy?"

"Nope. 'Sides, the m-more help we g-get, the less I ha-have to do."

"Andrew James." Sofie gave a loud huff. "We have always gotten by without anyone else's help."

His tiny grin vanished. "I th-think we could use s-somebody's help once in a while."

That sobered her into silence. She faced forward and let out a long breath through flared nostrils. "Oh, alright," she said after a moment's hesitation. "I suppose we could accept your help, Doc—Eli."

"Great. It's settled, then. Oh, and one more thing."

She turned narrowed eyes on him. "I'm afraid to ask."

"Don't be. What if I picked you two up tomorrow morning and took you to church with me?"

"What?" Sofie started. "No, I don't think—"

"Yes!" Andy shouted with enthusiasm. "I usually g-go with Georgie and his f-family, but I'd rather go with you. I'll run over there and tell them I'm goin' to a d-different church." Eli was impressed that he had spoken in almost perfect syllables.

Andy urged Buster out of the car, then bounded out himself, shut his door, and ran around to the other side. Before Sofie could issue another word, he relieved her of the picnic basket, looping his arm through the handle. He then reached inside the car and yanked her out. "See you in the morning, Eli!" He closed the door with a loud thunk.

Sofie stood there, looking confounded, mouth agape.

Before setting the gearshift in place, Eli leaned across the seat and hollered out the passenger window, "Thanks again for a great time today! See you tomorrow, around nine thirty."

Andy waved, but Sofie had already turned away, her arms folded across her rounded midsection, her plaid skirt flying in the breeze, granting him another glimpse at those awfully pretty calves. He shifted the car into drive and jostled up the bumpy road, chuckling all the way to the corner. Before making the left turn onto Mill Creek Pike, he noticed a beat-up black truck parked in the brush alongside the road. He thought he'd stop and see if the fellow was having car trouble, but a glance in the driver's window indicated that the cab was vacant.

Chapter Nine

Oh how great is thy goodness, which thou
hast laid up for them that fear thee....
—Psalm 31:19

That night, Sofie lay in bed, wide-eyed as an owl, and stared at the ceiling while a zillion worrisome thoughts whizzed through her head. She couldn't possibly go to church tomorrow with Eli, even though a small part of her soul hungered to hear God's Word preached again. The last time she'd attended a service had been in December, when she'd gone with Bruce and Tildi Walters to see the kids—their three sons and Andy—perform in the children's Christmas pageant. She'd wanted to enjoy the occasion for Andy's sake, but the brutal attack only weeks earlier had made her a regular basket case. Of course, she'd put on the bravest of smiles, even though her raw nerves had been prone to jump at the slightest sound or movement.

Now, seven months later, she carried a baby by some raunchy man, and no one had a clue. Instead, most people seemed to assume she was a loose woman who'd freely given herself away outside the bonds of marriage. How could she possibly go to church knowing that folks perceived her as practically the worst of sinners? Why, even Eli must wonder how she'd gotten herself into this pickle, and yet he'd invited her to church. What on earth had he been thinking? And, more important, why? Maybe he wanted to lead the efforts in her "reform." Or maybe he considered Andy to be a mission, of sorts—one small step in his campaign of world change. It wasn't a hard case to make, considering the way he'd befriended Andy and used his visits in order to check up on her, ask how she was feeling.

Even so, he couldn't possibly intend to sit with them in church and make a bad name for himself, just weeks after taking over his grandfather's practice.

Outside, the wind picked up and played continual tricks on her mind, making her believe someone lurked outside, when, really, those shadowy figures moving up the wall and across the ceiling were nothing more than the silhouettes of moonlit tree branches. She tugged her sheets up around her neck and squeezed her eyes shut, as if in deep prayer. Come to think of it, why didn't she pray?

Lord? I know I haven't talked to You in a long time; haven't read so much as a sentence from my Bible in... well, You know how long. I've prided myself on independence and self-sufficiency for so long, but the truth is, I'm scared. Scared of yesterday, scared of today, and terrified of the future. How will we ever survive once the baby comes? Is adoption the answer, after all? Margie doesn't think I should keep a baby conceived in such a way, but I'm afraid of passing my child to a couple who won't provide the love he or she deserves. Help me to trust You, Lord. Please.

She waited for a sign, or some special feeling— perhaps a "gentle nudge," as Eli had described. But none came. She did, however, drift off to sleep, and the next thing she knew, a dazzling ray of golden sun shone through a small opening in the bedroom curtains.

"Sofie? You awake?" Andy rapped on her door. "Don't forget, we're g-going to ch-church today."

Moaning, she pulled the sheets up over her head. "Go away."

"Nope. Get up! Eli'll be here in an hour. Don't you wanna take a b-bath?"

Sofie was struck by the sudden role reversal. "I took one last night."

"Good. Then, all you have to do is get dressed and eat some breakfast. I already ate. Oh! What're we havin' for lunch today?"

She rolled her eyes. "Is that the only thing eleven-year-old boys think about? Food?"

"Guess so. Now, get up."

"Alright, alright, just give me a second." Sofie's nocturnal work schedule had always been a bane when the weekend arrived. Accustomed to working week-nights, she usually had a tough time falling asleep on Saturday and Sunday evenings, and, regardless of how many hours of shut-eye she got, she had to fight off a foggy mind in the morning. One would have expected her body to adjust, after all these years, but it never had. What would happen when the baby came? The lump in her chest from last night returned as the nagging idea of adoption resurfaced.

Doing her best to suppress her uneasiness, Sofie put on her finest dress, a baggy yellow dotted swiss getup from the secondhand store, and slipped her feet—more like squeezed them—into her white pumps, which had grown tighter due to her swollen ankles. She was not at all eager to appear at church—she dreaded the disdainful looks she was sure to receive when she walked through the doors—but she also didn't want to disappoint Andy. She consoled herself with the following plan: sit in the back row to avoid notice, and then, at the close of the service, make a beeline for Eli's car, whether he followed her or not.

᯽

When Eli parked in front of the Rogerses', Andy ran to the car and jumped in the backseat before Eli had even opened his door to get out. Sofie's steps were marked by significantly less enthusiasm, but when Eli held the passenger door open for her, she thanked him politely and even granted him a smile—a dry one, to be sure, but a smile nonetheless. The poor girl could do with a few new clothes, Eli observed, but he wasn't about to ruin a perfectly beautiful Sunday morning by suggesting it.

After she was settled, Eli closed the door and started whistling a snappy tune as he walked around front and climbed back into the driver's seat.

"You seem real h-happy t-today, Eli."

"I'm happy every day—at least, I try to be." Eli shifted the car into gear, compressed the gas pedal, and started south on River Road. "It doesn't always come naturally, and in those times, I remind myself, *'This is the day which the* LORD *hath made,'* Andy; *'we will rejoice and be glad in it.'"*

"Huh?"

Eli laughed. "It's from the Bible. Psalm one hundred eighteen, verse twenty-four. I recite it every morning when I wake up."

"Is my name in it?"

"What?"

"You said, 'Th-this is the d-day which the Lord hath made, Andy.'"

Sofie giggled softly. "No, silly." She turned around. "He was just directing it at you."

Eli grinned at Andy in the rearview mirror. "I'm almost certain I read your name in another Bible verse, though." He slowed as they approached the corner of River and Mill Creek Pike, preparing to make the turn.

"You did? Wh-which one?" The boy sat so far forward, Eli felt his breath on the back of his neck.

"Let's see...it was another verse from the Psalms, and it goes like this: *'Delight thyself also in the* LORD; *"Andy" shall give thee the desires of thine heart.'* There! Did you hear your name?"

He heard Andy slump back in his seat. "Oh, you're j-joshin' me. It's supposed to say 'and he,' not 'Andy'!"

They laughed and made light conversation all the way into town, and Sofie even joined in. Of course, it helped that the drive to his grandfather's house lasted only ten minutes.

"Why are we stopping here?" Sofie asked when he pulled the car into the driveway and shut off the engine.

Eli turned in his seat to face her. "I thought you might feel more comfortable walking into church today if you rode over with Grandfather and Winifred."

Her eyebrows arched.

"Me, too?" Andy asked.

"Yes, you too, Andy. That way, no one will put the three of us together. I spoke to Grandfather about it last night, and he said he and Winnie would be happy to take you."

Sofie lowered her eyebrows again. "Oh. I see." He couldn't read the expression in her eyes, since she had dropped her gaze to her lap. "That's probably best. I was actually hoping to sit in the back row, in order to make a fast exit."

"No need to hurry out afterward. Maybe you'll see some folks you know."

"I can't think of anyone who'd want to spare me a word. In fact, your grandfather doesn't need to show up with me in tow. Just drop me off a block from the church, and I'll walk the rest of the way. That way, no one will think ill of you."

"It's not me I'm concerned about," Eli rushed to say. Or was it?

"Can I sit w-with you, Eli?" Andy asked.

"I think it would be best if you sat with your sister."

"Wh-why don't you want to s-sit with us?"

"It's not that I don't, Andy, but...well, we don't want folks getting the idea that...." Why bother finishing the thought? He already sounded like a pompous schmuck. And he felt like one, too.

Sofie took a long, deep breath, then exhaled slowly, with a sigh. "You know, I think it might be better all around if you just took me back home. I don't belong in church. Clearly, you agree."

"What?" A frantic feeling stirred in his gut that he'd gone about this all wrong. "No, I don't want to do that. I invited you, and I want you to come, both of you." Good grief! He had a notorious talent for sticking his foot in his mouth, and it had never been his intention to alienate them. He tried to imagine how Jesus might have handled this kind of situation. In a way, it was similar to the Samaritan woman at the well, who'd been rejected and shunned for sexual immorality. Jesus had sought her out and asked her for a drink—from the same cup, in fact. He knew the sins of her past, yet it never occurred to Him to distance Himself from her.

"There won't be any embarrassment on your part or your grandfather's if you just take me home," Sofie went on. "I knew from the start this was not a good idea. Andy can stay, but I don't want to put your grandfather and Mrs. Carmichael out. My situation is awkward, to say the least. As I've said, it isn't proper, my going to church, especially in light of the way most folks view me."

"Sofia, please. No one is perfect. In fact, church is no place for perfect people! All of us are sinners saved by grace."

"Well, you haven't seen the way folks look at me, saved or not. I'm sure the members of the Wesleyan Methodist church aren't any different. I am a woman scorned, no matter how you look at it."

Eli recalled his interaction with the two gossipy ladies he'd met at Murphy's Market, and newfound anger surged up like a tidal wave at the memory of their holier-than-thou attitudes. But then, he had to aim that anger back at himself, for hadn't his suggestion that Sofie and Andy ride to church with Grandfather and Winnie implied that he harbored the same attitude? Hadn't he as much as admitted he was afraid of being seen with her? That he worried what folks would think and, worse, imagined their conversations behind his back: *If that new fellow is going to associate with the likes of Sofia Rogers, I'll have to switch doctors*? "Wait here." He opened his door.

"Why?" Sofie demanded. "What are you doing?"

"I'll be right back." He vaulted up the front steps, opened the door, and stepped inside, finding

Grandfather and Winnie seated in the front parlor. Grandfather looked classy, as always, in his dark brown three-piece suit. Next to him, Winnie was the picture of refinement in her floral print dress, her gray hair pinned beneath a feathery hat.

"Ah, there you are." Grandfather smiled. "Are we ready to go, then?"

"Yes," Eli replied, "but I'll be taking Sofia and Andrew, after all."

"Oh." Grandfather's white eyebrows arched severely. "Do you think that's wise?"

"If it isn't, I don't care. It's the only kind thing to do. I'm the one who invited them, after all, and I don't want Sofie thinking I'm judging her. Enough people make her feel that way. Plus, Andy wants to sit with me, and I can't bear to tell him no."

Winnie smiled. "You have a sensitive spirit, Elijah. I've always liked that about you. We'll see you at church, then. Oh, you should know that Reverend White is going to announce our engagement from the pulpit this morning. We wanted to forewarn you."

"Well then, congratulations are in order. Have you set the date yet?"

"Next Sunday at two. It will be a quiet affair, held right here in the living room."

"That soon? Man alive! You two don't waste any time, do you?"

Grinning sheepishly, Grandfather stood and offered an arm to his bride-to-be.

The plumpish woman rose to her feet and gazed lovingly into Grandfather's eyes. "When you get to be our age, time isn't exactly on your side."

Back at the car, Sofie and Andy both sat like solemn soldiers.

"Ready to go?" Eli asked as he slipped into the driver's seat.

"Where?" Andy asked.

Eli met his gaze in the rearview mirror. "Why, to church, my man."

"With you or your grandpa?"

"With me." He started the car and began backing out of the driveway.

"I told you, I'd prefer to go home." There was a hint of ire in Sofie's voice.

He cast her a lazy smile. "Sorry, no can do." He proceeded east, toward the center of town. Out the corner of his eye, he noted Sofie had taken to wringing her hands in her lap, and the strongest urge came over him to reach across the seat and cover them reassuringly with one of his own. He resisted, but just barely.

Lord God, help me. I think I'm falling for this girl.

Chapter Ten

Oh that men would praise the LORD for his goodness, and for his wonderful works to the children of men!
—Psalm 107:8

As expected, murmurs and curious stares from every direction greeted the unlikely trio as they entered the little white clapboard church, followed by Doc Trent and Mrs. Carmichael. Sofie didn't know why Eli had insisted on bringing her to church when she'd specifically requested to be taken back home. She found he could be just as stubborn as she when he wanted to.

She kept her gaze lowered, staring at her scuffed shoes, even though she felt embarrassed that she had nothing nicer to go with her dress—not that it was anything special. She looked the poorest of waifs. At least Andy had some decent clothes. She'd purchased them secondhand, at the Salvation Army store, but at least they were still in good condition. She hadn't wanted to waste more than a few cents on her maternity clothes, knowing she'd wear them for only a short time, so she'd bought three or four outfits that she wore again and again. Already they showed a great deal of wear and tear. She could have sewn something new, but fabric wasn't cheap. Nothing was cheap these

119

days. To pull herself out of the mire of self-pity, she silently thanked the Lord for her job, when so many folks across the country had lost their means of income.

Eli's hand touched the center of her back, and she jumped. "How are you doing?"

"I'd rather not be here. Everyone's staring."

"No one is staring," he insisted. "You have a vivid imagination."

"They're gossiping about us, too."

"Again, your imagination is hard at work."

He urged her forward, but she shook her head. "I want to sit in the back."

"That's fine, if it'll make you more comfortable, but Grandfather and Winifred usually sit toward the front. They might be disappointed if we don't sit with them. Besides, the preacher is going to make a special announcement concerning them, and I should be with them when he does."

That tidbit spiked her curiosity, but not enough to convince her to sit toward the front. "You go sit with them, then."

Andy looped a hand through her arm. "C-come on, sis. Let's g-go sit with Doc Trent and Mrs. Carmichael. W-we're used to p-people p-pokin' fun at us, r-remember? How m-many times have y-you told me to b-b-be brave and not l-let people's w-words c-cut m-me down?"

She hated when her brother preached at her, almost as much as she hated to hear his speech impediment worsen, as it often did when he was nervous. Her own anxiety had probably made his worse. Shame on her. She pulled back her shoulders and raised her chin, resolved to be strong, despite the stares of onlookers. "Alright, then. Lead the way."

She hadn't heard singing like that of the Wesleyan Methodists since...well, maybe she never had. They raised their voices with gusto and heart, and the pianist, why, she accompanied them with such skill and precision. The music refreshed her soul as fresh rain pouring from an open sky. Whenever she caught herself singing along, though, she silenced her voice, reminding herself that she had no business celebrating such subjects as joy and redemption, in her present state. She'd been so lax about all things spiritual. What must God think of her standing here, sharing a hymnbook with Andy and Eli? She imagined Him pointing a finger of divine rebuke and disdain. And then, there were the people singing around her, all of them probably marveling at her audacity in filling a pew at their fine, untainted church with her unwed, pregnant self.

When the enthusiastic music director finally invited the congregation to take a seat, Sofie wished she could crouch low enough to vanish from view. As if Eli had read her thoughts, he reached an arm around Andy's back and touched her shoulder, as light as a feather. She angled him a second's glance and, in that instant, discovered in his eyes a calming look that nearly brought her to tears. *Oh Lord, what is happening to my heart?*

In his sermon, Reverend White spoke on the topic of trust, and it seemed that every word he uttered was aimed directly at her. He explained that people feel safest when everything is "under control," but, more often than not, life is topsy-turvy, and the only way to weather the storms is to trust in the God of order. He said that God's love is wide and long and high and deep and sometimes almost too overwhelming to believe, and that instead of accepting His love for what it is—genuine, tender, forgiving, and gracious—many folks run away from it, choosing to settle for a mediocre existence. Mediocrity, he said, offers a degree of comfort and predictability, but it also leads to fear and uncertainty. Without the "divine lifeline," as he called it, folks struggle to stay afloat, unsure which way to swim when the rivers rise. He encouraged his congregants to venture out in faith, taking hold of God's strong hand with confidence, for only then would they experience His abundant joy and boundless love.

The reverend closed his sermon with Psalm 63:8: *"My soul followeth hard after thee: thy right hand upholdeth me."* Sofie thought it was one of the loveliest verses she'd ever heard, and she snatched the piece of paper Andy had been doodling on for the duration of the sermon, asked to borrow his pen, and hurriedly scrawled it down.

Listening to his closing words with rapt attention, she could almost forget about her circumstances. She could almost trust that God had carved out a pathway just for her. Almost. Until the preacher scanned the congregation to acknowledge any visitors and invite them to return. Her blood ran hot and then cold with terror at the thought of having to raise her hand or, worse, stand up.

Thankfully, he issued a blanket welcome, followed by what he called a "most exciting announcement": the recent engagement and upcoming nuptials of Dr. Wilson Trent and Widow Winifred Carmichael. At his declaration, many oohs and aahs rose up from the pews. Someone started clapping, and others followed suit, so that the entire assembly was soon on its feet, applauding in a show of approval. Sofie slowly stood, as well. When Eli glanced over Andy's head at her and smiled, she smiled back, with a wave of relief that the center of attention had shifted to the happy couple. Now, hopefully, she could slip out unnoticed.

＊

As soon as the service ended, folks flooded the front of the sanctuary to offer their well wishes to Grandfather and Winnie. Eli felt torn between remaining with them, as a show of support, and chasing after Sofie, who'd grabbed Andy by the hand and was pushing her way like a pit bull to the outside aisle, away from the throng.

"Sofia, wait!"

Eli turned at the voice and spotted the woman who had yelled. He recognized her, but he couldn't recall her name. She seemed to be in a great hurry to reach Sofie and stall her exit, and she squeezed her way past the other people in her narrow pew, bumping knees as she went, pulling along by the hand a boy who appeared to be about two or three.

Sofie stopped at the door to the lobby and waited for the woman, who detained her with a wide, friendly smile and launched into an animated conversation. Sofie returned the smile, reticent as it was, and Eli observed her talking to the woman as though she knew her well. Rather than rush to her side, he decided to allow the woman to engage her for now. If there was one thing Sofie Rogers needed, it was the companionship of other females. She had mentioned several friends, such as that older woman, Margie, and the neighbor lady named Tildi, but he doubted she had much time for socializing, given her rigorous schedule working nights and sleeping days, not to mention that she spent every spare minute with Andy. Maybe making some new friends would keep her coming to church.

His musings were interrupted by a little gray-haired woman who scuttled up to him. "Isn't that somethin' 'bout your granddad and Mrs. Carmichael?" She gave him a good-natured slap on the arm. "I been seein' Doc Trent for years, and that Mrs. Carmichael's been in his employ for as long as I can recall. Never had a clue them two had a thing for each other."

Eli grinned down at the woman. "I don't think they had a clue, either, until just a few months ago."

"Well, bless my stars. I guess one never can tell when the love bug's gonna sneak up and take a big bite right outta your heart. I'm Mrs. Don Jonas, by the way." She extended a hand. "But you can call me Pat."

Eli shook her hand. "Nice to meet you."

Still pumping his arm, she added, "'Spect I'll be comin' to you, now that Doc's retirin'. I'm right healthy, though, so, chances are, you'll just see me at church."

"Let's hope it stays that way, Mrs.—er, Pat. You have a nice day, now."

Someone else came up to shake his hand, and then another, and before he knew it, a regular crowd had gathered around to meet him after speaking with his grandfather and Winnie. Eli spoke with each one for what he believed to be a reasonable amount of time before excusing himself and making his way to the foyer, where he'd last seen Sofie, talking with that young woman.

But the foyer had cleared, save for a small circle of ladies chatting about an upcoming craft bazaar, as well as a frazzled-looking mother and father struggling to round up their children, who'd taken to running up and down the staircase. The Reverend and Mrs. White still stood by the propped-open doors, where they always greeted the parishioners as they exited the building. The reverend offered Eli an outstretched hand. "Good morning, Dr. Trent."

"Morning, Reverend, Ma'am." He nodded at each of them. "Wonderful message this morning, Reverend. You gave me much to chew on this week."

"Well, that's usually my mission." The reverend chuckled, his belly jiggling beneath his unbuttoned suit coat. "Mighty fine news about your granddad and the widow Carmichael, don't you think? I didn't see that one coming, but they'll make a fine match."

"I didn't see it coming, either, but I'm happy for them, as well." He peeked out the door at the parking lot and noticed Sofie talking with a couple of other ladies. The sight warmed him, even though her stance— arms folded, shoulders slumped—seemed to indicate she didn't feel the same. Still, he was glad that she'd stopped insisting he take her back home. She needed to leave the confines of the familiar once in a while, and what better place to venture to than church?

He thought about their picnic yesterday, relishing the brief glimpses he'd gotten of Sofie in a relaxed frame of mind. He resolved to make next Saturday's workday a fun one for her and Andy. Their lives had been so fraught with strife, they were more than deserving of help, especially given Sofie's condition. He couldn't imagine her crouching down to remove a splintered step or climbing a ladder to fix the sagging shutters. He wondered why no one else had stepped forward, but perhaps it was that no one was aware of her needs. It was clear that she prided herself on being independent, and it occurred to him that most people probably assumed—correctly—that she didn't want their help. But he wasn't about to let that stop him from lending a hand.

"So, Dr. Trent." The reverend cleared his throat, drawing Eli out of his daydream. "How did you come to know Sofia Rogers and her brother?"

"Well, Sofia is a patient of my grandfather's, and I met her when she was hospitalized a little while back. Andy and I struck up a friendship in the process."

"That's wonderful. That boy could really use a strong role model."

"I agree," said Mrs. White. "And I'm delighted you brought them both to church. I rarely see Sofia, and I was mighty surprised last month to learn of her... condition. I didn't realize she had a...a male friend."

"She doesn't. Never did, to my knowledge. I know the common assumption, but...well, it's my personal belief that someone took advantage of her."

Mrs. White gasped, covering her mouth with her hand. "Gracious me! You mean, in some vile attack? Has she gone to the authorities?"

"I doubt it. To be honest, this is strictly a hunch. She hasn't shared any details with me or even with my grandfather. As a matter of fact, she never even sought prenatal care. The only reason she was admitted to the hospital was a bout of the flu."

Eli realized that he had probably said more than was wise on the matter, but he felt a sense of relief at having confided in the reverend and his wife. Sofie needed more people on her side, and he figured spreading awareness was the first step.

"Well, now that you have established an acquaintance with her, I'm sure she'll receive the finest medical attention from both you and Doc," said the reverend.

Andy raced past the open door with two other boys on his tail, the laughter of all three rising to the treetops. "Looks like young Andrew has found some new friends in Alex and Nathan Taylor," Mrs. White observed, batting a pesky fly that buzzed around her face. "Those two belong to Will and Livvie Taylor. Have you met them yet?"

"No, but I've heard all about them, and their restaurant."

"There you are, Elijah." His grandfather and Winnie descended the staircase and greeted the Whites. "We've been invited to Livvie's Kitchen for lunch. I don't think I told you, but Livvie and Will often ask people from the congregation to a meal after the service on Sundays, when the restaurant is closed to the public."

"That sounds nice. I'd welcome the opportunity to meet some other church members."

Grandfather stepped closer and whispered, "Sofia and her brother have been invited, of course. Do you think she'll accept?"

Eli grinned. "Well, I am her ride home, so I guess she doesn't really have a choice."

Grandfather stepped back with a wily grin. "Now, there's a servant with a strategy."

Will and Livvie Taylor and their two oldest boys turned out to be servants in the most biblical sense, tending to their guests' needs, putting everyone at ease, and serving an exceptional dinner of roast chicken, mashed potatoes and gravy, fresh green beans, home-baked rolls right from the oven, and a choice of apple, cherry, or chocolate cream pie for dessert. No wonder Livvie's Kitchen was known as the most popular restaurant in town. Eli made a mental note to return one day soon as a paying customer.

They sat at a long table with Gage and Ellie Cooper and their four children—"four and a half," Ellie clarified, since she'd reached the halfway point in her pregnancy. "Maybe you and I could get together and compare notes sometime, Sofia," she said. "Although we have a slew of kids, this is my first pregnancy, too—I'm Gage's second wife, as you know—and you and I seem to be in the same age bracket." She spoke with a southern twang, leading Eli to believe she wasn't originally from Wabash.

Sofie smiled shyly. "Congratulations to you both. It would be...nice...to talk with another woman who's in the same boat as me. Sort of."

The conversation had taken an awkward turn, so Eli stepped in to steer it elsewhere. "What is it that you do, Gage?"

Soon, Gage had told him all about his furniture business, with Grandfather chiming in, on occasion, about various pieces he'd purchased from him and how his reputation as a talented craftsman had spread far and wide.

It wasn't long before everyone was begging Will Taylor to serenade them with a couple of tunes on the harmonica. His talent on that mouth harp took Eli by surprise. He'd rarely heard the instrument played with such precision, and it intrigued him, even got his toe to tapping. And when he stole a glance at Sofie, his heart soared at the look of pure elation on her face.

Around two o'clock, folks began pushing their chairs away from the table. The womenfolk started carrying dishes to the kitchen, where Will and a couple of other men had already begun washing and two women had taken up towels for drying. They had a regular system in place, and Eli gathered that this group had been invited to the Sunday meal on many occasions. He hoped he'd be included again sometime soon, as he'd thoroughly enjoyed himself.

On the drive back to Sofie's, Andy chatted at a faster than usual rate, stuttering some, but not as much as Eli might have expected. He talked about the fun he'd had and asked if they could go back to the Wesleyan Methodist church next Sunday.

"What about going to church with the Walters family?" Sofie asked him. "Don't you think Georgie would miss you?"

"I'm not in Georgie's S-Sunday school class. C-can't I go to Sunday school at Eli's ch-church, instead?"

Sofie gazed steadily out her window, probably to avoid Eli's occasional glance. "Oh, I don't know. We'd have to think about that."

"I could pick you up again," Eli said. "And I wouldn't mind checking out the adult Sunday school class."

Andy leaned forward excitedly, his chin propped on the top of the front middle seat, as had become his habit. "Okay, then! It's settled."

Sofie turned and glared at him with pursed lips. "Nothing is settled, young man."

Before making the turn onto River Road, Eli noticed a black truck parked off to the side, the same place he'd seen a similar vehicle, if not the same one, yesterday. This time, at his approach, the engine roared to life, and the truck sped away with a squeal of tires down Mill Creek Pike.

"Look at that guy," Eli muttered. "Cut right in front of me."

When he set the brake and shut down the engine outside Sofie's house, Andy shouted, "Hey! There's

Georgie on his p-porch. C-can I g-go play with him, Sofie? P-please?"

"I suppose. But, first, what do you say to Dr. Eli?"

"Um, thanks for t-takin' us to church, Eli. I'll s-see you tomorrow night when you p-pick up Sofie for work."

"You got it, buddy."

The boy jumped out, slammed the door shut, and made a dash for the house two doors down, leaving him alone with Sofie.

"Well, thank you for taking us to church," Sofie said, reaching for the door latch. "It was...nice." She opened the door and climbed out.

Eli was two seconds behind her.

"I can walk myself to the door," she said without turning around.

"I know you can, but it wouldn't be very gentle-manly of me to let you do that."

She heaved a sigh and set off at a brisk pace, and Eli couldn't help but grin when he noticed the slight waddle in her gait, common among women entering the latter stages of pregnancy.

At the foot of the steps leading up to the stoop, she halted abruptly, causing him to run smack into her back. He followed her gaze to the front door and immediately saw what had stopped her in her tracks. Smeared across the door in black paint was this message:

Stop talking to that doctor,
or someone will get hurt.

Prickles of alarm pinched his skin like so many needles. "What is that?" he whispered.

"Oh, dear. Oh, no." Sofie covered her mouth with both hands and made a couple of frantic spins, her eyes brimming with tears.

"Who did this?" He steadied her by the shoulders, turning her to face him. She looked down, avoiding his gaze, so he crouched lower and tilted his head to meet her eyes. "Who, Sofie?"

"I...I can't say." She wriggled away, spun around, and ran up the stairs. In seconds, she had unlocked the front door and disappeared inside.

Eli followed on her heels. "Please, Sofie." He closed the door behind him, then moved through the house, making sure no one was lurking inside. When he was satisfied that they were alone, he returned to where Sofie was in the kitchen and fixed her with a stern look. "Sit down. We need to talk."

"I need to get that paint off the door before Andy sees it. He'll get scared, and I don't know what all will happen. What should I do? Do you think it'll wash off?" She ran to the door, pulled it open, and touched the paint. "It's still a little sticky. Oh, dear Lord, he must have just been here."

He went to her, took her by the hand, and walked her across the room to the sofa, where he gently pressed his hands to her shoulders and eased her down. "We'll take care of the door, but first, we are going to talk."

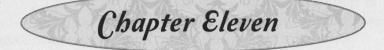
For thou, LORD, wilt bless the righteous;
with favor wilt thou encompass
him as with a shield.
—Psalm 5:12

Sofie could not steady her pounding heart. Would her attacker's threats never cease? And now, they extended to Eli, who had nothing to do with any of this. Was the goon afraid that she would tell Eli what had happened, and that he would launch an investigation? She rued the day she'd come down with the illness that had compelled Andy to summon the doctor, thereby bringing Eli into her life. All of them would be better for it, especially Eli. She had a sinking feeling that his almost daily visits could somehow lead to his ruin, and it would be her fault. A sharp stab in the side made her wince in pain and clutch the spot. Lately, her baby's kicks had been stealing her breath.

She picked up a round brocade sofa pillow and hugged it close to her. Eli sat on the edge of the chair across from her, leaning forward with his elbows propped on his knees. She dared peek at him, only to find his blue eyes piercing her like two sharp pins. "Okay, Sofie, it's time you opened up about a few things. Who painted that message on your door? I'm guessing it was the guy in the black truck, but I need to know his name."

"I don't know."

"You expect me to believe that?" His voice didn't contain anger as much as frustration, and she could hardly blame him.

"I think I should heed what it says, stop talking to you. Starting tomorrow, I'll find my own way to work, and I'd prefer it if you didn't come over here next Saturday or pick us up for church again. It's for the best."

"No, it's not for the best." He stood up and crossed the distance between them, plunking down on the couch next to her.

His nearness disarmed her. She dropped her gaze to her clenched fists, and only then did she realize that her fingernails were nearly penetrating the flesh. She forced her hands to relax.

"Telling me the truth would be for the best."

"The truth?"

"Come on, Sofie." He spoke her name in a melting whisper. "Who is the father of your baby?"

His comportment, gentle and soft-spoken, nearly did her in, but she thrust back her shoulders and sniffed, desperate to remain resolute in keeping her secret. "I can't...I don't...."

"Why? Are you afraid of something? Or deeply hurt? Was this someone you cared about?"

"No!" Her answer shot out faster than she'd intended.

"That can only mean one thing." He paused. "It wasn't consensual."

That he'd figured it out was almost a relief. Almost. Because what if her attacker discovered it and then followed through with his threats? She gulped down several mouthfuls of air, trying to avoid hyperventilating.

"Sofie, please. Be honest. Who did this to you? He should be sitting in a jail cell."

She rumpled her brow to the point of pain, frantic to hold her tears at bay. "I can't tell you, and you can't make me. He's threatened to hurt Andy, to hurt Buster. He will, too. And now, he's miffed because you've been coming around."

"Tell me who he is, and I'll take care of the rest."

"I can't, because...." Tears began to fall. "Because I don't know," she whispered. "I must have been drugged, because I woke up when it was over, and... and...."

"Oh, Sofie."

"It happened at one of my job sites." She wiped her eyes and gave a bitter chuckle. "The only way I stayed sane was by convincing myself that it never happened. That it had been nothing more than a terrible nightmare."

He held out his arms, inviting her into an embrace.

At first, she resisted, sitting there stiffly. She wasn't ready to feel a man's arms encircle her body. Didn't want to feel the warmth of his strong, solid chest against her cheek. And certainly didn't want to hear his heartbeat beneath his soft cotton shirt.

"Sofie, Sofie," he repeated. "I'm so sorry."

She didn't want his sympathy, either. Yet the effort she might have spent on pushing back from him fizzled away at the feel of his hand circling softly, gently, on her back. It was then her tears mounted up, brimmed over, and cascaded down her cheeks like a waterfall, and she fell into his arms.

He lifted his other hand and cupped the back of her head as a sob came rolling out of her, followed by another and then another, sounding like someone else altogether. She didn't recognize her own voice, and figured the last time she'd cried like this had been at her parents' funeral. "Let it out. Just let it out," Eli whispered soothingly.

And so she complied.

After five minutes or so of frenzied wailing, she composed herself enough to sit up. She wanted to move away from his overwhelming presence, but there was no hope for it. On the one hand, his nearness soothed her fearful spirit like a cool, healing salve; on the other hand, it frightened her, because she didn't like admitting to herself how nice it felt to be held, comforted, reassured. A sigh shuddered out of her chest.

Eli sat up and scooted forward again, elbows resting on spread knees, eyes directed downward at the floor. "So, you're going to let this guy off, even if he haunts you for the rest of your life? Take this secret to the grave?"

"I...don't know."

"What about bringing him to justice? Think of the other women he might hurt. Or already has. Don't you want to keep that from happening?"

"Of course." She sniffed. "But you saw the message he left. He's been warning me ever since it happened that I'm not to tell anyone, or he'll hurt Andy. Kill him, even." Another wail escaped her lips. "You have to go now, and don't you dare tell anyone what I've told you. I have some white paint in the shed out back. I'll paint over the message before Andy comes home."

When she threw down the pillow and rose, he stood up also. He placed his hands on her shoulders and looked into her eyes, as if to search her soul. Then the unthinkable happened. His face lowered ever so slightly—was he giving her a chance to skitter? Of course, she should have skittered. She should have wriggled away from his grasp and run to the door, flung it open wide, and insisted he leave immediately. But something about him made her feel valuable, worthy, and, for the first time, desirable.

Ten seconds of silence ticked away between them, and she thought she might explode like some distant star. In an instinctive yet irresponsible move, she parted her lips, and he accepted the unspoken invitation to bring his mouth within an inch of hers. Her mouth formed his name, but a vague utterance was all that issued forth.

It wasn't a passionate kiss—just a brush, laden with timidity; more a mingling of breaths than of skin, two tentative mouths touching while hearts hammered against one another in a timeless drumbeat.

Eli pulled back first, and she looked into his blue eyes, an ocean of inexpressible warmth and tenderness. She marveled that one so good, so pure, inwardly and outwardly, and so Christlike could have the slightest jot of desire to touch her so tenderly—she, plain and pregnant and carrying a tarnished name among those who presumed her to be promiscuous.

Yet he kissed her again, another featherlight brush of her lips, this one carrying a hint of longing. Her fingertips flattened against his chest, and the kiss deepened as they sought a more intimate fit, their heads tilting and nodding, the kiss escalating into something far more intense than she ever could have imagined.

When Eli broke away and studied her face, his eyes glittered with something like wonder. "Well now, that was something I didn't plan on."

She could have said the same. And she couldn't decide how to take his remark. Did he regret kissing her? If so, then she shared his remorse. She stepped away and walked to the door, turning the knob and pulling it open, the black painted words across the door bringing her sense of reality back with a cruel thud. "You'd better go now."

"Sofie, I'm not going anywhere. Not until I know that you'll at least consider going to the authorities and starting an investigation to bring your attacker to justice."

She inhaled deeply through flared nostrils. "I'll think about it. Happy? Now, please go. And don't come back."

"Let me at least paint the door first. You said there's a can out in the shed?"

"I can handle it just fine, Eli, and I don't think you're grasping the full meaning behind that message. I don't doubt that he will bring you harm if you don't distance yourself from me. He's already threatened to harm Andy."

"I'm not afraid of him, and I'm not about to leave you alone."

"I'm not alone. Andy's here, and so is Buster."

"Neither of them would be any help to you, and you know it. Besides, you don't want Andy trying to come to your rescue and getting in the middle of any scuffle."

Sofie felt a swell of defiance rise up from within. Elijah Trent seemed to assume that a few kisses earned him the right to step in and take control of their lives. But they'd been on their own for more than six years, and she was not about to sit back and let anyone else take the wheel, never mind how well he kissed. The feel of his lips on hers mere minutes ago was already a fast-fading memory.

She opened the door even wider. "I don't need your help, Eli; I need you to leave. I—*we*—will be just fine." She sounded harsh, but she didn't know another way to get her point across. They couldn't afford to take any chances with her attacker. Who knew the lengths to which he would go to keep his identity a secret?

Eli stood there in silence, eyes narrowed, shoulders slightly drooped. Finally, he released a slow sigh. "Alright, Sofie. I'll leave, but only because I don't think that brute will come back right away. But if you think I'm going to stop driving you to work at night, you're plumb crazy. I also don't like the idea of Andy staying here alone at night. Maybe he should come stay with me for a while."

"No. We belong together, Andy and me."

"I'm not talking forever, and I'm only suggesting he spend the evenings with us, at least for a little while."

She raised her gaze to the ceiling. "How many different ways can I put this? I don't want you interfering in our lives any longer, Dr. Trent. After I paint this door, I'm going to walk over to Tildi's and ask if she'd mind driving me to and from work, just until the baby's born. I know she'll do that for me. She's always offering help, and she'll be thrilled that I'm finally ready to accept it. Please let your grandfather know that I've appreciated the rides home from work, but they're no longer necessary. Of course, I thank you, as well. Now, would you please go?"

"What about Andy? Do you think he should stay home alone? You've just said your attacker threatened him."

Her stomach tied itself in knots, pushing a wad of bile to the back of her throat. She swallowed it down. "I'll ask Tildi if he can stay with her awhile. Georgie would like that."

"That would be good." He stood there, stalling. "I make no promises to stay away."

"You'd better."

"Andy will wonder."

"I'll tell him he can go visit you when you finish your workday...if you want him to, that is."

"Of course I do. But I want to see you, as well."

"Eli...." She heaved another sigh. "You have your reputation to consider. Associating with me will only drive away your patients, and the last thing I want to do is bring down the practice your grandfather worked so hard to establish."

"In case you didn't notice, I'm not particularly worried about my reputation. Plus, I know the truth: you never asked for this pregnancy. And I give you a lot of credit for sticking it out. There are ways you could have...you know. Ended it."

Sofie felt sick to her stomach. "That was never a consideration."

Eli nodded. "Life is a precious gift, no matter how it comes about." He paused. "But keeping your baby after the birth is bound to be difficult without another parent to help shoulder the load."

"You should really consider adoption." Margie's advice crept across her mind, as it always did whenever she was reminded of her impossible future. A pounding pang started in her temples. "Please, just go. I have to paint this door."

He shook his head at her, then pinched the bridge of his nose. "Sofie."

"Go."

"Okay, I'm going." In the doorway, he paused and turned to her again. "Be sure to lock your doors and windows."

"I always do."

"I wish you had a telephone. I see some wires, so it looks like a few of your neighbors have them." He gazed out over the sparse neighborhood.

"I've managed without one this long; I think we'll be alright." She knew she sounded curt, but she had to protect her heart against him, and brusqueness seemed the only way.

"How will I know if you can't find a ride tomorrow?"

"I'll find a ride. Don't worry."

"Did anybody ever tell you you're hardheaded?"

"Good-bye, Eli."

Before she had time to duck, he bent down and touched his lips to her cheek. "You know where to find me." The kiss left a searing, smoldering burn long after he got into his car and pulled away. When he disappeared down the road, she had to walk through a blur of tears to get to the ramshackle shed where she kept the paint and brushes.

❁

On the way back to town, Eli decided to stop in at the sheriff's office. He didn't expect to find the sheriff there on a Sunday afternoon, but he figured he could at least speak with a deputy. Sofia Rogers might put up a regular fuss, but he was not about to let another day go by without reporting the crime she'd fallen victim to.

He maneuvered the car alongside the vacant curb in front of the sheriff's station. Inside, the office was deserted, save for a woman crouched beside a tall metal file cabinet, shuffling through the bottom drawer.

When the door shut behind him, she turned her head, then promptly jumped to her feet, brushing off her navy blue pencil skirt with her palms. Her face was vaguely familiar, but he couldn't quite place it.

"Well, goodness gracious, if it isn't the fine young doctor." She extended a hand over the counter. "I'm Clara Morris. We met in the grocery aisle at Murphy's Market some weeks ago."

"Yes, I remember." How could he forget the gossiping twosome? He offered a smile as they shook hands.

Clara Morris's grin never left her face, and her grip lasted a little longer than he thought appropriate.

When she finally released his hand, Eli glanced around. "Business is slow today, huh? No crime allowed on the Sabbath, I guess."

"There is the occasional offense," she said, matter-of-factly. "Deputy Fett is actually responding to a call right now. Some domestic dispute...oh, you!" she tittered. It must have just dawned on her that he'd been kidding. She cleared her throat. "I don't usually come in on Sundays, but I was a little behind on paperwork, so I decided to spend a few hours catching up."

"Must be nice, working for your husband."

She wrinkled her nose. "I prefer to think of it as working for the citizens of Wabash."

"I see." He smiled. "When do you expect the deputy to return?"

She glanced back at the clock on the wall. "Hard to say. Maybe another half hour or so? But the sheriff's in, if you want to see him. He's here every other Sunday afternoon, and today just happens to be his weekend to work."

"Well, that's perfect. He's actually the one I wanted to talk to."

"I hope there's nothing terribly wrong."

"I'm sure it's nothing he can't handle."

A dubious expression crossed her face. "Why don't you follow me, then? I'll take you to his office."

Eli followed her down a short hallway to an imposing oak door, which she tapped lightly and then pushed open. The heavyset fellow seated inside jerked his head up and dropped his feet from the desktop.

"For heaven's sake, Buford!" Clara put her hands on her hips. "You're on duty. No napping!" Paired with her scowl, her scathing tone of voice reminded Eli of a hissing alley cat.

"You could knock, you know."

"I did, you fool. This is Dr. Elijah Trent, Wilson's grandson. He wants to talk to you."

"Well, come on in." The man gestured to the battered brown leather chair situated across from his equally weathered desk. "Clara, close that door on your way out, would you?"

"Thank you," Eli said to Clara as he stepped inside and sat down.

"Hear you're takin' over your granddad's practice. That's mighty fine. S'pose ol' Doc's sick and tired o' hearin' 'bout everybody else's woes. Feel the same way myself, sometimes." He chuckled, but Eli wasn't inclined to laugh. He did, however, follow the big man's gaze behind him to the door, where his wife lingered. "What do you want?" the sheriff barked.

"I wanted to see if I could get the good doctor something to drink. Coffee, tea...."

"Oh. What about it, Doc?"

"No, thank you, but I appreciate the—"

"That'll be all, Clara," her husband gruffed before he could finish.

When the door closed, the rotund fellow reached across his desk for a cigar box. He flipped open the lid, selected a stogie, and offered it to Eli.

"No, thanks." Eli had learned the hard way how sick those things made him, when, as a young boy, he'd smoked a pack with his pals behind the neighbors' barn one night. And that had been before he'd studied medicine and developed his doubts as to their innocuous nature.

The sheriff stuck a cigar in his mouth, struck a match, and lit the end. "So, what can I do for you, doctor?" He took a long puff.

"I've come to report a crime."

"A crime, you say?" His nonchalance hardly seemed staged as he leaned back in his chair, opened a drawer, and produced a notebook, which he laid on the desk. "What sorta crime?"

"I'll be blunt. I have reason to believe there's been a...a sexual assault in town."

The sheriff whistled, a pungent ring of smoke escaping his lips. "Well now, that's a mighty serious allegation." He plucked a pencil from a canister on the desk. "Why hasn't the victim come forward herself?"

"I think fear is to blame. Her attacker has threatened to hurt her and her brother if she breathed a word about it."

"Hurt her brother...who're we talkin' about here?"

Eli took a deep breath. "Sofia Rogers. She takes care of her little brother, and—"

"I know who she is. Heard-tell she's a bit of a loose woman. Got herself in a motherly way."

Eli figured the sheriff was privy to the latest gossip his wife was spreading. "You don't really take stock in what you hear through the grapevine, do you, Sheriff?"

The stocky fellow took a long drag off his stogie, his narrow eyes firmly fixed on his target, Eli. "Hard not to when it's all over town." He looked down at his tablet and scribbled something on it. "Miss Rogers and her brother still live out on River Road?"

"That's correct."

"So, she tell you about this...this supposed assault?"

He didn't like the man's arrogance. "She did. She's kept quiet about it until now, though, because she doesn't know who's responsible. She was drugged while it happened, you see. She's also been afraid of what her attacker might do if she goes to the authorities. I took her to church this morning, and when I drove her home this afternoon, we discovered a note painted in black letters on her front door. I believe she's probably covered it up by now, as she didn't want her brother to see it."

"What'd it say?"

"Something to the effect of, 'Stop talking to the doctor'—that's me—'or someone gets hurt.'"

"Pfff. Fool's jealous. My guess is, the two of 'em had somethin' goin', she dropped him like a hot skillet, and now he's thinkin', if he can't have her, nobody else can, either. I'm not about to get involved in a lovers' spat. She got herself in a family way, and now she wants to point blame. That don't go over too well with me."

Remembering Sofie's tears of anguish while she'd talked about the attack caused a rash of anger to sizzle under his skin at the sheriff's coldhearted demeanor. He fought to hold his anger at bay. "I believe you have it wrong, sir." He inwardly prayed for the right words to say—and for the self-restraint not to strangle the sheriff. "Maybe you could at least go out there and talk to Sofia. Get a feel for things."

He sniffed. "I guess it couldn't hurt. What's your connection to her, anyway?"

Not that it was any of his business, but Eli supposed that it might prove helpful, if the sheriff were to conduct any kind of investigation. "I'm her physician."

"I see. I guess you've prescribed church attendance as a part o' her regimen?"

His ire went up another notch. "I invited her, if you must know, along with her brother, whom I'm committed to helping overcome a speech impediment."

"Humph. Can't cure a stutter, as far as I know."

"That hasn't been proven. Aside from that, we've also struck up a friendship."

"That right?" With his teeth clamped around the cigar, which was sticking out of his mouth at an angle, he jotted something down, then drummed the eraser end of the pencil on the grungy desktop. "Just with the boy, eh?"

Eli didn't appreciate the insinuation one bit. "I'm here to report a crime, sir. Are you going to look into it or not?"

"Just hold down your dander, doc. I'll look into it. Not sure I'll find anything, but I'll pay Miss Rogers a visit." He glanced down at his notepad, then peered up at Eli with raised eyebrows. "She give you a description of her alleged attacker? Age? Build? Weight? Any birthmarks or other telltale signs that would make him easier to track down?"

"As I've said before, she was unconscious while it happened, so she wouldn't be able to provide you with any such details."

"Well, that's a big help, huh?"

A sigh of frustration slipped past Eli's lips. "I know you don't have a lot to go on right now, but maybe there's something Sofie hasn't told me. Isn't it your job to investigate the matter? See if you can pick up any clues?"

"Even if she's willing to talk, I'll be hard-pressed to find as much as a trace of evidence at this point. Plus, if she was assaulted, as you say, and that's how she got pregnant, a good six or seven months have already gone by. It's a little late for her to be making accusations, don't you think?"

"The least you can do," Eli stated evenly, "is question her."

The sheriff scratched the back of his gray head. "Yeah, yeah. I'll go out there first thing in the morning."

Today would have been better, but tomorrow would have to do. The sheriff's lackadaisical attitude was rather irksome.

"You got anything else for me to go on?"

"There is one thing. I've noticed an old truck parked along the shoulder just before the turn onto River Road."

"Probably a hunter."

"A hunter? Sitting in his vehicle?"

"What make is it?" the sheriff pressed.

Eli's frustration hit another high. "I don't know. It's old. And black."

"Well, you've just described about half the trucks in town. Not many farmers driving around new vehicles."

"Who said he was a farmer?"

The sheriff stood up dismissively and extended a hand over his desk to Eli.

Eli got to his feet, as well, and was tempted to decline shaking hands. But then, he reminded himself that civility went a lot farther than hostility. He grasped the sheriff's hand and looked him in the eye. "Thank you for checking in with Miss Rogers tomorrow. I'm sure you'll do whatever it takes to get to the bottom of this."

Sheriff Morris gave a chilly smile. "I'd say I'm pretty much there already."

With gritted teeth, Eli turned around and left the office. He found Clara in the hallway, holding a stack of papers and smiling sheepishly. She must have eavesdropped on the entire conversation. "Ma'am," he said, nodding as he passed.

"You have a good afternoon, now," she said. "Stop in again anytime."

"I would like to think I won't have need."

Outside, gray clouds had started gathering in the sky. Eli spotted a long string of blackbirds perched on a telephone wire—a sure sign of rain, his grandmother would have said. The humid air felt heavy, but it wasn't the only weight bearing down on his shoulders. A meeting he had hoped would put his fears to rest had only magnified them.

Chapter Twelve

Enter ye in at the strait gate:
for wide is the gate, and broad is the way,
that leadeth to destruction.
—Matthew 7:13

*O*wen slouched on the couch, listening to the radio. A couple of comedians bantered back and forth, while the live studio audience periodically burst into laughter in the background. He didn't find the show particularly funny, but it helped to while away his boring Sunday afternoon. A drenching rain pounded on the upstairs roof and whistled down the rain barrel on the side of the house. His mother rattled pots and pans in the kitchen, while his sister set the supper table and talked to her mother about some birthday party she planned to attend next Saturday. His dad walked through the front door just as the station broke for a commercial about Quaker Oats. Owen didn't bother greeting him.

His dad took off his hat and tossed it on the coffee table, then slipped out of his jacket and gave it a shake, sending rain droplets in every direction, before hanging it on the coat tree. "Don't you have anythin' better to do with your time?" He picked up the Friday paper and then settled into the leather club chair he barred everyone else from using. "Whenever I come home, I find you lazin' around. Did you mow the lawn like I asked you?"

"I forgot. Besides, it started raining."

"What do you mean, you forgot?"

"I mean, my memory isn't perfect. Gosh! It's no tragedy. I'll mow it tomorrow night when I get off work."

"Ah, so you're finally going back to work tomorrow?"

"I didn't have to work this weekend. What's the big deal?"

"The big deal is that on those weekends you don't work, you should be chippin' in around the house. There's always stuff to do."

He couldn't help lifting his lip at the corner. "Yeah, yeah."

"That was an interesting visit from the new doctor," his mother interrupted as she stepped out of the kitchen, wringing her hands in her floral apron. Owen felt himself jolt upright. Was she talking about the same guy he had in mind, or had Wabash acquired more than one new doctor?

"What were you doin', nosin' around by my office door?" His dad unfolded the newspaper and gave it a few snaps before burying his nose inside.

"Well, I couldn't help but overhear your conversation. Those walls are paper-thin, you know."

"Sure, especially when you put your ear to the door," he muttered from behind the paper.

"Well? Do you believe him?" she persisted.

The radio program resumed, and it was all Owen could do to keep from jumping up and turning the blasted thing off so he could better hear what his parents were saying.

"I don't have an opinion, one way or the other."

"That wasn't what I gathered. Seems to me you thought that girl got what she deserved."

His dad lowered the newspaper to his lap and gave her a beady-eyed glare. "I'm sure you want to tell me what you think on the matter, so go ahead. State your view." He made a sweeping gesture with his hand.

"Well...." She stepped further into the living room. "It does seem odd to me her getting in that...that female predicament...when I've never seen her with a man before. I know what folks been saying, that she's a hussy and all, but what if there's some truth to the doctor's words? I think it was commendable of him to come in and file a report."

"Well, good. I'm glad you think it's commendable. Now, may I get back to my paper? And when's dinner? I'm famished."

She scowled and spun around, her plaid skirt flaring. "In another five minutes or so," she called back before disappearing through the kitchen door.

Owen's stomach twisted into a pinching knot. He sat forward and stared at the patterns in the blue brocade wallpaper on the far wall. Then, his eyes veered to the newspaper that blocked his father's ugly mug from view. "Who's she talking about, anyway?"

"What?"

"Who got herself in a 'female predicament'?"

He lowered his paper again and sighed louder than usual. "Why do you care?"

"I'm curious, is all. Why'd the new doctor drop by your office today?"

He sighed again through his fat nostrils. "Oh, that girl named Sofia Rogers got herself in a family way, and now she's cryin' rape. Guess she told young

Dr. Trent about it. I don't know, maybe she told his grandpa, too. I'll have to drive out there tomorrow and ask her a few questions." He lifted his paper, then lowered it again, his eyes trained on Owen. "You remember Sofia Rogers? She's near about your age, I'd think."

"Me?" Owen tried to remain calm, even as fury foamed in his gut. "Well, I remember her—sort of, I guess. I never paid much attention to her, though. She was a couple o' years ahead of me in grade school." He used to think she was the prettiest girl in town. Of course, she'd never given him a second's glance. No girl ever had. "Yeah, I heard she got knocked up. She's a hussy, alright."

"What makes you say that?"

"Oh, just stuff I hear."

"Such as?"

"I don't know. I just heard fellas talk."

"Fellas like to talk," his dad groused. "That don't mean it's true."

Owen twiddled his thumbs for a moment. "She didn't give a name, did she? Of who done it to her, I mean."

"I thought you just said she was a hussy."

"She is," he blurted out, suddenly feeling pinned.

"Humph. Well, I s'pose I'll get to the truth one way or the other, and, nope, she didn't pass out any names, far as I know." He picked up the newspaper and resumed reading, signaling the end of their conversation.

Owen stood and made for the stairs. He needed to escape to his room.

"Where you goin'? You heard your ma. Supper's almost ready."

"I know. I'm just goin' to wash up."

"Turn off that blasted radio, will you?"

He switched off the radio, then climbed the stairs, his heart pounding with rage. Apparently, the message he'd left for Sofie hadn't been clear enough, and now, that goody-two-shoes doctor was sticking his nose where it didn't belong.

Both of them would learn their lesson in due time.

❧

Sofie awakened on Monday to a yellow predawn glow peeking through her curtains. Outside, water from the overnight rain still dripped from the eaves, while the birds began their morning symphony, their wee chirps calling from tree to tree, as if to alert one another of the new day.

Weary from a restless night's sleep, she emerged with reluctance from her bed and walked to the window, opening it to let in some fresh air. She leaned forward and breathed deeply as her memory drifted back to the previous afternoon. Whatever had possessed Eli to kiss her? Worse, what had gotten into her that she'd allowed it? She couldn't give herself permission to care about a man, not in her state—and certainly not with her attacker lurking around every corner, threatening to do them harm.

The smell of paint still lingered in the air, as did the memory of that awful sign it had taken her three coats to obscure completely. Of course, Andy had wanted to know why she'd painted; "It needed to be done" was as creative an explanation as she'd been able to concoct. The truth was, the surface had been severely marred, and so he'd accepted her answer without asking further questions.

After painting the door, she'd gone over to Tildi's and arranged for a ride to and from work. She'd also asked if Andy could spend the nights at her house for a time. Tildi had agreed with enthusiasm, even scolding Sofie for waiting so long to accept her offers of help.

She'd thought Andy would be excited to stay at Georgie's house. But when he'd found out that Buster would remain at their house, he'd pouted, saying that the dog would get lonely sleeping without him every night. He didn't understand the sudden shift in routine, had refused to accept her explanation that it was for the best, and had chosen instead to mope for the rest of the night.

Letting go a heavy breath, she made a slow turn, her eyes landing on her nightstand and the Bible perched prettily atop it—the Book she dusted twice a week but rarely opened. She walked over and ran her fingers along its worn leather cover, remembering how her mother would sit in her rocker and read for hours on end, underlining various passages with her pen and jotting notes in the margins. A dog-eared bookmark jutted out from its pages, and Sofie opened the tome to see what was written there. Her eyes focused immediately on a passage underlined in bold. It was Psalm 9:9–10: *"The LORD also will be a refuge for the oppressed, a refuge in times of trouble. And they that know thy name will put their trust in thee: for thou, LORD, hast not forsaken them that seek thee."*

Those two verses were at the same time comforting and convicting. "I wouldn't blame God if He forsook me," she muttered. "You could hardly call what I've done 'seeking.'"

She flipped ahead a few pages, until another underlined verse caught her eye. It was Psalm 27:14:

"Wait on the LORD: be of good courage, and he shall strengthen thine heart: wait, I say, on the LORD."

She sat back and clutched the open Bible close to her heart. It was as if Mother was sending her a message through the verses that had meant the most to her. She decided she ought to begin at the beginning of Psalms. So, choosing to ignore the hundred other things she should have been doing, she settled into the rocking chair beside her bed, flipped on the floor lamp, and started to read.

Before she knew it, bright sunlight was bursting through her north-facing window. She checked the clock and saw that a full hour had passed since she'd started reading, yet she felt fully refreshed and, if possible, more awake than ever. It was hard to define the keen sensation stirring inside of her, but she embraced it, praying that it would not disperse as soon as she started her long list of chores. She found a purple ribbon to mark where she'd left off, closed the Good Book, and headed to the kitchen to start breakfast.

Shortly after the teakettle whistled, Andy padded barefoot out of his room, still dressed in his pajamas. "Good morning, sleepyhead!" Sofie greeted him as she filled her teacup with steaming water. "It's about time you got up! Today's wash day, remember?" She dropped the metal infuser into the cup, draping the tiny chain over the rim.

He groaned, brushing a hand through his messy hair. "Do I have to h-help? I'd rather work in the garden than hang clothes any day, even though they're both g-girl jobs." Ah, so he'd decided to remain in his grumpy slump, showing her nary a smile.

"Hey, mister. Around here, there's no such thing as 'girl jobs' or 'boy jobs.'" She reached out to tweak his nose, but he ducked, dodging her. "You want a hard-boiled egg? I made a few extra."

He wrinkled his nose. "Yuck. You know I h-hate those things. C-can you flip me a couple of p-pancakes, instead?"

"I will, on one condition: you retrieve my laundry baskets from the shed. They'll come in handy later, when you carry the wet clothes outside and hang them to dry. Yes, I did say 'you.' Being as big as I am with the baby, I'm finding it impossible to lift things."

His brow furrowed in a show of annoyance. "T-tell me again when that baby's comin'."

"Sometime in August. I can't tell you exactly when. You'll be going back to school around the same time." *And your niece or nephew might not come home to live with us.* The thought of giving up her child pained her heart as much as ever, but she had to maintain a practical mind-set. Did she have a choice, really? Someone had to work to put food on the table, and she could hardly take a newborn baby along with her while she cleaned offices. Moreover, if she gave up her child, maybe the father would quit hassling her. Of course, it would be best to find a deserving couple outside of Wabash.

"Is he g-going to s-sleep at Georgie's house, too?"

She blinked twice at him, unable to come up with an adequate comeback, his sarcastic retort so out of character that she had to pause, mouth agape. "No," she finally managed, deciding not to expound. "Now, go get my baskets, and I'll get the pancake batter going."

She had just cracked an egg for the flour mixture when Andy burst through the door, his face as white as the milk she'd just added to the mixing bowl. In one hand, Andy held a strange-looking bottle of something; in the other was a piece of paper.

"What's that?" Sofie asked, icy dread already moving up her spine.

"I f-found it outside the sh-shed, next to B-Buster...he looks awful sick, Sofie." He held it out to her. "What's Red Squill?"

A chill coursed through her veins. Town officials had approved the use of the poison two years ago to treat a rat infestation. According to the newspaper, the state, which had funded the program, had disposed of any leftover poison. "Go put that outside, and then come back in and wash your hands." She wiped her palms on her apron and snatched the note from his hand. As he walked to the open door and set the bottle on the front step, she proceeded to unfold the paper, her eyes frantically scanning the message typed therein.

Stop talking to the doctor, or I'll give your dog a lethal dose next time. There's plenty more where this bottle came from.

Chapter Thirteen

*For God hath not given us
the spirit of fear; but of power, and of love,
and of a sound mind.*
—2 Timothy 1:7

After carrying Buster inside and laying him on a blanket, Andy wiped his hands on a towel, then rubbed his tear-dampened eyes. "Why would s-somebody poison Buster? H-he...he isn't gonna d-die, is he, Sofie?" He sniffled. "What's th-this all about?"

Sofie folded the note and stuffed it into her pocket, unsure how to proceed. So many questions, yet no answers—none she was ready to give, anyway. She crouched beside the ailing pup and rubbed his stomach. "Sorry, boy. We'll have you feeling better in no time." She stood and took a step closer to Andy, amazed that she had to lower her gaze only slightly to meet his eyes. Laying both hands on his shoulders, she focused on the green flecks in his eyes.

"Andy, you cannot tell Georgie or anybody about this note. It could cause more harm than good. I'm sure Buster will be okay; let's give him some water to flush out his system. The person who wrote this note...he's up to no good. Oh, I may as well tell you. He's the one...." She lowered one hand to her abdomen and sucked in a breath for courage. "He's the one who

157

put me in this family way. I don't know how to tell you
without alarming you, but you deserve to know the
truth...he attacked me sometime before Thanksgiving.
I don't remember the date."

Andy's eyes took on a wider, brighter hue as her
words sank in. She had no idea the degree to which he
comprehended the situation, as naïve as he was, but
she vowed to do everything within her power to shield
him from the worst of it. And yet, she'd grown so weary
of tiptoeing around the truth.

"So, he kissed you lots of times?"

"No, no. At least, I don't think he did. The truth
is, I was unconscious the entire time. He must have
slipped something into my coffee before I went to work
that night. He did other, far, far worse things to me,
but they are the kinds of things you don't need to
know about right now. Someday, I'll tell you more, but
for now, just know this: women deserve respect and
utmost care, and I want you to always remember that.
Promise me you will, okay?"

He nodded, slowly at first, but then more heartily.
"I would never do a b-bad thing t-to a girl, and I hate
that somebody did that to you. If I ever g-get my hands
on him, I'll...I'll...choke him. Yeah, th-that's what I'll do."

She lifted one hand and cupped his cheek. "Please
don't talk like that, Andy. I admire your desire to protect me, but I never want you resorting to violence.
And if this man should ever come around here and
threaten me, I want you to jump on your bike and
make a beeline for town. This note comes as a warning
to us that if we don't abide by his wishes, that is, keeping quiet about his identity, he will hurt us further."

"Startin' with B-Buster." His voice trembled, and
the corners of his eyes still brimmed with tears.

"We won't let anything else happen to Buster. We'll have to keep him inside, though, for the time being."

"But he loves to run off into the fields an' such."

"I know, Andy. But we can't run the risk of letting that...that evil brute get close to him again, or he may do something worse."

The sound of an engine outside drew them both to the window. Sofie's heart took a gigantic plunge at the sight of the sheriff's car.

"W-what's he d-doin' here?" Andy asked.

"I don't know, but I'm sure I'll soon find out. I want you to stay in the house."

"Why? I wanna hear what he has to s-say."

"I need to talk to him in private. I'm sorry, Andy. Do you understand?"

He hung his head. "Y-you always treat me like a b-baby."

The truth stung, but she didn't have time to deal with it now. "That may be so, but you are to stay inside anyway, and I don't want any arguments. Understood?"

His lower lip jutted out as he gave a slow nod.

Sofie stepped outside, clutching her cardigan closed at the top in response to the brisk morning air. As the sheriff climbed out of his car, she couldn't help thinking that his belly, bulging over his belt, was just about as big as hers. "Good morning, Sheriff," she called from the stoop. "What can I do for you?"

"Morning, ma'am." He tipped his hat and folded his flabby arms across his chest. "Nice day, huh?"

"Indeed." She lifted a hand to shield her eyes from the sun, which silhouetted the sheriff's corpulent frame.

"Is there somewhere we can talk? Inside, maybe? Or would you prefer standin' out here?"

"As long as you don't mind, sir, outside suits me fine. May I ask what this is about?"

"Well, I won't beat around the bush." He shifted his weight from one foot to the other. "I had a visitor yesterday—the new doctor in town. Dr. Trent."

"Oh?" Her chest constricted, but she forced herself not to react visibly. "And how does that concern me?"

He gave a chilly half smile. "I believe you know the answer to that." He nodded at her pregnant belly. "He says you were attacked last fall—November, per-haps—and that's how you found yourself in the family way. Is that true?"

She held her breath until the onset of dizziness forced her to empty her lungs. How dare Eli go run-ning to the sheriff, when she'd expressly asked him not to! Anger stewed in her stomach as she scrambled for an appropriate response. "He shouldn't have filed a report without my consent."

"Well now, he didn't file a report, per se. There's nothin' to file, till the victim comes forward. He did express his concern, and his suspicions, based on the particulars you told him. Problem is, those particu-lars have to come from the horse's mouth, so to speak, if they're goin' to hold water."

She snapped her shoulders back and lifted her chin. "I have nothing to say."

He glanced to the side and took a sniff before re-turning his gaze to her. "Are you tellin' me you weren't attacked, then? That whatever went on between you and your baby's daddy was consensual?"

She gulped. "I...I don't believe I'm required to an-swer that. Am I?"

He tilted his head and studied her through nar-rowed eyes. "If you don't plan on pressin' charges, you don't have to speak a word. But if a crime's been committed against you, ma'am, then I suggest you come forward with the truth."

"What do you mean by 'come forward'?"

The sheriff sighed. "Did you, or did you not, suffer an attack?"

Her brain raced in several directions. Of course, she had no choice but to remain quiet on the subject, especially since she believed that her attacker had ties to the sheriff's office. "I...I really can't say."

"And I can't force you to, I'm afraid." He kicked at a stone with the toe of his boot. "Dr. Trent told me he's seen an old black truck parked up around the corner." He nodded in the direction of Mill Creek Pike.

"I wouldn't know." It pricked her conscience, lying to the law, especially after a morning spent reading the Scriptures and praying.

He sighed. "I figured as much. I told the good doctor there's a ton of black trucks around town. He'd have a tough time tryin' to identify just which one he saw. Folks are always parkin' up and down this road, fishin' in the creek and huntin' in the woods."

To keep from fidgeting with her hands, Sofie interlocked her fingers behind her back.

The sheriff narrowed his eyes. "What's this I hear 'bout somebody paintin' a message on your front door yesterday?"

"Oh." She would never forgive Eli. "That was a harmless prank, I'm sure."

He eyed the door behind her. "You must've painted over it already."

She nodded quickly. "Yes, it was quite unsightly."

"Too bad. That would've been a legitimate act of vandalism. Not much I can do, though, if you destroyed the evidence. You got anything else to show me?"

She unclasped her hands and shoved them inside her skirt pockets, squeezing the note Andy had found by the shed into a little ball. She shook her head.

"Humph. Well, I s'pose I'm 'bout done here, then." He paused, his eyes locked on something at her feet.

Slowly, Sofie looked down. Her heart sank when she spotted the bottle of Red Squill, sitting where Andy had left it on the stoop.

The sheriff came up the walkway and snatched the little bottle. "Where in tarnation did *this* come from?"

"That? Oh, my brother found it somewhere."

He frowned. "You know what this is?"

"I think so. Wasn't it used to rid the city of rats a number of years ago?"

"That's right. It's a dangerous poison. And only a few folks have access to it. Where'd you say your brother found it?"

"I didn't. I mean, I really have no idea. Please, feel free to take it with you. I surely don't want it around here."

"Hmm. Your brother home?"

"Uh, yes, but he's…not feeling well, and I'd rather you didn't disturb him." All this deception made her queasy. "I'm sorry I haven't been very helpful, Sheriff. I appreciate your concern, but, really, what happened to me"—she put a hand to her protruding belly—"is, well, a private matter, and something I can't discuss."

He raised an eyebrow. "At least not with me, huh?"

Determined not to let him unnerve her further, she raised her chin a notch and matched his stare.

With a tip of his hat, he turned and headed back toward his car. "You're kind of stuck out here in the boonies, aren't you?" he said over his shoulder. I imagine it'd be hard to call for help if you needed it. No car, no tellyphone. If I were you, I'd talk to the law while I had the chance." He opened the driver's door and draped an arm over the window, studying her for a few more seconds.

She shifted her weight, wishing he'd drive away before she changed her mind and told him everything she knew—which wasn't much. But what good would that do? He wouldn't believe her, and he'd want to wash his hands of any crime that might be tied to his office. She decided not to grace him with a reply.

Inside again, she stood with her back against the closed door, trying to catch her breath and get her bearings, as the sound of an engine revving and tires squealing faded down the street.

Andy crept out of his room, his pajamas still on. "Is he gone? What'd he want?"

"He wanted to know if...um...." How could she bear to continue lying? "If I had anything to tell him."

"A-about what?"

"About...how I got pregnant."

"Well? Did you t-tell him?"

She sighed. "No."

"Why n-not? I knew I should have c-c-come out there. I w-would have told him myself."

"That's precisely why I told you to stay in the house. Don't you remember what I said about not breathing a word about this to anyone? I don't want to put you in danger." She moved away from the door, her head swirling with a mess of worries. "By the way, the sheriff took that can of Red Squill. I told him you found it, but I didn't give him any details about how you came upon it. And I don't want you telling him, either."

"What am I supposed to do if he c-comes back and asks? L-lie?"

"No, just…I don't know. Be vague."

"H-how do I do that?"

She squeezed her head between both hands and made an about-turn. "I'm going to ride my bike into town."

"Can I c-come along?"

"No. I want you to stay here and keep watch over things. Don't open the door for anyone, you hear?"

"What if it's Georgie?"

"I guess he can come inside, but I don't want you going out till I get back."

"Why do you have to go to town?"

She hesitated a moment but decided she was done telling falsehoods. "I'm going to pay Eli a quick visit. And I already said you can't come, so don't you dare start begging."

"Is that s-safe? You know you're not s-supposed to be riding your b-bike anymore. Eli said so."

She sucked in a stream of air and blew it back out through her nostrils. "Eli is not in charge of me, and it's high time he got that straight." She glanced at the clock on the wall. "Sorry about your pancakes. I'll make them when I get back, if you can wait that long to eat."

He shrugged. "It's okay. I'll get s-somethin' else. Maybe we c-can have pancakes for supper. What about the l-laundry?"

His compliance shocked her. "We'll tackle it later. You can at least gather up your dirty clothes and put them by the washing machine."

"Can I listen to the radio?"

"Fine, but make your bed first, okay?"

Minutes later, situated in as comfortable a position as possible on the hard seat of her bicycle, Sofie started pedaling toward town. She was out of breath before she reached the first corner, but there was no time for worrying about how awkward she must look or for lamenting over how her constitution had regressed. She had a speech to prepare.

Chapter Fourteen

Happy is the man that findeth wisdom, and
the man that getteth understanding.
—Proverbs 3:13

By ten thirty, Eli had already treated Mrs. Kaiser's cough, listened to old Mr. Swineherd drone on about his awful gout, wrapped a sprained ankle, stitched up a finger of a factory worker who'd been injured on the job, and administered an ice pack to the goose egg on the forehead of young Darrell Niswander, who'd had the misfortune of picking the wrong girl to chase on the playground before school and been struck square between the eyes with a well-aimed rock. His mother hadn't been overly concerned, though, confiding in Eli that he'd probably had it coming.

It had seemed as if the number of cases was beginning to quiet down, but when he started down the short corridor connected to the small waiting room, it sounded like it was filled with crying babies, coughing kids, and wheezing adults. *Lord, give me grace and compassion for each patient here*, he prayed. *And please grant me wisdom and strength to carry out the tasks set before me.*

Taking a deep breath for fortitude, he opened the door and came eyeball-to-eyeball with several patients all vying for his attention. Some even leaped to their feet, begging to be seen next. A new wave of folks came streaming in, most of them without appointments. Somehow, Eli needed to tighten the way he managed this office. But Winnie was running errands for the wedding, and so he was on his own. He wasn't about to turn anyone away, however.

Suddenly, he laid eyes on Sofie, sitting quietly in a corner, looking neither desperate to see him nor ill, for that matter. His heart soared at the sight of her, and the memory of the kisses they'd shared yesterday swam rapidly to the surface. He raised his hands to hush the crowd of clamoring patients.

"Excuse me, folks, but I'm going to have to invite you back on a greatest-need basis. Anybody here bleeding?"

It seemed an awkward way to arrange his appointments, and even as he stood there, faced with a vast age range, three more people came ambling through the door: a middle-aged man with a hacking cough and a young woman leading a whimpering toddler by the hand.

"Allow me, Doctor." Sofie rose to her feet then walked—waddled, rather—to the desk situated next to the outside door.

The room went silent as Sofie assumed her post behind the desk. "Who here has a scheduled appointment with the doctor?"

A few hands shot up.

Sofie picked up the file folders lying in a neat stack on the desk and thumbed through each one. "Well, unless you are bleeding, as Dr. Trent said, or perhaps are suffering chest pains or some other potentially life-threatening condition, he will see you in the order in which your appointment was made, beginning

with…"—her eyes scanned the top of the stack—
"Walter Deeter." She looked up again to address the
room. "The rest of you will wait your turn. There's only
one of him, as you know."

As if the queen herself had spoken, everyone kept
his mouth shut and sat down. Even the children nestled
compliantly in their mothers' laps, a kind of peace set-
tling over the room now that order had been restored.

Eli cast her a grateful glance, not sure if she read
it or not, and ushered Mr. Deeter to the examination
room.

The remainder of the morning went off without
a single glitch and by the time the clock on the wall
registered exactly 12:05, he had seen every person—
except for Sofie, who'd insisted on being last. "Where
did everybody go?" he asked Sofie after releasing his
final patient of the morning. She was sitting in one of
the waiting room chairs.

"I made up a sign."

He walked to the door and opened it. Sure enough,
taped to the knocker was a piece of paper that read, in
neat block letters, "OFFICE CLOSED TILL 1:15."

"I locked the door at eleven thirty, and if folks
tried to slip in while another patient was leaving, I directed them to come back later, or to go to the hospital
if they had a serious injury."

"That's incredible. Thanks for lending a hand.
You wouldn't want to come work for me, would you?"

Sofie remained seated, hands folded, expression
solemn and unmoved. "I already have a job, thank you
very much."

He couldn't help it; her sober face invited humor,
if not a little flirtation. "I can offer you excellent benefits." He arched his eyebrows in a mischievous grin.

"That isn't why I'm here."

"Then, why?" He hesitated. "Is it wishful thinking to hope you came to collect a few more kisses?"

Her face went pale before the blood returned as a full-out blush. "It's not only wishful thinking, it's preposterous."

Apparently, she'd come on business, then. No matter. He was still delighted to see her, stern-faced and all. He lowered himself into the chair next to her. When their shoulders touched, she made a point to move away, propping her elbow on the other armrest. "Okay, if it isn't my kisses you long for, it must be my company," he joshed.

"I'm afraid not. First, I have no idea why I kissed you yesterday, but I can assure you, it won't happen again. Second, I'm disappointed in you."

"I figured that out on my own. I guess my visit with the sheriff must've upset you a little."

"More than a little, Elijah Trent! I trusted you."

"And rightly so. But I cannot sit back and ignore a horrendous crime."

"It's none of your business."

He tilted his head at her, eyeing her tenderly. "It is now. Those kisses we shared have made it my business."

A loud breath escaped through her nostrils, and in it he detected frustration. He wanted to put her at ease. "Look, Sofie. You suffered a terrible wrong, and you can't just let the guy off the hook because you're worried what he might do if you report him. Can't you see? You're letting him have full control."

She drew back her shoulders and straightened her spine. "I'm not your charge, and neither is Andy."

He sat back and straightened his legs, crossing them at the ankles. "Did Sheriff Morris come to see you, then?"

She folded her arms tightly across her chest. "Yes."

"Did you answer his questions honestly?"

"You saw that note painted across my door, Eli. I'm not to say a word to anyone, not even the sheriff. I'm also not supposed to have any contact with you."

"And here you sit. What if that creep followed you here? Did you think about that?"

"No one followed me. I took the side streets, mostly."

"You didn't bike here, did you?"

"I most certainly did."

When he opened his mouth to protest, she added, "And don't bother telling me I shouldn't have. Like I said, I am not your charge."

He cleared his throat. "Sofie, you can't go on letting everyone think this pregnancy was your choice."

"People can think what they want, Eli. That's their business. Just as what happened to me is *my* business."

"You're wrong. It's much more than just your business. Someone else could be in danger because of that maniac. Don't you feel some responsibility to the other young women of this town?"

A tight gasp whistled through her teeth, and the urge to give her hand a reassuring squeeze nearly overtook him, but he forced himself to keep his arms folded across his button-down doctor coat. "I wouldn't wish what happened to me on anyone else." Her voice faltered.

"I know you don't like me hovering, Sofie, and that you've made it on your own for years. But it doesn't hurt to accept help every once in a while. And you can trust me. I would never divulge a confidence unless I thought you were in grave danger, which, by the way, I happen to think you are."

There was no sound, save for the wind rustling through the leafy trees outside and the distant whistle of a train. With the house situated right next to the tracks, locomotives whizzed past all day long, but Eli had grown so accustomed to the sound that he often couldn't remember when the last one had passed through, despite the way they tended to shake the house to its very foundation.

She studied her feet, pointing the toes of her worn brown loafers. "I don't like having to depend on other people."

"You've made that more than clear."

She looked over at him. "Is that so bad? That Andy and I have managed well on our own?"

"On the contrary, it's commendable. But nobody can be self-reliant forever. We all need one another. Sometimes, we give help; other times, we receive it. And, right now, it's your turn to be on the receiving end. You're about to have a baby, Sofie."

She angled her face upward, meeting his gaze. He thought he read a hint of mischief in her eyes. "You're kidding, right?"

He laughed, and when she giggled along with him, a kind of camaraderie grew up between them like a blossoming flower—one so delicate, he feared a single unbefitting word could hamper its growth or even uproot it altogether. So, he opted to say nothing.

The silence stretched out between them until Sofie cleared her throat. "Do you think I should give my baby up for adoption?"

The question nearly knocked him over. He never would have expected someone so doggedly independent to invite his opinion on such a serious matter. He collected his thoughts for a moment. "I think you should pray good and hard about it. That's between you and the Lord."

"You don't have an opinion?"

"Shocking, I know. But this is an issue that you must decide for yourself—with the Lord's leading, of course."

The thought occurred to him that it would be a lot easier for her to keep the baby if she were married. Having a husband would solve many problems, from many perspectives—financial and logistical, not to mention that it was preferable for a child to grow up under the auspices of a mother and a father. Of course, that assumed she married a man of the highest Christian character, one who worked a steady job and was committed.

You match that description. Why don't you marry her?

The notion raced through his head as fast as a bullet. Instead of passing through, however, it seemed to lodge in his heart like a steely lump, as outrageous as it was. He cared for Sofie, of course, and he'd certainly enjoyed her kisses. But marrying her? What was he thinking?

If only he could uproot the absurd idea, as he might surgically extract a bullet embedded in a flesh wound. As nonsensical as it sounded, he couldn't shake it. He was attracted to Sofie, but did he love her?

"Love suffereth long, and is kind; love envieth not; love vaunteth not itself, is not puffed up, doth not behave itself unseemly, seeketh not its own, is not provoked,

taketh not account of evil; rejoiceth not in unrighteous-
ness, but rejoiceth with the truth." Like a soothing
balm, the truth of 1 Corinthians 13:4–6 surfaced in
his mind. When it came to Sofie, he certainly sought
her good, more than his own. Who was to say that he
wouldn't come to love her, in time?

Lord, if this is coming from You, I'm going to need a
lot more to go on came Eli's quiet confession.

He pushed the whole thing aside and tried to
concentrate on Sofie's voice. She sounded a thousand
miles away.

"...hard to know what's right," she was saying.
"My heart tells me one thing, while my head says something else altogether. I know I will berate myself until
I'm old and gray if I give up the baby, no matter the
circumstances through which he was conceived, but,
at the same time, I have to be realistic. Margie says I
shouldn't even want him; that it would be a blessing
for the child and for all concerned to let some well-
deserving Christian couple take him off my hands. I
know that, in some ways, she's right. But...."

His heart ached for her with a pain that pressed
like a heavy rock. "Have you made a list of the pluses
and minuses of both options?"

She frowned at him. "You make it sound like I'm
trying to decide between two cars I'm thinking of pur-
chasing. Not that I could afford one, anyway. This is
about a baby, for goodness' sake!"

Without thinking, he slipped an arm around
her shoulder and squeezed. "I'm sorry, honey. I didn't
mean it like that."

She slid out of his embrace and moved away from
him one chair. "Don't touch me. I can't think straight
when you do that. And don't call me 'honey.'"

He chuckled under his breath. What else could he do?

She buried her face in her hands. "I need to think."

"I could come over tonight, if you wanted to talk this over further."

She lowered her hands and gawked at him. "You haven't listened to a word I've said, have you?" She jumped to her feet and started for the door. "I don't want you coming over anymore," she said over her shoulder. "Tildi was more than happy to agree to drive me to and from work, and she said Andy could spend the nights at their house."

He followed her outside. "At least let me drive you home."

She took up her rusty bike, hoisted her skirt slightly, and threw one leg over the bar. The maneuver gave him a nice view of her pretty calves. She mounted the seat, one foot on the ground to maintain balance. "I've been biking everywhere for years."

"Not pregnant, you haven't. Remember?"

She rolled her eyes. "You're a real pest, Dr. Trent, you know that?"

"Proud of it." Eli gave a wry smile. "And you, Miss Rogers, are a mulish young woman."

Huffing, she pushed off with her foot and pedaled away, not giving him even the briefest of backward glances. The searing sun burned through the fabric of his white coat as he watched her go south on Cass Street until she disappeared from sight. When he turned to walk back inside, a beat-up black truck, much like the one he'd seen parked alongside Mill Creek Pike, slowed at the corner and turned onto Sinclair. He could have sworn that the driver had eyeballed him, but, with the noonday sun blinding him, he wasn't able to make out the fellow's expression, much less identify him. Had the guy decided to travel further south on Cass, Eli would have jumped in the car and followed him, just to ensure Sofie's safety.

He gave his head a hard shake. "I think I'm losing my mind. Why am I so bent on protecting her?"

"Love...beareth all things, believeth all things, hopeth all things, endureth all things. Love never faileth."

What? He squinted in the blinding sunlight. *Lord, is this coming from You, or is the heat of the day just messing with my brain?*

When no further revelations came to him, he retreated inside, the coolness a welcome refuge from the scorching sun—and from those hallucinations. Good grief! He had a long afternoon ahead of him, and no time to worry about Sofia Rogers, let alone further contemplate marrying her. Where had his common sense run off to? He couldn't hope to fill his grandfather's shoes if his head wasn't properly screwed on. And he couldn't afford to put off any longer his search for a secretary, someone who was organized, experienced, and competent. Preferably, someone like Winnie Carmichael—in other words, of an age and appearance that didn't distract the sense out of him.

Chapter Fifteen

The Lord *redeemeth the soul of*
his servants: and none of them that trust in
him shall be desolate.
—Psalm 34:22

On Monday afternoon, Owen headed to Livvie's Kitchen on his lunch break for hamburgers with the gang—Elmer, Lester, and Marvin. It was a much-needed escape from the service station where he worked. His boss, Wilbur Godfrey, was a cranky old codger who was always harping on him for his "lack of motivation" and his short fuse with customers. What, did he really think Owen wanted to work at a service station the rest of his life? "Good luck finding a friendly genius to spend his days pumpin' gas," he told the fellows over lunch.

"A genius you ain't," Elmer affirmed.

Lester and Marvin hee-hawed as if they'd never heard anything funnier.

"Laugh all you want," Owen said. "I'm the one with the high school diploma."

"Yeah, from a school for delinquents," Elmer put in. "Don't be surprised if you're pumpin' gas the rest o' your days, 'cause nobody else'll hire a certified hooligan. Least I'll get my daddy's farm someday."

"I thought that was goin' to your brother," Owen sneered.

"That's prob'ly what he thinks. But I've got a plan."

"If it don't pan out, looks like you'll be haulin' wood at the lumberyard for life," Lester observed.

The foursome kept up their mocking banter for the remainder of the meal. Their connection wasn't affable, by any means, but they'd gravitated toward one another because of the obvious qualities they shared—discontent, disruptiveness, and defiance. They were habitual lawbreakers, and although they mostly worked alone and kept their conquests to themselves, they were happy to pool their knowledge and expertise for one another's benefit. They talked about having their way with various women, but Owen doubted any of them had pursued their desires as far as he had. All talk and no action, they were.

After lunch, Owen drove back to the gas station by way of Doc Trent's massive house. Lo and behold, his grandson, the good doctor Elijah, was standing right in the front yard, gazing down Cass Street. If only he'd thought to pack one of his dad's revolvers, he could have shot off a couple of rounds and then sped down Sinclair and vanished in a cloud of smoke, just to give that busybody a good dose of fear. What a perfect beginning that would have been to the string of events he'd been dreaming up to drive the fellow out of town! It would serve him right for taking matters into his own hands and talking to the sheriff about Sofie. She better not have talked. His dad was no brilliant gumshoe, but it wouldn't take long to assemble the clues—his leaky alibi; his mother's missing bottle of Veronal, which she took for her bouts of insomnia—and Owen couldn't afford to have them pieced together in a way that pinned him as the perpetrator.

He pulled into the parking lot of Godfrey's Garage and hadn't even shut off the engine when he heard the familiar, gruff voice bark, "You're late."

He turned and met the steely grimace of old man Godfrey, whose face, hands, and overalls were black with grease, and whose sparse gray hair stood up straight from hours spent horizontal beneath the bodies of automobiles.

Owen glanced at his watch. "Only by fifteen minutes. Gosh."

"You get forty-five minutes for lunch. That's it."

Rolling his eyes, he climbed out of the truck and slammed the door shut. "Then, why do they call it lunch *hour*?"

The guy wiped at the side of his nose with his sleeve. "That ain't the term I use. When your daddy convinced me to hire you, I told him there'd be conditions, the first of which is punctuality. If you can't arrive on time in the mornin' and after your noon break, I'm afraid I won't be able to keep you on."

Rage boiled in Owen's belly, giving him the strongest urge to throw something. Day after day, he bent over backward to do his job, but it was never enough. Sure, he'd been late a few mornings, but he had his mom to blame for that. Fool woman never woke him up on time, probably because she was still under the effects of her sleep aid. "Cut me a break, alright? I'll try to do better." He detested the apologetic tone in his voice. As if he owed Godfrey a thin dime. He ought to sic his dad on him—that'd silence his hollow threats. Wilbur Godfrey liked his hooch, and if he feared the discontinuation of his supply, he'd let up on Owen in fast order.

He had all manner of tricks up his sleeve, and he'd use every one of them, if need be. Nobody pushed Owen Morris around and got away with it.

※

Sofie heard a knock on the door at nine o'clock—Tildi Walters, come to drive her to work. "I hope you don't mind leaving a little early, Sofie," Tildi said when she opened the door. "I'm happy to drive you, but I need to get back in time to put the kids to bed. Andy and Georgie are having quite the time playing with their cars and trucks, making roads all over the living room floor. Hopefully, they'll have tired themselves out by the time I get back."

Guilt yanked at Sofie's conscience for imposing on her neighbor in this manner. "I could just as well ride my bike," she said, feeling obligated to at least offer. "And it isn't necessary for Andy to stay with you every night. Why, he's spent the nights at home alone, sleeping, ever since I took a job."

"No, absolutely not. I won't hear of it. Bruce even said yesterday, 'It isn't safe, that boy being alone at night.' It's always bothered him. And you know what else he said?"

"I'm almost afraid to ask."

Tildi giggled. "He said, 'It's about time that woman asked for help. She's so darned independent, it's a wonder she lets a chicken give her eggs.'"

"Oh, gracious." Sofie couldn't hold back her sudden burst of laughter. "Well, tell him I don't. I pay for my eggs at Murphy's Market." She chuckled softly. "At any rate, I do appreciate you taking Andy overnight, and I can't thank you enough for driving me to and from work. I'm afraid I'm reaching that awkward stage in my...condition." Speaking of awkward, that was exactly how it felt, speaking to Tildi about her pregnancy. She was a friend, yes, but not someone Sofie felt very comfortable confiding in. It wasn't that she didn't trust her, but she didn't want to burden her with problems and pain that weren't hers to bear. It struck her as odd, though, how easily she'd confided in Eli, even expressed openness to the idea of adoption—something she hadn't told Margie, one of her oldest friends.

"And you shouldn't be riding your bike at this stage," Tildi agreed. "If you fell, you or your baby, or both, could suffer serious injury. We don't want that to happen."

The two women didn't want for casual conversation on the drive to Spic-and-Span. They talked mostly about Tildi's boys—the youngest one's antics, in particular—and avoided anything too personal, including mention of Sofie's pregnancy and any pertinent questions. Sometimes, she wished she could just blab something about the situation to Tildi, but doing so would only open another can of ugly worms and force the entire truth to come spewing out. In some ways, keeping Tildi in the dark was to her benefit, for it released her of any responsibility. Maybe Tildi realized this, hence her silence on the matter. And who could blame her? She had enough worries of her own, trying to keep her husband happy and her three young boys in line.

When Sofie walked through the door of Spic-and-Span Cleaning Service, Mr. VanDyke looked up from his paperwork and nodded, a little less amiably than usual, if she read him correctly. In fact, his demeanor was downright edgy. She tried not to let it bother her, thinking he must have a great deal on his mind.

"Is my assignment ready, Mr. VanDyke? I thought I could get a head start, since I'm a little early."

He scratched his ear and glanced at her, avoiding eye contact, from the looks of it. "Not tonight, I'm afraid. I need to hold a meeting when the others arrive."

"Oh."

The tension in his voice gave her a jittery stomach, but she pushed the possibly unfounded feeling aside and walked to the back room, where she stashed her meager sack lunch in her private cubby and retrieved her apron and cap from a hook on the wall.

Delores, Edith, and Francine filtered in next, plenty ahead of schedule, and Mr. VanDyke greeted each of them in much the same way as he had Sofie, without his usual warmth. Although the four women had always maintained a friendly relationship among themselves and with their boss, it was strictly professional. They did their jobs and went home to their families, rarely ever talking shop for lack of time. Thus, while Sofie was sure they all sensed a difference in Mr. VanDyke's deportment, none of them would have thought to voice her concern. Instead, they just waited for "the meeting" to convene.

They all sat at a round table, two with hands folded on the tabletop, while the others, like Sofie, perhaps twiddled their fingers in their laps.

"I'm afraid I have some news for you ladies that might not go over too well," he said.

Delores, the eldest, released a tiny gasp.

"And since there's no point in putting off telling you any longer, I may as well give it to you straight."

Sofie's heart took a wild leap to her throat. What sort of bad news could he possibly have in mind to tell them?

He drew in a breath. "There's just no easy way to tell you this," he said, looking at each one individually. "Spic-and-Span Cleaners is closing up shop. I'm not selling the business, because...well, we've been losing profits on a monthly basis. In fact, it's belonged to the bank for some time now. I just haven't had the heart to tell you. It's these hard times we're living in. As you know, I've lost a number of clients over the past year, and I just can't stay afloat. My wife and I are moving to Atlanta to join forces with my brother, who runs a similar business, only he's managed to keep it going. He's actually buying out another company. Being there for the merger will be an excellent opportunity for us. I'm sorry it doesn't extend to you ladies, as well."

Sofie's mind raced in a dozen directions as she looked around the table from one woman to the next. Each of them wore an expression of disbelief, confusion, and sheer panic.

"I'm sorry I kept our recent losses from you until now. The truth is, for the longest time, I believed I could pull the business back together." Beads of perspiration exploded on his forehead and started dripping down his face.

In spite of the blow of loss Sofie felt, she couldn't help but sympathize with the poor man. Somehow, she had to believe God had another plan in mind. For now, it seemed that she would be forced to give up her baby. Maybe this was God's way of revealing that to her.

"How much longer will you be in operation?" Edith asked, her voice quaking with apprehension.

Mr. VanDyke's face fell even further, and he drummed his pencil against the edge of the table. "I'm afraid it will cease to exist completely, as of tomorrow. The bank has already found another buyer for the property, and they intend to use the building for some other purpose entirely; don't ask me what. I'm hopeful you ladies can find employment elsewhere, perhaps at one of the other cleaning services in town."

"None of them is hiring," Francine whined. "I've got friends working for Tidy Tim's, and she's been afraid of being laid off for some time. Seems everybody's tightening his belt."

Mr. VanDyke cleared his throat. "Well, I'm sure some of my clients will be switching to the other services, so there may be a need for new employees. I'd be glad to put in a good word for any of you, wherever you decide to go. You've served me faithfully over all these years." He turned to Sofie with a cheerless smile. "I know you count on this job, Sofia. Something else is bound to come along."

The three other women wore matching expressions of pity as they looked at Sofie, and although no one said a word, Sofie knew what they were thinking. *No one's going to hire an unwed woman so close to giving birth. No one.*

Chapter Sixteen

As for God, his way is perfect;
the word of the LORD is tried: he is a buckler
to all them that trust in him.
—2 Samuel 22:31

By Thursday, Eli had interviewed no fewer than fifteen women for the position of secretary, and that had been after weeding through the thirty-nine résumés he'd received in the previous two days. During the interviews, he'd asked strategic questions and had taken detailed notes, yet his head still spun as he tried to recall each applicant's personality and weigh whether she might be a good fit. The primary qualities he sought, besides work experience, were a confident, easygoing nature and an apparent compatibility with his style. This enabled him to eliminate ten applicants easily. Several of them were overbearing; one woman knew everybody else's business and was proud of it; another couldn't stop bragging about her strong points; and yet another insisted on receiving, in addition to her salary, complimentary care for her family— a husband, five children, four aging parents, and six grandparents. Eli had resisted the temptation to ask her why she didn't throw in her entire neighborhood.

There were also more than a few single women who had applied with blatantly ulterior motives. One fluttered her eyelashes with every answer she gave, made sure to show him some leg, and continually tossed her long, flowing hair over her shoulder. Yet another became so flustered in his presence that she broke out in a sweat, and Eli had to pause the interview to get her a damp towel and a glass of water.

Still, after reviewing their applications and the notes he'd taken, there were a few remaining candidates that he would consider calling back for a second interview. At day's end, he found himself exhausted, hungry, and in need of a break from all things medical.

He rose from his desk and proceeded to close and lock every window in the medical wing, including the street entrance. He started down the corridor to the living quarters just as the clock at the end of the hall chimed seven times. In the front parlor, he came upon Grandfather and Winnie sitting together on the sofa, holding hands, and speaking in hushed tones.

"Oh! Sorry to interrupt."

Grandfather looked up. "Good grief! No interruption. We were just sitting here making last-minute wedding plans and marveling at how fast this week has gone. Sit, sit." He gestured at the wingback brocade chair opposite the sofa. "Has it flown by for you, as well? You look spent."

"Flown by?" Eli collapsed in the chair and released a long, loud sigh. "More like catapulted through the air at the speed of a hurricane-force wind."

Grandfather chuckled. "I'm afraid I've been of very little help to you." He winked, then turned to Winnie and pressed his forehead against hers. "My bride-to-be has been running me into the ground with so many errands."

"I thought you were planning a simple affair."

"Oh, we are, we are," Winnie said, flicking her wrist. "Don't listen to him. I merely asked him to arrange for the flowers to be delivered on Saturday and to collaborate with Will and Livvie Taylor on a menu for the intimate dinner party afterward."

"And to hire Marcia Tisdel to play the piano," Grandfather put in. "But the grand piano hasn't been played in years, and I had to run all over the county to find someone to tune it. I finally found a piano tuner over in North Manchester, and he graciously agreed to come tomorrow, even though his schedule was already booked." He gave an exaggerated huff. "And let's not forget that I also made arrangements to have the drapes professionally cleaned, which reminds me: I went to speak to Peter VanDyke about doing the job and learned he's no longer in business. After all these years, Spic-and-Span Cleaning Service is closing its doors."

Eli nearly shot out of his chair. "What does that mean for Sofia Rogers?"

Grandfather furrowed his brow. "As I understand it, he had to let everyone go. Word is, the bank foreclosed on the business and the building. Apparently, they'd been struggling for some time. It shocked me to drive up to that little shop and see the big 'Closed' sign nailed across the door. Looks plain gloomy inside."

"I hate to see businesses go bad. It's such a sad thing. But I'm more concerned for what will happen to Sofia," Winnie said. "I can't imagine she'll find another job, at this point. Who's going to hire someone so far along? There must be something we can do."

Eli rose from his chair. "I'll go see how she's doing, for starters. She must be devastated. Maybe I can encourage her. She doesn't want to see me, but that's just too bad."

"Not want to see you? Why ever not?" Winnie asked.

He sighed. "It's a long story, one I probably shouldn't start right now."

Grandfather cast him a sly smile. "You aren't developing feelings for this girl, are you, Elijah?"

The man had never been one to dance around an issue. "You could say that," Eli confessed. "She's a special woman, and I admire her something fierce."

Grandfather stroked his goatee pensively. "But is it love?"

The question thundered in his chest. How to respond when he didn't fully know the answer himself? "I know that I care deeply for her, even if the feelings are one-sided. Don't lecture me, please; I already know what I'm up against. She's got a brother and a baby on the way."

"I wasn't about to lecture."

The two men studied each other for a long moment, while Winnie looked on silently. Eli almost wished she would share her perspective.

But a train rumbled past, giving all of them a chance to ruminate.

"I trust your judgment, son," Grandfather said when the engine whistle had faded into the distance.

"And I trust both of you implicitly." He dropped into his chair again. "I may as well tell you that last Sunday, when I dropped Sofie and Andy at their house after lunch at Livvie's Kitchen, we found a nasty message painted across her front door."

Grandfather's eyes registered alarm. "What did it say?"

"Something to the effect that if she knew what was good for her, she'd stop talking to the new doctor in town, or somebody was going to get hurt."

The old man straightened. "You!"

"Precisely. Sofie panicked and insisted I leave. Her biggest concern was painting over the message before Andy had a chance to see it."

Winnie's brow furrowed in concern. "Does she have any clue who might have left such a threat?"

"No. You see...." Eli drew in a cavernous breath and let it out through thinly parted lips, his elbows pressed into the chair arms, his hands steepled under his chin. "Our suspicions were correct. She was attacked, last fall, right around Thanksgiving."

A hissing gasp rushed past Winnie's lips.

"The worst part is, she has no clue as to her attacker's identity. Seems he drugged her before the whole thing. The only positive aspect is that she has no recollection of the actual event. But her attacker has been sending one threat after another not to breathe a word about it to anyone." He took a deep breath, processing the information even as he shared it. "When it became clear that she wasn't about to go to the authorities herself, I left her house and went straight to the sheriff's office to start an investigation. Then, on Monday, I got a visit from Sofie, who made it more than clear she didn't appreciate my butting in."

Winnie wrung her hands. "I should think she'd be thankful you reported the crime."

"You would, wouldn't you? Yet she was downright angry. And she won't agree to file a report. She must think that her attacker means business about following through with his threats. I don't like that she and Andy are stuck out there in that tiny run-down house with no car, no phone...no means of escape, really."

Grandfather ran a hand down his face. "Do you have a solution to propose?"

He chuckled. "Funny you should say 'propose.' It's occurred that I could ask her to marry me. That would solve a world of problems."

Grandfather's expression was stern. "That's not rational, Elijah. You can't marry her strictly to protect her and her brother. You need a better reason than that for making a lifetime commitment."

Eli nodded. "I know. But I've sensed the Lord speaking to me, nudging me gently."

"And this nudging—you think He's telling you to marry her?"

"The idea of marrying her planted itself deep in my mind the other day, like the seed of a giant oak that won't stop growing. I've been digging into my Bible before bed each night, and everything I've read has confirmed my inclination to marry her. I have this nagging need to protect them, that baby included. Marriage seems like the best solution."

"Marriage is not a 'solution,' son. It's a union of two people in love. And you can't count on marriage to fix anything. That was never God's intention."

"Poor choice of words," Eli conceded. "I'm not viewing it as a solution as much as the best option. I'm thirty-two, and I've known a fair share of women, but none have captured my attention quite the way Sofia Rogers has, pregnant or not."

Grandfather and Winnie sighed in unison, but his tone was frustrated, while hers was whimsical.

"I think it's romantic," Winnie gushed.

Grandfather gawked at her, as if her nose had developed an unsightly mole, but then his expression shifted to one of quiet deliberation. He tilted his head at Eli and blinked twice. "Knowing you, Elijah, I'm sure you'd make it work. If you don't fully love each other now, you will in time."

"Thank you, Grandfather." Eli pushed himself off of the armrests to a standing position and headed for the door. With one hand on the knob, he stopped and turned back around. "I don't know what, if anything, is going to happen tonight, but I'll ask you to pray for me. Sofie's in a precarious position right now, and I'm plain worried about her and Andy."

"We'll pray," they assured him with one voice.

Chapter Seventeen

The LORD is good unto them that wait for him,
to the soul that seeketh him.
—Lamentations 3:25

*O*wen seethed with anger at the sight of that doctor's car sitting in Sofie's driveway. He'd thought that, between the painted message, printed note, and poisoned dog, the fellow would have been deterred from visiting her. Apparently, he needed to take more drastic measures. He drove past River Road for the third time, deciding he'd wait till dark set in before making his move. Fool doctor had a lesson to learn, and he intended to teach it in such a way as to make it unforgettable.

※

Sofie stood at the counter, hands coated in flour, kneading bread dough as if her life depended on it. Her hope had been that baking would be a helpful distraction to her fraying nerves. Andy and Eli were engaged in a game of checkers at the kitchen table. Eli was winning, but Andy didn't seem to mind, the way he kept jumping up on his chair, speaking in stops and starts.

"Slow down, buddy," Eli chided him gently. "Remember how we said that you should think about what you want to say before you speak? Form the words in your head and then say them aloud, slowly and deliberately."

"I know, b-but I'm s-so excited to see-ee you. Sofie said you w-weren't c-coming back."

Eli looked up at her, keeping his blue eyes trained on her while he spoke. "Well, she should have known I would miss you and wouldn't be able to stay away for long. It's been a busy week, but I'm here now."

Flustered by his penetrating gaze, she lowered her head and focused on the large lump of bread dough before her. Why had Eli come, when she'd specifically asked him not to, in light of the risks involved?

She had a headache, her third this week, and she knew it stemmed from stress and worry over her lack of a job. It surely hadn't helped that she'd pedaled all over Wabash looking for a new one—to no avail. And now, with Eli here, the tension had only mounted. She placed the dough ball in an oiled bowl, covered it with a towel, and then went to the sink to wash her hands.

"Sofie doesn't got a j-job anymore. She got f-fired."

She whipped her head around. "Andrew James! I asked you not to be telling other folks our business. And I didn't get fired. Mr. VanDyke had to close his doors."

Andy stared at the checkerboard, his face flushed. "That doesn't mean we can't tell our f-friends. Mrs. Walters knows."

Sofie turned back to the sink and held her fingers under the flowing faucet, closing her eyes to stanch the flow of tears. All week, she'd tried, time and again, to give her worries to the Lord. But, whenever she succeeded, it was temporary; she'd take them right back again. "That's because she's been kind enough to drive me around to a few places to look for a new job." Of course, Tildi didn't know she'd also ridden her bike on the days she didn't want to bother her. She couldn't impose on Tildi all of the time.

"I'm sorry to hear that."

Sofie turned around, and there was Eli's gaze again, moving over her tenderly, like wispy feathers brushing her skin. "Actually, I'll confess, Grandfather told me earlier this evening. That's one of the reasons I came out here."

She kept her body averted, wondering if he meant to talk to her again about that office job he'd mentioned on Monday. She would turn him down if he did. She hadn't the proper qualifications, and, besides, her attacker would never stand for it. The responsibility for keeping the matter of his identity undisclosed lay heavy on her shoulders, which also meant she had to keep her distance from Eli.

"I hope she finds another job, 'cause that's how we eat," Andy said.

"We're not going to starve. Something will come up."

"Yes, it will," said Eli. "Gotcha!" With three loud thumps on the checkerboard, he jumped the last of Andy's black checkers with his red king. "Why don't you get ready for bed? Maybe read a book or something." He slid the checkers into the box, folded the board, and placed it on top.

"Aww, no fair! It's not even all the way dark yet."

"Skedaddle, mister. Don't worry, I won't leave without a decent good-bye."

"Will you be back?"

Sofie wanted to answer that question with a firm no, but Eli spoke first. "You can count on it."

With an inward growl, Sofie turned off the faucet, picked up a frayed towel and dried her hands on it then turned to watch Andy shuffle out the kitchen door, move across the living room, and enter his bedroom.

"Could you close your door, bud?" Eli called after him. "I'd like to talk to your sister, and I don't want to keep you up."

The door closed with nary a complaint from Andy, and Sofie marveled at Eli's ability to get the boy to do his bidding without a fight. She wanted to ask him his trick, but she already knew it. Andy worshipped the ground beneath his feet and wouldn't dream of doing anything that might put him out of favor with the doctor.

Flustered by the knowledge that they now shared the kitchen minus Andy's unstoppable chatter, Sofie's heart stepped up its rhythm. Eli pushed back his chair and stood, then fitted the lid on the square box containing the wooden game board and checker pieces. That done, he gazed up at her with his crooked, almost sheepish, grin, which always served to trip her up. She wrung out a wet dishcloth over the sink and set to wiping down the floury counter where she'd been kneading the dough, pouring all her concentration into her efforts, even as he moved away from the table and came to stand behind her.

"I have a proposition for you." His voice came off low and whispery, tickling the nape of her neck. "A proposal, of sorts."

"I can find a new job myself, Elijah."

"Elijah? I had a hard enough time getting you to drop the 'Doctor' and call me 'Eli.' Now it's Elijah?"

She didn't grant him a reply.

He stepped aside and leaned back against the sink, mere inches away, his arms folded across his chest. "So, how did your job search go this week? Has there been any talk about another cleaning company moving in where Spic-and-Span was located?"

"No. Mr. VanDyke said that someone did purchase the building, but all of his equipment was bought by another cleaning company."

"Hmm. Did you inquire at the other cleaning services in town?"

She pursed her lips and fixed him with a sullen glare. "Of course, I did. But it was a lost cause. One look at my near-to-bursting belly, and they said they weren't hiring."

"Near-to-bursting?" He tossed back his head and laughed, which made her want to slap him. "I'm not sure you've quite reached that point, Sofie. Not yet, anyway. Where else did you go?"

She moved away from him and started wiping down the porcelain pull-down lid of the white cast-iron kerosene stove. Heat from the oven below, where the loaf of bread was baking, seeped through her baggy, knee-length cotton skirt. It had been a hot day, hence her decision to hold off baking until evening.

Eli maintained his post at the sink, but she could feel his eyes following her every move. "I went to almost every establishment on Market Street, a couple of cafés—Livvie told me she would have hired me two weeks ago, but they just filled a position—the Honeywell Heating Company, some beauty shops...."

"Beauty shops? What would you do there?"

"I don't know. Sweep floors, maybe. I thought the girl who cuts my hair might be able to use me, but they don't hire out for cleaning."

She stopped scrubbing and let her shoulders droop—a mistake, since Eli noticed and came over to rub her back. "Sounds like you exhausted your options."

"I'm not done looking, by any means. Something will come up." She straightened and tried to move away from his touch, but her feet remained firmly planted in place. Her heart throbbed so loud in her ears she wondered if he could hear it.

"Why didn't you apply for the position at my office? I had thirty-nine applicants, but none of them exactly bowled me over."

"Thirty-nine? See, that just goes to show you how desperate people are for jobs. No wonder I couldn't find anything. I bet that for every application I filled out, there were a hundred more girls all vying for the same position."

He turned her around by the shoulders and lifted her chin with his index finger. "You could always come and work for me. No interview necessary. I saw you in action on Monday. You'd suit perfectly."

"That's ridiculous, Eli, and you know it." She wriggled away from him. "I am far from qualified to run an office, and besides, I don't have an interest in sorting files and setting up appointments. I would, however, be glad to dust your bookshelves."

"You're hired!"

"I was kidding." Bewildered, she headed into the living room.

Eli followed and then passed her, pushing open the front door. "Will you show me your garden?"

Reluctantly, Sofie followed him outside. The first stars had just started twinkling in the expansive sky, and a slice of moon peeked out from behind a slow-moving cloud. Two bats swooped low, probably to snatch a few bugs hovering around the neighbor's gas lantern.

Eli took her clammy hand in his. Gracious, it was hard to breathe when he touched her. She let him lead her around back, even as she wondered what she was going to do with this sweet, impossibly stubborn man.

❧

At the slam of a door, followed by quiet voices, Owen hurried to flip off his flashlight and then stilled himself, waiting to see what would happen. Thankfully, the doctor wasn't headed to his car, or he would have caught Owen crouching behind it.

He held his breath, his pulse pounding in his ears, and listened, but the sounds seemed to be more distant. He sneaked a peek around the fender for a better view, but the best he could figure, Sofie and the doctor, and possibly the kid, had walked around to the backyard. With beads of sweat rolling down his brow and dripping off his nose, he turned the light back on and made his way along the side of the car toward the front, then carefully lifted the hood. Nothing but a bunch of rubber tubing, wires, and huge parts he couldn't identify. How was he to know what sort of damage he was inflicting when he went to clip this wire and that with his knife? He didn't want to make the car impossible to start. What would that accomplish?

Across the road, a dog must have noticed him, and now the blasted beast wouldn't shut his big trap. Owen lowered the hood and tried to improvise his plan—no easy feat, with the dog's relentless barking. Just then, he remembered watching old man Godfrey fix a customer's car after a collision with a cow, of all things. He'd replaced a hollow tube—a steering shaft, he thought it was called—which had been bent something terrible in the accident, so that the automobile's direction was impossible to control.

Owen raced around to the driver's side door, opened it, and lay down on the seat, shining his flashlight up under the dash. A surge of pride welled within him when he spotted the steering shaft. He pulled his knife from his front pocket and started to cut the tube with a sawing motion. But his labors failed to make more than a narrow slit in the metal. Whether it was enough to impair the vehicle, he couldn't tell. He perused the area in the light of his lamp and found that the shaft was attached by two end brackets. If he loosened the brackets and then cut through the strap holding the shaft in place, it might disable the steering, to some degree. It was worth a try, anyway. Again using his knife, he hastened to the task. After he'd finished, he sat up, slid off the seat, and gently closed the door, taking care not to latch it, for fear of the noise it would make. Then, he took off at a run down the sidewalk, passed by the barking mongrel, and trotted down River Road to his truck, which he'd parked along Mill Creek Pike. When he reached the vehicle, he jumped inside, started the engine, and sped out onto the road, his stomach aflutter with anxious butterflies as he anticipated the front-page headline of tomorrow's *Daily Plain Dealer*: "Young local doctor dead after violent vehicular collision."

❧

Eli picked his way through the rows in Sofie's garden, lit only by a bright moon and a host of stars, and listened as she talked about the various berries and vegetables she'd planted: cabbage, sprouts, beets, summer squash, potatoes, cucumbers, strawberries, and so on.

"And these are tomato plants?" Eli crouched beside a sea of vines.

"Yes. They're already getting tiny little tomatoes, see?" Sofie pointed to a cluster of diminutive green globes. "Of course, it will be a little while before they're ripe."

He stood up again and followed Sofie down an aisle of cornstalks. "It looks like your corn crop's off to a great start."

"'Knee-high by the Fourth of July' is what they typically say, but it's already past that point. It should be a good season for corn." She looked out over the field bordering her yard. "I'd say mine's growing every bit as fast as Mr. Hoffman's, wouldn't you?"

"Yes. Sofie, I—"

"We've had a good balance of rain and sunshine this year, which always helps. Of course, the weeds like it, too, so Andy's been particularly busy at that task. He isn't overly fond of the assignment, mind you."

"I was wondering if we—"

"You surely have a way with him. He would probably kiss your feet if you asked him to. I'm not saying you would." With a nervous giggle, she folded her arms across her chest and wrapped herself for warmth. "Golly, I think it's getting a trifle chilly out here. Never thought I'd say that, as hot as it was today, but once that sun goes down, it—"

"Sofie!" He hated interrupting, but it appeared to be the only effective way of halting her incessant chatter.

"Oh."

He lowered his head so that their gazes were level. "We can go back inside, if you're serious about being chilly, but I thought it might be better to talk without Andy in earshot. Would you mind?"

She gathered a big breath. "I've already told you I'm not going to work for you."

He grinned. "Is that because you're holding out for a better opportunity?"

She expelled a long sigh and looked skyward, and it was all he could do to resist leaning forward and kissing the hollow spot in her elegant neck.

She lowered her head again, meeting his gaze. "I'm not going to work for you, because...because of another threat. Andy found it out by the shed, next to a canister of Red Squill. And Buster, who'd been given some of the poison. Poor dog's been suffering, though I think his system's almost clean. But, the implication was that, next time, he'd give him enough to kill him. Needless to say, Andy went into a regular dither."

Eli's blood boiled with a mixture of alarm and red-hot anger. "When did Andy find it?"

"First thing Monday morning."

"Before or after the sheriff came?"

"Before."

"Then, you told him about it, right?"

"No. I burned the note soon after he left."

"What?" Spasms of unease erupted in his mind. "That note was evidence, Sofie. Hard proof the sheriff needs to go on."

"Well, it doesn't matter. Hard proof or not, I'm not about to tell the sheriff anything. I can't."

He clutched her upper arms, firmly but gently. "That doesn't make sense, Sofie."

"I wouldn't expect it to make sense to you."

"Then, explain it to me."

"I can't."

Eli dropped his hands and started pacing, trying to come up with a way to make Sofie understand the error in keeping quiet. It wasn't easy to think clearly, though, with the cacophony of croaking tree frogs and barking dogs. He shook his head in frustration. "Well, you can at least tell me what the note said."

"Pfff." She blew through her teeth. "Fine. It was another warning to stay away from you. I guess he's afraid you're going to persist with the investigation, somehow. And I have no doubt he will follow through on his threats. That's why I told you to stay away. I truly wish you hadn't come tonight. Furthermore, you had no business promising Andy you'd come back. You can't." A desperate tone swathed her every word.

But he ignored it, because he was just as desperate to keep her safe. "Listen to me, Sofia." He searched her face for a sign of comprehension. "We have to get you out of this house. You're not safe here."

"What? I can't afford to—"

"Yes, you can. You may feel that you have no choice but to comply with these threats, but I certainly don't. He can't go on thinking he's in control of your every move. Not while you're in my care."

"What do you mean?" She stiffened, sticking out her pert little chin. "I already told you, I'm not your charge."

"That may be. But I'd like to make you my charge."

Her chin protruded even further, her brown eyes glimmering like gold dust in the increasing starlight. "What is that supposed to mean, exactly?"

"I want to marry you, that's what!"

Chapter Eighteen

Thou wilt keep him in perfect peace,
whose mind is stayed on thee:
because he trusteth in thee.
—Isaiah 26:3

You *what?* Are you crazy? I'm about to have a baby."

"I know. And that's one reason why getting married makes a great deal of sense. You can live in my house—my grandfather's house, actually, until I purchase it from him—raise your child in a safe environment, and have all your needs met, medical and otherwise."

Her head felt ready to spin right off. It was one thing for him to offer her a job, but the whole package—marriage, a home, permanence, and security? She couldn't imagine why he would make such an offer, when she had nothing to offer in return. No—she knew. He felt sorry for her. "I've told you before, Eli, I don't need your sympathy."

"I'm not asking out of sympathy, Sofie. I know it may sound strange, especially considering how little we really know each other, but I was attracted to you from the start, and I actually believe God has been prompting me to marry you ever since."

"God? Why hasn't He prompted me?"

"I don't know. His voice is extremely quiet—usually inaudible, in fact—and the only way I've come to recognize it is by spending time reading His Word and praying."

A lump of guilt rose in her throat. She'd been reading her Bible only recently, having dusted it off after years of disuse. "Marrying you would really rile the father."

"Please talk to the sheriff, Sofie. I know you're afraid, but I'm not. Together, we can put that creep behind bars, where he belongs."

She couldn't help it: a single tear trickled out the corner of her left eye and rolled down her cheek. Eli reached up and dabbed it with his thumb, which only precipitated the escape of yet another, and then another. "You have...no idea...what you're saying," she sputtered between fretful sobs. How she longed to believe everything would be okay. But someone at the sheriff's office was tied to the attack. She had no doubt the sheriff would do anything to protect his staff, since they were a reflection of his own reputation.

He gathered her in his arms, so close that, had the baby decided to kick, he probably would have felt the movement against him.

"I care a lot about you, Sofie. Truth is, I might even—"

"Stop right there, Elijah Trent!" She pushed him away and ran as fast as she could toward the house, her chest so full of tension she thought it might explode. On the stoop outside the kitchen door, she turned around and shouted, "Leave and never come back. I mean it!" With that, she slipped inside and locked the door, then leaned against it, panting heavily. Had he wanted to, he could easily have walked right into the living room, as that door stood wide open to the unlocked screen. But he made no effort to enter uninvited. "Sofie, come here," she heard him say in a low voice from outside the screen door. After catching her breath, she pushed away from the kitchen door and shuffled tiredly into the living room.

On the other side of the screen, with his nose pressed against it, he resembled a lost pup begging for shelter. "I didn't mean to scare you."

His honey-colored hair, ruffled by the breeze, drooped over one eyebrow, and her heart caught. She breathed easier and sighed. "You didn't," she said, meaning it. "It's just that you took me by surprise, and the notion of us marrying, it's...well, it's plain absurd."

"I don't know why you'd say that. You need help, and you know it."

"Needing help is no reason to get married."

"You're right. My grandfather said the same thing."

Her lashes flew up. "You told your grandfather about your scheme?"

"And Winnie."

She sucked in a sharp breath. "I can't imagine what's going through their minds. Your family would want you marrying your own kind, not somebody from the...the other side of the tracks."

His eyes reflected off the glaring living room lamp and glimmered with humor. "Actually, the tracks are over there"—he pointed off to the east—"so we're on the same side."

She managed a tiny smile. "You know what I mean."

"May I come in? I did promise Andy I wouldn't leave without saying good-bye."

She gave the screen a gentle push and stepped
back. He entered, and she had that sensation of standing next to a strong tower. He put his hands on her
shoulders, and her resolve started crumbling as she
watched the play of emotions on his face.

"Don't worry, I'm not going to take advantage of
you," he said in a low, composed voice.

She sighed. "I wasn't worried." Nothing about him
scared her, except for her lessening ability to resist
him, which made no sense. They came from two different worlds, and getting married would be nothing
short of disastrous.

He dropped his hands to his sides and walked
across the room, pushing open Andy's door. With his
back to her, he motioned her over by way of a hooked
finger. She came up behind him and peered around
him. Andy lay sound asleep, with Buster curled at the
foot of his bed. "The picture of peace," he whispered. "I
guess you could tell him I intended to say good night."

"Of course."

He turned and put a light kiss to her lips, a quick,
feathery kiss, and it left her wanting more, but she
knew encouraging it would only put them right back
where they started, with him arguing that marriage
was the answer, and with her rejecting his pity.

"You better go," she said in a choked voice.

"If you insist," he said in a discontented one.

A moment later, she watched the glow of his tail-
lights retreat down the street toward the intersection
of River Road and Mill Creek Pike. Emptiness and
confusion filled her instead. *Oh Lord, what am I to do?*

*"Wait on the Lord: be of good courage, and he shall
strengthen thine heart."* Like a gentle whisper, the verse
she'd read not so long ago pulsed through her mind.

Was this how He spoke, then? *Is that You, God? Wait on Me.*

✳

When Eli got home, he found Grandfather and Winnie where he'd left them, only now, Winnie was pacing the floor frantically, while Grandfather sat perched on the edge of the sofa. On the pedestal table beside him sat a tall glass of milk and a plate of homemade cookies, both untouched. Eli was amused that they'd waited up for him like two worried parents.

"Well?" Winnie rushed to greet him.

Eli shrugged. "Let's just say there isn't going to be a wedding anytime soon. Aside from yours, that is."

"What did she say when you asked her?" Grandfather wanted to know.

Eli chuckled bitterly. "More like, what didn't she say?" He sighed. "I can't force her to say yes."

"Why not? It worked for me," Grandfather said with a mischievous wink.

"Oh, you!" Winnie walked over to him, poised to deliver a playful slap, but he snagged her by the arm and pulled her down beside him. Their flirtations reminded Eli of two smitten teenagers, and he tamped down a pang of jealousy.

"I'll leave you two lovebirds to fight it out." He headed for the stairs but paused on the bottom step and leaned over the banister. "By the way, there was something strange about the way the car handled tonight. It seemed to want to keep pulling to one side."

Grandfather sobered. "Really? That's odd. I had it checked at Godfrey's Garage just last month. I'll have him look at it again. It might be something as simple as a tire gone bad. Take my Packard next time."

"Thanks. I might actually purchase a car in the next week or so, since I'm in a buying mood—you're still planning to sell me your house, aren't you?"

"Indeed, I am. And you may purchase one of my cars, if you're of a mind to."

"Yes, please do!" Winnie said. "Only the good Lord knows where we're going to put all his vehicles once we're both living at my house."

Eli laughed. "But, Grandfather! I'm already buying you out of house and home."

"I've reached the age where it's wise to pare down. Take your pick of my cars, and I'll cut you a good deal."

He shook his head in mock dismay. "I think falling in love has severely impaired your business sense. You need to stop giving away all your possessions."

"That's what love does to a man, son—turns him inside out till he hardly recognizes who he used to be. You'll discover the truth of that soon enough."

On his climb up the stairs, he wondered if he hadn't made that discovery already.

❧

Well into the wee hours, Owen wobbled into a dimly lit house, thankful for the quiet. He'd been out in the barn with his buddies and had managed to imbibe more brew than usual. Not only was it affecting his gait, but he wondered if he might have revealed more than was wise regarding Sofia Rogers. He remembered telling them that she'd caught his eye in elementary school, and that she'd always been untouchable "until recently." The words had tumbled out in a spurt of arrogance, during a session of bragging about who'd done what with which girl. It had seemed only fitting that he air his feat. The problem was, his comment had been followed by an uncomfortable silence, everyone exchanging glances, an unasked question hanging in the air like a hangman's noose.

To cover up his blunder, he'd attempted a joke, but he keenly remembered the seriousness in the three gazes fixed on him, despite the amount of liquor they'd consumed. Truth was, most of them had a high tolerance—Lester, in particular. He probably heard every word—and the deeper meaning—loud and clear. And that worried him.

He stumbled on a clunky shoe in the doorway, so he kicked the thing across the room. A big, shadowy figure bent to pick it up, and he froze.

"You're out late. Aren't you scheduled to work tomorrow?" His dad's voice carried an icy undercurrent of warning. He tossed the shoe aside.

Owen let out his breath. He refused to be bullied. "Yeah, but I had things to do."

"That right?" His dad sniffed. "You could smell the hooch on your breath from clear up in Elkhart."

"So? I can smell it on yours just as well."

"No sir. Haven't had a drop o' the stuff for days. Sit down, Owen."

"Why?"

"Because I told you to, that's why."

Owen was never one to obey, but that warning tone hadn't left his dad's voice, so he figured he'd better go along with it for now. He plopped into the nearest chair and stretched out his legs, propping his feet on the coffee table, his boots depositing a small mound of dirt on the glass surface.

His dad made no objection. Whatever he was about to say must be serious, then.

"I got a question for you, and I want a straight answer."

"Fire away."

"Where's the pistol I keep in the back of the gun cabinet?"

"How should I know?"

His upper lip curled back. "Oh, you know, alright. Carolee saw you sneaking around the cabinet a few weeks ago. I didn't even realize I was missing my M1911 until yesterday afternoon."

"That conniving little—"

"Watch your tongue."

"I don't have your pistol."

"Maybe not right now, but you did, didn't you?"

An uneasy sensation slithered like a snake through his stomach, and he found himself shifting in his chair. "I've got no idea what you're talking about."

"Sure, you do. Did you look under the seat of the truck today?"

He drew his eyebrows together to make the beads of sweat on his forehead stay put. "No. Why?"

He reached in his side pocket and pulled out the pistol, the dim lamplight reflecting off of its barrel.

A shiver started at the base of Owen's neck and moved down his spine.

"Because you would have discovered I removed it first thing this mornin' before you set off for work."

A string of silent curses sounded off in his head. Still, he would fight to the finish to deny all accusations. "Carolee put it there to set me up, then. She's always trying to get me in trouble. I can't stand that tattling little twerp."

"She didn't put it there, and you know it. What sort of trouble are you gettin' yourself into now, huh? Didn't you learn anything at Peterford?"

He narrowed his eyes at the fool. "More than you know. And I ain't in trouble."

His dad scratched his head. "There's somethin' else. I didn't make much about it, at first, but now I'm wonderin'...."

"What?"

"I had four cans of Red Squill out in the garage up on a high shelf. Been holdin' on to 'em ever since the town trustees did away with that rat infestation awhile back. Not many folks have it in their possession. It just happens I confiscated a container of it from Sofia Rogerses' place the other day, so I brought it with me and put it up in the garage with the others. That's when I noticed there were only three cans up there."

The nerves in his gut tightened. "Why should I care?"

"Because I think you might know somethin' about it. What's your business with Sofia Rogers?"

He squeezed the ends of the chair arms. "I got zero business with that floozy. I hardly know what she looks like. Maybe you should question her about how she came to be in possession of it. Isn't that stuff illegal?"

"Don't play dumb with me, boy." The man stood, towering over him, still wielding the pistol in one hand. It was loaded, Owen knew. He swallowed.

"Let me be perfectly clear. I intend to be reelected sheriff. And if you lose me so much as one vote, by gum, I'll...." He shook the pistol several times. "Folks think I can't control my own son, they'll wonder if I can keep the peace about town. You just watch your step, you hear?"

Owen felt his back go rigid against the chair. Bygone memories of long-ago beatings resurfaced, and he fisted his hands, preparing to defend himself, if need be. He'd like to show his brutish, bad excuse for a father what he'd learned in reform school. But, with all the alcohol he'd consumed that evening, this wasn't exactly an opportune time. He'd be at a disadvantage. So, he steeled his gaze for a stare down. After sixty seconds, the oaf sneered, swiveled on his heel, and stalked off toward the den.

"Just so you know, Mr. Smart Guy," he called over his shoulder, "I changed the lock on the gun cabinet, so don't get any ideas about stealin' anything else. If somethin' else goes missin', don't think I'll wonder who's responsible."

Owen wasn't worried. He'd basically majored in lock-picking at Peterford. He dragged his booted feet across the coffee table and planted them on the floor.

That hadn't been bad, as confrontations went. At least his dad didn't suspect him in the case of Sofia Rogers. He walked upstairs to go to bed. In the hallway, he paused outside Carolee's door, half tempted to sneak inside and press a pillow to her face. He'd give her a good talking-to first chance he got and make her plenty sorry for opening her fat trap.

Chapter Nineteen

*Being confident of this very thing, that he
which hath begun a good work in you will
perform it until the day of Jesus Christ.*
—Philippians 1:6

On Friday, after a long morning seeing patients in his office and a long afternoon doing the same at the hospital, Eli finally called it quits at eight o'clock. He drove straight to Sofie's house, determined to make her see the wisdom in marrying him. When he arrived, he was disappointed, and somewhat alarmed, to find the house dark, with no sign of her or Andy anywhere. He walked around the building, trying to peer inside through the windows, but the curtains were drawn. Finally, he decided to scrawl a quick note on a piece of paper from his doctor's tablet and tuck it in between the front door and the frame.

> *Stopped in to see you two. Sofie, may we talk
> some more?*
>
> Fondly,
> Eli

He returned the next morning after making a quick stop at the hospital but found the same scene. His note from yesterday was just where he'd left it, and their bicycles were still propped against the side of the house. At least they hadn't pedaled off somewhere. That gave him a measure of relief, however small.

This was to have been the day Eli came to help with the various weekly tasks, and it saddened him that Andy didn't greet him at the door, as eager as he'd been a week ago when Eli had made his offer. Granted, Sofie had told him not to come, but she needed help, and he wasn't about to let her win on this one, especially since some of the tasks were risky for a woman, pregnant or not. He decided to do what he could, despite their absence.

From the trunk of his grandfather's Packard, he retrieved his toolbox. Hopefully, he'd brought everything he'd need to repair the sagging shutters, mend the broken step, and tend to any other areas screaming for attention. Any supplies he lacked, he would scrounge around for in the shed.

Other repairs called for advance planning—and a trip to the hardware store. The tiny house desperately needed new shingles, a fresh coat of paint, and several replacement windows and doors. Of course, all those things would be irrelevant if he could talk her into marrying him and moving into his future house.

He didn't know why she had to make such an ordeal of it. In his eyes, it seemed a simple matter. Get married—sleeping in separate bedrooms, of course—and let their relationship grow at its own pace. Apparently, for Sofie, and probably for most women, practicality wasn't king.

But then, he had to admonish himself for his lack of sensitivity. The only man she'd ever loved—her father—had been killed in a train wreck, and another man had assaulted her in a way from which she might never fully recover. To make matters worse, he continued his torment with bullying threats. Was it any wonder she hesitated to commit her life to some man she'd known for only a few weeks? He shouldn't have expected to earn her trust overnight.

Sighing, Eli set the toolbox on the ground, then fished around in the trunk for a couple of rags, a bucket, and a pair of work gloves.

"Who're you?"

The youthful voice behind him gave him such a start that he jumped up and bumped his head on the open trunk door. Turning, he met the eyes of a lad who looked to be a trifle younger than Andy, though certainly stockier. He had a football tucked under one arm, and Eli could picture him playing for a college team someday. "Georgie?" he ventured.

The boy screwed up his round face and pushed a lock of brown hair out of his blue eyes. "How'd you know my name?"

"You're Andy's friend, right? I saw you standing on your front steps last Saturday when I brought Andy and Sofie home from church. Andy went over to play with you, I think."

"Oh." A light dawned in his eyes. "Are you that doctor guy?"

Eli chuckled. He liked this kid. "I sure am." He set the toolbox on the roof of the car and extended a hand. "My name's Eli Trent."

The boy hesitated a moment, then shook hands. He immediately released Eli and tossed his football several feet in the air, catching it easily when it came back down. "Andy's not here right now."

"I figured that one out. You wouldn't happen to know where he went off to, would you?"

"Not uh-zackly." He tucked the ball back under his arm and scratched his head with five dirty finger-tips, making that pesky lock of hair stand straight up. "Him and his sister went to stay with a friend."

"No kidding." He didn't know whether to be of-fended that Sofie hadn't thought to tell him they were leaving, or relieved that she and Andy were somewhere safe. "Do you know who they're staying with?"

The boy shrugged his shoulders. "Nope. Andy just tol' me he'll be gone a few days. That's why I wondered who you was, 'cause I thought maybe you were brin-gin' him home early or sumthin'. I was gonna see if he wanted to play with me. We like t' throw the football." He held the ball out in front of him. "I got a new one for my birthday. I'm nine now. I'm gonna be in third grade. In case you were wonderin'."

"I was wondering just that, actually. You're pretty tall for your age. Congratulations on being another year older."

He wrinkled his nose. "Don't you mean 'happy birthday'?"

Eli laughed again. "Yes. That, too." He picked up the toolbox again. "Well, I'd better get to work. I'm go-ing to do a few repairs around the house. You have a good day, young man."

"I will. Hey, you want to throw—?"

"Georrrrr-gie!"

The lad turned in the direction of the bellowing voice. A thin woman with long brown hair about the shade of Georgie's stood on her front porch, the palm of her hand shielding her eyes, as she scanned the neighborhood.

"That's my ma. She might got sumthin' for me t' do. I better go."

"Bye, Georgie." As he watched the sooty little lad take off at a gallop, he couldn't help feeling grateful his mother had summoned him home when she had. It was awfully hard to turn down an invitation to play catch with a nine-year-old, especially one with pleading blue eyes, when he had a good deal to accomplish. He couldn't stay long, since his parents and sisters were due in on the three o'clock train. Indeed, he looked forward to the reunion, and the happy occasion that had precipitated it. His only regret was that he wouldn't have the opportunity to introduce them to Sofia and Andy. He could almost envision his parents' and sisters' eye-popping expressions if he met them at the train station with a very pregnant woman, announcing his intentions to marry her. Laughing to himself, he made for the house, prepared to do as many repairs as he could in a couple of hours.

⁂

Sofie stood at the sink in Margie's kitchen, peeling carrots. She glanced out the window and watched Andy follow Howard to the barn. They paused, and Howard pointed at something off in the distance, perhaps explaining something about the bald eagle perched atop a scarecrow in the middle of the Grants' cucumber patch.

Margie came alongside her and put an arm around her shoulders, tugging her to her side. "He's a fine boy, that Andrew. Your parents would be so proud of you both."

She gave a reflective nod. "I like to think so."

"It's hard to believe he's going to be in the sixth grade this fall. Even more so how much his speech seems to have improved."

She paused in her peeling and looked up at her friend. "Do you really think so?"

"Absolutely. Do you think it's because he's on summer break?"

"Possibly. But I think it's also been the influence of Dr. Eli Trent in their time spent together. Eli tells him to think through his words before blurting them out—that if he lets his brain process exactly what he wants to say, and he proceeds to speak the words slowly and deliberately, rather than spouting them off, he'll have a lot less difficulty. Of course, it requires major concentration on his part, not to mention patience on both our parts. I tend to jump in and coax him along, finishing his sentences and such, but Eli says that's the wrong approach."

Margie gazed out the window again. "Hmm. This Dr. Eli seems to be quite the expert."

"Not really. A friend of his did his doctoral thesis on speech pathology, with an emphasis on the problem of stuttering, and he's read a lot of his work."

"I'm quite anxious to meet this fellow—your young doctor friend, that is."

"Andy thinks he can walk on water."

"So you told me yesterday."

In fact, she'd told her a good deal when Margie had dropped in on her the previous morning, while Andy had been playing over at Georgie's house. They'd sat at the little wooden table in the kitchen, sipping coffee and nibbling on toast topped with strawberry preserves. Having read an article in the *Daily Plain Dealer* about the demise of Spic-and-Span Cleaning Service, Margie had wanted to see how Sofie was holding up. She'd also asked her what plans, if any, she'd made for the future.

Sofie had told her about Eli's marriage proposal—his *preposterous* marriage proposal.

"I'm not convinced it's all that preposterous," Margie had said. "He sounds like a fine Christian man who also has strong feelings for you. I think I would latch onto him if I were you."

"I don't know if I'll ever marry, Margie," she'd said, meaning it. "I have nothing to offer. Besides that, I'm damaged goods. Eli may think marrying me sounds like a good idea right now, but what will he think one or two years down the road? He may very well resent my lack of education and low social standing. Or, worse, despise me for the child I will have brought into the world."

"Against your will, don't forget," Margie had pointed out. "Does Dr. Eli know about the circumstances regarding your pregnancy?"

"Yes, he knows."

"And still he wants to marry you. There's something very noble about that. You've got to be realistic, honey. He's offering you a wonderful opportunity."

"Margie Grant!" Sofie had nearly slammed down her coffee cup, rattling the saucer. "I don't like looking at marriage as an opportunity. If and when I ever marry, I want it to be for love alone."

Margie had tilted her head slightly, a few strands of salt-and-pepper hair coming loose from her bun, and angled her a penetrating look. "Is it possible you might already love him, but you're too afraid to admit it?"

Her heart had skipped a beat, but she'd tamped down her emotions. "It doesn't really matter how I feel." She'd fingered the rim of her coffee cup. "Marriage is simply out of the question."

"But does he seem like the sort of man you could spend your life with? Someone you could come to love, in time?"

The question had tripped her up. "I suppose, but what difference does it make? In the end, I'm still not a good match for him. For anyone. In time, he'd surely grow bored, even disgusted, with me."

"Sofia Rogers, you severely underestimate yourself."

After a few more minutes' conversation, Margie had insisted that Sofie and Andy pack their bags and come to stay with them for a while. "Why, you could stay with us until the baby is born—and longer, if you'd like!" she'd exclaimed. "You know that we've always considered the two of you like our own children, and heaven knows we have more than enough room in our big old farmhouse." She'd clapped her hands together and smiled at the ceiling. "It would be such fun to hear a baby's cry echo off the walls again. The boys have been grown and gone for so long."

"Margie, I don't even know if I'm going to be able to keep the baby. The idea of adoption keeps popping into my head at the most unexpected times." Tears had filled her eyes at the mention of the word, and she'd covered her face with her hands. "I don't know what to do," she'd wailed. "I'm so confused."

"Oh, honey." Margie had stood and come around the table to give her a comforting hug. "I know you're confused right now, and I can't blame you. I know I've encouraged you to consider adoption, but I'm no longer convinced it's the best answer. God can work miracles beyond our wildest imaginings, and I'm certain He has a big one up His sleeve right now." She'd paused. "That's why I'm telling you not to close the door on young Dr. Trent's marriage proposal." With that, Margie had scooted away and started clearing the dishes.

She'd felt her shoulders slump as a shuddering sigh escaped her lips. Silence had prevailed in the following minutes, Sofie pondering the situation, Margie bustling about the kitchen, tidying up.

"Well, if nothing else," Margie had finally said, sitting back down at the table, "I believe the young doctor made a good point when he said that it isn't safe for the two of you to be living here, all alone, on the outskirts of town. You're vulnerable, and being without a telephone makes your situation that much more hazardous, especially the further along you are in your pregnancy. Please, won't you come stay with Howard and me? As long as you want. Stay forever, in fact!"

"Goodness, Margie, I don't know."

Margie had frowned. "Are we that difficult to get along with?"

The remark had elicited a tiny giggle from Sofie. "You know what I mean. I couldn't impose like that." The thoughtful gesture had touched her, but she could no more accept her offer to live with them than she could Eli's offer of marriage.

"Well, we'll talk about that later," Margie had said. "For now, we'll just look at it as a visit. You need a change of scenery and a chance to relax. Take a break from this job search and let me pamper you a little. My stars, when was the last time you sat back and put your feet up?"

She'd had to think a bit. "When I was sick, I guess."

"Right. You were laid up in bed for a few days, and then you jumped headlong into work again, weak as you were. I'm talking about relaxing for no other reason than that you're pregnant and you need a few days' decent rest. You'll feel so much more refreshed afterward."

The offer had been so tempting that she'd finally given in. What could it hurt to take a few days off from the thankless job search? She'd set aside enough money to last them a month or so. "I'm not sure I know how to put my feet up," she'd admitted.

Margie had laughed and planted a light kiss on her cheek. "I'll be happy to teach you how."

And so, after a Friday morning of packing clothes and toiletries, the brother and sister had been spirited away in Margie's red Chevy Superior to the Grants' farm, where they'd been given the royal treatment since their arrival. Why, Sofie had almost had to beg Margie to let her help in the kitchen, but she needed to do something to earn her keep.

Three days, she told herself. *That's the limit*. After three days, she would hit the streets running again— pedaling, rather—in search of some kind soul willing to hire an unwed pregnant woman.

I shall supply all your needs, according to My riches in glory.

"What?" She dropped the carrot she'd been peeling in the sink and swiveled to look at Margie, who was leaning over the icebox, rummaging around inside.

Margie lifted out a head of lettuce, then slanted her a curious gaze. "Hm?"

"Did you say something?"

"No, why?"

"Oh, no reason." She started gathering the carrot peelings from the sink. Had the Lord just spoken to her again? This time, as before, the message was based on a Scripture she'd read. She'd pored over the book of Philippians just this morning, and she remembered reading something along those lines.

Be confident of this very thing: I began a good work in you, and I will complete it until the day of Christ Jesus.

She pivoted again to look at Margie, but she was merely humming to herself as she prepared a salad.

Was that You again, God? Oh, I pray that You would do a good work in me! This new experience of His still, small voice was at the same time thrilling and frightening. But she prayed that it would continue.

Chapter Twenty

The LORD will give strength unto his people;
the LORD will bless his people with peace.
—Psalm 29:11

*F*emale chatter and children's laughter filled the Trent house on Saturday afternoon. Eli had his arms full, literally, with Ruby Lynn, his three-year-old niece, bouncing up and down on his knee and talking faster than a rabbit runs for cover, and Ruby Lynn's two-month-old brother, Robert John. To be honest, he felt somewhat trapped while planted in his grandfather's overstuffed chair next to the fireplace, his brothers-in-law and father engaged in political talk across the expansive room. Clyde, Ruby's older brother by two years, scampered past, while the little dog his parents had brought with them from Grosse Pointe Park barked and nipped at his heels.

When the baby started squirming, his mother, Francine—Eli's oldest sister—snatched him up. "It's time to feed this little button! I must say, he looked quite at ease in your arms, Eli. I guess doctoring has given you a bit of experience, brother dear."

Francine was a beauty, as always. She'd gotten married and had kids later than most women, but, at forty-one years of age, she maintained a trim figure and hadn't a single gray hair to her name. She took after their mother, with her brown eyes, dark hair, and olive skin. His other sister, thirty-five-year-old Constance, also attractive, was like Eli in that she favored their father's features, with a bigger-boned body frame, blue eyes, flaxen hair, and fair skin.

Folks had always said that he and Connie looked the most alike, especially with their matching chin dimples, a signature Trent trait. When he was a young boy, his great-aunt used to poke the spot with her long pointer finger and say, "Dimple in chin, many hearts you'll win." Considering his record of past sweethearts, it seemed she'd had a point, except when it came to one Sofia Rogers. A lot of good a silly dimpled chin had done him in winning her affections.

Grandfather entered the room from his study and announced he intended to take the Ford over to Godfrey's Garage so Wilbur could look under the hood.

"Now?" Winnie asked from the dining room archway. "We're going to sit down to dinner before long, and I know how you and Wilbur get to talking."

"It needs looking at, Win. Something's not right with the steering column." He looked at his watch then back at her and winked. "Don't worry, I'll time myself."

She frowned. "You know I don't believe you. You'd better take someone with you."

"Then we'll both be late," said Francine's husband, John, with a knowing grin.

Grandfather strolled over to Winnie and kissed her cheek. "I will be back in thirty minutes, I promise. Just in time to sit down for dinner. The rest of you carry on." He turned and headed for the door.

Eli set Ruby Lynn on the floor, and she immediately joined in the chase around the house with Clyde and the puppy. "I'll follow you in the Packard,

Grandfather. Otherwise, you'll have to walk back from the garage."

Grandfather lifted his bearded chin. "I was going to ask Wilbur to give me a lift back, but if you do that, then I won't be putting him out."

"I'll tag along with Eli," said Charles, Connie's husband. "Truth be told, I'd like to see Wabash again. It's been a couple of years."

"Truth be told, you just want to escape all the racket around here," John teased.

"I'm the one who should be following in the Packard," Eli's father, Thomas, chimed in. "I can see my grandkids any day of the week. Eli, why don't you stay here and keep visiting with everyone?"

Grandfather glanced around at the lot of them and shrugged. "Well, frankly, I don't care who follows me, as long as we can leave right now. I don't want to upset my bride-to-be and spend all of dinner seeing her look of disappointment."

Eli took his dad's advice and stayed to visit with "everyone"—the women and children, that is, since his dad and both brothers-in-law decided to go along with Grandfather. To make the most of it, when his older niece and nephew, Henry, ten, and Virginia, eight— Connie's children—came bounding down the stairs, he volunteered to take all the kids to the backyard for a game of hide-and-seek, followed by tag, if they had time. Naturally, they all approved the idea.

As he held the door open and watched five rambunctious kids ranging in age from ten to three file past, followed by the scraggly little terrier, he thought how well Andy would fit in with the group.

Somehow, he had to figure out where Sofia had run off to so he could give her a good dressing-down for leaving without so much as a see-you-later.

Not twenty minutes later, the children were all hiding, and it was Eli's turn to start the search. Already, he spotted Ruby Lynn peeking at him from around the trunk of the big walnut tree, which concealed only half of her body. At three, she hadn't fully grasped the rules of hide-and-seek.

Just then, he spotted his mother come out the back door, her face awash with deep anguish. She beckoned him silently with bent index finger.

His concern mounted as he made his way over to her. "What's wrong?" he asked, his voice low.

"I don't want to alarm the children," she whispered, "but there's been an accident...involving your grandfather."

His stomach did a sickening flip. "What do you mean? What's happened?"

Her face went suddenly ashen.

He took hold of her elbow. "Mom! Are you alright?"

"Yes, yes, I'm fine, and I understand that your grandfather is, as well, only he's shaken. His car veered off the road and into a ditch. It was a frightening accident."

A wave of guilt washed over him. "So, it wasn't just my imagination—something was wrong with the steering mechanism! Why didn't I take the darn car to Godfrey's myself?"

"Now, Eli, don't blame yourself. John's in the living room talking to Winnie. He can give you the particulars. Your grandfather will need your medical assistance. I'll stay out here and watch the children."

After a brief rundown from John, Eli grabbed his medical bag, and they both jumped in the Packard and headed back to the scene, which happened to be a quarter mile east of Godfrey's Garage, off Cass on

Highway 24. John talked a blue streak all the way there, relaying as best he could how the accident transpired. "Dad, Charles, and I were following Grandfather, and when we got up to twenty-four, he stopped at the intersection, then proceeded left. When he got his speed up around thirty-five, the car started swerving. We could see he was having difficulty maintaining control. Next thing we knew, he ran off the road. Looked like his right front wheel got caught in a gutter, and that's when he went off into the ditch, ultimately crashing into a fence bordering a cow pasture. Broke right through the thing and sent a couple of cows running. Thank goodness he wasn't going any faster. He did get a bloody nose and bruised lip out of the deal, when his face collided with the steering wheel. And I expect he'll be sore for a few days from being jostled around inside that Tin Lizzie. I'm just thankful he didn't get thrown out, or his injuries would have been far more serious. I drove to Godfrey's Garage to get help before coming back for you."

"Praise God there wasn't another vehicle involved."

"Amen to that!"

When they arrived on the scene, Sheriff Morris was already there, standing beside a tow truck with the words "Godfrey's Garage" painted on the side. Two fellows were down in the ditch, fastening a chain to the Ford's rear bumper. Grandfather, holding a bloodied handkerchief to his face, stood with Eli's father and Charles, all three of them talking with the sheriff. As soon as John stopped the car, Eli grabbed his black bag, jumped out, and hurried over.

"Grandfather! Are you alright?" Upon reaching him, he removed the handkerchief to have a look at his face.

"I'm fine, I'm fine," Grandfather insisted. "No need to fuss."

"You got yourself a dandy little cut there." He nodded to the gash above his lip. "It might need a few stitches." He tried to separate the mustache whiskers to get a better view of the wound, from which blood still trickled, but the man pushed his hand aside.

"Not if that requires shaving," he groused. "I can't go without a mustache. I'm getting married tomorrow."

Eli wasn't about to argue with him. As a rule, doctors made the worst patients. "At least keep applying pressure to stop the flow of blood. When we get home, I'll treat the area with some antiseptic. You should put a cold compress on it, too. Come over and sit in the car so I can look at your pupils."

"I don't have a concussion, Elijah."

"Just the same, I want to do a quick exam."

"He's right, Pop," said Eli's dad. He took Grandfather by the arm and led him toward the Packard. As he did, Eli noticed a definite wobble in his grandfather's gait.

The sheriff followed behind. "Don't seem like there's much to do in the way of investigation, Doc. Appears your car had some sort of malfunction. Hopefully, ol' Wilbur, there, will figure out what went wrong."

Eli tossed a backward glance at the ditch, where the two men he'd spotted earlier looked to be about ready to haul the car out.

"Is that your son helping out?" Grandfather asked.

The sheriff craned his neck around. "Yeah, that's Owen. He works for Godfrey." Under his breath, he murmured, "If you can call it 'working.' Kid's about as motivated as a bag o' rocks."

"Well, at least he's employed," said Grandfather, ever the diplomat.

"I guess. He's a freeloader, though. I'm about ready to throw him out on his ear."

It was too bad the sheriff felt such blatant disdain for his own son, but Eli didn't give it much thought. Right now, his grandfather's well-being was his primary concern.

"Sit, Pop," Eli's dad ordered when they'd reached the car. Charles held the front door open.

"You fellas sure are bossy," Grandfather muttered as he lowered himself onto the front seat, keeping his legs outside the car, feet planted on the ground. "I told you, I'm fine. It's my car I'm worried about." He gazed wistfully at his beloved automobile as Wilbur Godfrey climbed inside the tow truck and gunned the engine. The chain went taut, and the rear tires of Godfrey's truck starting spinning, sending dirt flying everywhere. Finally, the Ford started inching forward, slow as a sloth. Everyone held his breath, willing the chain to hold and the bumper to stay intact.

Once the Ford was free of its temporary grave, Godfrey climbed out of his truck and gave the vehicle a once-over. "It don't look too bad," he called.

Eli reached into his medical bag for his flashlight, but Grandfather stood up and pushed his way past him. "I'd like to see for myself," he announced.

Elis shrugged at his dad and brothers-in-law. "I should have known he wouldn't sit still for more than a minute."

❧

Well, this was a fine fix. With Owen's latest design against the young doctor gone awry, his mind was already spinning other schemes to run him out of town permanently, whether dead or alive. At least Owen had plenty of time to launch his next plan. Spying on Sofie's house the other day, he'd watched her pile into a car with her brother, and he'd followed until he'd figured out their destination: the home of Howard and Margie Grant. They hadn't been back since, so it appeared they were staying there. If Sofie were going to spill the beans to Mrs. Grant, she would have done so by now. Still, Owen had to act quickly. He snarled under his breath.

The elder doctor walked stiffly in his direction, still pressing a bloodied handkerchief to his lip, and perused the damage to his car, beginning with the crumpled front fender. When the rest of the group gathered around him, Owen stepped away, keeping to the background. No one paid him any heed—not even his dad. Fine by him. He no more wanted to associate himself with the law than his dad wanted to fraternize with a juvenile delinquent.

"I'll give her a thorough check," Godfrey said, scratching the back of his balding head. "Don't know what could've gone wrong in the time since you last brought her in. Had her purrin' like a kitten. You say the car was swervin' out of control?"

"It was something with the steering apparatus," Doc's grandson put in. "I noticed it pulling to the side the other night. My grandfather thought it might have been a tire gone bad. Obviously, it was something more serious. I only wish I'd had the brains to bring it to you first."

Yes, if only, Owen thought.

"Let me take a quick look," Godfrey said. He opened the driver's door and leaned inside. When he peered under the dashboard, Owen's stomach took a nosedive. He stuck his hands in his back pockets and swiveled his body to look out at the moving traffic, not wanting anyone to sense his discomfort.

"Well, I'll be a long-toothed swine."

Owen snuck a hurried glance at old Doc Trent as he stepped forward. "What is it you see there, Wilbur?"

Godfrey didn't readily answer; he just kept monkeying with something under the dash. Finally, he came out, carrying a long tube. "Here's your culprit."

"What is it?" the young doctor asked.

Godfrey turned it several different ways in his hands, peering at it with one eye closed. "It's the tube that goes around the steering shaft. If you look real close, here, you can see it's been tampered with." Everyone moved in for a better view. "See here? It's been sawn with some type of tool. Somebody did just enough damage to create a real problem in the steerin' apparatus." He paused, then chuckled nervously. "You got any enemies, Doc?"

Owen noted his dad's brow knit into a tight frown. He rubbed the back of his neck in that way he did when something troubled him. Owen knew no one would have any reason to suspect him, but, even so, he had to play it cool. "Ain't that somethin'?" he murmured.

His dad turned a scowling face on him and edged him out of the circle of observers. "After you've done a thorough assessment of the vehicle, Wilbur, I'll need you to report your findings to me. Looks like I might be in for an investigation, after all. This appears to have been a criminal act."

"Yes, sir." Wilbur nodded, throwing back his shoulders with self-importance. "I should have an answer for you later today. I'll check under the hood and elsewhere to see if I can find evidence of any other tinkerin'."

Owen could have told him not to bother, but at least the assessment would keep old man Godfrey off his case for the rest of the afternoon.

Chapter Twenty-one

*These things I have spoken unto you, that
in me ye might have peace. In the world ye
shall have tribulation: but be of good cheer;
I have overcome the world.*
—John 16:33

Do you want to come to church with Howard and me?" Margie asked Sofie on Sunday morning. "Or shall we drop you off at the Wesleyan Methodist church?"

Sofie might have known she'd be expected to attend church today. It would be the right thing to do, especially out of respect for her hosts. But the idea of making another appearance at Eli's church made her stomach do a couple of flips. "We'll go with you" was her firm reply.

"Aww!" Andy whined from his seat at the breakfast table. "Can't we go to Eli's church? I miss him."

She also might have known Andy would object. He wasn't alone in missing Eli, but she wasn't about to share that information. Gracious, his proposal of marriage still rang as clear as a crystal bell in her mind—and sounded just as harebrained now as it had then.

Margie took a sip from her coffee cup and then set it down. "Why don't we all go together to the Wesleyan

Methodist church? That way, I can visit with my sister, Livvie. I haven't seen her or her boys all week."

Sofie tried not to scowl. "Oh, but I don't mind going to your church. Actually, I—"

"Nonsense. We'll worship with the Wesleyan Methodists," Howard insisted between bites of bacon. "Besides, I'd prefer to hear Reverend White over Reverend Groot. His sermons always put me to sleep."

Margie clicked her tongue disapprovingly. "Howard, don't say such things in front of Andrew. You'll have him thinking church is boring."

"The preaching part is boring," Andy affirmed. He'd finished chewing his food before speaking, no doubt using that time to think through what he wanted to say, as Eli had taught him to do. "It's hard to un-understand what he's t-talking about. Last week, Eli gave me a pen and some p-paper so I could draw a p-picture. I made three crosses on a hill." This he said with slow, deliberate pauses between his words, stumbling only a few times. Sofie appreciated the way Margie and Howard had waited patiently for him to finish his sentence.

She thought back to last Sunday, recalling how she'd absorbed every word of the preacher's decidedly "un-boring" sermon and even scribbled down his closing Scripture, Psalm 63:8, which she'd repeated in her head again and again this past week: *My soul followeth hard after thee: thy right hand upholdeth me.*" She'd spent some time reflecting on ways in which the Lord truly had upheld her that week, from sending Margie to her house at just the right moment to encouraging her through gentle reminders of His promises. Was it possible that He had sent Dr. Elijah Trent to Wabash for that very purpose—upholding her? She dared not dwell on that notion, lest her resolve to resist him begin to weaken. Surely, by now, he'd kicked himself a dozen times for posing that outlandish marriage proposal!

And now, they were about to go back to his church. What if she ran into Eli at the service? Would he avoid her out of sheer embarrassment? Perhaps, the Lord would uphold her again with a pounding headache before the time came to leave for church.

❧

The Trent home buzzed with activity on Sunday morning as everyone got ready for church and also prepared for a busy afternoon—the two o'clock wedding ceremony, followed by a dinner for family and close friends. At Eli's prodding, Grandfather had agreed to forgo the morning service in favor of resting. He wouldn't be alone, though; Winnie had arrived at the house at seven thirty and didn't plan on leaving until she was a married woman, while Francine had opted to remain at home with little Robert John.

Although Grandfather had escaped yesterday's car accident with only a few bruises and some minor bodily aches besides the cut on his upper lip, his lip had swollen to twice its normal size, despite his constant application of an ice pack. It was actually the skin between the lip and nose that bore the gash, but with the mustache covering it, Eli couldn't assess the wound, and, try as he might, he couldn't convince his patient to shave his mustache off in order to give him a better look. "You might need stitches," Eli had reminded him, "and if we don't tend to it, it might not heal properly, not to mention you'll be left with a scar. Shoot, you'd say the same thing if I was the one with the wound."

"I'm not going to shave off my mustache so that you can come at me with a needle and thread."

"Ah, so that's it. You're afraid of a little extra pain," Charles had teased him.

"No, it's simply that I've had a mustache for more than three decades, and I'd like to keep the record going. Besides, my mustache will hide any scar that remains, and I'll keep applying salve to prevent infection. I'll be fine, so stop fussing over me." There'd been an edge to his voice, very unlike the soft-spoken, jovial tone everyone was accustomed to hearing. Eli suspected his nerves had bundled up into a tight little ball, thanks to his upcoming nuptials. Even Winnie couldn't convince him to let Eli tend the wound, and Eli finally surmised that Charles was right; the thought of any further pain factored into his uncharacteristic stubbornness. That, and not wanting to draw further notice to himself on a day when the bride was supposed to be the center of attention.

Eli's mother and sisters scurried about the house, making preparations for the event. They'd vowed to have everything in order—the house decorated, the long oak table set with the finest china—before Will and Livvie Taylor arrived to unload the components of the catered meal planned for afterward.

The thought that someone had tampered with his grandfather's Model A troubled Eli more than anyone knew. Grandfather had dismissed it as a puerile prank that had gone a bit too far, whereas Eli saw it as something deeper and far more vindictive. He'd expressed his concerns privately to Sheriff Morris, saying he felt certain that someone had deliberately compromised the steering shaft with the intention of harming him rather than his grandfather. The sheriff had promised to "look into it," not that Eli knew exactly what that meant. How exhaustive would his search for the perpetrator really be? Would he interrogate Sofie further? And, if he did, should Eli insist on being present? He didn't want to cause her unnecessary stress, but he also didn't want her to suffer in his place because of a devious plan that miscarried. It was bad enough that injury intended for him had befallen his grandfather, instead.

Two vehicles were needed to transport everybody to church. They decided that Charles would drive the maroon Packard, with Eli leading the way in Grandfather's prized midnight black 1928 Chevrolet Imperial Landau sedan. He was half afraid to drive the thing, considering how rarely it saw the light of day, but Grandfather insisted he take it, saying it was "just" a car. *Right,* he thought, *and the sun is "just" a little glimmer.* But the only alternative was the truck, which had space for no more than four passengers, and even that was a tight squeeze.

So, they piled into the cars, the kids dressed in freshly pressed shirts and pants or frilly dresses, their faces spotless, the boys' hair combed perfectly flat, the girls' done up in curls with ribbons of yellow, pink, and red, to match their outfits. When they reached the church, they made for quite the spectacle when they filed out of the vehicles and paraded across the parking lot and up the steps.

The tiny sanctuary was packed, making the air stuffier than the average first day of July. Yes, Grandfather and Winnie would have a scorcher of an afternoon for their wedding, and if the heat wave of the past few days continued, the townsfolk might cook their catches from the river just as easily on the blistering sidewalk as on the blazing grill during the annual Fourth of July Fish Fry this Wednesday.

Standing just inside the sanctuary doors, Eli made a quick survey of the space. He spotted Sofie almost immediately, seated with a middle-aged couple on the right side of the church, four rows from the back. Andy was sandwiched between the man and woman, the man sitting at the end of the pew. Facing front, her spine as straight as a pin, Sofie had no idea how it mesmerized him just to stare at the back of her pretty head of curls. Was there any hope for him? Pregnant and all, she'd hooked him without having to bat an eyelash. In truth, he hadn't expected to see her today, and, now that he did, his crazy stomach sizzled and flipped like a pancake on a hot griddle. *I'm a goner, God, plain and simple.*

❦

Sofie noticed Eli walking down the center aisle, leading two small children by the hands, with several others trailing behind. After them in the procession was an elegant-looking older woman—his mother, perhaps—a beautiful lady who had to be his sister, and then an older man, perhaps his father, and last a couple of other fellows, probably his brother-in-law and perhaps another brother. *My, what a striking family,* she remarked, *and all of them so smartly dressed and sophisticated-looking.*

All around them, folks murmured quietly, and Sofie could imagine many of the conversations centered on the attractive family making a regular grand entrance. She didn't see Doc Trent or Winifred Carmichael, but that was no surprise, considering their wedding was that afternoon. No doubt they were

busy making final preparations. Indeed, she was surprised to see the rest of the family at church.

"I wonder who they are," Margie mused, close to
her ear. "Do you know them?"

She should have figured Margie would ask. "The
one in front is Doc Trent's grandson, Elijah," she whispered back. "Those others must be his family who
traveled here for Doc Trent's wedding."

"Sofia Mae! That, there, is the man who asked for
your hand in marriage?"

Sofie put a finger to her lips. "Margie Grant,
shush! Someone will hear you."

"Sofie, look! There's Eli!" Andy pointed ahead.
"C-can I go sit with h-him?"

"No, you may not. It looks like his family is taking
up the whole row as it is. Besides, those are probably his
nieces and nephews, and they'll want to sit next to him."

He put on a mopey face, crossed his arms, and
slouched in the pew. Howard put an arm around the
boy's shoulders and whispered something in his ear,
after which Andy smiled up at him. Sofie wondered
what magic words Howard had whispered to erase
that frown.

"My stars, Sofia, he is one handsome man. I could
look at him for about a thousand years."

"Oh, stop it, Margie. And mind those manners."
Why did she suddenly feel like the more mature one?

Upon sitting down, Eli turned around and met
her gaze—a quick glance, to be sure—and gave her
a tiny grin. It rankled her that she'd failed to smile
back before he had faced forward again. What would
he make of her apparent coldness?

Margie jabbed her with her elbow. "Did you see?
He just looked at you!"

If her nerves weren't so jumbled, she might have giggled at her friend's unchecked enthusiasm.

"You must introduce him to Howard and me after the service."

Before Sofie could reply, the song leader stepped up to the platform and announced the first hymn, inviting the congregants to stand. While Margie thumbed through the hymnal, Sofie focused her attention on Eli. Margie was right. He was probably the handsomest man in all of Wabash, maybe even throughout the Hoosier State.

At the conclusion of the musical part of the service, everyone sat down, and the preacher approached the podium. He made several announcements about various upcoming events and then shared specific prayer requests of multiple congregants. Sofie gasped in alarm, as did many others, when he informed them of Doc Trent's brush with death when his car went into a ditch and rammed into a fence. "Police are investigating the incident, as they have reason to believe it was not accidental," the reverend said, setting off a wave of hushed exclamations. "Let us pray that the sheriff will be able to determine what really happened and that justice will be served. On a lighter note, I am happy to inform you that I visited the family last night and discovered that Wilson did not suffer any great harm, aside from a minor facial wound and some bruises. His grandson, Dr. Elijah Trent, reports he is doing well and that the wedding will go on." Several people seated around her let out sighs of relief. "Speaking of the wedding, let us welcome Wilson Trent's family to our service. May I ask them to stand?" They did so, including the children, and Sofie was struck anew at what a fine picture they made.

Regrettably, she didn't hear much of Reverend White's message, as she was haunted by the dreadful announcement of Doc Trent's auto accident. She couldn't help suspecting that her attacker had somehow played a part, and it pained her to realize that, if her suspicions were valid, then she herself carried a degree of blame for the incident.

※

After the service concluded, the first thing Eli did was fight through the crowds to get to Sofie. Of course, it was slow going, as several people stopped him along the way to inquire about his grandfather, and his nieces and nephews insisted on following close behind, the littlest two clinging to his pant legs, and he had to keep an eye on them, lest they get lost in the throng. Ever since their arrival, he'd felt like a child magnet, the way they all stuck to him, vying for his attention. It was his own fault, though—he loved teasing them, chasing them around the yard, and hearing their squeals of delight. His mother kept saying she couldn't figure out who the real kids were, they or he.

At the top of the stairs, he finally caught up with Sofie. She was standing with the woman she'd sat with, both of them chatting with Livvie Taylor. Andy was nowhere in sight, and Eli figured he must have scooted outside to join the children who always ran around the churchyard after the service. He moved up behind an unsuspecting Sofie and tapped her lightly on the shoulder. With a tiny jolt, she whipped her head around, then quickly blushed. He loved getting that girlish reaction from her.

Livvie laughed. "Don't you know the risks of sneaking up on a pregnant woman, Dr. Eli? It's potentially dangerous—for both of you."

"I'm willing to take my chances," he answered with a smile. When no one made a move to introduce him to the other woman with them, he extended a hand to her. "Sorry to intrude. I'm Elijah Trent."

The woman grabbed his hand and pumped it for all she was worth. "Goodness gracious, no intrusion whatsoever. Isn't that right, Sofie?" She didn't let her hazel eyes waver from him. "I'm Margaret Grant, but you can call me Margie. My husband, Howard, is... well, I don't know where he went off to, or I'd introduce him, as well. Livvie, here, is my baby sister. Of course, you know Sofia." She elbowed Sofie in the side.

That seemed to bring her to life. "Hello, Eli. Nice to see you." Her eyes darted to the children clinging to his calves. "Your nieces and nephews?"

"Yes." He hefted little Ruby Lynn up in his arms. "This is the youngest of the girls, Ruby Lynn." Looking down, he added, "And that's her brother Clyde. Their mother, my sister Francine, is at home with their baby brother, Robert John." On the other side of him, he put a hand on the shoulder of the taller girl. "This is Virginia and her brother, Henry. They belong to my other sister, Connie." He took a deep breath and grinned from one woman to the next. "Now that I've completely confused all of you, where is Andy?"

He noticed a smile pass over Sofie's face. "I think he went outside with Howard."

"Ah. I was hoping to introduce him to Henry, as they're right around the same age. Maybe next time." He ceased with all the small talk and looked at Sofie. "I stopped by your house yesterday."

Her eyes rounded into big brown moons. "You did?"

"Yes." He raised his eyebrows. "Our workday, remember?" Ruby Lynn squirmed in his arms, so he set her back down.

"Oh. But I told you there was no need—"

"I know. Are you telling me you still haven't figured out I don't listen very well?"

There came that cute little blush again.

"I fixed the step, for now; what you really need is a brand-new set. And your roof...well, it isn't in good shape."

She frowned. "Thanks for noting that."

"I thought it might make your day," he said with a wink. "Oh, I washed the windows, as well."

She gasped. "You did? I—I don't know what to say."

He leaned forward. "'Thank you' will suffice. I—"

He was halted mid-sentence by the commotion of his family exiting the sanctuary, his mother and Connie chatting a mile a minute with the reverend's wife and a couple of other women about the details of the wedding, his brothers-in-law engaged in a discussion of their own, and his father discoursing affably with another man. The group glided past Eli, oblivious to his proximity. His nieces and nephews chose that time to dart down the steps and out into the beckoning sunshine. "The rest of my family," he said in an apologetic tone.

"Would you excuse me?" Livvie said to him. "I need to speak with your mother about the dinner."

"Of course. Go right ahead."

She told Margie she'd see her soon, and then she gave Sofie a quick hug. "Come and visit me," she said before scampering down the stairs to the entryway, where she caught up with Eli's mother.

Sofie gazed down at his slew of relatives. "You have a lovely family."

"They're a lively bunch, for sure," he said. "I'd like to introduce you—"

"That isn't necessary." Her answer shot out quicker than a bullet.

"Well, okay, then. Another time. They'll be back in a few months, I'm sure."

Margie put an arm around Sofie's shoulder. "In case you wondered, Sofie's been staying with Howard and me. I insisted she needed a good rest."

"Ah, so that's where she's run off to. Well"—he dipped his chin at Sofie—"I'm glad to hear it."

"I'm sorry about your grandfather, Eli." This she said in a hoarse, broken voice, and he wondered if she shared his suspicions—that her attacker had tampered with the car in hopes that Eli would be the one behind the wheel when the steering failed. But he wasn't about to bring that up now. She looked ready to run as it was. "Is he really doing as well as the reverend said?"

"You know my grandfather; nobody can keep him down. He'll be as good as new in no time. Besides, he's getting married today. Weddings have a way of healing all ills."

"Yes." Her cheeks flamed pink, probably at the fresh memory of his own marriage proposal. She returned her gaze to the open doorway, where folks lingered and talked, allowing their children to run around and burn off some of their pent-up energy before they piled into their stifling-hot cars for the drive home.

"How long will you be staying with Mrs. Grant?" Eli asked her.

"Call me Margie, please," the woman spoke up. "She'll stay as long as she—"

"Just a few days," Sofie interjected. "I can't afford to wait any longer to look for a job."

Margie shook her head, exchanging glances with Eli. "She seems to think she needs to find a new gig right away, but I keep telling her—"

"Margie!" Sofie's head jerked up.

"I offered her a job, but she doesn't seem to want it." Eli kept his tone straight and calm, directing his words at Sofie, even though she insisted on looking past him.

"Gracious me! Doing what?" Margie asked, her eyes bulging with curiosity.

"I need a secretary."

"Well, my stars. I hope you take him up on it, Sofie."

Sofie's forehead puckered into a frown as she gazed at her friend. "I don't know the first thing about secretarial duties."

"But you could learn," she said. "You're a highly intelligent, capable young woman." She turned to Eli. "Did you know she graduated from high school at the top of her class?"

"Margie...."

Eli raised his eyebrows and rocked on the balls of his feet. "That's very impressive."

"Don't," Sofie growled.

"And she completed two years of schoolwork in one." Margie put an arm around Sofie's shoulder and drew her to her side.

Sofie merely closed her eyes and crossed her arms, and Eli couldn't help delighting in how they rested so nicely on her round little shelf.

"Now, I'm triply convinced she ought to work for me." He enjoyed watching her squirm under all the attention.

She rubbed her belly. "I think I need to get off my feet."

"Good idea!" Eli held out his arm. "I'll walk you to the car."

"No, please. Your family's probably waiting for you, and I'd rather not...you know...." Her voice broke into a whisper, and she looked down. "I'd rather not meet them like this."

"I think you look lovely, but I understand if you'd rather wait to meet them."

She nodded.

"I'll drop by to see you as soon as I can, alright?"

"It'd be better if you didn't."

Grinning, he inclined his head. "I don't turn my back on the people I care about."

She blinked twice as another blush climbed up her neck. "I hope your grandfather and Mrs. Carmichael have a lovely wedding."

"I'm sure they will, but I'll tell them you said that."

Sofie turned to Margie. "I'll meet you outside. I need to visit the ladies' room."

He watched her walk away. "There goes one of the most complicated women I've ever met."

Margie followed his gaze. "She's not the least bit complicated once you find her ticking mechanism. She may be a bit bullheaded in her self-sufficiency, and she wears a tough façade, but underneath all that, she's not nearly as sure of herself as you'd think. If anything she lacks self-confidence and either doesn't recognize or chooses to ignore her brilliant qualities. Plus, poor thing believes she's about as plain as a peanut."

"She's anything but that."

"Don't I know it? She's beautiful, inside and out, but I have a hunch she's scared off more than a few men with that independent air of hers. That's just what it is—an air. It's a sort of defense against hurt and rejection, and, by consequence, against love. Deep down, she feels completely unworthy of male attention, most of all yours. And it's only gotten worse since...."

"I know what happened."

Margie nodded. "Now it's become a trust issue, as well."

"How can I convince her she has value, and that I'm worthy of her trust?"

She winked at him. "I'd say you need to do some serious wooing."

Chapter Twenty-two

And the work of righteousness shall be peace; and the effect of righteousness quietness and assurance forever.
—Isaiah 32:17

*E*li's family stayed in town until Tuesday afternoon, when the four o'clock train arrived to transport them back to Chicago. On the platform at the station, some of the children erupted in tears, while the adults all exchanged hugs, kissed cheeks, and gave another round of well-wishes to the newlyweds. Eli would miss the commotion that had enlivened the expansive house over the past several days. Still, a big part of him looked forward to a good dose of peace and quiet before he jumped back into his hectic work schedule. He'd closed the office Monday through Wednesday, which was a national holiday. This meant that patients would come hobbling through his door in droves first thing Thursday morning. And that would be above and beyond the patients he would visit at the hospital, where he was to fill in for Dr. Stewart, who'd graciously agreed to cover Eli's weekend shift.

He belonged to a group of six doctors in Wabash who coordinated a monthly schedule, taking turns being on call after hours or covering the overnight shift in the emergency room at the hospital. The graveyard shifts always made for an exhausting morning the next day, but Eli hadn't yet developed a schedule that would enable him to accommodate his patients and still get adequate sleep. What he needed now, more than ever, was a secretary. But Winnie wasn't around, and he wanted her to train whomever he happened to hire. She and Grandfather had decided at the last minute to honeymoon in Chicago and then travel east to visit some of Winnie's cousins in Ohio and Pennsylvania. There was no telling when they'd return to Wabash.

They'd shared their plans with the family this morning over breakfast. "I can see it now," Grandfather had said in a loud aside to Eli. "She's going to drag me all over the countryside. Truth is, I think she married me mainly in order to secure a travel companion."

"That, and your money," Winnie had said, planting a playful kiss on his cheek.

Frankly, Eli wouldn't miss their nonstop smooching one bit. They were no better than a couple of love-struck teenagers. He decided to join in their banter. "It appears that your wound is healing nicely, Grandfather, the way you've been using those lips lately."

Grandfather had turned twinkling eyes on a pink-cheeked Winnie. "What can I say? My wife's kisses are like a healing balm."

Everyone groaned, and Charles quickly changed the subject, talking about the weather.

Later that night, after everyone had gone, Eli sat at the kitchen table with Grandfather and Winnie, sipping coffee and finishing the crumbs of a chocolate cream pie someone had dropped off yesterday. "When are you going to hire that secretary you've been talking about?" Grandfather asked, scraping his fork across his plate to loosen every last ounce of filling.

"Yes, when?" Winnie asked. "And what about Sofie?"

"Sofie's made it clear she doesn't want the job, so I've had to go back over my list of applicants. One who looked a little promising was a Mabel Downing. She came to see me last week."

"Oh, I know Mabel," Winnie said, dabbing her chin with a linen napkin. "She worked for Dr. Stewart some years ago. She'd do an excellent job, I'm sure of it."

"Yes, I'm certain she would," Grandfather affirmed. He pushed his empty plate aside. "Truth be told, I don't know that Sofia could manage a full-time job and raise a baby."

"If she keeps the baby," Eli inserted. "She's been thinking about adoption."

Winnie's mouth formed a tiny frown. "I hope it doesn't come to that. Not that I'm opposed to adoption, mind you. There are so many worthy couples who can't conceive. But, knowing Sofie, I think it would tear her apart."

Grandfather shot Eli a conspiratorial wink. "What she really needs is a loving husband."

The nine o'clock train rumbled past, shaking the house. As the screeching wheels and the shrieking whistle faded into the distance, Eli gazed absently at the window. "Margie says I need to woo her."

"Well, then?" Winnie lurched forward and folded her hands on top of the table, her eyes brightening like two stars. "What are you waiting for?"

"I can't say I've ever wooed a woman in my life." He wasn't bragging, just stating a fact.

"Goodness gracious, Elijah," Grandfather scoffed. "Don't tell me that, at age thirty-two, you need schooling in how to do it."

He gave a sheepish smile. "I might. I'm not sure she wants anything to do with me. She keeps telling me to stay away."

"Well, can you blame her?" Winnie asked. "Consider what she's been through. She needs time to learn how to trust men again."

"Now you sound like Margie. Have you two been talking?"

"Of course not, silly. But, as women, we understand these things in the same way. Think about it, Eli. Stability leads to trust. So far, much of Sofia's life has been unstable and difficult, so it stands to reason trusting others doesn't come easy. By the sweat of her brow, she has managed to give Andrew a halfway decent life, but she's also spent a great deal of energy shielding him from the taunts of others. Young people can be so cruel, as can adults. Why, I remember one time, when Sofia brought her brother in with an earache, she told me that one of his teachers had written across the top of his penmanship exercise, 'Andy, this is very sloppy. Try printing better than you speak.' Such caustic criticism only makes the problem worse.

"And something else; one of the reasons she stopped going to the church her parents raised her in was because a few children in particular teased him about his stutter, and their parents laughed it off, saying, 'Kids will be kids.' Without her parents there to intervene, the weight fell upon Sofia's shoulders, and she just got tired of it. She started thinking it would be a lot easier to just stay secluded as much as possible.

"Unfortunately, her seclusion didn't go unnoticed, and many started thinking of her as a recluse, cold and unfriendly. Some have gone so far as to call her unchristian, especially now that she carries some awful man's baby, no matter that it was out of her control."

Grandfather cleared his throat and set his hands on the table's edge then pushed back, causing the chair legs to scrape against the floor. "The biggest concern I have is that she won't agree to an investigation." He took his empty coffee cup to the stove, picked up the percolator, and refilled his cup. "What will it take for her to finally come forward and admit what was done to her?" He held the pot out by its black handle. "Anybody want a refill?"

"No, thanks," they chimed in unison.

Eli wrapped his hands around his cup, lukewarm from the coffee cooling inside. "I'm convinced that the creep is the same one who messed with your steering column. He wanted me behind the wheel, not you. I took my suspicions to the sheriff, but I don't know what he's doing about it."

Grandfather set his cup on the table and sat back down. "I'm afraid Sheriff Morris seems to be more concerned where his next bottle of booze is coming from than he is about upholding the law. Even so, I fear his name will appear on the ballot yet again this fall."

Winnie rubbed her arms as if chilled. "Dear me. Nobody's safe in this town."

Eli's gaze flitted to the bouquet of flowers in the center of the table left over from the wedding. Outside, the voices of children at play carried from across the road, a bike horn jingled, and crickets pulsed the air with their high-pitched song. "Do you suppose the Grants have a telephone?"

Winnie slapped the table and leaped up like a jack-in-the-box. "Indeed! Let me just check my directory." She pulled open the drawer closest to the telephone box hanging on the wall and started shifting items around inside. After a moment, she drew out a soft-bound book and started leafing through its pages. "Ah, here it is. Four-one-nine." She took the receiver off the hook and held it out to him. "Here you are."

Eli grinned and shoved back in his chair. "Well, I didn't necessarily—"

"Of course, you did. Here." Turning to Grandfather, she said, "Come on, Wilson. Let's give Eli some privacy."

⚜

After supper, Sofie had spent the evening curled up on the Grants' living room sofa, reading her Bible, while Margie sat in an overstuffed chair, knitting. Whenever Sofie had a question about a specific passage, she would pose it to Margie, who would patiently put down her project and answer as best she could. Sofie's interest in spiritual matters had sprouted wings since she'd come to stay with the Grants, and she found herself gobbling up every morsel of biblical truth like a baby bird.

Their companionable silence was interrupted when the telephone rang—one short, two long. Margie laid aside her ball of yarn and hurried across the room to the end table where the Western Electric sat atop a lace doily.

When Margie answered the phone, the kitchen screen door opened with a squeak and closed with a thwack. Sofie could hear Andy speaking in his usual excited tone about the new foal, his stutter more pronounced the faster he spoke.

"Slow down, there," Howard urged him gently.

If her conscience would only allow it, Sofie would never leave the comfort of the Grants' house. But she and Andy were going home on Thursday. The rest and relaxation their stay had afforded had been long overdue, but it was time to resume her search for a job. Tildi had promised to look after Andy during the day, which was a major burden lifted.

As tempted as she was to accept Eli's job offer, Sofie knew that seeing him every day would only rile her attacker, and who knew what he'd do next. That, or Eli would wear down her defenses and end up escorting her to the sheriff's office to file a report—a futile effort, since the sheriff, whose scruples were hardly above reproach, would do whatever it took to protect the reputation of his staff. From there, things would go further downhill, and she wouldn't be surprised if the entire town turned against her, maybe even forced her to leave. She couldn't bring that sort of shame on Andy or the baby—unless she chose the adoption route.

As if sensing her recent bent toward that option, the baby gave a hearty kick, putting her in mind of that little foal in the barnyard. She rubbed her side, then glanced up at Margie.

She was holding the receiver against her shoulder, a little glimmer in her eyes. "It's for you, honey."

"For me?" She pushed herself up from the sofa and crossed the room, her forehead wrinkling. "Who is it?"

But Margie only smiled and handed her the phone. "Hello?"

"Hi, Sofie."

Her heart thudded against her ribs. "Eli!"

"Surprised?"

"Yes."

"Well, you shouldn't be. You should know I've been thinking about you."

She dared not admit the same. "How was the wedding?"

"Short and sweet. I guess when you're older, you don't want to waste any time. There was no special music—just a processional and a recessional on the grand piano—and Reverend White delivered the shortest homily I've ever heard. After the vows were said and the rings exchanged, there were lots of hugs all around."

"That sounds lovely."

"Livvie and Will Taylor put on a nice spread for about twenty people, most of them family members, along with a few of Grandfather and Winnie's closest friends. My family left today on the four o'clock train."

"You must miss them terribly."

"It was great to see them, and we had a wonderful time, but I have to admit I'm enjoying the peace after the storm." His laughter that followed was rich and resonant. "Part of the reason I'm calling is that tomorrow's the Fourth, as you know, and I'd like to invite you and Andy to accompany me to the local festivities."

"Eli, I've already told you, I don't think—"

"I won't take no for an answer. How does noon sound? Bring a sweater. You might need one by the time they set off the fireworks."

"Fireworks?"

"I'll bring a blanket and everything else we'll need for a picnic."

"But...I'm just not sure this is such a good idea. What if...what if *he* sees us together?"

"Let him. I'm not about to spend my life running scared, and you shouldn't, either. Trust in the Lord, sweetheart."

Sweetheart. The endearment made her insides flutter with warmth.

"Tell Andy I missed seeing him at church on Sunday."

"He missed you, too. He'll be so excited to see you tomorrow."

"Until tomorrow, then. Good night, little mother."

Little mother. More tickles of warmth moved through her. *Lord, what is he doing to me? And why on earth didn't I give him an adamant no?* "Good night." But he had already hung up. She placed the receiver back in its cradle and turned around, finding herself face-to-face with an anxious-looking Margie, hands clasped under her chin, eyes hopeful.

"Well?" her friend asked.

Sofie blew out a breath. "I guess Andy and I are going to spend the day with Eli tomorrow."

"Oh, I just knew it!" She jumped up and down and then danced in a circle, clapping her hands all the while.

Andy and Howard emerged from the kitchen, each of them holding a tall glass of lemonade. "What's going on?" they asked in unison.

While Margie kept up her whooping, Sofie tried her best to mask her own excitement as she calmly offered an explanation.

As soon as Andy heard the plan, though, and joined Margie on the dance floor, Sofie couldn't help but grin from ear to ear.

Chapter Twenty-three

Trust in the LORD *with all thine heart; and*
lean not unto thine own understanding.
In all thy ways acknowledge him, and he
shall direct thy paths.
—Proverbs 3:5–6

Last week had been a long succession of hot, cloudless days, so when July 4 dawned with peals of thunder, streaks of lightning, and a torrential downpour, Eli was both surprised and dismayed. Not only had he been looking forward to spending time with Sofie and Andrew, but he'd also been eager for an opportunity to get out into the community and meet the fine folks of Wabash—with Sofie at his side, forget what anybody thought about seeing them together. He could only hope Sofie wouldn't use the rain as a reason to cancel their plans.

If he thought the weather had put a damper on his spirits, he could only imagine the effect it was having on the committee that had spent weeks planning the events advertised for the holiday celebration, which included baseball games, three-legged races, cakewalks, and musical chairs.

He found the aging lovebirds in the kitchen, conversing quietly while sipping their morning coffee and munching on slices of sweet-smelling cinnamon toast.

Their mood was unaffected by the weather, if their affectionate smiles were any indication. While rain battered the windows, lightning streaked the dark sky like fingers of fire, followed immediately by thunder booms that rattled the house clear to its foundation.

When Eli entered the room, Winnie released Grandfather's hand and smiled over at him. "Beautiful day, isn't it?"

"Just lovely," he muttered, making a beeline for the coffeepot.

"It's bound to clear up. I wouldn't worry, if I were you."

Eli filled a cup to the rim and then carried the steaming beverage to the window, where he stood and gazed out at the pond-sized puddles forming in the front yard. Very few cars traversed the road, and those that did resembled giant ducks swimming against the stream. He glanced back at them. "At least you two are getting out of here this afternoon. Maybe you'll take the rain with you."

Grandfather gave Winnie a mischievous wink. "It makes no difference to me. I've got all the sunshine I'll ever need, right here in this woman."

Winnie flushed crimson. "Oh, Wilson! Flattery won't get you anywhere."

Eli chuckled at the pair, then sobered as he shifted his gaze outside again. "You think the river's rising?"

"Not yet," Grandfather said without hesitation. "It'll take a lot more rain for that to happen."

Eli remembered all too clearly the times when the river had risen to such a level as to cover streets several blocks north and south, flooding houses and stores and sending people in droves to higher ground.

He thought about the little house on River Road and knew a slight pang of worry.

At eleven o'clock, the rain still came down as steadily as ever. So much for their picnic. He called the Grant household to propose a backup plan: lunch at Livvie's Kitchen, after which they would assess the weather and decide what to do next. Sofie agreed, and so, after bidding Grandfather and Winnie good-bye, with wishes for a safe and happy honeymoon, he left in the Packard, intending to stop first at Godfrey's Garage, on the rare chance Wilbur was around on a holiday. He wanted to see how the repairs to the Ford were coming along and, more important, ask if Wilbur had found any more evidence of intentional tampering.

When he reached the service station, he slowed and pulled into the lot, which was riddled with rain puddles. The place looked quiet, but he noticed a light on in the garage, so he parked near a roof overhang and turned off the engine. There was an old black truck parked between the station and the house next door, which he presumed to be the Godfrey residence. And while the truck bore a resemblance to the one he'd noticed along Mill Creek Pike, he reminded himself what Sheriff Morris had said about old black trucks being a dime a dozen in Wabash.

He opened his door and stepped out into the heavy, humid air, glad for the overhang, which kept him mostly dry. Water overflowed the gutters and gushed along the downspouts like waterfalls, forming miniature rivers of runoff in the soggy soil. He tried the door and found it unlocked, so he ducked inside, causing the bell above the door to emit a loud jingle. "Hello? Anybody here?"

The tiny station had a grimy, marred counter with a cash register atop it bearing signs of grease and dirt. A wrinkled, sloppily folded edition of the *Wabash Daily Plain Dealer* lay next to the register. On the wall hung several metal signs advertising goods or services and their prices. Across the room stood an icebox, with a sign that said "Coca-Cola, 5 cents." "Hello?" he called again.

"Out here." Wilbur Godfrey, no doubt.

Eli walked across the sandpaper-textured cement floor, which probably hadn't seen a broom in months, and opened the door to the service garage. Sure enough, there was Wilbur, as well as the sheriff's boy—whose name escaped him now—both of them bent over the fender of an automobile, staring down into the hood.

"Hello, there. Just stopped by to see how you're coming along with my grandfather's car since that run-in with the fence."

"Ah." Wilbur wiped his hands on a rag, then stuffed the dirty thing into his hip pocket and approached.

The kid glanced around, then straightened and sauntered to the back of the garage, completely ignoring Eli's friendly nod. *Ill-mannered teenager.*

"I planned to call Doc Trent as soon as I had a minute. Got me a few other cars needin' various repairs, as you can see. This economy has actually been a boon for business, as folks're tryin' to hold on to their cars instead of buyin' new. Hope it keeps up. Anyway, car should be ready to go by mornin'. You want me to drop it off?"

"You could do that?"

"Sure. Let's see…tomorrow, I got Ned Burns and Chip Franklin comin' in. I'll have one of 'em follow me out to the house, and then we'll both ride back to the station. Shouldn't be any problem a-tall."

Eli reached inside his hip pocket for his wallet. "I sure do appreciate that. How much do I owe you?"

Wilbur waved him off. "Nothing right now. Doris, that's my wife, will mail a statement when she does the monthly billin'."

He tucked his wallet away. "That sounds fine with me. How extensive was the damage?"

Wilbur raised his arm and wiped the perspiration from his brow with a dirty sleeve. "Well, besides fixin' that steerin' issue, I had to install a new bumper, replace the headlights, and make a few other minor repairs. Engine's good in that critter. They make them As pretty darn solid. Wouldn't mind gettin' one myself. Wonder if old Doc would be interested in sellin' it."

"He's interested, alright, but he already has a buyer." Eli chuckled. "And you're looking at him."

"That so? Well, you're gettin' yourself a nice li'l machine, not to mention dependable transportation. Guess you'll need it for all them doctor calls."

Eli nodded. "Now if we can just keep it tamper-proof." For whatever reason, he glanced back at the boy to see if the remark provoked any reaction. But it was impossible to tell, the way the fellow stood with his back to him.

Wilbur rubbed the back of his neck. "That was an odd thing. Sheriff Morris says he's lookin' into the matter. Don't know as your granddad has a single enemy in all of Indiana. He's one well-respected man. Why anyone would want to mess with his steerin' mechanism is beyond me."

Before Eli could reply, a powerful streak of lightning lit up the space, followed by a thunderbolt that fairly shook the little building.

"Whoa," the men said in unison.

Wilbur shuffled across the gritty floor to gaze out the window. "I guess we done got our fireworks for the day."

⚜

When that big maroon car pulled into the driveway, and Eli climbed out and dashed up to the door, head down to avoid the beating pellets of rain to his face, Sofie's pulse began to thud. For a man whose occupation required minimal physical exertion, he certainly maintained a muscular physique. She admonished herself for noticing. Their plans for the day may have resembled those of a courting couple, but then, they'd have Andy tagging along. Moreover, Sofie was not about to let her guard down and admit attraction to this man.

Andy ran to the door, Buster at his side, and opened it wide. "You're here!"

Laughing, Eli stomped his wet shoes on the rug, then bent to untie them.

"Don't even think of taking off those shoes!" Margie scuttled to the door, bright as a posy in her floral print dress, with her long sleeves rolled up to the elbows and her salt-and-pepper hair pulled into her typical, tight bun. For the moment, Sofie hung back, shyness taking over. "This house is meant to be lived in, and it is simply unnecessary to remove one's shoes at the door—unless it makes one more comfortable, of course."

"Well then, you run a very different ship from Winnie." He turned his gaze on Sofie and smiled. "Wow. Two lovely ladies in one room—it's almost more than I can bear." He reached down and patted Buster's flat head. Satisfied, the lazy dog sauntered back to the braided rug he'd claimed as his own upon arriving at the farm.

"Oh, he is some kind of man, Sofia, passing out compliments like candy. I think I'll keep him around!" Margie giggled. "And where did Howard get to? He should be taking notes."

Andy cleared his throat, pulled back his shoulders, and drew in a breath. "He's...in...the...barn...do-in'...his...chores."

Eli crouched down and opened his arms for a hug. The gesture warmed Sofie clear to her toes. "Hey! Great job there, buddy. I can see you've been practicing your speech. Keep up the good work!"

Thunder blasted the four corners of the old farmhouse.

"Good gravy!" Margie exclaimed after leaping almost a foot in the air. "When is this storm going to let up?" She slanted her head to look out the window toward the road. "It sure is nasty out there. Are you sure about venturing back out into it when you could just as easily eat lunch here? I've got plenty of food in the pantry."

"Ma'am, my grandfather's Packard sails straight through those puddles like a big barge. We'll manage fine." He turned to Sofie. "That is, unless you'd rather stay here."

She opened her mouth to get out her first words since his arrival, but Andy beat her to it. "We wanna go out!" he declared.

Eli laughed. "I guess that settles it, then. Are you ready?"

"Yea!" Andy cheered, then grabbed his raincoat and raced to the car.

Sofie turned to Margie. "We'll be back soon."

"Or...it might be a while," Eli said, grinning.

What did he have up his sleeve?

※

Despite the rain, Livvie's Kitchen buzzed with a lunchtime crowd. In fact, Eli had to give the place a good looking over before his eyes finally lit on an empty table at the back of the restaurant. Andy spotted it simultaneously and led the way through the maze of tables and chairs of diners.

"Sofie!"

At the sound of a female voice, he and Sofie both turned their glances to a nearby table seating four kids and two adults, the woman sprouting with a pregnant belly about the size of Sofie's. He recognized the family—they attended the Wesleyan Methodist church and had attended the recent after-service supper at the restaurant—but he'd forgotten their names. Sofie had spoken all of four sentences to him in the car, so he wondered if she would introduce them to him or if he'd have to take the lead. He couldn't figure out her sudden timidity, assuming that's what it was. "Aloof" might have described her state more accurately. *Women.* If only he could read them better. As they approached the table, Eli glanced over at Andy, who'd sat down at their table. Livvie walked up to him and started a conversation as she set the table for three.

Thankfully, Sofie reminded him of the couple's names: Gage and Ellie Cooper. They were a friendly bunch, and Eli and Sofie visited with them for a few minutes, until the family's food arrived.

As he followed Sofie to where Andy was waiting for them at the rear of the restaurant, Eli noticed more than a few sets of eyes following them. Briefly, he entertained the notion that, for all he knew, these people assumed they were a young married couple with a baby on the way. But anyone who recognized them might have been more than a mite curious why the new doctor was hanging around the likes of Sofia Rogers, that "loose woman." The latter notion formed a knot of anguish in his gut. If only the townspeople knew the whole story. Shoot, if only he did.

Andy gobbled down his hamburger and French fries faster than a starved bear and monopolized most of the mealtime conversation. He stuttered more, as fast as the words came tumbling out, but he seemed determined to share every last detail about their time at the Grants' farm: news of the foal born three weeks ago, the chicken coop, the hog named Ornery, the many cows needing milking, the litter of kittens birthed by a cat aptly named Mama, and the four horses, nineteen-year-old Flame being his favorite, because of her gentle nature. "Mr. Grant let me r-ride her yesterday. She w-walked real g-good for me. Mr. Grant says I'll b-be a good r-rider someday."

Rather than interrupt his chatter by reminding him to think before speaking, Eli just sat there and took in his enthusiasm. There would be plenty of time later for getting back into their speech lessons. He would *make* the time.

When Andy finally ran out of things to say, Eli decided to direct the conversation for a change. He turned to Sofie. "How have you been feeling? Have you experienced any odd pains or unexplained symptoms? Is the baby moving a lot?"

She smiled and placed a hand on her abdomen. "Yes, doctor. Everything feels normal, and the baby's been kicking up a regular storm. I think my insides must be black-and-blue. Margie's been telling me what kinds of things to expect."

"That's good to know. I'm glad you've been staying with the Grants."

Andy looked at his empty plate. "We have to go h-home tomorrow so Sofie can start lookin' for a j-job."

"Is that right?" Eli kept his voice relaxed as his eyes wandered back to Sofie, who started pushing her food around on her plate.

The cacophony of clattering silverware, boisterous laughter, fussing babies, and hamburgers sizzling on the grill made conversation difficult, so he leaned forward and gently asked, "And just where do you expect to find a job at this stage in your pregnancy, Sofie Rogers?"

She lifted one shoulder in a shrug. "I don't know, but I have faith that the right thing will come along."

He reached across the table, laid his hand on top of hers, and gave it a little squeeze. "I have that same kind of faith."

❧

In a sour mood, Owen maneuvered his truck into a narrow parking space in front of Livvie's Kitchen and cut the engine. Not for one second had the rain slowed, and he hated that he'd gotten soaked on his jaunt from the station to his car—and that he'd had to listen to Godfrey warn him not to be late coming back to work. Of course, his dander had really gotten up when he'd set eyes on that young doctor over at the garage, and it still ruffled him that his entire plan for disposing of him had blown to bits. "I hate my job," Owen groused.

Marvin Duran stared straight ahead, taking the final puffs of his cigarette. "You should quit and find somethin' else." A sudden peal of thunder put an ex-clamation point to his statement.

"Yeah? Like what, dimwit? Jobs are scarce these days, or haven't you heard?"

"Okay, okay. Don't blame me. Let's go eat."

"I'm not gettin' out till the rain lets up."

Marvin sneered, taking another drag of his nico-tine stick. "Then you'll be sittin' here all day. Come on; it's just a few steps."

They shoved open their doors with their shoulders and made a hurried dash to the door, Marvin drop-ping his cigarette butt on the sidewalk beneath the awning and grinding it out with his boot. When they walked inside, several heads shot up. Blamed place was crawling with people—noisy, to boot—and there wasn't a spare table in sight. They were probably tak-ing their sweet time eating, being in no rush to brave the elements again. Besides, it was a holiday, so most folks had the day off—except for him, of course. Old man Godfrey had insisted there'd be travelers passing through, and they'd need gas.

"Looks like there might be a table for two, way in the back corner," Marvin said, pointing.

Owen followed his finger and froze at the sight of Sofia Rogers and her little brother, seated at a table with the young Dr. Trent, the three of them chatting it up with Livvie Taylor and two of her boys. He ought to walk right up to Sofia and give her what for. What was so hard about following his demands to stay away from Dr. Trent? He wanted to wring her neck. The doctor's, too.

"Come on, before somebody else snags it," Marvin said, setting off for the table in back.

Owen grabbed his arm. "Let's go to a different joint, one that's not so blasted noisy."

"Since when did a little noise bother you?" Marvin sneered. "I'm stayin' right here. I'm starvin'."

"Suit yourself. But you can find your own ride home. I've got to get back to work within the hour, but I'm not eating here."

Marvin made one last glance at the back of the room and the little unoccupied table. Then whirling his head back around, he set his narrow gaze on Owen. "Ah. I see who's sittin' back there. You got somethin' for that knocked-up floozy?"

"Shut up!" He whirled on his heel and shoved his way out the door, slogging through deep puddles to reach his truck, Marvin on his tail. Back inside the truck, they tugged their doors shut. The rain sloshed down the windshield, obscuring their view. Owen slammed the steering wheel with his palm.

"What's gotten into you?"

Too enraged to reply, Owen started the truck and sped up Market Street, his wipers waving as fast as they would go. Sofia Rogers was *his* conquest, and no dumb doctor had any business being around her. High time he knocked some sense into her skinny little skull.

Chapter Twenty-four

Therefore being justified by faith,
we have peace with God through
our Lord Jesus Christ.
—Romans 5:1

It was nice of Livvie to invite Andy to stay and play with her boys," Eli said after lunch. "I'm sorry we couldn't spend more time together, but he'd gotten bored with us in no time. Besides"—he reached across the seat and gently grasped Sofie's hand—"I rather enjoy having you all to myself."

An odd mixture of caution and yearning turned her stomach upside down. She knew she ought to pull her hand away, but she found the warmth of his touch oddly irresistible. While Eli traced tickling circles on the palm of her left hand, she rested her right on her belly and stared straight ahead at the torrents of rain streaming down the windshield, the wipers working as hard as they could to create a clear view of Market Street. "Where are we going?"

"I thought we'd sit for a few minutes at the park and talk." He slanted her a grin. "In the car, if you don't mind."

He drove a block till Market Street ended, then crossed over the railroad tracks and maneuvered the sedan into a parking space just beyond the circle and overlooking the bulging Wabash, its swift-moving currents creating a symphony of rhythm. Dropping her hand, he turned off the engine, then shifted in his seat, angling his body toward hers. The rain had cooled the air considerably, making the temperature inside the car comfortable, if not a tad chilly.

"Grandfather and Winnie should be pulling into the station in another hour or so. They're leaving on the three thirty train for Chicago, and then, after a few days there, they'll head east, to Ohio and Pennsylvania. Winnie wants to show off her new husband to her friends and relatives."

"That's sweet. They certainly picked the perfect day to leave. Who wouldn't want to escape this weather?"

"Exactly." Eli looked out over the river, his left hand flung lazily over the steering wheel. "She's a beauty, isn't she? Even in the middle of a raging storm."

Sofie followed his gaze. "Fiercely beautiful. You never can tell what she's going to do."

"Sort of like a woman."

She jerked up her head at his remark, and she caught the twinkle in his eye. "If you say so."

"I do. I've never met a creature more complex."

"You must have known many women, then."

The rich timbre of his laughter erased some of her nervous tension, and she relaxed her shoulders into the soft cloth of the seat back.

"There've been a few." He reached a hand up and fingered one of her curls, sending a shiver down her spine. "But none like you. Have you had many boyfriends?"

She glanced at him, the movement causing his fingers to graze her cheek. "I've never had time for one."

"Never?"

How was she to answer him? She could not, would not, admit that he captured her attention like no other. What good would that accomplish? They made a terrible match. She clasped her hands in her lap.

"Not one single boy ever caught your eye?"

"Nope." She dared to angle him a glance. "Unless you count Eddie Caldwell."

He blinked twice and arched his brows. "Eddie Caldwell?"

"Yes. He sat across from me in the sixth grade, and he used to pass me notes when our teacher wasn't looking. I always stuffed them inside a book to read later, for fear the teacher would see and read it aloud to the class."

Eli's mouth twitched at the corners. "And what sort of things did this Eddie fellow write to you?"

She fiddled with one of her sleeves. "Oh, goodness. Childish things. I can't remember."

"Come on. You probably still have those letters tucked away in a box somewhere."

"What?"

He looked closer. "You do, don't you!"

"Don't be silly." But how could she lie? "Well, maybe a couple."

His smile broadened. "Were they love letters?"

She felt her face color deepen. "Good grief! We were only eleven or twelve. If it was love, it was the puppy kind."

He cast her a sidelong glance. "I think I'm a little jealous."

Her heart skipped a thump. "You're silly."

"I don't think so." He leaned across the seat and touched his lips to her cheek.

She shuddered, a gasp of air whistling out of her lungs. "Don't do that. Please."

"Why not?" His breath tickled her ear. "You aren't afraid of me."

"How do you know?" She scooted closer to her door.

"Because we've spent enough time together for you to know I'd never hurt you." He paused. "Look at me, Sofia."

She complied, albeit unwillingly.

"I know you've been hurt in the worst kind of way. But I am not at all like him."

"I know that."

"You can trust me."

"Yes, I know, but…you shouldn't, we shouldn't…."

He cupped her chin in his hand and studied her with those intense blue eyes. "Won't you go to the sheriff and report what happened to you? An investigation could free you from having to live in fear. The sheriff would throw him right in jail."

"No, he wouldn't." As soon as she had uttered the retort, she wanted to take it back.

His blue eyes dimmed under a frown. "Why do you say that?"

She looked over his shoulder out the window, at the rain pouring down like a waterfall. "I don't want to talk about it."

He moved his hand to the back of her neck and gently rubbed. She closed her eyes, nearly melting at his touch. Oh, how she longed to let down all the barriers that kept her from exposing the truth. But the ramifications could be deadly—case in point, Doc Trent's automobile accident. What devious plot would her attacker devise next? Again, she hoped and prayed he hadn't spotted her with Eli at the restaurant. She should have known better than to go out in public with him. Her chest constricted with worry.

I am nigh unto you when you call on Me in truth. I will hear your cry and will save you, My child. Her spirit was moved by the gentle words, which reminded her of a passage she'd read in Psalm 145 that very morning.

Eli's tender ministrations, along with the still, small voice, were enough to coax a few tears. She clamped her eyes shut to prevent more from following. He reached over and brushed her damp cheek with the pad of his thumb. "What makes you think the sheriff wouldn't throw that creep in jail?"

"I don't know." She fussed with her pale yellow skirt, straightening each little wrinkle as best she could. "He doesn't put much stock in my story. I'm sure that, like everybody else, he just thinks I got what I deserved."

"I think you'd be surprised what most folks think. Haven't the people you've seen at church treated you kindly?"

"Yes, but...."

"But what?"

"They're just being good Christians. Deep down, their minds are probably made up, but they're choosing to overlook what they perceive as true and treat me with mercy."

"Then, let's get it all out in the open so people won't draw the wrong conclusions. Think of how freeing it will feel to have that load off your shoulders. Secrets can get heavy after a while. Don't you want to let it go?"

"You don't understand. Look what he did to your grandfather's car. I've no doubt he intended you to be the one involved in an accident."

His hand on her cheek went still. "That's exactly what I suspected, and I've told the sheriff as much. He said he'd look into it. Has he been over to question you further?"

She flinched at the mention of Sheriff Morris. "No, and I wish you'd stop talking to him."

"Sorry, honey, I can't do that. Not until the perpetrator of this heinous crime is behind bars."

She swallowed hard, then heaved a long, jagged sigh. "Okay," she finally muttered.

"Okay?"

She nodded and cleared her throat. "Yes. But could we talk about something else now?"

To avoid his penetrating stare, she looked out over the river again, blurry as her view was because of the rain.

"Alright," he said. "How's this for a change in topics? Come sweep my floors for me."

She couldn't help but let loose a hearty laugh.

"You told me yourself it's your strongest area. As desperate as I am for an organized office, for a doctor, a clean office is even more important."

She couldn't tell if he was jesting. "You never give up, do you?"

His mouth quirked up at the corners. "I can't help it, Sofie; I enjoy being with you. And it would be nice to see you on a daily basis."

His words stirred in her a silent longing. "It's actually a tempting offer, but you already know I can't. *He* would find out."

"Aww, Sofie. Have you noticed *he* tends to come between us an awful lot? I wish you'd give up your resignation to live in fear."

His words revealed a world of heartache, and it worried her that her unnamed attacker would haunt her forever. Eli stretched his arm across the back of the seat and cupped her shoulder with his hand. "Come here." He gave her a gentle tug, and she slid closer, her pulse pounding. Was he about to kiss her?

"I'm going to pray for you."

Her insides swelled with emotion as he held her close and began addressing the Lord aloud. First, he thanked Him for the privilege of knowing her and Andy, and then he asked the Lord to bless and encourage her heart, to keep her precious baby safe, and to grant the wisdom to discern, and the courage to carry out, His will for her. Last, he asked God to grant her freedom from the bondage of fear that kept her so tight-lipped. By the time he uttered the final "Amen," a torrent of tears to match the rain was pouring down her cheeks.

And he dutifully and tenderly wiped away each one.

Chapter Twenty-five

*Your Father which is in heaven...maketh his
sun to rise on the evil and on the good, and
sendeth rain on the just and on the unjust.*
—Matthew 5:45

On Friday morning, the skies had finally closed up, and the sun had emerged against a backdrop of blue, as if to spotlight the damage wrought by two-and-a-half days of incessant, pounding rain. Along the banks of the Wabash, for a quarter mile in every direction, the terrain had taken on the appearance of a large lake, forcing the closure of many roads and businesses and necessitating evacuations from homes. People who lived and worked further from the river had to contend with overflowing ditches and drowned gardens. Farmers worried over flooded fields and ruined crops, and with Factory Street completely flooded, many industries had to close their doors temporarily. For now, instead of earning their wages in the factories, dozens of workers were making money through the cleanup efforts, hauling away debris and digging up deposits of mud.

Homeowners able to make it back to their houses had been faced with the challenge of emptying basements of water by the bucketful, a daunting task that often required a team of several family members, friends, and neighbors. Household items called for disinfecting or disposal, and electric fans ran round the clock to speed up the drying process. Nowhere in all of Wabash or its surrounding towns could one find a single fan for sale, so folks did what they could to ventilate their homes by keeping all the windows open and praying for a dry spell.

Thankfully, Grandfather's house was situated far enough from the river that it had suffered no real damage, but that wasn't to say there hadn't been pond-sized puddles in the yard. And there had been a veritable deluge of patients in the waiting room, many of them with problems stemming from the flood: aches and pains from overworked bodies; infections long ignored, in light of more pressing concerns; broken bones, cuts, and bruises sustained from slipping on mud or falling off ladders; and the usual suspects of heatstroke and chest pain.

If only Eli had hired a secretary before the storm struck. He was nearly drowning in paperwork, the stacks of which had mounted his desk to the extent that he couldn't see over them. He'd also been running on very little sleep. From what he'd heard, doctors all over town were in the same boat: patching up the wounded, doling out pills, and filling hospital beds faster than they could be emptied.

He hoped that Sofie and Andy had stayed on at the Grants', for their house could hardly accommodate them in its present condition. After leaving the park on July 4, they'd driven out to check on her little house, where they'd discovered leaks aplenty—proof it needed a new roof. They'd spent a couple of hours positioning pans, bowls, and buckets under numerous drips; moving furniture; stripping beds of soggy linens; and moving books, photographs, and other important items to a cabinet where they would remain dry. The ceiling sagged in spots, and Eli had worried that it might collapse under the weight of standing water. So, although Sofie had been determined to move back home again and keep up with the leaks, Eli had practically ordered her to return to Margie's because it wasn't safe. She'd finally acquiesced, albeit begrudgingly.

During supper at the Grants' that evening, Howard had promised to go over to the house the next morning to assess the situation. This had eased Eli's mind, but it had appeared to do little to erase the worry lines around Sofie's eyes. It seemed that even if that little house were falling in around her, she would fight to the end to keep it upright. He understood, considering it was all she had to her name, as well as the only place where memories of her parents lived on.

When the meal was over and the kitchen had been tidied, the five of them had sat in the living room and talked until almost nine, when Howard had excused himself and gone up to bed. Margie told Andy that she'd run a bath for him, to which he'd argued, "I s-stood in the rain; d-doesn't that mean I'm c-clean enough?" Eli chortled at the memory. "Boys" and "baths" didn't belong in the same sentence. He remembered well the arguments he'd had with his mother about the very same subject. Andy had finally said good night and then, ever so slowly, dragged himself up the stairs after Margie, Buster on his heels.

That had left him alone on the couch with Sofie. He'd put his arm across the back of the sofa, taking care not to touch her. While he delighted in kissing her, he didn't want her to think that his affections were primarily physical in nature. They'd talked quietly, and he'd even made her laugh a few times, especially when relating his embarrassment at stumbling upon Grandfather and Winnie in the midst of a passionate embrace.

She'd been particularly interested in hearing reminiscences about his past—his college days, his years of medical school, the church he'd attended in Detroit, and the like. By the time the clock had chimed ten thirty, her eyelids had begun to flutter with fatigue, so he'd decided to make his exit. He'd stood, then taken her by the hands and helped her up. They'd remained there, facing each other, her belly grazing his chest, and he'd fought the urge to touch it, knowing he wouldn't be doing it out of doctoral concern.

He'd abstained from kissing her, as well, despite her uplifted face, and thought he detected the slightest disappointment in her eyes. Good. He wanted to woo her in such a way that she was left wanting more.

He'd bidden her good-bye, asking her to promise him not to return to her house unless accompanied by Howard. She'd given him a halfhearted nod, and he'd figured it had been insincere, a mere attempt to appease him. Goodness, but she could be a real handful.

Three days had passed since then, and he hadn't found a spare second to pick up the phone and place a call to Sofie. After locking his office doors at the end of each day of back-to-back appointments, he'd gone straight to the hospital for his rounds, then come back home and collapsed on the sofa, only to rise before dawn and repeat the process. Today, Saturday, had been no exception. And tomorrow would be more of the same, as Dr. Stewart had fallen ill, and Eli had agreed to look in on his patients who were recovering from surgery. He'd never imagined that one river could wreak so much havoc, even after the floodwaters had begun to recede.

He glanced at his watch. Ten minutes of ten. Probably too late to call the Grants. Howard had said he kept an early bedtime because his daily farm chores began at the crack of dawn. Still, Eli had an insatiable urge to talk to Sofie. He decided to dispense with decorum and make the call. It was the earliest he'd gotten home in three days. Hopefully, she was still awake.

The phone rang three times, and he was about to hang up the receiver when he heard a soft "Hello?"

"Margie? It's Elijah Trent. I'm so sorry if I woke you."

"Woke me? Heavens, no. You did catch me with flour up to my elbows, though. Saturday night's when I bake bread. I'll be up for some time."

"How have you fared in the aftermath of the storm?"

"Oh, we're fine here. Howard's a little worried about his corn crop, though. The north field looks like a lake. But that's minor compared to what others have suffered. And, now that the rain's let up, it's already starting to dry out. Would you believe Livvie's Kitchen stayed open the whole time? My sister said that everybody was comparing injuries they'd gotten from heading for high ground or making repairs after the waters had receded. I heard you and the other doctors have been up to your chins in patients."

He chuckled. "That's one way of putting it."

"But, sweet mercy, I'm sure you didn't call to listen to me rattle on. You're wanting to talk to Sofie, aren't you?"

"Well, now that you mention it, is she available?"

"Sorry to say, she and Andy both went to bed already. When I walked past her door a few minutes ago, I could hear her snoring lightly. Poor girl is plumb tuckered out. I've been encouraging her to rest, but she insists on going above and beyond with help around the house. She can't seem to accept that I don't expect anything in return for her staying here. I love her and her brother like they were my own, you know."

"They're blessed to have you in their lives."

"I just wish she wouldn't worry so. Besides carrying around that baby, she carries a huge financial burden. Howard went over to look at the roof; sure enough, he agrees that she cannot move back until it's been replaced. And now, her ceiling needs repair, as well. We'd be happy to loan her the money, but she won't hear of it. She says she'd take out a bank loan before borrowing from us. She can be so obstinate about accepting help, and it's downright frustrating! If she had even an inkling we picked up her hospital bill, she'd have a regular fit. And here's another thing you should know: she thinks she can birth that baby at home and avoid further hospital costs. She's been reading up on it."

"Well, you know I'll never let that happen. In fact, my grandfather will probably want to do the honors of the delivery, since he delivered both her and Andy. But I can promise you that he'll insist on a hospital birth."

"I'm relieved to hear you say that." There came a pause on her end. "She's seems to be leaning more and more toward adoption…and I feel partly to blame. Early on, I encouraged it, but I know now she would only regret it."

"I plan on persuading her to marry me before she makes that decision."

"I've been praying for that very thing!" she tittered. "Gracious, if only it were up to Andy. That boy adores you from the top of your head to the soles of your feet."

He grinned. "The feelings are quite mutual."

"Actually, I think Sofie feels the same way; she just won't admit it because she's too afraid. She still doesn't think she's good enough for you—or anybody decent, for that matter."

Hearing how Sofie really felt about him quickened his heart, even as sadness set in at the thought that Sofie's self-regard had been damaged so deeply by the circumstances of her life.

After a few more minutes of conversing, they said their good-byes.

He picked up the newspaper and tried to read but soon found he couldn't concentrate. So, at the clock's eleventh gong, he tossed it aside with a yawn and padded barefoot up the steps. When he reached the upstairs hallway, he heard a loud thump on the porch, followed by racing footfall. Turning, he saw a yellow-orange glow through the glass panels. He ran back down the stairs and threw the door open wide. Fire! He had no time to chase after the culprit driving away in a truck, engine sputtering. He grabbed the nearest thing he could find, a folded blanket draped over a wicker rocker, and jogged down the steps to slap at the small fire set in the middle of the yard. Across the road, a screen door slammed.

"Need some help there?" came a male voice. "What happened?"

With no time to look up, Eli smacked the flames several times before the fire finally petered out. He bent over to examine the ashy remains, but, without a flashlight, he couldn't make it out. As far as he could tell, it was nothing but a pile of clothes, and the stench of gasoline indicated whoever had started the fire wanted to assure they burned. He glanced up at the neighbor.

"You must be Wilson's grandson," the fellow said. "Name's Allen Pickford." He stuck out his hand, and Eli shook it, studying his face by the light of the moon. He looked to be in his mid-fifties, with gray hair and a beard to match.

"Yes, sir. Elijah Trent. Nice meeting you, although we might have chosen better circumstances. Did you happen to get a look at who did this?"

"I'm afraid not, but the truck—"

A woman in a long robe with her hair pinned up in a hundred little curls came running up the street, waving her hand. "Everyone alright there?" She reached them, breathless, and pointed back at her house. "I just happened to be sittin' on my porch, mindin' my business, when I saw a fellow drive up and get out of his truck with a small bundle in his arms. I thought he might be bringin' a little kid in for medical treatment because I saw him walk up to your door. But then he came back, dropped his armload of stuff on the ground in a heap, lit a match to it, and then ran back to his truck and drove off." She paused and caught her breath. "I'm Betsy Hack, by the way. I live two doors down." She turned to Allen Pickford. "Hello there, Allen. How's Wilma?"

"Oh, she's just fine. Upstairs sleepin', as we speak. Han't got any idea I'm over here."

"Nor does Steve. He's sawin' logs far as I know. Like I said, I was just mindin' my business, sippin' a nice hot cup of tea, not quite ready to go to bed." In the midst of their chatter, she looked at Eli. "So, you're Doc Trent's grandson. Sorry I haven't been over with a platter of cookies to welcome you to the neighborhood."

"That's quite alright," Eli assured her. He was anxious to get to the real reason they both stood in his soggy front yard.

"My mother stopped in to see you yesterday. Florence Meadows. She had that terrible cough."

"Ah, yes. I hope she's feeling better."

"Indeed she is, thanks to that cough medicine you prescribed. She said you'll do just fine replacing Doc, and that's saying a lot for Mother, who thought the sun rose and set just for the ol' guy."

The truth was, Eli couldn't exactly recall the woman. He'd seen so many patients over the past few days, his brain had turned to pudding. "Back to the fellow who started this fire...you didn't happen to recognize him, did you?"

"Nope. Too dark for that. But I made out his stature. He wasn't a fatty, or anything like that, and I figure he wasn't too old, either, the way he took off running."

Allen Pickford pushed some hair off his forehead. "I'm pretty sure I've seen that truck before."

That spiked Eli's interest. He tilted his head. "No kidding. How could you be sure in the dark?"

"I've seen it go by here more than once just lately. A couple of weeks ago, I was standing outside, smoking a cigarette—the wife won't let me smoke inside—when he came around the corner, slowed down in front of your place, and then drove on. It was gettin' real close to dark, so he had his headlights on. Correction: *light* on. The one on the passenger side must not be workin' 'cause the fender's all bent in."

The back of Eli's neck prickled with tension. He'd seen a truck that fit that description over at Wilbur Godfrey's place and figured it belonged to that young boy who worked for him, the sheriff's son. He shifted his weight and squinted at the man. "What color truck was it?"

"Oh, black, for sure, kind of a beat up ol' thing. I saw it a week or so ago in broad daylight, too—before the rain started, I'd say. Maybe Monday or Tuesday. Yep, I was standin' right over there, talking to Larry Ritsema, your next-door neighbor. Same truck, bent fender, broken headlight. He slowed right in front of your place before speedin' away. I can't say the driver looked familiar, just that he's on the young side."

"That's an odd one," Betsy remarked. "Now that you mention it, I may have seen that truck myself. 'Cept, I saw it on the Fourth, during that dreadful storm. I was standin' at the front window, watchin' the rain come down in sheets, when that old jalopy made the turn off Cass. The engine stalled when the guy drove through a deep puddle. I can't tell you what made me remember the dented fender. Both boys had to get out and push the truck out of the water. Then, they climbed back in, and the truck restarted. I remember thinkin' how lucky they were to get that old thing goin' again."

Eli looked at the charred clothes and wondered whose they were, his stomach tied in a knot of dread. "I think I'll go inside and get a flashlight."

After retrieving a flashlight and slipping on some shoes, he returned to find the pair conversing quietly while Allen used a fallen branch to dig through the smoldering heap. With the stick, he pulled something off the top and held it out. Eli shone the light on it and immediately took a sharp breath.

"Why, it looks like a—a dress!" Betsy said. "What in the world?"

"It sure enough is, with little flowers on it," Allen said, leaning in. He wrinkled his nose. "Stinks to high heaven of gasoline, too."

Eli tried to rub the tension from the back of his neck. He'd seen that dress before. Sofie had worn it to church on the day of Grandfather and Winnie's wedding. He thought about her and Andrew asleep at the Grants'. The need to protect them surged strong in his chest.

"You goin' to report this to the sheriff?" asked Allen.

"I would if I were you," Betsy said. With a shake of her head, she added, "The world sure is full of strange people. Don't know why anyone would want to burn a lady's dress in Doc's front yard. You don't suppose it was a prank intended for his new wife, do you?"

Eli's ears buzzed like a wasps' nest. "I have no idea," he muttered, even though he knew full well this had nothing to do with Winnie. "But I do plan to speak to the sheriff."

He thanked his neighbors for their concern and bid them good night, then turned and used his flashlight to navigate his way back to the house. On the porch, something on the floor off to the side caught his eye—an envelope weighted down by a rock. He bent over and picked it up, then opened the screen door and stepped inside, letting it thwack behind him.

He collapsed into a living room chair and stared at the envelope for several minutes. Then, cautiously, so as not to tamper with the evidence, he removed the seal. Something fell out and landed on the hardwood floor and then started to roll, but Eli stopped it with the heel of his shoe. Picking up the small, rounded object, his body convulsed with a wave of shock, followed by a fire of indignation. It was a bullet. He set it down on the coffee table and then reached inside the envelope, pulling out a folded piece of paper. He opened it and read the simple message scrawled inside.

> *Stay away from Sofia Rogers.*
> *Next time, there'll be blood.*

Unholy anger boiled up in Eli's stomach as he tucked the note back inside the envelope and then slid it into his pocket. It would be a hot day at the North Pole before he gave in to the whims of that coward.

Chapter Twenty-six

*For I the L*ORD *thy God will hold*
thy right hand, saying unto thee,
Fear not; I will help thee.
—Isaiah 41:13

*O*wen awoke to a quiet house, which meant that his mother and sister had gone to mass, and his dad was either puttering around in the garage or had already left for the office. The two of them had exchanged barely more than two words over the past several days, which suited him fine. Even now, he intended to dress and beat it out of here before he roped him into doing some stupid chore.

The sun shone through his window and reflected off the wood floor, zeroing in on the dust balls his mom had told him to sweep out of the corners a couple of days ago during that rain storm when he'd been glued to the house due to impassable roads. Cleaning was woman's work, he'd told her, and besides, dust didn't bother him. From there, an argument erupted, she telling him if he didn't help more around the house he'd have to leave, and he spouting back that Carolee didn't do half as much as he did, but he didn't hear his mother telling her to leave. Carolee bugged the life out of him, and he'd been sure to tell her so on Thursday night, when he'd gotten stuck working alongside her, hauling water out of their flooded basement by the bucketful. He'd been tempted to push her down the rickety steps for snitching on him about the pistol in the cabinet, but then he thought of the possibility of her surviving the fall and ratting on him again, so he refrained.

He would gladly hightail it out of this godforsaken place if he could, but Godfrey didn't pay him nearly enough to cover rent, food, gas, and other expenses, like cigarettes and hooch. And he didn't much feel like slicking himself up and pretending to be somebody he wasn't just to find different work. Nothing really appealed to him, anyway. Not that he enjoyed pumping gas, but it beat working in some sweat factory. At least at Godfrey's he enjoyed the benefits of sunshine and fresh air.

He threw on a well-worn T-shirt and the same holey pair of jeans he'd worn yesterday, then stepped into his favorite boots and slipped downstairs, glad he didn't have to report to work today. Through the window, he checked the backyard for any signs of his dad, but the only activity was a couple of squirrels scurrying up and down a tree trunk.

He opened an overhead cupboard and grabbed a tall glass, which he filled to the brim with cold, sparkling water from the spigot. He took a couple of long, refreshing swallows then stopped short at the sound of a car door slamming, then pounding footsteps on the porch. The front door opened and banged shut, after which thundering strides rocked the house and came to a halt at the foot of the stairs. "Owen Morris! Get down here. Now!"

With forced calm, he set down the glass, swallowed a thick wad of dread, and answered, "I'm in the kitchen. What do you want?"

His dad came to the kitchen doorway, chest heaving, eyeballs bulging. "Exactly where were you last night at eleven o'clock?"

He shook off his trepidation. "At home. Why?"

The giant man stepped into the kitchen and came within inches of him. "Are you sure?"

His pulse skipped as he scoured his brain for an alibi. "You saw me go upstairs at nine thirty."

One thick eyebrow arched. "How do I know you didn't go out after your ma and I went to bed?"

"Why don't you ask your favorite little informant? Carolee can tell you I was home all night. You still haven't told me why you care."

His dad's upper lip curled in a snarling fashion. "Carolee spent the night at a friend's house, so her word has no bearing on your alibi this time." He stepped closer. "You might be interested to know who came to see me this morning."

"I seriously doubt it." Owen folded his arms across his front and feigned indifference, even though his chest constricted at the vengeful glare in the man's eyes.

"That new doctor, Elijah Trent, showed me something rather disturbing. Maybe you'd like to see it, too."

He shrugged, concentrating on keeping his breathing steady. "Again, I doubt it."

His dad drew out a piece of paper from his front shirt pocket and thrust it under Owen's chin. "Don't play dumb with me, Owen. I'd know your chicken scratch anywhere."

He stared at the folded note and blinked twice, his pulse racing faster than a herd of gazelles. "I got no idea what you're talking about."

"I think you do," he growled. "And it's all startin' to add up: the missing can o' Red Squill that showed up at Sofia Rogers'; Doc Trent's car ending up in a ditch on account o' somebody tamperin' with the steering shaft; a dress belongin' to Miss Rogers, burnt to smithereens.... And, don't forget, your ma's missin' bottle o' Veronal." He crowded closer, his eyes glinting with hatred. "If these pieces add up the way I think they will, and you had somethin' to do with Sofia's pregnancy...why, I'll...I'll...."

Owen stepped back until his hind side bumped against the sink. "You're mad," he scoffed. "You don't have a single piece of evidence to pin on me. And what about the election?" He nodded coolly. "If you rat me out, your hopes of getting reelected go straight down the drain. Who wants a sheriff who can't enforce the law in his own home?"

His dad plunked his hands on the counter on either side of him and brought his face within inches of Owen's, his rancid breath making him cringe. "I've covered for you through plenty of scrapes, Owen, and saved our family from a heap of embarrassment. But this time...." He shook his head. "What you've done is beyond coverin' up. You won't stand a chance in a courtroom. One simple paternity test, and your cover's blown. And there ain't a thing I'm willin' to do to get you out of this muddle. In fact, I'll be glad to put you behind bars. Folks'll respect me even more for putting my own son in jail—for prizin' justice above protectin' my kin when they commit unspeakable crimes." He narrowed his eyes in a hateful gaze. "What you did was unspeakable, Owen. You're despicable, you know that?"

"I take after you, then, don't I?" Owen dared to say, to tamp down his panic at the prospect of a paternity test.

His dad didn't take his fiery eyes off of Owen for even a second, his upper lip curling in utter disgust. "You don't take after me one bit. I wouldn't be surprised to find your ma was seein' somebody behind my back when she got pregnant with you."

Owen sneered. "I'm your son, true as day. I just learned from watchin' you, you big hypocrite."

"Why, you little—"

"You lay one finger on me, and it'll be the last thing you ever do," Owen growled, bracing himself with two fisted hands. "I've taken enough beatings from you to last a lifetime."

"You deserved every spankin' you ever got. And now, you deserve life in prison for what you done."

"Yeah? Well, don't think I'm going down alone. If you're worried about the election, you should be, 'cause I'll make sure everybody knows about your secret stash you keep stocked, thanks to the likes of Orville Dotson and company." He was gaining the upper hand. "You rat on me, I'll rat on you."

Catching him off guard, his dad snagged him by the front of the shirt with both hands and hauled him close enough that their breaths meshed. Something in those cold, cruel eyes sparked the worst kind of hatred in the depths of his soul. In a single flash of fury, he broke free from his father's hold, raised his fist, and drove it hard into the man's beefy jaw, hearing the crack of bone and feeling the burst of pain in his hand. He watched the oaf stagger backward, his face registering shock and horror, and, in that moment, Owen felt a burst of pleasure, as years' worth of pent-up anger had exploded out of him in that single, satisfying strike.

The man's expression fast went from dread to dull, though, when he lost his battle with gravity and started to plummet, his skull slamming hard against the stove's sharp corner and his body slithering down the white enamel, a trail of blood following after. Surreal and drawn out like a movie reel in slow motion, Buford Morris fell unconscious in a disfigured heap that hardly looked human, and, for a moment, Owen could do nothing but stand there and stare at the motionless mound.

Seconds later, Owen came to life. He bent over the body and felt the neck for a pulse. "Wake up, you idiot!" he screamed.

No response. No rise of the chest to take in air; not a single flick of a finger or a twitching eyelid.

Sudden terror gushed through Owen's blood, running hot and then icy cold. *Don't panic*, he told himself. *Keep your cool. Breathe.* He did all those things, but they didn't ease the alarm that made it hard to take his next breath. What to do? Run? Wait for his mother and sister to get home and tell them he'd hit his father in self-defense? He might be able to pull that off, considering all the thrashings he'd taken in the past. They'd believe him, wouldn't they? But what if they didn't? He refused to rot in jail. Peterford had been as close to a prison as he cared to experience. He figured he'd done his time.

He wiped away the beads of perspiration rolling down his face and fought the urge to retch. In another flash of panic, he leaped up and ran to the den, his heart hammering in his chest. He picked up a lead paperweight from his dad's desk and slammed it into the glass door of the gun cabinet, then reached through the gaping, sharp-edged hole and grabbed a revolver and a box of cartridges. Next, he ran to the living room and snagged the key off the nail by the door.

Then, turning, he gave the house a final glance before sprinting down the porch steps and beating it to his truck. He had one stop to make before blowing this town for good.

※

The church service was especially good that morning, the singing heartwarming and the sermon convicting and inspiring. But Eli was absent, and Sofie left the service feeling somehow incomplete— silly, considering how hard it was to admit how much he meant to her. Oh, how she'd wanted to react with elation when Margie had told her he'd called last night, but she'd managed to remain calm.

"He loves you, you know," Margie had said over a quick cup of coffee in the kitchen before they'd left for church.

"More likely he pities me," she'd replied. "He's proposed marriage but never spoken of love. We're worlds apart, Margie."

"That's because you don't let him get close enough to bridge the gap between your two worlds."

They pulled out of the church parking lot around noon, with several folks still milling about in the churchyard, no doubt discussing the storm and the damage it had wrought. At least the river had receded quickly once the rains had let up. All that remained now were puddles in low-lying areas, and the unending chore of emptying wet basements.

Livvie and Will had invited a number of people to Sunday dinner at the restaurant, including Margie, Howard, Andy, and Sofie. But Sofie begged off, asking if Howard would mind driving her out to her house instead so she could check on things and then swinging by to get her afterward. Margie wasn't in favor of the idea, saying she didn't want Sofie getting any ideas about moving back until they repaired the roof, while Howard forbade her from lifting anything or attempting any fixes of her own. Of course, Andy was eager to accept the invitation, as it would give him a chance to play with Livvie's boys, as well as exempt him from any chores Sofie might have assigned him at the house.

Finally, Sofie managed to convince them that she wanted to check the garden. Howard told her he'd pick her up one hour later, and Margie promised to bring her a plate of food, reminding her of the danger of skipping meals with a growing baby inside of her.

Gracious, what an ordeal, she thought when at last they dropped her off at her little house on River Road and drove away. They were worse than a mama bear with her cub, and she felt a measure of relief to be out from under their thumbs for an hour, though she knew they meant well.

When she unlocked her front door and stepped inside, she was greeted by the smells of mildew and mold. She lamented that her little home had fallen into disrepair in so short a period, and it pained her to think what would be required to bring it back to a livable state. Scattered around the house were the pots, bowls, buckets, and other vessels Eli had helped her place strategically on the floor to catch the drips. She also noticed a few damp areas, indicating places they'd missed. A sob caught in her chest, but she held it at bay. There was no point in crying over something she couldn't control. Plus, she feared that if she gave in to the temptation, she might never stop the waterworks.

Instead, she swallowed the lump in her throat, blew out a loud breath, and walked to the kitchen, stepping over a couple of pans to get there, and peered out the window at the side yard. The grass was overgrown and needed a good cutting, a chore she'd passed off to Andy a couple of years ago. A tender breeze made the rose bushes growing along the neighbor's picket fence bob and sway like lovely ladies.

Sighing, she turned away from the window and headed for her bedroom, hoping her mattress had stayed dry. Indeed, it had, but what she found was far worse than a wet bed. The window had been broken, with shards of glass scattered everywhere, and the evidence of a break-in was unmistakable: her dresser drawers had been pulled out and lay, overturned, on the floor, with clothes strewn everywhere. Dismay and disbelief overcame her, followed by the certainty that her attacker was the culprit. She dashed over to Andy's room and felt a small measure of relief to see that it was untouched. The chest of drawers had been moved away from the wall, but Eli had done that in order to protect the piece from two leaks up above. In its place, Sofie had positioned two pans, which now brimmed with water.

"Lord, what next?" she moaned as a lone tear trickled down her cheek. "How much more can I take from the man who spoiled my chastity, broke my spirit, and filled me with fear?"

Be careful for nothing, came a whisper in her spirit, *but in everything, by prayer and supplication, with thanksgiving, make your requests known to Me. Then My peace, which passes understanding, shall keep your heart and mind through Christ Jesus.*

Stirred by her memory of Philippians 4:6–7, Sofie fell to her knees, her elbows propped on Andy's bed. "Oh, Lord," she cried out, lifting her face and raising her hands, "I need Your peace like never before. Yet I struggle to take my worries and requests to anyone else, including You, preferring to deal with them in my own strength. Forgive me, Lord, for I am sadly inadequate for the task.

"I don't know what the future holds, especially concerning my finances or the child I carry, but I know that You hold my tomorrows, and so I surrender them into Your capable hands. Please take me, Jesus—all of me—and forgive me for the many times I've trusted in myself rather than in You."

She knelt there for a moment and took in the wonder of what it meant to finally surrender everything, and then she pushed herself back up and glanced around the house. *Gracious,* she thought, *my heart feels lighter already. Yes, everything is in total disarray, but I don't sense the same hopelessness I did just moments ago. Thank You, Lord.*

A smile tickled her lips as a wave of giddiness washed over her. If this was what surrender felt like, she couldn't imagine why she'd waited so long to do it. Still reveling in this frame of mind, she went outside.

Even though her garden looked a mess, with many of her plants lying shriveled against the soggy earth, to the point where she wondered if they would survive, she found herself rejoicing in the beauty around her: the scorching sunlight, which penetrated the cotton of her short-sleeved dress, warming her shoulders; the wind whistling through the trees overhead, where a chorus of birds chattered and sang. "Thank You, Lord," she whispered. "Thank You even for this predicament, because I know that You'll see me through it somehow. My garden may not make it, but I will survive, by Your grace."

Sofie was bending to uproot a weed, however futile the effort might be, when she heard a car door slam. Just as she started to turn, she heard an eerie voice say, "Hello, Sofia."

She whirled around, sudden terror surging up her spine. What was Owen Morris doing here? "What do you want?" Suddenly, understanding dawned, the weight of it heavy and horrible.

He approached, but he wasn't himself. He smiled like a lunatic, his eyes wild, his manner frenetic. "I'd hoped to find you here, since you weren't at the Grant farm."

She stood slowly and faced him, her hand instinctively moving to her abdomen. *Lord, keep me calm. Protect me and my baby.* "You...you went to the Grants'? Why?"

"I had to find you. Come on. We don't have much time." He snagged her by the wrist and started tugging.

"Wait!" She dug her heels into the soil. "Where are we going?" Something in his expression warned her not to push beyond a certain point since he looked near to breaking. Had he lost his mind? If he hadn't, he was surely bordering on it, judging by the feral glint in his eyes.

"We've got to get out of town. No time to waste." His eyes darted to the road. "They're coming."

"What? Who?"

"You know."

"No, I don't. And I can't go with you. I...I have to tend my garden. See all the weeds?" She pointed at the scrawny plants pushing up from the soil. "I need to get them uprooted so they don't crowd out my vegetables. Do you want to help me?" She wasn't sure where that question had come from, even as she posed it. What was she thinking?

Yet Owen seemed to consider her proposition, his gaze fluttering back and forth from her to the garden to the yard, as if afraid someone would jump out at him.

Something—or *Someone*—kept her from hyperventilating as she stood face-to-face with the man she feared most, the man whose identity she finally knew. "Come on, Owen. You can help me," she coaxed him, shocked by her sense of calm, which she attributed fully to the prayer of surrender she'd uttered not ten minutes ago.

Owen started to kneel, as if preparing to weed, but then he jumped up again and shook his head at her. "No! What are you trying to do, play with my mind?"

He brought his hand to the hip pocket of his pants, and that's when she saw the grip of a pistol poking out. *Oh, God!* "But, Owen, I can't go anywhere just yet. I...I have to get ready first."

His eyes swept her quickly from head to toe. "What do you have to do?"

"That depends on where you're taking me."

He looked pensive for a moment. "I haven't quite decided yet. All I know is, I'm leaving town and taking you with me."

"You haven't decided where you're going?" Sofie forced gentle enthusiasm into her voice. "Well, maybe we should sit down and talk about it."

"Talk about it?" He furrowed his brow, the frown lines glistening with drops of sweat.

"Yes...and we should eat first, don't you think? I'm famished. How about you?" She had to find a way to stall him at least until Howard returned, hopefully within the hour. Owen was far from stable, for whatever reason. She didn't detect alcohol on his breath, but his behavior put her in mind of someone standing on the edge of lunacy.

He swept a hand through his hair in a nervous gesture and blinked, as if trying to get his bearings. "Yeah, yeah, I guess I'm kinda hungry. Make me something to eat, and then we'll go. Just don't think you can talk me into hangin' around any longer than necessary. We've gotta get going."

"That's fine, Owen. Just relax, okay?"

"Why're you tellin' me to relax?"

"You seem jumpy, that's all."

He looked around again, then grabbed her elbow, pinching hard as he pulled her toward the house. "I'm not jumpy, I'm just...."

"What?" She didn't attempt to free herself from his grip. For now, going along with him seemed like the safest course of action.

"Nothin'. Let's just get inside."

"Okay. I'll fix us something nice to eat, and then we'll talk about where you want to go."

"Good, that's good. But we've gotta make it snappy." Once inside, he shoved her toward the kitchen. "What you got in the icebox?"

"Not much, I'm afraid. I've been away, as you know."

He sneered. "Yeah, out and about with your lover."

"What?"

"You heard me. You're always out with your lover, the young Dr. Trent." He spoke Eli's name almost in singsong.

"Dr. Trent is not my lover. He's just a friend."

"And a tattletale," he spat. "Fool can't keep his mouth shut. He's always runnin' to the sheriff, my good-for-nothin'—" A spooked look crossed his face, his eyes bulging in a deranged sort of way. "Hurry up with that food, girl."

His tone joggled her into action, and she started opening cupboard doors in search of something to fix for lunch. *Lord God, give me courage and wisdom,* she pleaded silently. *Give me the words to say and the actions to take to keep this situation from escalating.*

Be not afraid of sudden fear, neither of the desolation of the wicked, when it comes. For I shall be your confidence, and I shall keep your foot from being taken.

Chapter Twenty-seven

Fear thou not; for I am with thee:
be not dismayed; for I am thy God:
I will strengthen thee; yea, I will help thee;
yea, I will uphold thee with the right hand of
my righteousness.
—Isaiah 41:10

Eli swerved into the Grants' driveway and jumped out of the car without shutting off the engine, leaving the door open as he raced across the yard to the front door and then rang the doorbell impatiently. Forehead pressed against the window, he peeked inside, but the only sign of life was Buster running to the door, tail wagging. Some watchdog he made.

Once he'd given up on finding the Grants at home, he dashed back to the car and headed for town, hoping to find Sofie and Andy at the Wesleyan Methodist church. His mind still reeled from the news of Sheriff Morris's sudden death, and the rumor that it hadn't been an accident sent waves of alarm rippling through his veins. Who could have killed him but Owen?

Eli had gone to the sheriff's office first thing that morning to report last night's incendiary episode, along with his suspicions that the sheriff's own son had been the perpetrator. After their discussion, he'd had reason to believe the sheriff was prepared to arrest

Owen. But if Owen had resisted, and somehow ignited a scuffle that had ended in his father's death, Sofia and Andy were also in danger. Anyone as volatile as Owen Morris couldn't be trusted any further than the length of his nose.

Only a few churchgoers lingered in the church parking lot, so Eli questioned each of them. One man said he'd seen Sofia Rogers and her little brother with the Grants, and, as far as he knew, they'd all gone to Livvie's Kitchen for a meal. Eli thanked him and proceeded to his next destination.

"Dr. Trent! Won't you join us?" called Will Taylor from a table near the center of the eatery. Seated beside him, Livvie looked up and waved him over. It was then that he noticed Margie and Howard Grant sitting at the same table. Where were Sofie and Andy? He breathed a sigh of relief when he spotted Andy among the group of kids at a table near the back of the restaurant. But where was Sofie?

Not wanting to make a spectacle of himself or to draw undue attention to the matter at hand, he casually walked past the other guests, nodding and smiling, even though his head told him to hurry.

When he reached the table, he forced a smile and spoke softly. "Hi, everyone. Just wondering if anyone knows where I might find Sofie."

Margie smiled back. "She's over at her house, checking on the flood damage. We tried to talk her into coming here for lunch, but I think she wanted to be alone for a bit."

Eli gripped the back of an empty chair. "You must not have heard, then, that Sheriff Morris...he's dead."

"What?" All of them gasped in unison, drawing the notice of guests at nearby tables.

Margie slapped a hand over her open mouth, keeping it there as she spoke. "What happened?"

"They're still trying to piece together a scenario, with the help of neighboring police departments. But, the evidence...." Eli lowered his voice to a whisper. "The evidence points to murder."

More gasps erupted around the table.

"Who would do that?" Will asked. "Do they have any suspects?"

Eli kept his voice quiet. "The sheriff's wife suspects her son did the deed, said there's definite proof of a struggle in the kitchen, and that the gun cabinet was broken into and a pistol removed. I reported some things to the sheriff just this morning concerning his boy, and I'm certain he had in mind to go home and place him under arrest."

Will ran a hand through his hair. "What sort of things?"

Without hesitation, he proceeded to tell them about the fire set in his yard and the note and bullet he'd found on his porch the night before. Before he knew it, the restaurant buzzed with anxious chatter. People left their tables and gathered around to learn what was going on. "I need to get out to Sofie's place. I have reason to believe she could be in harm's way."

Without missing a beat, Howard swiped a napkin across his mouth then pushed up from the table. "I'll go with you."

Margie scooted back in her chair, but Howard gripped her shoulder. "You stay here with Andy."

Her face had turned a pasty white. "Alright, but... be careful."

"You need any help?" said a man Eli didn't recognize.

"Yeah, we could form a posse," said another.

"That won't be necessary," Eli assured them. "The last thing I want to do is take the law into our own hands. I merely want to check on Sofie and make sure she's safe."

Seeing the commotion, Andy and the Taylor kids came across the restaurant to join the circle. Andy pushed through the crowd. "Eli! Is everything all r-right? How come everyone looks so w-worried?"

Eli wrapped an arm around the boy's shoulder and drew him close. "A few things have come up in the town, son." Deciding it useless to hide the details from Andy when it would be front-page news tomorrow, he went on to share with him and others what information he'd managed to gather. "I was at the hospital making my rounds this morning when the news started spreading that Sheriff Morris had been brought to the hospital by ambulance. I went over there myself and learned he'd died. Police cars were parked outside the hospital. Apparently, Robert Humes, the superintendent of the state police division, is putting together a team right now. I'm sure it won't be long before the town is swarming with cops—and with every manner of rumor imaginable. The one thing I want all of you to know, and you can spread this far and wide, is that Sofia Rogers is not a loose woman. She was attacked back in November, and, while everyone is innocent until proven guilty, I can tell you beyond a reasonable doubt that Owen Morris is the culprit."

A few more gasps whistled through the little diner. Andy slipped away and disappeared in the crowd, no doubt desirous of finding a corner where he could let this latest information digest. At eleven years of age, he'd already suffered a lifetime of hurt.

Eli searched for the boy and spotted him at the back of the restaurant, walking shoulder to shoulder with the oldest Taylor boy, who looked to be consoling him.

"Please pray for Sofie," Eli said to the crowd, "and for all of Wabash, for that matter. No one is truly safe while Owen Morris is roaming free." He looked at Will. "Would you mind contacting the police and telling them we're headed out to Sofie's place and that they should meet us at the corner of Mill Creek Pike and River Road?"

Will jumped up. "Consider it done."

᠅

Owen fingered the gun in his pocket, trying to collect his bearings. He had to get Sofie away from here before they came after him and forced them both to submit to a blood test. Without either of them around, there was no way of proving anything. Plus, she carried his kid. Yes, sir—Owen Morris was going to be a dad. And he'd be darned if anybody kept him from fulfilling his fatherly role, raising his kid with a lot more love and affection and training than he'd gotten. His original plan had been to do away with Sofie as soon as the kid came out of her, but a new sense of possessiveness had come over him, and now he really wanted her for himself. She was his, and no one else's.

Soon, it would be just the three of them. They'd go someplace far away, like Oklahoma. As much as Owen had despised the years he'd spent in the state, he knew it had plenty of open space—the perfect hideout for him and Sofie.

"You just about done in there?" Owen moved away from the front window, where he'd been standing sentry, gazing down River Road for any signs of vehicles approaching. Sofie jolted at the sound of his voice, and he liked that he wielded such power over her. She stood at the stove, stirring some kind of meat-and-potato concoction that smelled awfully good.

"It shouldn't take too much longer. You can sit down and relax, if you'd like." She looked about as relaxed as a caged cat herself.

"I'd rather stand here and watch you." He leaned against the doorframe and removed the gun from his pocket, then studied the upturned barrel before pointing it at her for effect. "Bang!" he said, laughing when she jerked with a loud gasp.

"Put that away, Owen."

"Why? Does it scare you?"

"Yes."

"Good answer. You should be scared. Guns are dangerous."

Her lack of a smile and the way she kept her eyes trained on her task said she wasn't amused. He walked up behind her and kissed the back of her neck. She went as straight as a broomstick, then quickly wiped away the wet spot he'd left there. "I thought we were going to discuss where you wanted to go."

"Not till we sit down to eat. What's taking you so dang long? And what is that you're making?"

"Beef stew, with onions and potatoes. I need to make some gravy next. Go sit down so I can finish up and then set the table."

"You're awful bossy."

"I'm sorry. I don't mean to be." She had a trembly quality to her voice. "It's just hard to work with you breathing down my neck."

"You should get used to it, you know. We're going to be together forever."

She snapped erect and turned to look at him, her dark eyes piercing him.

"Does that excite you as much as it does me?" He played with his gun, cocking and uncocking it, enjoying the way it made her twitch every time she heard the little click.

"I...I suppose."

"How do you feel about Oklahoma?"

"Oklahoma?" She stopped stirring but didn't look up. "I've never been there."

"I thought that would be a good place to settle."

She resumed her stirring, although she didn't appear to be in any great hurry.

Growing impatient, he walked to the window again. Two cars turned onto River Road. He held his breath and then sighed with relief when they continued past the house. He shuffled back into the kitchen and sat down at the table, laying down his revolver. "That's where I went to high school, you know. Oklahoma. My parents shipped me out there."

She shifted her weight to the other foot. "I'm sure they both had your best interests in mind."

He passed over the remark. "Would you believe my dad made one of his deputies escort me to Oklahoma by train?"

"Really? That must have been terrible."

"It was, but then I came home and laid eyes on you, the pretty gal who cleaned my daddy's office. You had such pretty eyes, and your short dark hair looked so soft. Why did you cut it short, by the way?"

"It became a nuisance when I started working."

He scratched his temple and gave his head a little shake. It was hard keeping all his thoughts in check, and he knew he was rambling. "Well, you'll need to start growin' it out again. I liked you better that way."

She touched one of her curls then stirred a little faster. "What was your school like?"

"Pfff. Boring. It'd have been more exciting to watch a banana ripen."

While the stew simmered in the pan, Sofie opened a cupboard and took down two plates, then pulled out a drawer. He watched her closely, in case she was inclined to pull a knife on him, but she merely lifted out a couple of spoons and some folded linen napkins. She approached and set the table in front of him. He sat back and started to relax. "You know, Owen"—pausing, she chewed on her lower lip—"I'm just learning again how much God loves me. I've started going to church again."

"Don't talk to me about God and church," he spat. "I don't believe any of that nonsense, and those who do are nothin' but hypocrites."

"There's no need to yell, Owen. I merely wanted to suggest to you that God forgives us our trespasses."

He lifted his upper lip at the corner and looked at her round belly. "What about you? Do you forgive me my trespasses?" He reached out and snagged hold of her wrist, squeezing until she flinched.

"Ouch. You're hurting me."

He ignored her complaint and tightened his grip. "Well, do you?"

"Yes, yes, I forgive you!"

"Wrong answer. You were supposed to say there is nothing to forgive. You know very well you wanted me as much as I wanted you."

Wetness formed at the corners of her eyes, and he had the sudden urge to slap her. Instead, he tossed down her wrist. "Hurry up with that food. We gotta get out of here."

⚜

Sofie's pulse thrummed with panic, despite her efforts to surrender her fears to her heavenly Father. *Help me, Lord. Keep me calm, and please, don't leave me.*

"I will never leave thee, nor forsake thee." The unshakable words of reassurance washed over her, providing her with a resurgence of courage and strength, in spite of her own weakness.

Still rubbing the sting from her wrist, she hastened to take down a serving bowl from the shelf and started spooning in the stew. As she did, she glanced through the doorway into the living room. With Owen sitting at the table, his back to the front window, his hand resting on his gun, she caught a quick glimpse of something or someone darting across the yard and prayed it wasn't Georgie coming to see if Andy could play. She held her breath, waiting for a knock at the door. A minute passed without a sound, so she began to breathe easier. Maybe it had been a dog. But then... could it be? Ever so slowly, Eli peeked over the windowsill, putting a hand to his lips to shush her before ducking out of view.

A mixture of relief and alarm coursed through her. *Lord, keep him safe.*

Chapter Twenty-eight

*The angel of the LORD encampeth round
about them that fear him,
and delivereth them.*
—Psalm 34:7

*E*li and Howard took the Grants' car so Owen wouldn't recognize it, and the five policemen who met them at the designated intersection arrived in unmarked cars. They parked about fifty yards from Sofie's house and then proceeded on foot between houses and sheds, trees and other parked cars, then stealthily preparing to secure a perimeter around the house. The police also evacuated several homes in the surrounding area, directing folks to drive north to the riverbank, where they were to stay until summoned when it was deemed safe to return. Eli prayed that Owen wouldn't suspect anything and rested easy when he peeked his head over the edge of the living room windowsill to make eye contact with Sofie and determined she had been successful in waylaying Owen by making him a meal. Smart girl. Nothing like offering a hungry man a home-cooked meal to keep him distracted. He asked the Lord to protect her while the cops made their move.

Crouching beneath the window, he signaled an "okay" to Howard, positioned behind Owen's truck. A policeman scooted up next to Eli, while three others crept around the house from both sides, one to station himself by the kitchen, the others to occupy the garden side. The last man hunkered down next to Howard behind the truck. It appeared they had their bases covered.

"When the time's right, I'll make my move," the one in charge informed Eli in a hushed voice. "Our main objective is getting Miss Rogers safely out of there." It was a relief to hear him say that. Eli certainly didn't want the lot of them to go barging in, only to have Owen turn a gun on Sofie. There was no telling what he'd do if cornered. "Get yourself back behind that truck with the others," the policeman added. "I don't want you gettin' killed tryin' to protect that girl."

Eli nodded, knowing it made little sense to argue with the experts. All he could do was trust they knew what they were doing. "You should know I plan to marry her."

The cop started to creep forward, then paused and looked over his shoulder. "Well then, I'll have to make doubly sure I deliver her to you safe and sound."

꙳

Owen had the jitters. He couldn't concentrate, especially with the vision of his old man smacking his head hard against the corner of the stove and then crumpling into a mangled heap on the floor replaying with merciless detail in his mind. His head had begun to pound. Had he really hit him hard enough to kill him? Shoot, he didn't know what had come over him. All he knew was that he needed to make himself scarce, the sooner, the better.

After Sofie had devoted so much time and preparation to the noon meal, she'd finally sat down across the table from him. When he'd picked up his spoon to dig in, she'd reached across and put a hand to his arm and insisted they say a prayer of thanks. Now he couldn't get the words out of his head, further clogging his befuddled brain and delaying his plans for escaping. He began to wish he hadn't wasted his time in stopping to pick her up before skipping out. Why, she'd dragged out the whole affair so much that his nerves jangled together like a bunch of out-of-tune piano keys. And, worse, he'd allowed it.

"Eat fast so we can get a move-on," he said between hurried bites.

She didn't do one thing about hastening along, merely cast him a casual glance and answered, "Well, I'll have to clean up the dishes first. I just hate messes. That's precisely why I came back to check on things. My leaky roof has posed such a problem and ruined so many of my belongings. Do you know I'm going to need a new roof and ceiling?" She shook her head. "Such a terrible expense, and without a job, it's going to take mc a while to save up enough cash."

He pressed a hand to his throbbing temple. "Stop talkin' about your dumb roof and cleaning up your kitchen mess. And shut up about getting a job, for pity's sake. Once we get to Oklahoma, none of that is going to matter one bit."

Frowning, she started pushing her stew around on her plate. "And that's another thing, Owen. I don't know how safe it is for me to travel at this stage of my pregnancy. Have you thought about that? You do want me to have a healthy baby, don't you?"

He slammed his fist on the table, resulting in giving her another big jolt in which her neck snapped backward, and she blinked hard. "We're leavin' today, no matter what! I don't care if you give birth on the way, but we aren't spendin' one more minute in this blasted town."

❊

Sofie had no idea how much longer she could keep up her front of composure. The way her pulse thrummed in a wild rhythm, she worried her heart just might explode through her chest. To make matters worse, her baby had set to kicking so hard, it was actually painful. The possibility that the pains were actually labor contractions crossed her mind, but everything she'd read indicated it was too soon. So, she laid aside the thought and blamed her nerves for making the baby especially agitated. Then again, she'd never been through childbirth before. Despite the number of books she'd read on the subject, no description seemed adequate to help her recognize the initial stages of labor.

It seemed that Owen had indeed crossed some sort of threshold into madness, given his jumpy behavior and the way his wild eyes flashed like burning coals. He had some very twisted ideas about love, and the notion occurred to her that he'd probably never felt the true thing from anyone. She didn't feel sorry for him, not after the horrific thing he'd done to her, but she could learn to forgive over time and certainly pray that someday, somehow, God would reveal Himself and His unconditional love to Owen.

She thought about Eli and wondered if the face she'd seen peeking over the windowsill had been real or imagined—a mirage, perhaps; the result of wishful thinking. Soon, she began to question her own sanity. She raised her head for a quick look out the window, then berated herself because the mere act spurred Owen into action. He grabbed his revolver, jumped up from his chair, and ran to the window, craning his neck to look left and right.

"What are you doing?" she asked. Howard would surely come driving up the road at any moment, and the thought that Owen might start shooting filled her with dread.

"Looking outside, like you just did. You expecting someone?"

"No," she fibbed. "Come back to the table and finish your lunch."

"I'm not hungry anymore, and neither are you. It's time to go."

"What about my brother? I can't just leave him without an explanation. He won't know what to do."

Owen turned away from the window and rushed at her, nabbing her by the arm and hauling her up from her chair. "You can and you will." The sudden move toppled the chair and made her scream out in pain.

A loud knock sounded at the door. "Owen Morris, come out with your hands up," a booming voice demanded. "We know you're in there. The house is surrounded by armed officers. You have no recourse but surrender."

In haste, Owen snatched Sofie up close to him, wrenching her other arm, one hand wrapped securely around her front, the other pointing his gun directly at the door. He fired off a single shot that ricocheted off the doorknob, cracking it in two and splintering a lower section of the door. Sofie screamed at the noise and the sudden spark of splitting metal, her heart racing fiercely.

"She's next if you don't call off your dogs!" he screamed past her ear.

"Now, just calm down, Owen," said the man outside. "Your father's dead. Hasn't there been enough violence for one day? We can make this easy, Owen, if you'll just put down the gun and come out."

"Owen! Your father...is he really dead?" she croaked.

He sneered in her ear. "Fool got what he deserved." Then, to the officer outside, he shouted, "Get off the property now, or I'll kill her, I swear!"

Sofie's head swirled with dizziness as a harsh pain exploded in her abdomen. She moaned, clamping a hand over the swell.

"What?"

"I don't know. I think I need to sit down, Owen."

"Are you crazy? There's no time for that. You're coming with me."

"Owen, be sensible," she said through gritted teeth. "You heard what he said. The house is surrounded. There's no way to escape."

His breath became ragged. "I'm not going to jail. I'm gettin' out of here, even if I have to shoot my way out."

She took a deep breath. "How do you propose to do that? They'll shoot back."

"Not with you in front of me. Come on, move." He started to push her forward, so she complied, afraid of the consequences of refusing.

Another rap came at the door. "Owen, if you won't come out, how about letting me in? We can talk this through, man to man."

When the icy metal barrel of the revolver touched her cheek, Sofie let out a deafening shriek. "Please! He has a gun to my face!"

"Hold on there, Owen," said the negotiator. "Let's talk about this. I'm not armed. Open the door and see for yourself."

Owen stilled for a moment, as if considering the officer's suggestion, but then he relaxed his stance and let out a coarse laugh. "You think I'm stupid enough to believe you won't blast me in the head as soon as I open the door? I have a better idea. Call off your dogs, every last one of 'em, and tell them to vacate the property. Then, and only then, will I talk to you."

"I can do that, Owen. But you're going to have to promise to open the door."

"Just get rid of everybody!"

"Men, listen up!" The voice bellowed loud enough to rattle the walls. "I want everybody back to your cars. Now!"

Another pain seized Sofie's womb, this time pinching with such pressure that she nearly fainted. "Owen, you have to let me sit down."

"Shut up and let me think!" he hissed. Seconds later, he dragged her to the window for a look outside, the gun still pointed at her temple. Three policemen started walking down the drive.

"They're leaving, just as you asked. Now, open the door, would you?" Sofie pleaded.

"How do I know that's all of them?"

"You can go look out the window and see for yourself."

The thump of Owen's heart pounded straight through the back of her cotton shirt. "Owen, let me sit down. Please."

"No! We're getting out of here, you and me, and the kid. You can sit in the truck."

Sweat drops made a stream down her face as her stomach clenched. "Owen, I'm having pains. I think...I think the baby's coming."

"I told you to shut up!" he growled. Then, he called, "We're comin' out, so you best step aside."

After a moment of silence, the officer replied, "Okay, I'm stepping aside. The coast is clear for you to come out."

Sofie couldn't imagine what the officer intended, but it didn't seem logical that he would just allow Owen to take her away. *Lord above, please keep my baby safe* became her new prayer.

Holding her so close, she felt his hot breath at the nape of her neck, Owen eased her toward the door. "No fast moves, now."

"Yes, Owen, I heard you. No fast moves. Easy does it."

"Open the door," he hissed in her ear.

Trembling, she reached for what was left of the doorknob, gave it a turn, and pulled.

The splintered door creaked open to blazing sunlight, silhouetting a tall man in uniform standing at the foot of the porch steps, arms outstretched, palms up. "No gun, see? Come on out, Owen, and you'll see there's no one about. They've all gone back to their cars."

Inch by dreadful inch, they stepped out into the sweltering heat of noonday, the pistol's cold tip pressed to her temple. The policeman looked Sofie square in the eyes "You alright, ma'am?"

"She's fine," Owen spoke up. "Now, don't try following us, 'cause I'm goin' to have my gun on her till we've cleared the city limits."

"I see," the man said, sidestepping to the left to make way for their descent down the porch steps. "And what happens after that? You know you can't get far. Your name and picture will be posted on every telephone pole across the country. Every department will be on the lookout for you. You'll never have a second's peace. Is that what you want?"

Owen moved her forward a step, and then another. Frantic, she scanned the yard but saw no sign of anyone. Where was Eli? Had he vanished at the sound of the gunshot? She wouldn't have blamed him one bit.

"What I want is for you to shut up and get out of my way."

The officer lifted his hands higher and took another sideways step. "Does it look like I'm stopping you?"

Sofie caught a glimpse of movement from behind Owen's truck and prayed he hadn't spotted it. Apparently, he must have been more intent on keeping an eye on the officer, because he kept nudging her down the steps.

When they reached level ground, Owen clenched her tighter, and they moved toward the truck as one, his steps matching hers, his breaths loud and ragged in her ear. The unnamed officer walked beside them, and Sofie wondered if he planned to allow Owen to sweep her away. Another painful cramp seized her, this one located more in her lower back, and she had to concentrate to keep from crying out.

Just feet from the front of the truck, a screeching yell brought Owen's steps to a sudden standstill. Horror raged like venom when Sofie caught sight of Andy racing across the yard, arms flailing. "You let my sister go!" he yelled. "Leave her be, you—you ugly monster!"

The officer made an about-turn and raised his hands at Andy in a halting gesture.

"Andy! Go back!" Sofie wailed.

After that, any semblance of order dissolved into instant chaos. Gunfire split the air, deafening Sofie for more than a few seconds, when Owen raised his revolver to fire at his moving target. Held now by only one of his arms, Sofie managed to wrangle free and then shove him backward. Out of nowhere, an airborne Eli dived at Owen, knocking him to the ground. With lightning speed, Sheriff Morris's chief deputy, Dan Fett, also emerged from behind the truck and jumped into the melee, wresting the gun from Owen's hand and sending it flying. Sofie screamed, and she couldn't help the gush of tears that splashed down her face when Andy rushed into her arms and squeezed like he never meant to let go. Even he let out a little sob. Howard then came on the scene and quickly guided Sofie and Andy several feet away from the scuffle.

The officers who'd retreated earlier came sprinting back to intervene in the tussle on the ground. One of them hauled Owen up by the back of his collar, and then another wrenched his arms behind him and shackled his wrists in handcuffs, with Owen moaning all the while. Everything happened in a matter of seconds, but those seconds seemed to play out in slow motion before Sofie's eyes, every image etching itself on her mind.

She set Andy back from her and then cupped his face in her hands, as if to study every freckle. "What in the world? Where did you come from? Are you alright?" Each succeeding question spilled out before he'd had time to answer the one before.

In a blink, his expression changed from fretful to sheepish. "I climbed in the back of Mr. Grant's car before him and Eli got in. I h-heard them s-say they'd b-be driving here. I l-laid way low so they w-wouldn't see me. I know it was wrong, b-but I was scared for you, Sofie."

She pulled him close, even as another cramp seized her. "You scalawag. I don't know whether to scold you or applaud your valiant effort."

He squinted up at her with that hangdog gaze. "I'd like the second one b-better."

Eli walked over and tousled Andy's red hair, then put both arms around Sofie, sandwiching Andy in between them. She relished her newfound sense of security—one she hadn't felt in more than seven months.

"Are you alright, sweetheart?" Eli searched her eyes, his filled with concern. "Did he hurt you at all?"

She shook her head. "I'm fine, really. I tried playing along, pretending to cater to his whims. Though, I'll admit, I got plenty scared when he pulled out that gun." She decided not to mention the cramping pains just now, in hopes that they were simply a result of stress and would dissipate once she'd had a chance to rest and recover from the ordeal.

He squeezed a little tighter and murmured over the top of her head, "You are a brave woman, you know that?"

To hold back another gush of tears, she bit down on her lip, backed out of his embrace, and returned her attention to Andy. "I don't know if you realized it, Eli, but this boy was a stowaway in Howard's car. Whatever are we going to do with him?"

"I suspect a good punishment is in order."

"Yes, I agree."

A flicker of worry washed over Andy's countenance as he looked from one to the other. "I din't mean to d-disobey. I only wanted to—"

"We're only teasing, silly." Sofie chuckled softly. "It was a dangerous thing you did—a foolish thing, too—but it was brave nonetheless. And I know you were only trying to protect me. I'm just so thankful you didn't get hurt...or killed."

Eli delivered a gentle punch to Andy's upper arm. "Your courage is impressive, indeed. I'm proud of you for wanting to protect your sister. Just goes to show how much you love her."

"Then, you must feel the same," Andy countered, casting him an upward glance, "'cause you wanted to protect h-her, t-too."

"You make an excellent point, my man."

Sofie's face grew hot, and she envisioned little red blotches popping out on her cheeks and neck, having nothing to do with the scorching heat and everything to do with her close proximity to the man she'd come to love, though she dared not admit it aloud. She couldn't imagine their opposing worlds ever intersecting—she, a working-class social misfit; he, a wealthy, well-read, highly respected physician.

Sofie was aware of an officer barking instructions pertaining to the suspect when another severe pain accosted her, prompting her to double over, both hands pressed to her abdomen.

"Sofie, what is it?" Eli's hand moved to the center of her back.

She tried to say something, but she found it impossible to release her breath, let alone speak through gritted teeth.

"Sofie, talk to me. What's going on? Are you having pains?"

Still clenching her jaw, she gave a quick nod, and the next thing she knew, Eli had picked her up, gently deposited her in the backseat of Howard's car, and climbed in next to her through the other door. Andy jumped up front with Howard, and off they went, toward the hospital and away from the man who would never meet the baby he'd fathered.

Chapter Twenty-nine

These things have I spoken unto you, that
my joy might remain in you, and that your
joy might be full.
—John 15:11

Gracie Joy Rogers came into the world at 6:32 p.m. on July 8, a full six weeks ahead of schedule, weighing five pounds, three ounces—a wee little lass with a full head of black hair, and as healthy and strong as if she'd come out weighing twice as much.

Eli had delivered Gracie. By the time they'd reached the hospital, Sofie's contractions were coming in two-minute increments, and there'd been no stopping them. Although she'd read everything she could about labor and delivery, nothing could have prepared her for the actual experience. "Beautiful" and "horrid" best described it when she tried to put it into words, but with every passing day, the memory of the excruciating pain faded a little more, and she forgot it altogether when she looked into the face of her perfect, precious baby. All along, she'd expected a boy, for some reason; but she could not have been more thrilled when Eli brought her the squealing girl and lowered her into her arms.

Every time Sofie looked at her tiny daughter, she couldn't imagine life without her. She prepared herself for the criticism many people were likely to give: *"She should have given that child up." "It isn't proper, her being unwed and all." "I can't imagine how she thinks she'll manage." "How can she love a baby that came about from such a violent event? She'll be a constant reminder."* That had been Margie's argument, at the beginning—but when she'd first laid eyes on the ebony-haired gem, she'd sighed, "Oh, Sofie, she looks exactly like you."

For her part, although Sofie had considered adoption, the notion had vanished altogether once she'd clapped eyes on her daughter for the first time. She believed that God would take care of their needs, just as was promised in His Word, and that they would thrive. In fact, He had assured her of this repeatedly, with an all-surpassing sense of peace, and with the way the pieces of her life had begun to fall into place.

At the Grants' insistence, the little family remained with them for two weeks after Sofie's release from the hospital. She didn't need to keep searching for a job, as Jackson Cleaners had telephoned her three days after Gracie was born and offered her a position that was hers whenever she felt strong enough to resume working. Margie insisted on watching the baby while Sofie worked, and she refused to accept any payment, claiming that Gracie Joy was as much her grandchild as if they shared the same flesh and blood.

After the two weeks, Eli came to pick up Sofie, Andy, and the baby and take them home to River Road. As he approached the corner of their street, Sofie was astounded by the number of cars parked along the side of the road—and even more by the enormous crowd of people standing in her yard. "What is this?" she asked, flabbergasted by the gathering.

"Yeah, what's going on?" Andy wanted to know, sliding forward in his seat to get a good view.

Grinning ear to ear, Eli pulled up directly in front of the house and parked, after which throngs of people pressed in around the car. "It's a whole town of people who want to express their love and support for you, and don't you dare say you don't deserve it, Sofia Mae Rogers. Not after all you've been through." It was the first time he'd called her by her full name, and she could only surmise he'd heard it from Margie.

"But…I thought most people would think ill of me for, you know, keeping her."

He reached across the seat and touched her arm. "First, you should stop worrying what folks think. And, second, do these people look like they came here to judge? Just accept this as their way of saying, 'We're here for you, and we want to lend a helping hand.' Look at your house."

The crowd separated, allowing Sofie a full view of her house. At first sight, she could barely take it all in—the siding had been painted a soft shade of eggshell blue; the front door had been painted a smart navy blue—in fact, the door looked new; the shutters were hung tidily and straight; the roof looked brand-new; and the front steps, also new, featured an array of terra-cotta pots brimming with beautiful flowers. "What in the world…?"

Eli's smile had grown, if it were possible. "It didn't take long for all of Wabash to hear the whole story, corroborated by a series of front-page articles in the *Daily Plain Dealer* detailing the charges against Owen Morris. And it took even less time for them to mobilize, under the leadership of the Wesleyan Methodist church, on behalf of the young mother they now knew to have been a victim of circumstances. They took up a collection, Sofie, and raised enough money to cover your hospital bill, replace your roof and ceiling...even purchase a crib and a few other essentials for baby Gracie."

Sofie couldn't believe the outpouring of kindness. "But why...?"

Eli laughed. "There's more. Your house has been cleaned from top to bottom, and I happen to know of more than a few women from the church who have been sewing and knitting round the clock, producing baby clothes, diapers, and blankets of all sorts. Your pantry was stocked and should last you for a while, and your garden's looking good—well-watered, with nary a weed to be found."

Of course, the tears that had welled in her eyes at first sight of her house had given way to outright waterworks. When Eli came around to open her door and help her out, the women and children pressed in closer, competing for a peek at the blanketed bundle in her arms, while the men stood at a distance, smiling broadly, their hands tucked under their armpits or shoved in their pockets.

Bessie Lloyd, the most notorious gossip in town, was among the first to get a glimpse of the newborn, swaddled in her soft, pink blanket. To Sofie's surprise, the woman didn't have one foul word to say. Clara Morris was noticeably absent from the crowd—and who could blame her? It was hard enough being widowed, but when you had your own son to blame—a son who had also forced himself upon a hapless local girl with the aid of a prescription drug prescribed to you...Sofie could only imagine the depth of her grief. In spite of all that she had suffered at the hands of Clara's son, she couldn't help but feel sorry for the woman, as well as for Owen's sister, Carolee. And, while she didn't have an ounce of compassion for Owen, she also found that she didn't hate him, and for that, she had only the Lord to thank.

Among the many items the church ladies had sewn for Sofie was an over-the-shoulder sling fashioned from soft, durable fabric, which proved a convenient way of carrying Gracie around. She could move freely from the kitchen to the bedroom to the washroom and even out to the clothesline, all with Gracie Joy in tow! In fact, about a week later, she had just fastened the final clothespin to the dozenth diaper on the line, Gracie still sleeping soundly against her bosom, when a horn honked, announcing Eli's arrival. At the sound of the front screen door thwacking shut, followed by Andy's gleeful shout, her heart took a familiar leap. It was a sultry Saturday night in early August, and Eli had come for supper. She'd neglected to ask his favorite food when she'd invited him, so she hoped he liked Swiss steak and mashed potatoes.

Since they'd come home to River Road, Eli had stopped by several times to visit with Andy and to check on her and the baby, but he'd never stayed overly long. She suspected he had a soft spot in his heart for Gracie, mostly due to the role he'd played in bringing her into the world. But there'd been no further mention of his earlier marriage proposal, nor as much as an attempted kiss. As for his persistence in offering her the position of secretary, he'd ended up hiring Mabel Downing one week after Gracie's birth. She had clerical experience, having served as Dr. Stewart's office administrator.

Was she to conclude that his reasons for wanting to marry her had all but vanished? It didn't seem that outrageous an explanation. He no longer required her services in his office, and with Owen Morris languishing in a jail cell, undoubtedly facing a lifelong prison term, there were no further worries over her safety. She had also been offered employment. Moreover, now that the townsfolk had put forth so much time, money, and effort into repairing her house, she had no need to move. Thus, all talk of marriage ceased. And even though she'd turned down his previous offers, her heart ached a little that he hadn't been a bit more persistent.

But, Grandma's good gravy, what was she thinking? Hadn't she told him repeatedly that she could manage just fine, that she enjoyed her independence, and that she wouldn't marry him simply because doing so seemed like a viable solution to a host of problems? She couldn't live with herself, if one or two years down the road, he started resenting her for their wide differences in background and education. Goodness knew they came from vastly diverse worlds. What possible reason could there be now—other than love—for marrying?

Even so, she couldn't shake the empty feeling in her heart every time he said good-bye. There was no explaining it away. She had fallen in love with him, and too late. He would never know.

She hoisted the empty wicker laundry basket by its handles and headed for the kitchen door, excited to see him, even if any sparks of romance that had once ignited between them were now mere embers aglow, barely warm enough to sustain a friendship.

❧

Good heavens, but she made a pretty sight in that yellow gingham dress. A curly wisp of hair had fallen across her dark chocolate eyes, and she whisked it away with a toss of her head, then smiled at him. It was almost enough to make him blow his cover right there, and he nearly confessed his love and dropped down on one knee to ask for her hand—this time, not for the sake of convenience, but because he loved her with every bone in his body.

But the timing was off, and he felt far from spontaneous enough, not to mention he hadn't bought a ring. It didn't help that his dumb ego got in the way, but he feared—not without reason—that she'd turn him down. What if she rejected him yet again? He'd almost lost count. Maybe she simply wasn't interested—never was, never would be. What if she knew that she could never love him? She seemed set for life in her newly remodeled house, and it was altogether possible she wouldn't want to leave, now that it was such a comfortable, secure dwelling. She was so blamed self-sufficient, it amazed him that she'd even agreed to stay with the Grants two whole weeks after leaving the hospital with Gracie.

If he were ever going to win her over, he had to play this game right. And the best way to do that, besides asking God for divine direction, was to take it slow and easy. He'd never imagined asking relationship advice from a seventy-eight-year-old, but his grandfather was doggone smart about a lot of things, including romance. "You've got to keep her guessing a little, son," he'd advised. "You've already proposed, and she's turned you down. Might not hurt to make her think she missed her chance."

Inside the house, Eli raced Andy across the room to baby Gracie.

"Aww, no f-fair," Andy whined when Eli won.

Eli laughed. "Yes, fair. You get to see her all the time."

"Fine. I'll b-be in the ki-kitchen." With that, Andy wandered off.

He went to relieve Sofie of her bundle, his arms brushing hers in the exchange.

Their eyes met, but she quickly lowered hers to the baby.

"How's she doing?" he asked, stroking Gracie's smooth-as-silk forehead. At his touch, she squirmed and let out a squeaky sigh.

The two of them laughed softly as they gazed down at her, as if she were the eighth wonder of the world. Oddly enough, Eli never thought of Owen when he looked at Gracie, considering her to be Sofie's child alone, and the warm spot in his heart grew a hundredfold every time he held her. *I need to marry this family,* he silently resolved, *because I'll be darned if I don't love all three of them!*

"She's doing very well." Sofie's reply jolted him back to his senses, and he put on his doctor cap once more.

"Is she sleeping soundly?"

"She wakes up only when she's hungry...which is pretty often."

"Remember, she's still supposed to be inside you, so she's busy growing in her sleep."

Sofie gave a slow nod.

He continued his informal exam. "It looks like the rash she had a couple of weeks ago has improved."

"Yes, it's almost gone." She leaned closer to him and peeked over the blanket.

Her floral scent was like an arrow from Cupid, shot squarely in the center of his chest. "And she's feeding well?"

At that, she stepped back, and he could tell by the tiny pink specks suddenly dappling her cheeks that he'd embarrassed her. Cupid's arrow embedded itself even deeper.

She recovered quickly, even producing a diminutive smile. "Like a hungry little racehorse."

He chuckled. "Excellent." He studied the babe's petite features. "She looks like you, you know."

"That's what Margie says."

"Which means she's a real beauty."

Her blush blazed down her neck. "Well...thank you."

Slow and easy, he reminded himself. *Not too fast with the compliments. "Keep her guessing a little, son."*

He turned toward the kitchen, where something simmered on the stove, filling the space with a tantalizing aroma. "Something smells mighty fine."

"Oh, I should check on our supper. I hope you don't mind Swiss steak and mashed potatoes. It was one of my mother's specialties." As Sofie moved into the kitchen, he couldn't help but watch the gentle sway of her hips and the flow of her skirt as it swirled against her shapely calves. She'd regained a fit physique in almost no time. In fact, to look at her, no one would suspect she'd given birth just one month ago.

He'd known her only with a protruding belly, to which he'd easily grown accustomed. But now that her petite figure was unencumbered with a baby, he thought it might take a while to stop gawking. Why, even her face seemed finer, her complexion fresher.

At the stove, she turned around to face him. "Eli? Does that sound alright?"

"What?" Good grief! He needed a hearty slap. "Oh, yes, I love Swiss steak!" *Among other things.*

She blew out a soft sigh. "Good. I was a little worried for a moment, there."

You should be, he thought, his eyes trained on her. "Since Grandfather and Winnie have transitioned to her house, I'm fending for myself and eating a lot of peanut butter sandwiches."

"The house is officially yours, then?" She opened the oven door and bent to peer inside.

"It is. We made it official with an attorney after they returned from their honeymoon. I still can't believe I'm living in that big old house. I've never heard it so quiet." *Careful, or she'll think you're making a not-so-subtle hint that you'd like her to fill the silence.* "But I enjoy the solitude," he fibbed.

A gentle laugh came out of her. "I enjoy solitude, as well, but I don't expect to enjoy any of that for years to come."

He finally took his eyes off Sofie and looked down at Gracie, squirming in his arms. It warmed his heart how her little fingers had wrapped themselves around his index finger. "Babies do have a way of keeping things lively."

"They surely do, but it's worth every second," she answered.

❦

The three of them enjoyed genial conversation over dinner, while Gracie Joy slept soundly in her cradle in the living room, where a gentle breeze drifted in through the window. Sofie congratulated herself on a steak that fairly fell off the bone at the touch of a fork, and she thought it tasted as good as Mama's, if not a little better. Sometimes, she missed her mother more than words could express, especially now that she had Gracie Joy. How she wished she could watch her parents hold their granddaughter. How she longed to share with them how God had taken such an appalling circumstance and turned it into something entirely sweet and precious and good.

Andy finished his meal first, and so, when Georgie stopped over to see if he could come out to play, Sofie allowed it, instructing him to be home by eight thirty, in time for his Saturday night bath.

Once he'd scooted out the door, leaving Sofie alone with Eli and the sleeping baby, she scrambled for something to talk about. "How is Mrs. Downing working out so far?"

She'd caught Eli between bites, and so he chewed, swallowed, and took a quick sip of water before replying. "Good! Very well, in fact. It helps that she has experience, and that she knows so many people in the community is a bonus.

"She organized the files to her liking within a week's time and also set up a better system for seeing patients. She keeps me on a tight schedule, which has been a relief. And she even tidies up the lobby area and my office with a dusting cloth and sweeper a couple of times a week, as well as keeps the exam room clean. I told her we could hire someone else to take care of the housekeeping, but she won't hear of it. I tell you, she's a wonder, the way she works circles around me. I'm blessed to have found her."

Sofie didn't know why it bothered her that he spoke so enthusiastically about Mrs. Downing, other than that she'd taken the job he'd offered—several times—to her. He must be thanking his lucky stars that he hadn't pressed her on it, considering her lack of clerical experience. "I'm glad you're so satisfied. It would have been disastrous to hire someone with no expertise."

He eyed her in a sideways manner and lifted one brow. "You're not regretting your decision to turn down the job, are you?"

"What? No! Gracious, no. I made the right decision, and so did you."

He took a quick sip of water, then wiped his chin with his napkin. "Good. I'm glad to hear you say that. Besides, you got that call from Jackson Cleaners. That must have been a relief. When do you think you'll start?"

"I haven't quite decided. Soon, though." She dreaded the thought of being away from Gracie Joy, even though she had confidence in Margie's care. For one thing, she would have to desist with nursing and resort to feeding her with a bottle, and she worried that she might not react well to the change. She quickly reminded herself that God had everything under control. She'd been having to do a lot of that lately.

"Have you figured out the logistics, like how you're going to get to work, whether Margie's coming to your house or if you'll take Gracie to her, what your schedule will look like, and if you're going to work a night shift again?"

He was certainly full of questions. Unfortunately, each of them was legitimate. With a long sigh, she rose from her chair and started gathering the dinner dishes. "It's a lot to think about right now, so I've been putting it off."

"Ah, the old 'If I don't think about it, maybe I won't have to make a decision' approach." He was teasing her, but his comment struck her at the core. She tried to smile but found she couldn't, so she turned and carried a stack of soiled dishes into the kitchen. He joined in her efforts, and they met at the sink. "If you had a car, I could give you some driving lessons."

She gave a soft chortle as she turned on the faucet, then began rinsing dishes, while he returned to the table and brought back an assortment of dishes and serving bowls. "I'm serious," he went on. "You could find yourself a decent used vehicle for an affordable price. Be sensible, Sofie. You can't possibly think that riding your bike to and from this new job is a good idea. It's even farther away than Spic-and-Span."

"Maybe I'll just get a newer, more reliable bike," she returned with a wink.

"Oh, there you go! That makes a lot more sense."

She laughed at his sarcasm, and he joined in, bumping gently against her.

They made quick work of the dishes, Sofie washing, Eli drying, and the matter of the car was dropped. Instead, they talked about a wide range of other subjects, from Doc Trent and Winnie's wedding trip to Owen's trial, scheduled sometime in early winter, to the upcoming church picnic. Eli asked if she planned to go, and she was half tempted to say, "Shall I consider that an invitation?" but she merely shrugged and said she'd yet to decide.

Andy returned at eight thirty, hot, sweaty, and red in the face from running through the neighborhood and playing hide-and-seek with Georgie and several other kids. He talked at a rapid pace as he relayed to them how he'd found a toad and dropped it into the side pocket of ten-year-old Rosie Mayberry while she was hiding behind a bush, and that her scream upon discovering it had blown her cover.

After laughing at his antics, Sofie told him to go take a bath.

"Aww," he complained. "C-can't I play a game of Ch-Chinese checkers with Eli first?"

She'd been about to grant him permission when Eli begged off, saying he needed to go home and spend a few hours studying one of his medical journals. Her disappointment ran deep that he didn't wait for Andy to exit the room before bidding her good-bye. He tip-toed over to the cradle for a parting peek at the sleeping babe, then ruffled Andy's hair and told him to be sure to wash behind his ears. Buster had come over, tail wagging, and he petted the pooch's head before opening the screen door and stepping outside, closing it behind him.

On the porch, he turned around and spoke through the screen. "Thanks again for the delicious dinner, Sofie. I had a great time. Will I see you two in church tomorrow?"

No offer to stop by and pick them up? Her throat developed a bit of a lump. "I...I believe we're going to Howard and Margie's church."

"Oh. Well, you have a nice Sunday, then." And no mention of spending tomorrow afternoon with them? Her heart took a little tumble.

With a smile, Eli turned and skipped down the steps, whistling as he walked to his car.

Blast that man! Sofie sulked. *He touched everybody but me. Even Buster got a pat on the head.*

As she stood at the living room window and watched him drive away, she couldn't help wondering if she had tasted the last of his lips.

Chapter Thirty

For thou, LORD, art good, and ready to
forgive; and plenteous in mercy unto all them
that call upon thee.
—Psalm 86:5

The days passed by in steady succession, and before Eli knew it, August was winding down to its final week. It had been relatively slow, for a Monday—Mrs. Downing had arranged to take the afternoon off, and she'd purposely planned a lighter schedule for him that day. So, when Grandfather stopped in to see if he had time to go to lunch, he jumped at the opportunity to get out of the office.

The afternoon was beautiful and balmy, with bright blue skies and low humidity, so they decided to walk the seven blocks to Livvie's Kitchen. While Grandfather often joked about the woes of growing old, it seemed to Eli that he still had the strength and energy of someone half his age, the way he walked so straight and tall, and with a rapid, even gait. He stayed active on the hospital board and at church, as well as devoted his time to reading, gardening, and various other hobbies. Eli suspected his marriage to Winnie had something to do with his youthful demeanor. Amazing how love could change a person's very countenance and even put a bounce in his step.

"It still seems strange, Buford Morris's being gone," Grandfather mused as they strolled west on Sinclair, passing beneath the shade of several sprawling oaks, the canopy of their long branches draping over the sidewalk and extending into the street. "Not sure why I keep thinking about him."

"I've have a hard time coming to terms with it myself," Eli remarked, "but I hear his chief deputy, Dan Fett, is doing a fine job in his stead and will probably win the upcoming election. Folks say Fett's an upstanding citizen who knows the law and abides by it—somewhat unusual for a sheriff in these parts, apparently." He paused. "Did you hear Clara Morris gave the authorities access to Buford's garage? They cleared out quite the stash." Eli turned to grin at his grandfather. "Mrs. Downing has been a faithful informant, in case you wondered about my source. I believe she even manages to stay one step ahead of the *Plain Dealer*."

Grandfather tossed back his head and chuckled. "Did she also tell you about Orville Dotson? He was arrested and charged with operating an illegal still. No doubt he'll serve a long sentence—longer than his previous term, which apparently wasn't enough to keep him out of trouble."

Eli shook his head. "She didn't mention that, but that's not to say she didn't know about it." A couple of young bicyclists pedaled past them, a black dog running alongside, and the sight made him think of Sofie and Andy. "What do you think will be the final outcome for Owen Morris?"

"Oh, he's had his last taste of freedom, I'd say. He'll be handed down a life sentence with no parole. I hear the public defender doesn't have much in the way of defense, and the prosecutor will probably attempt a plea bargain, which will serve only to keep that boy from getting lynched. If the prosecutor can talk Owen into a plea, it would eliminate the need for a trial and save the taxpayers a good deal in court costs. Only time will tell. I'm confident Sofie will be up to the task if she's called to the stand, though. She's a strong young woman."

"She is that," Eli said with a bit of a sigh. He hadn't driven out there in almost a week, due to his busy schedule, what with daily appointments back-to-back with nights spent on call at the hospital. He missed the little family terribly. "She was to have started her new job today. I'm anxious to learn how it went."

"Is she working days this time?"

"Yeah, Jackson Cleaners advertises office and home cleaning services, so, for now, she'll work days cleaning homes for private clients."

"Well, that's a nice switch for her, working days. I hope she's not planning to ride that broken-down bicycle to work."

"Mrs. Grant's offered to take her to and from work every day. Of course, she doesn't like the idea, considering Margie's already going to watch Gracie Joy and Andy, and she won't take any money for her troubles, either. Margie's like a mother to her. As you can about imagine, Sofie hates being so reliant on her, but I told her it's that or buy a car—something cheap yet reliable. To be honest, though, I don't think she'll earn enough to purchase a vehicle, certainly not to maintain one."

He felt his grandfather's assessing gaze. "Well, it's certainly a blessing Howard and Margie are so faithful in looking out for them. They always have been, ever since the death of Sofia's parents. But what that girl needs now, I'm afraid, is a loving husband and father for Gracie Joy."

Eli kicked a small pebble and watched it skitter several feet. "I'm working on that, Grandfather."

Livvie's Kitchen buzzed with customers, though Eli didn't think the restaurant had ever seen a slow day. He liked the Taylors, found them to be genuinely kind and generous individuals who contributed a lot to the community.

An aged loyal customer named Coot Hermanson and a couple of his cronies sat at a table by the window, sipping steaming mugs of coffee. His faithful black dog lay curled on the floor at his feet. From what Eli had heard, the dog had played a major role in saving Livvie's life, and the mutt had been a welcome visitor at the restaurant ever since, sleeping away the hours and receiving meaty snacks between his naps. On the front door hung a sign that read:

> *No Pets Allowed,*
> *Unless You Happen to Be a Black Hound*
> *Dog Who Answers to the Name of Reggie.*

They found a small table and got themselves situated. A middle-aged woman whose name tag read "Cora Mae" approached, all smiles, and plunked down two glasses of water in front of them. "Afternoon, gentlemen. What can I get for you today?"

They placed their orders of chicken sandwiches, and off she went to the next table full of customers.

They covered a variety of topics, from medicine to last Sunday's sermon, from last month's flood to the current utter lack of rain, from Mrs. Downing's clerical skills to Winnie's cooking, which was as fabulous as ever.

"I sure miss her meals," Eli confessed.

"You know you're welcome to dine with us as often as you have a hankering."

"And impose on the newlyweds?"

"The old newlyweds," Grandfather said with a wink. "So, do you have a plan for popping that all-important question to Sofia? For the second time, I mean."

"I've been formulating one, but I have to fine-tune the timing if I'm going to pull it off."

Grandfather finished off his water and set the glass back down, expelling a loud breath. "Be sure to let me know if you need someone to bounce ideas off of. I may be seventy-eight, but I haven't lost my touch, and it never hurts to keep honing my skills."

Eli gave a hearty chuckle. "As you've said before, at thirty-two, one would think I'd be a little less bubble-headed when it came to women, but I tell you that girl rattles me so much, I can't even think straight. I'll certainly keep your offer in mind. In the meantime, you might pray for me—around the clock, if at all possible."

The old man grinned. "Winnie and I will take shifts."

❧

The weekend before Sofie's new job was scheduled to start, Andy, baby Gracie, and she had stayed with Margie, mostly to keep her company while Howard was in Indianapolis for an agricultural convention. On Monday morning, Sofie'd had to borrow her friend's bicycle, since Margie's car had refused to start, and, with Howard out of town, they'd had no alternate vehicle at their disposal. The trek to Jackson Cleaners had been more exhausting than she'd bargained for—no wonder, since she hadn't had opportunity to engage in much physical activity since the baby's birth.

She hoped with every push of the pedals on her way back that evening that Margie's car would be fixed. That way, not only would she have a ride to work in the morning, but she and the baby and Andy could return to their little house on River Road. Margie would be glad for a little peace and quiet.

Oh, she could use a car. She could use a husband, too, as adamantly as she'd always denied the fact. But it appeared Elijah Trent had lost interest, probably since his earlier motivation for marrying her had all but dissipated. They hadn't seen him for several days, so he had yet to learn that Gracie Joy had started rewarding Andy and her with the tiniest of smiles, and that she had made an almost seamless transition from breast to bottle—not that Sofie would be eager to divulge that information. The weaning process hadn't been as difficult as she'd expected, and now, with Andy able to help feed the baby, Sofie was enjoying greater freedom, both to rest and to accomplish the household chores more efficiently.

Her first day of work had been fine—and tiring, to be sure. She'd been paired with another woman to clean three different residences, all of them stately mansions with ornate furnishings and décor, requiring much more bending, stooping, scrubbing, and polishing than Sofie was accustomed to performing. She'd even had to climb a ladder to dust the chandeliers, which seemed to adorn most of the rooms. Her workmate—a rather plaintive sort, who seemed to have an ache or pain in every part of her body—had essentially supervised, giving her feather duster a shake from time to time, while Sofie had done all of the hard labor. She would have to find a way to be more assertive if they were to continue working together, and she found herself worrying her lower lip as she pedaled along, the breezes blowing her cotton skirt every which direction.

She reached Margie's at precisely 5:35, happy to have finally arrived and half tempted to drop the bike and collapse beside it on the ground. Instead, she parked it along the side of the house and dragged herself inside, feeling rejuvenated with every step closer to seeing her daughter again.

Upon entering the house, she found Margie standing in the kitchen, laboring at the stove. She lifted her face and greeted her with a cheery smile. "There's the working woman! How was your first day?"

"Positively dandy." But she found that her attempt to match Margie's smile utterly failed.

Margie chuckled. "Well, that's to be expected, I guess. Everything went fine here. Gracie's sound asleep in the crib upstairs, and your brother's spent most of the day outside, helping Joe Striker, the hired hand. Don't ask me what all Joe's been having him do. All I know is, every time that boy comes inside, usually for a glass of lemonade or a cookie, he says he wants to be a farmer when he grows up. I'm sure we'll hear all about it at the dinner table."

"Dinner? I...I guess I'd hoped you could take us home before then. We've already eaten you out of house and home, Margie. I can easily make a simple supper at my place. Really."

"Nonsense! You'll eat here. Besides, I can't drive you home just yet. Wilbur Godfrey called a bit ago to say that the car isn't finished. Guess he had to order some part or another. He said he expects to be able to deliver it sometime tomorrow afternoon." Margie gave her a thorough perusal. "You have time for a bath. Supper's at six. And we're having company."

"Company?"

Margie went back to stirring a kettle of gravy, her eyes focused on her chore. "Yes. Dr. Trent is coming for dinner."

"Eli!" Her pulse quickened as a wave of elation washed over her, and she nearly lost her ability to breathe. "I haven't even seen him in a week or more! Was this your idea?"

"No, honey. He called here, wanting to know how you were doing. He said he's been so busy in the office, plus working double shifts at the hospital the last four nights."

A sigh of relief mixed with joy wafted out of her.

"He offered to take you all home after supper, and he also insisted on picking you up in the morning, dropping Andy and baby Gracie off here on your way to work."

"Oh." Another time, she might have objected, but, really, why protest? Besides, the idea of sitting next to him in the front seat again highly appealed, and actually, the notion of actually depending on him had become a welcome idea.

Dinner was pleasant, with tasty food and amiable talk. Andy did not dominate the conversation, for a change; evidently, a long day spent working in the barn had robbed him of most of his energy. Eli inquired about Sofie's new job, and she asked him about his busy week. While gently rocking Gracie back and forth and patting her back to coax a burp out of her, Margie told about the farm convention Howard was attending, and Andy declared what Margie had already told her: he wanted to be a farmer when he grew up.

"I think farming would suit you just fine," Eli told him. "In about ten years, you'll buy yourself a nice chunk of acreage if you start faithfully saving every cent you make between now and then. It's a nice goal to work toward."

Sofie could envision it herself, the way Andy and nature went together like French fries and ketchup. He would purchase a land parcel, find a wonderful woman to marry, and build a successful farming business. But what was she doing orchestrating her brother's future when she couldn't even figure out her own? She spent the remainder of the time listening to Eli and Margie converse and dreamed of what life would be like if the four of them were a family.

Around seven o'clock, Sofie rose and started to gather the dishes. "You lay those right down, Sofia Mae," Margie insisted. "I intend to clean up later, after my radio program. It's time Eli took you home so you can rest up for tomorrow. You look plumb tuckered out, if you ask me."

Now it was Sofie's turn to act out of character. She didn't protest.

When Eli made the turn onto River Road, Andy pointed at the house. "Who-s that?"

Squinting against the fast-descending sun, Sofie made out the figures of two women retreating down the walkway toward a car parked along the curb in front of the house. She gasped, nearly choking on her own breath. "It's Clara Morris and her daughter, Carolee."

Eli put his foot to the brake pedal. "Do you want me to drive on by?"

She hesitated a moment. "No, it's alright. I'll see what they want, but...you'll stay with us while they're here, won't you?"

He delivered a reassuring pat to her arm. "You know I will. Don't worry."

"Yeah, don't w-worry, Sofie," said Andy with an air of authority. "We'll protect you."

A dozen or more thoughts ricocheted through her brain, each more dreadful than the one before. Had Clara Morris come to give her a piece of her mind? To cast blame on her for the awful things that had happened? Perhaps she intended to testify in court that Sofie had seduced her son, or, worse, maybe she planned to lay claim to her grandchild and argue that Sofie was unfit to care for her. The possibilities multiplied in her mind, making her quiver with fear and dread.

Eli parked behind the Morrises' car and cut the engine. Clara Morris and Carolee stopped in their tracks, their chins dropping, their expressions marked by mortification, apparently at having been caught lurking about. Eli got out of the car and came around to Sofie's door to help her and the baby out, and Andy climbed out after them. The two parties stared at each other, unmoving, unspeaking.

"I'm sorry to bother you, Sofia," Clara said after a moment. "Carolee and I didn't mean to alarm you. I merely wanted to bring over something for...the baby...just a small gift. We left it up there on your porch." Across the distance, she cast a longing look at the bundle in Sofie's arms, and she felt a surge of emotion, albeit unidentified, rush through her. Eli's hand, pressed supportively against the center of her back, lent her strength, but he remained quiet. He must have been just as shocked that Clara Morris had come bearing gifts.

The woman shifted uncomfortably. "I also wanted to say I...I'm sorry for everything you've suffered at the hand of my son. I'm sorry, too, for the way I treated you. The other ladies and I...we were wrong to shun you. I had no idea my own son...and with my own prescription, no less...well, it's plain awful, that's all. And...and now, I've said my piece, so...good-bye."

With a sad smile, Carolee gave a tiny nod, then walked to their car, opened the passenger door, and started to duck inside the vehicle, her mother doing the same through the driver's door.

Perhaps it was the identical slump to their shoulders, the utter lack of joy on their faces, or just the sheer irony of it all—Sofie didn't know. She knew only what she needed to do. "Wait!"

They both hesitated and looked back at her, their eyes emitting hopeful glimmers.

"Would you like to see my baby?"

They lingered only a few minutes, as the situation was awkward, to say the least. But, at the same time, it was right. It hardly seemed possible, Sofie standing face-to-face with the mother and sister of her attacker, and yet she didn't see Owen in them, any more than she saw him reflected in her precious, innocent daughter. Still, she didn't invite them inside. Even if she had, she doubted they would have accepted.

"She favors you," Clara said, gently folding back the pink blanket to get a better glimpse of the babe. "And I'm happy that she does." When their eyes met, Sofie understood what she meant and nodded silently.

"She's beautiful" was Carolee's wonder-struck declaration.

Andy and Eli stood protectively on either side of Sofie. Even so, she didn't offer to let Clara or Carolee hold the baby. Perhaps, she was being selfish. And, perhaps, in the future, things would be different. But today was not that day. Her wounds were too fresh, her scars still too raw.

She turned her focus to the Morrises' miserable state of affairs. For the life of her, she couldn't think of anything else to say than, "I'm very sorry for your loss."

Clara gave a glum smile. "Ours was hardly a model marriage, but the circumstances of Buford's death...well, it's quite difficult to deal with, as you can imagine."

Sofie could do little but nod—and be ever so grateful for Eli's presence.

"I'm just sorry we didn't do a better job raising Owen. He was always a hard one to figure out. My husband lost patience with him time and again, and I...well, there came a time when I didn't know what to say or do to make him mind, and then he became so combative that he often frightened me." A tremor in her voice led Sofie to fear the woman might be standing on the brink of an emotional breakdown. Carolee put a steadying arm around her mother's shoulder, showing a depth of maturity Sofie had witnessed many times, in her brother.

Compassion overtook her. "Everyone has been given the gift of free will, Mrs. Morris." She paused. Dare she say it? "You are not to blame for Owen's poor decisions. You did the best you could, and now, you must forgive yourself. And pray that God will touch his heart and change him."

The woman gazed at her through moist eyes. "You are quite amazing, Sofia. Thank you for your display of faith and courage."

"It's never too late, you know. You can release your feelings of disappointment and sorrow to the Lord and let Him breathe His peace into your very lungs. He did it for me, and I know He can do it for you both, as well. I don't know if this will be of any help, but you should know that I don't hate Owen, nor do I harbor any bitterness against him. The only reason I am able to say that is because of the way God redeems awful circumstances and turns them into something good. I hope that, someday down the road, you, too, will find a measure of peace and comfort in your storm."

Tears trickled down Clara Morris's face. "I...we... we thank you for saying that...and for allowing us a glimpse of your little girl. Perhaps, another time,...I don't know...?"

"Yes, another time, I'm sure of it." Sofie smiled. "I'll let you know, how is that?"

"That would be very nice," said Carolee, turning her mother around by the shoulders and directing her to the car. When they reached the vehicle, they both glanced around once more before climbing inside.

As they pulled away from the curb and started down River Road, Carolee rolled down her window and gave a tentative wave of her hand.

Sofie hesitated, then gently lifted the arm of the sleeping Gracie and moved it to return the gesture.

Chapter Thirty-one

By mercy and truth iniquity is purged: and
by the fear of the LORD men depart from evil.
—Proverbs 16:6

I want to thank you for staying while Clara and Carolee Morris were here," Sofie said to Eli as they stood at the door after tucking in a whipped Andy and laying the baby in her crib. Eli had expressed a need to head home for some more studying. "I really didn't know what to expect," Sofie went on. "All manner of things ran through my mind as to why they might have come to see me. Knowing Clara Morris's fondness for gossip, I imagined that she'd come with a vengeful spirit. Truly, an apology was the last thing I'd expected, but I'm glad she said what she did. I didn't need it to hear it as much as I think she needed to say it, and I hope she found a measure of peace as a result. I feel sorry for Carolee. She must be brokenhearted, poor thing."

Eli gazed down at Sofie's weary face, finding it most difficult to keep his hands at his sides. "It's tragic on many, many levels, Sofie. It's almost too tragic to come to terms with. But you seem to be doing a pretty good job of it. What you said to Mrs. Morris was profoundly gracious. You could have told her from the beginning to leave the premises, and I wouldn't have blamed you. In fact, I would have personally seen to it that she complied. But it was words of love and forgiveness that seeped through your spirit and out of your mouth, and it was an incredible thing to see. I've come to admire you more than you'll ever know, and I think you're pretty doggone special, too."

"Oh, pooh!" She wrinkled her nose at him. "I don't think there's anything very special about me."

"Well then, you're just blinded by your own humility."

She dropped her head and let it fall against his chest. The act sent a shock of joy straight through him.

He raised his arms and enveloped her softness, drawing her close and delighting when she acquiesced.

"You are far more special than you will ever know." He kissed her hair, then drew back and lifted her chin, kissing one closed eye and then the other. Next, he moved to her cheeks and, finally, her mouth. But he didn't prolong the kiss, and for good reason. "Oh, man, Sofia Mae." He spoke in a low voice he hardly recognized as his. "I'd better go now. You need your sleep." He wanted her to get some much-needed rest before a hungry Gracie woke her up.

She opened two pouty brown eyes, and he nearly caved in. He hadn't expected to feel such a powerful need for her. "Already?" she whispered.

He pressed his face against her soft curls and inhaled the scent of her. Vanilla bean and something floral. He sighed, knowing that if he didn't leave right now, he would regret it later—he might even have cause to beg the Lord to forgive him for departing from His statutes on love and marriage. So, he planted another kiss, soft and quick, on her lips and then set her back with a humorless laugh. "Yes, already. I'll pick you up tomorrow at seven. How does that sound?"

Despondency raced across her countenance, but there was no hope for it. He simply had to go before he gave in to her. He touched her cheek and quietly closed the door behind him, knowing he'd left her wondering if she'd done something wrong.

On the way to his car, he looked up at the stars and laughed in near jubilation when a realization dawned on him. *She wants me, and I'm about to steal that independent streak right out from under her.*

As promised, he arrived at Sofie's house at seven on the dot. Andy dragged himself out to the car, not quite awake yet, accompanied by Eli, carrying a large bag of various supplies for Gracie. Eli tousled the boy's tangled head of hair. "Wake up, kiddo. I bet there're going to be some eggs that need gathering and a certain foal that needs some attention when you get to Margie's place."

That brought him to life. "Yeah! An' Mr. Striker told me he'd let me sit up on the tractor with him today, maybe even drive it around the field on my own, when we finish the chores."

"Well, see? There you go."

"And I'm prob'ly going to feed the kittens and the goats, too."

Eli stopped the lad with a hand and stared down at him. "Do you know you just said two entire sentences without a single stammer? Good job!"

They resumed their trek to the car. "Th-that's s-somethin', ain't it?"

Eli chuckled to himself. He'd spoken too soon. Actually, he'd made the mistake of drawing attention to Andy's success. Best to ignore it most times and let the boy work it out himself. He suspected that by the time Andy reached adulthood, no one would be able to tell he'd had an impediment, unless he became overly excited. By then, he would have developed a track record of triumphs enough to overcome any insecurity. And Eli wanted to be around when that day came.

He opened the rear door and hoisted in the bulging bag. Andy climbed in the backseat just as Sofie walked out of the house and locked the door, carrying Gracie, asleep against her bosom.

At the top of the steps, she looked up, surveying the cloudless sky. "Looks like we're in for another hot one. We could do with some rain, couldn't we? My poor lawn has gotten so brown."

It was the same way at Eli's—a yard of beige, bone-dry grass, despite his efforts with the water hose on the rare night he was at home. Even his flower beds could do with a little more attention, although they had a way of flourishing on their own. Sofie would have them in tip-top shape if she got her hands on them. He supposed he could hire a gardener, but he much preferred the idea of having the "live-in" kind.

The time for "popping that all-important question," as Grandfather had worded it, was drawing closer, and his plan unfolded in greater detail in his head with every passing day.

❧

Lying on his back atop the narrow cot in his nine-foot-square cell, Owen brooded as he counted the flies circling overhead. He hated this place—the malicious guards, the stinking food, and the cold, damp floors. He also hated Lester, Elmer, and Marvin. Some friends they were, tattling to Deputy Dan Fett that they'd heard him slip and say something about Sofie while they'd been drinking out at the Chester farm. A person couldn't trust anybody these days, not that he'd ever really trusted those fools in the first place.

A door at the end of the hall opened, and the sound of approaching footsteps brought him to a sitting position. "Wake up, Morris. You got company."

He swept a hand down his face. Who would have come to visit him? His heart dropped a little at the sight of his mother and Carolee. His mother looked weary, her tired-looking eyes bloodshot, the skin beneath them sagging. She was a weak woman, always had been. He remembered how she used to jump at the sound of his dad's voice. After a while, she'd grown more comfortable when she'd learned to let him have his way. She'd put up a fight, from time to time, but his dad had emerged from every argument the clear victor.

Owen wondered if she'd come to thank him for ending her years of misery. It was the first he'd seen her and Carolee since he'd delivered that well-deserved blow to his dad's jaw. He hadn't meant for him to die, of course, but it was what it was.

His mother gave a tentative smile. "How are you, Owen?"

"Oh, I'm livin' the high life. You like my outfit?" With a sour laugh, he gestured at the striped, one-piece getup they'd dressed him in on his arrival at the prison. Every week, they issued him a new, "clean" one that reeked of bleach. "Anybody want to trade places with me?"

There was no response, just blank stares. Much fun they were.

"I've come to tell you I'm sorry for the way your father treated you," his mother said, "and I wish I'd done more, but I never knew what...how...I don't know. I'm just sorry it came to this."

He hadn't expected an apology, and, for a second, he didn't know how to respond. Somehow, he needed to regain the upper hand. "Yeah," he finally said, "and I'm just sorry I didn't do it a lot sooner."

His mother and sister gasped in unison. Just the reaction he was looking for.

Carolee recovered first, drawing her shoulders back. "That was a terrible thing you did to Sofia Rogers, Owen. Despicable."

"Shut up. I didn't do nothin' to her she didn't want to happen."

His mother bristled with another look of shock, from which he derived great satisfaction.

After a few moments, her expression sobered, and she cleared her throat. "You know that isn't true. But Sofie told us that she doesn't hate you, Owen, or hold any bitterness against you. She forgives you, because of God's grace and mercy."

"Pfff, yeah? When did she tell you that?"

"Mama and I went out to visit her," said Carolee. "We got to see the baby."

A stupid knot stuck in the center of his throat. "Well, good for you."

His mother stepped closer and clutched the bars of his cell with both hands. "Owen, in his homily last Sunday, Father Harry said that bitterness brews hatred. He's right. The only way to let it go is to surrender your life to Jesus. I've made a lot of mistakes over my lifetime, but, for the first time, I feel I'm experiencing God's forgiveness, and I pray that, one day, you'll experience the same thing. It doesn't matter the extent of one's sin. Salvation is a free gift. Father Harry said—"

He put up a hand. "Don't say another word about Father Harry, or any other religious quack, for that matter. It's all a bunch of baloney. Why don't you both just go?"

"You're wrong, Owen." Carolee shook her head. "But we'll leave it to God to convince you. Mama and I just wanted to stop by and see how you were doing. We also brought you something." She slipped a book between the bars.

He looked at the tome but made no move to reach for it. "I don't want no Bible."

"It's a book of prayers and short Scripture passages. You might want to read a page or two every now and again."

He took the dumb book, just to get them off his back, and tossed it on the cot behind him.

"We'll be going, now. Come on, Mama."

They turned to go, but his mother paused and glanced back, her eyes now damp in the corners. "I love you, Owen. Regardless of the terrible things you've done, you're still my son, and you aren't unredeemable."

He could have spouted off a nasty retort, but he didn't. Instead, he stepped up to the bars and watched the guard usher them back down the hall. When the big steel door closed, he lurched at the thunderous sound. His mouth went as dry as sand, as unquenchable thirst suddenly overtook him. He turned and shuffled over to the tiny sink. As he did, he glanced down at the book his sister had given him, lying coverside up on his cot. *Streams in the Desert* was the title.

Thirst of a different nature began to well up in a dry, dark, and desolate region of his soul—a place where no light had ever shone. And, for the first time in his life, he wondered if there might be something more.

❋

Sofie didn't love her job. She barely liked it, in fact. But it paid enough to cover their needs—they had food on the table, and their bills were paid on time—and, for that, she praised God every day.

Margie continued to drive her to and from work most days, with Eli filling in once or twice a week, when his schedule permitted. Today was one of those days, and Sofie found herself standing expectantly at the front window, awaiting a glimpse of his car coming down the street. Not that their brief travel time allowed for any deep conversation, but she relished every second spent with him.

If he felt the same, he didn't say, and the kisses he'd been dispensing had amounted to nothing more than short pecks that always left her wanting more. Whenever he drove her home from work, he stayed for supper, but he spent the moments before and after mealtime outside with Andy, coaching him with his baseball swing or his football throw. Recently, Georgie and several other neighborhood kids had been coming over whenever Eli was around, and they'd choose teams and play ball till the sun went down.

Sofie thought it wonderful that Eli was so fond of children, and she especially appreciated the attention he paid little Gracie, showering her soft cheeks with kisses and coaxing smiles from her. But she couldn't help thinking she could do with a few showers of kisses, herself, and she began to wonder if he didn't drive her to work just to see Andy and Gracie. Could it be that his heart for the downtrodden—a category in which he surely placed them—kept his affections platonic rather than romantic? She couldn't figure him out, and it plain irked her. He'd proposed marriage, after all, but now it seemed that the matter was closed altogether. Maybe she ought to just ask him herself—come right out with those four little words: *Will you marry me?*

❧

Today was the day, and Eli carefully reviewed every detail in his head, to make sure he hadn't forgotten anything. He had the jitters, to be sure, so much so that he couldn't keep up with Andy's incessant chatter on the drive to the Grants' house. Sofie sat in silence in the front seat, gazing out the window, with Gracie Joy asleep in her lap. She had something on her mind, he could tell.

When he'd asked her about it, she'd assured him that everything was fine, but her curt tone had convinced him otherwise. Had he said or done something to set her off? Her silence made him wonder if he ought to go through with this thing, but, doggone it, he'd made all the arrangements, and he loved her! He couldn't turn back now. *Oh, Lord, please don't let my little plan go awry.*

When they arrived at the Grants', Eli and Sofie visited with the couple for a few minutes before saying their good-byes, getting back in the car, and heading toward town. Again, Sofie kept her gaze directed out the side window.

"Is everything alright?" Eli had to ask.

"You already asked me that, and I said I was fine." There came that terseness again.

"Oh." *Lord, have I pushed too far?* "Have I said or done something to upset you?"

"No, nothing. It's just...."

He cast a quick glance at her as he veered the car onto Mill Creek Pike. "What? It's just what?"

"Oh, I don't know. I feel stuck, I guess."

"Stuck? What do you mean by that?"

"It's hard to put it into words. My job...I just wish things could be different, that's all."

"How so?"

She gawked at him as if he'd grown a second nose. "You really don't know?"

He hated it when a woman expected him to read her mind. "No, I guess not. Why are you looking at me like that?"

"I'm not looking at you in any particular way."

"Yes, you are."

She folded her arms across her slim stomach and stared straight ahead. It was hard to keep an eye on her, with all of the curves in the road, plus all of the turns he had to make onto various side roads to put them, at last, on Wabash Street.

"What's wrong with your job?" he ventured to ask.

"I don't currently happen to like it."

He decided to play along, see if he could get a hint of how things would go for him later. "I thought you wanted a job so you could support your family. You said you liked your independence."

"I did? I mean, yes, I do—I guess. I don't remember actually putting it in just that way."

He chuckled. "One of your favorite lines is, 'I can manage.'" She didn't seem to find any humor in that. "What exactly don't you like about your job?"

"It's hard. Not the job itself, but having to be away from Gracie all day...I never imagined it would take such a toll."

"I can understand that, with her being so young; not to mention, she's your own child. You raised Andy from the age of five, but he was your brother, and not a baby."

"She needs me."

"Yes, she does." *And later I'll tell you how much I need you, as well, if you can just hold on.* "I wish life didn't have to be so hard. But, if we look around, we can always find someone who's a little worse off than we are, you know? You just have to learn to rely on God for strength and guidance to get you through the tough times. Things will get better, you'll see."

She tilted her face at him and chewed her lower lip. "I don't think that's the problem, though. I'm confident that God will take care of me, and I know that if I keep on trusting Him, He'll see me through the rough patches. He always has. But...."

"Yes?"

She folded her hands in her lap and looked down, giving him a glimpse of a tear in the corner of her eye. He hated that he couldn't offer the comfort she needed—not yet, anyway.

After a moment, she shook her head. "I'd rather not talk about this anymore. Never mind what I've said."

He reached over and patted her arm. "It's okay. We can talk about it more when you're ready."

She took a heavy breath loaded with frustration, then released it toward the window, causing the glass to fog up momentarily.

Eli kept his gaze on the road ahead, the corners of his lips twitching as he resisted the temptation to smile. This episode had been just the confirmation he'd needed that Sofie didn't want to live the rest of her life without him.

Chapter Thirty-two

Be glad in the LORD, and rejoice,
ye righteous: and shout for joy, all ye that
are upright in heart.
—Psalm 32:11

As she entered Jackson Cleaners, Sofie put on a cheery face, in spite of her dismal mood. What else could she do? She didn't really know her coworkers, and she couldn't afford to expose her anguish that she'd fallen hopelessly in love with a man who didn't have any idea. Maybe aloofness was the price one paid to be a brilliant doctor—adept at diagnosing and treating physical ailments but absolutely clueless when it came to matters of the heart—emotional matters, that is. How close she'd come to blurting out, "Do you still want to marry me, or have you changed your mind?" But she couldn't bring herself to be so bold, so she'd simply sat and stewed, praying the blinders would fall from his eyes.

Rich Jackson, her new boss, greeted her with a friendly grin. "'Mornin', Sofia. You're looking fine today."

She'd found her employer to be a well-mannered gentleman with a no-nonsense approach to business. "Thank you. Good morning to you, as well."

"Looks like I've got a busy lineup for you today."

She tried to appear enthusiastic. "You know I like to keep busy!"

Along the wall were several hooks on which workers could hang their belongings, so she chose one and draped the collar of her cardigan over it. Under the hooks were cabinets. She opened a door and set her sack lunch on a shelf, slid her purse in beside it, and then straightened, wiping her sweaty palms on the front of her skirt. It already promised to be a hot day, making her glad she'd donned her yellow sleeveless scoop-necked dress. It was one of her nicer outfits, and not exactly a work dress, but her options were limited, especially now that her maternity clothes were out of the question. Moreover, much of her pre-pregnancy wardrobe no longer fit; for some reason, she'd grown above the torso but shrunken from the waist down. "You are ladies, and I expect you to dress as such," Rich Jackson had explained during her orientation. Of course, the company provided aprons and caps, which they were also encouraged to wear since they displayed the company logo.

She stepped up to the desk that Mr. Jackson sat behind and others had gathered around so she could receive her orders for the day.

Every morning, Mr. Jackson delivered a pep talk to his employees about presenting a positive image to their clients, most of whom were from the upper crust of society. He urged them to go above and beyond the assignment, maintain a cheerful attitude at all times, and always, *always* strive to put the client first. The company motto, "It Isn't Clean Until Our Clients Say So," was painted in black above the door of the little brick building on the corner of Walnut and Wabash that housed Jackson Cleaners. Mr. Jackson expected his employees to commit the phrase to memory, and sometimes, when she closed her eyes at night, Sofie pictured the printed words or imagined her boss's voice recite them in singsong.

He began listing the various locations needing service that day and whom he intended to send where. Normally, they worked in teams, and Mr. Jackson transported them in his six-passenger sedan to their assigned sites. On hot days, it made for a most uncomfortable commute, as some of the ladies were anything but petite. Sofie generally found herself as good as seated on someone's lap.

He left her for last, dismissing the others to go out to his car. When the room emptied, he looked at her over his reading spectacles. "Sofia, I'll ask you to stay behind today and clean our office. After that, I'll take you to the home of a potential client who's asked for a top-to-bottom clean starting at eleven. He's requested you, specifically, and if he's satisfied after this trial run, he plans to contract with us on a permanent basis."

"But…I don't understand. Why would someone request me in particular? Wouldn't you feel better sending someone with more experience?"

He thrummed the eraser end of his pencil on the desk and studied her over the rim of his spectacles. "More experience, Sofia? You're one of my best workers, and I've received more than several client commendations of your meticulous attention to detail. News gets around, I guess."

"I'm humbled by that, of course." She felt herself blush. "May I ask whose house I've been requested to clean?"

He glanced down at the printed schedule. "Dr. Elijah Trent."

She jerked her head back. "He's hired me to clean his house?"

"Appears so. Now, remember our motto: 'It Isn't Clean Until Our Client Says So.' I expect you to keep that in mind. "

Why, that—that Mr. So-and-so! Sofie suppressed a groan of indignation. *He doesn't want a wife; he wants a housekeeper, and a hired one, at that!* She could have requested that someone else be sent in her place, but then, she rather looked forward to giving Eli what for.

※

Eli was about as nervous as a nun in a bar while waiting for Mr. Jackson to drop Sofie off at his house. He hoped the man had done a convincing job with his part of the scheme. A final scan of the area seemed to indicate that everything was in place. Not only that, he'd swept the floor for the first time since taking over the house, shaken the rugs, dusted all the surfaces, straightened pillows, and cleaned every last dish—mostly crumb-covered plates and a bunch of knives slathered with leftover Peter Pan, as he'd basically been subsisting on peanut butter sandwiches. He had even less of a knack for household chores than for cooking. Even so, he'd managed to make the house nearly glisten, in his humble estimation.

For at least the twentieth time, he stuck his hand inside his pocket, breathing a sigh of relief when his fingers touched the gold ring he'd purchased at the jeweler last week. Good grief! Was he afraid the ring would jump out and roll away? He shook his head and ran a hand through his hair, ashamed at how shaggy it had grown. He needed to ask Mrs. Downing to schedule him an appointment at the barbershop. He didn't know what he'd do without that woman. When Eli had decided to close the office today, she had managed to appease all of the disgruntled clients by rescheduling their appointments for later that same week. She'd even been a sounding board for his strategy, and she'd just about swooned when he'd relayed the details. After being assured that his plan was "so very romantic," he'd asked her to pray for him as it played out.

Even now, she sat in the office down the hall, filing paperwork. Hopefully, she wouldn't try to spy on his proposal. He didn't want an audience, just in case it was a flop.

A car door slammed, which made his pulse quicken by a few beats. He raced to the window, pulled back the curtain, and caught sight of Sofie coming up the sidewalk, a purpose in her stride and a steely expression on her face that said she meant business.

Uh-oh was all that came to mind.

᙮᷒

Sofie raised her hand to the buzzer at the same time the door swung open, unexpectedly. One look at Eli, and all of the steam she'd built up inside, with the intention of spewing it forth when she next saw him, fizzled away to a fine mist. My, oh my, but he made for a pleasant sight in that dress shirt, the sleeves rolled up to his elbows, and those baggy trousers.

But what was she thinking? He'd hired her to clean his house, and that was just what she intended to do—with minimal conversation.

She turned around and waved at Mr. Jackson, giving him the okay to leave, and then, without so much as a greeting, she whisked past Eli into the foyer. "Where shall I start?"

"What?" He tilted his head. What had he expected, a kiss hello?

"I asked where I should start. The kitchen? The living room? Upstairs? Downstairs? I'm at your service, Dr. Trent."

"Dr. Trent?" His mouth twitched in one corner.

He had better not start laughing, or she would hightail it back to the office. She put her hands on her hips, awaiting his list of instructions.

"Why don't I give you a brief tour. Have you been in this house before?"

"Only in the office, but a formal tour won't be necessary. If you'll just tell me where to begin, I'll start there and make my way through, ending up in the same spot. Did you want a thorough clean, from top to bottom, or more of a surface clean? The latter should take only two hours or so, whereas a more thorough clean will require four to five, I'd guess."

He cast her a devilish grin. "Hmm. I'll go for the one that takes the most."

She took several deep breaths and engaged him in a stare down, silently daring him to lower his gaze first. When he didn't, she gave a surrendering huff. "You'll need to show me where you keep your cleaning supplies."

"Gladly. Follow me, madam."

Madam? If she was going to follow him, she may as well give him a good kick in the pants while she was at it. They entered the kitchen, the sight of which nearly stole her breath, not for the hours it would take to clean it, but for its sheer beauty and size. "Blessed stars above!" she exclaimed. Butter-yellow walls, miles of butcher-block countertop, a big bright window over the deep sink that looked out onto the lovely backyard, a white steel GE refrigerator with freezer, and an enormous cookstove were just a few of the features that caught her eye and nearly made her drool with envy. Oh, the things she could make in this kitchen—Mama's lasagna, her own yummy sweet potato casserole, Will Taylor's chicken enchiladas...oh, and she mustn't forget her grandmother's creamy wedding potatoes. Prepared in a kitchen such as this, they'd be sure to taste even better. "Gracious me! This kitchen is more than half the size of my whole house, yet it's arranged so efficiently."

"Is it too much for you?"

"What? No, of course not. I've cleaned bigger kitchens...I think." She noticed a crystal vase of red roses set in the center of the spotless counter. "But it hardly seems like it needs a cleaning. And everything is in its place."

"You really think so?" There was a teasing note to his voice.

"Eli!" She put her hands on her hips. "Do you want me to clean for you or not?"

He chuckled softly. "Come on, let me show you the rest of the house." He ushered her out with a hand at her back, and she couldn't help suspecting he had something up his sleeve.

❦

He led her through the entire house, showing her every bedroom and bathroom; the front parlor to the right of the main entrance; the expansive living room and elegant dining room, each with a fireplace set in floor-to-ceiling brick; the library, with shelves upon shelves of his grandfather's medical journals, which Eli had inherited along with the deed to the house;

and the laundry area, just off of the kitchen, with its window overlooking the garden.

Sofie made all kinds of exclamatory noises in every doorway, remarking on the fine choices in color schemes, the pretty patterns of wallpaper, the elegant furnishings, and the tall-as-treetops ceilings. And Eli loved every minute.

"Who's been tending that vegetable garden?" she asked, bending down for a better view.

"I told the neighbor to have a go at it, asking only that he share some of the harvest with me."

She straightened and gazed up at him. "That's very generous of you."

He shrugged. "I'm no gardener. I'd just as soon give that chore to someone else, along with most of the bounty."

She peered out the window again, gazing at the plants with such longing, as if those six-foot cornstalks were calling to her, that he wanted to heave all his plans out the door and get down on one knee right then. But he knew he'd regret it later if he didn't practice patience and see his plans through to the end.

After a few more seconds of garden-gazing, she straightened. With the little house tour over, only one thing remained. He stepped closer and wrapped one of her curls around his index finger. "So, what do you think? Could you give this house a thorough cleaning?"

"Well, of course. That's why I'm here."

"How about cleaning this house for the next...oh, I don't know...forty years?"

"What?" She frowned. "I hardly think I can make that sort of commitment. Forty days, maybe, but forty years?"

She wore a look of perplexity, and he found he enjoyed stringing out the mystery. "Yes, forty years. That sounds about right." His hands moved to her shoulders and began a gentle massage. "What do you think?"

He felt her muscles tense. "I think you should talk to Mr. Jackson. This type of arrangement most certainly falls under the jurisdiction of my employer."

He laughed. "You think I should ask Mr. Jackson's permission for your hand?"

"What?" She pushed his hands off her shoulders, but when she tried to exit the kitchen, he playfully blocked her path. "I don't know what to think of you, Dr. Trent. Are you playing games with me?"

"Not at all, Miss Rogers. I'm making a simple proposition. I think you know what it is."

She blinked twice. "Well, I guess I'm denser than you thought. You'd better say it straight."

"Alright, you dense damsel, you." He cupped the back of her head with his hand. "You are a precious woman, and do you know what else?"

She gave a quick shake of her head.

"I love you. There! You couldn't possibly have misunderstood that."

She stepped back and tilted her face upward. "Oh, my! What did you just say?"

He tossed back his head and laughed, adoring everything about her, especially her innocence, her spunk, her resilience, and her tender spirit.

When he recovered and looked at Sofie, she blinked her dark lashes again.

He took her by the hand and ushered her toward the door. "Come on, sweetheart."

"What? Where are we going?"

"You'll see."

"But I have to go clean your house. I'm still on the clock, remember?"

"No, you aren't. You have the rest of the day off. I worked it out with Mr. Jackson."

"You did? So, I was never supposed to clean your house?"

He laughed again and then led her—more like dragged her—out of the house to the car. He opened the passenger door for her.

"What's going on? Are you taking me to Margie's?"

"Nope." He closed the door, then jogged around to the driver's side and slid in.

"What are—?"

This time, he put two fingers to her mouth to shush her. "You ask far too many questions, Sofia Mae Rogers. Just sit back, relax, and enjoy yourself."

Chapter Thirty-three

*For of him, and through him, and to him, are
all things: to whom be glory for ever. Amen.*
—Romans 11:36

Did he actually expect her to sit back and relax?
Her teeth chattered and her body shivered with excitement, even though the air sizzled with oven-like
heat.

Several minutes later, Eli maneuvered the car
into a parking space of his own making on a grassy
patch near the river. She couldn't stop replaying in her
mind those three words she'd heard him say—or had
thought she'd heard him say: *"I love you."* Surely, she
had dreamt it. *Oh, Eli, I love you, too, but I haven't the
wherewithal to speak those words aloud, for fear I'll
break this magical moment and wake up from the most
delightful dream I've ever had.*

He cut the engine and gazed ahead, his arms
resting on the steering wheel. "What do you think of
the scenery?"

Before them stretched the beautiful Wabash.
"Splendid."

"I packed us a picnic lunch. Let's go enjoy it on
the riverbank."

"You did? My, you're full of surprises today."

With a slanted smile, he reached over and tapped her nose with a fingertip, sending a tremor through her. "And to think I'm not even done yet," he whispered huskily.

They spread a red and white checkered tablecloth on a plot of gently sloping ground so that, when they reclined, they would still have a nice view of the river, dancing along in slow motion, barely making a ripple as she flowed. They feasted on chicken sandwiches and a tasty cherry salad, both recipes from his mother, and then, for dessert, Eli produced a blueberry coffee cake. He'd thought of everything, and she was quite impressed. She couldn't help but quiver with excitement at the thought of yet another surprise, though she dared not venture a guess as to what it entailed. "I had no idea you knew how to cook," Sofie exclaimed, dabbing her mouth with a napkin.

"I don't." Eli chuckled. "You have no idea how nervous I was. The entire experience was further proof that kitchen chores are best left to others. And I might as well confess that, while I managed the salad and sandwiches, Mrs. Downing made the coffee cake."

"Mrs. Downing? So, does she know...? I mean, did you tell her you were kidnapping me for the day?"

"Indeed I did. It was the only way I could get her to chip in on the meal."

She giggled. "You're a cunning, conniving man, Dr. Trent."

"I'll take that as a compliment, Miss Rogers."

When they'd finished their meal, they returned the plates, silverware, and other items to the wicker picnic basket. Eli then closed the lid, picked it up by its handles, and moved it on the other side, so that no obstacles stood between them.

Sofie's heart thudded so hard in her chest, her ears could hear the reverberation. She folded her hands in her lap and tried to find something in the distance to set her eyes on, so as to forget the acute awareness of his gaze on her.

"I seem to recall a time we sat in my car in a drenching rain down by the river, and I inquired if you'd ever had a boyfriend. You told me no, except for that Eddie Caldwell fellow—the little creep—and also said you had no time for men. Do you remember that?"

"Yes, I remember. It was the Fourth of July, the day we were supposed to have a picnic lunch and watch the fireworks. The rain didn't let up for—"

"I'm not recalling the rain part as much as the part about the men...and your utter lack of use for them."

"Oh." She ventured a glance at him and was almost entranced by those vivid blue eyes.

"I know you've had some serious setbacks, Sofie. You've handled more pain in twenty-one short years than most people are dealt in a lifetime. And I would imagine it's hard, trusting a man...after what Owen did to you. I just hope you know that I'm a man you can trust."

Trust. Sofie had to admit, it didn't come easily to her. Over time, though, the Lord had taught her to place all her trust in Him, which somehow freed her to trust others, and to trust Him when those she trusted let her down. "I do trust you, Eli. You're a wonderful man—generous, kind, and God-fearing. I never thought I would meet someone like you."

"Did you believe me when I told you I loved you?"

Her heart tripped over itself. "You mean, that wasn't a dream?"

"No, sweetheart. It wasn't a dream." He slid closer, wrapped an arm around her shoulder, and lowered his head, dropping several feathery kisses on her neck.

"But, Eli"—against her desire, she sidled away— "I come from a completely different world. Your family is so big, and beautiful, and perfect. My family is just...well, me, Andy, and now, Gracie Joy. What on earth would your parents think if they found out you'd fallen for someone of my lowly estate?"

"They would cheer me on, and they would love you even more for all you've endured and for how you've persevered through your trials. I can't wait for them to meet you. How does next month sound?"

"Next month?"

"They'll love you right into the fold."

"Into the fold?"

"Yes, into the family. I want you *in* it, Sofie, not looking at it from a distance. Do you understand what I'm saying?" He reached into his pocket and pulled out a tiny black box.

A shiver shot up her spine. She dared not envision what might be inside, but it was a pretty sure guess. Could it be? Was this truly happening to her?

"It wasn't long after I met you that I felt that gentle nudge from God again. And do you know what His nudge told me to do?"

She shook her head as tears welled up in her eyes, blurring her vision.

"It said, 'Marry her.' It said, 'She is the one.' And, 'Love takes time.' You see, I got the 'Marry her' part right. 'She is the one' was a no-brainer. But the 'Love takes time' thing? That one threw me off balance. I thought I had His timing figured out, but I was wrong. The first time I asked you to marry me didn't really

count. I was in such a hurry to make you mine, convinced I was the solution to all your problems, that I
came darned near to demanding it. That wasn't the
way God ordained it to be. And I had to learn to back
off and give our relationship a chance to mature from
the ground up, starting with a foundation of friendship. I sent for you today because I wanted you to
walk through my house and see if you could see yourself living there, calling it home. I didn't send for you
so you could clean it. I spiffed it up myself, as best I
could. Granted, I know you could do a much better job
without even trying."

He lifted the lid off the box and revealed something brilliant and glimmery. In slow, purposeful
moves, he released it from its little slot, tossed the box
aside, and clutched a sparkling diamond ring protectively between his thumb and index finger.

Sofie tried to speak, but her throat was clogged
with thick emotion.

He swiveled his body around and, in one fluid
move, was up on one knee.

She gasped for air, but her lungs took in only a
thin slice, just enough to take a shallow breath. She
seized the collar of her dress with a closed fist. "Oh,
Eli. Is that...? Are you...?"

"Sofia Mae Rogers, will you marry me and be my
wife? Will you live in that big old house with me and
fill it up with more babies?"

She kept clutching her chest as she found her
voice. "All this time, I thought you didn't want me. I
thought you'd asked me to marry you only out of a
sense of compassion, even pity. I thought maybe you
just had this strong need to protect us, and then I even

thought...well, I thought you wanted a housekeeper. Goodness gracious, Eli, I thought—"

"Sofie?"

"What?"

He grinned. "This is the part where you're supposed to stop talking. After saying yes, that is."

Quite by surprise, a nervous giggle erupted out of her. "Oh! Then, my answer is yes, Eli—unequivocally, indisputably, most assuredly, yes!" She threw herself into his arms, knocking him off his bent knee and causing them both to roll down the incline, like two smitten children rollicking on the playground.

When they finally came to a stop, just a few feet from the river's edge, they stayed like that for all of five heartbeats, nose touching nose, breaths intermingling, and then he swiftly rolled her to the side and kissed her with a thoroughness she'd never known, his kisses so sweet, yet tinged with sensuality, as a sort of promise—a promise that would not see its fulfillment until they'd spoken their vows. The thought must have struck Eli at the same time, for he ended the kiss abruptly and sat up, then helped her to a seated position.

He gazed at her with a loving intensity, until a look of another kind altogether overtook him, and she recognized it instantly as panic.

"What is it? What's wrong?"

"Two things," he said as he scanned the surroundings, his eyes darting to and fro. "One, you haven't told me you loved me, and, two—where is the ring?"

Together, they climbed the incline on all fours, slowly and deliberately, their eyes trained on the ground, examining every inch of soil, separating blades of grass, looking far, looking near, and casting the occasional fearful glance at the glistening waters below.

"I love you, Eli. Lord, help us find the ring."

"I love you, too, Sofie. Yes, Lord, lead us straight to it."

"I can't believe I lost the ring," Sofie moaned.

"You didn't lose it, honey."

"I did. I lunged at you like a female lion."

"And I enjoyed every second of it. Keep looking."

"I also can't believe I waited so long to tell you I love you," Sofie sighed. "I've loved you for...actually, I don't know when I first knew. It may have been as early as when I first saw you, at Murphy's Market."

"That's when it started for me," Eli said. "I took one look in those chocolate eyes, and I just knew."

"And when I saw yours, blue like the ocean, I nearly melted into a pile of mush."

There was no gazing into one another's eyes right now, of course.

"How could you have known you loved me at Murphy's Market?" Sofie wanted to know. She lifted a leaf—no ring. She checked under the tablecloth— no ring. Her dress kept bunching under her knees, making crawling difficult, but she would not give up. "You could see I was pregnant, but how did you know I wasn't a married woman?"

"I asked Mr. Murphy about you when I went up to the counter."

"You didn't."

"Ah-ha!"

She whirled at his elated exclamation and then laughed in relief. "Where did you find it?"

"You'll never guess," he said, holding it out to her. "Come here and I'll show you." A teasing twinkle in his eyes beckoned her to him. When she reached him, he pulled at the front pocket on his shirt.

She gasped. "How did it get in there?"

"It must have bounced inside by some miracle during our downward tumble. I suppose stranger things have happened."

She held out her left hand and lifted her chin. "I'm ready."

He laughed, then quieted. "I'm ready, too," he said in that husky tone. He slid the ring on her finger, giving it a gentle push to get it past the knuckle. "The jeweler said he'll fix it to your liking if the fit isn't quite right."

Their eyes met, hers damp, his glistening. "It's perfect," she said. "You're perfect. And, by the way, I would love to fill your house with more babies—as many as the Lord wills."

"And if He doesn't will it right away, then we'll have lots of fun trying."

She giggled and drew back to give him a playful slap.

He blocked her hand. "And something else. It isn't my house; it's *our* house."

She stood on tiptoe to kiss his tiny chin dimple. "I'll try to remember that."

He drew in a deep, wobbly breath, then lowered his face to shower her with more kisses, on her forehead, around her temples, and along her jaw, landing at last on her mouth, where he spent a good deal of time exercising his rights. Some time later, they came up for air. "I love you, Sofie."

"I love you, too, Eli."

He tweaked her nose. "No more secrets, you hear? We're done with them."

"None. You have my word."

Some ducks swooped down and camped beside them, no doubt checking for any morsels of food that may have scattered around that covered basket. Overhead, a few clouds passed in front of the sun, lending a bit of relief from the unrelenting heat.

Eli reached down for the tablecloth, folded it, and placed it inside the basket, then removed an uneaten chicken sandwich. He and Sofie took turns breaking off pieces and tossing them on the ground for the ducks to grapple over.

When every last crumb had been consumed, he brushed off his hands and then extended one to Sofie. "Ready, Mrs. Trent?" He picked up the basket with his other hand.

"Mrs. Trent?"

"I'm just practicing."

"Sofie Trent...it does have a nice ring to it, doesn't it?" She held out her left hand for another look at the dazzling diamond. Later, she would take an even closer look.

They clasped hands, and with the lazy Wabash River to their backs, they sauntered to the car, hearts ablaze with hope and promise.

My dear readers,

I can't tell you how much I've enjoyed writing this three-book series, set in lovely Wabash, Indiana. I always grow a little nostalgic when winding down a series because my characters have a way of wrapping themselves around my heart, and reaching the end of a beloved series is almost like saying good-bye to family.

Speaking of family, I've asked my cherished mother-in-law, sisters-in-law, nieces, and two darling daughters to contribute tried-and-true recipes, the ones that glean the most praise from others and have become family favorites at gatherings. (A few of these recipes even had a cameo role in *Sofia's Secret*.)

Family is everything, and food has a wonderful way of bringing people together. What better way to celebrate life and love than to sit around a dinner table with loved ones, enjoying lively conversation and partaking of delicious fare?

May God grant His richest blessings on you and yours.

—*Shar*

Shar's Family Favorites

Breakfast and Brunch

❧

Overnight French Toast Bake

Contributed by Wendy Baker Hodgin (Shar's niece)

Ingredients:

¼ cup (½ stick) butter, melted
¾ cup packed light brown sugar
1 loaf French bread, cut into slices 1½ inches thick
8 eggs, beaten slightly
1 cup whole milk
1 tablespoon vanilla extract
1 teaspoon ground cinnamon
¼ teaspoon ground ginger
½ cup pecans, chopped
1/8 teaspoon salt
*Optional: maple syrup and/or powdered sugar for topping

Directions:

In a small bowl, combine brown sugar and melted butter; spread over the bottom of a 9×13 baking dish.

Arrange slices of bread in the baking dish, overlapping if necessary.

In another bowl, combine milk, eggs, vanilla, salt, cinnamon, and ginger; pour evenly over bread slices.

Sprinkle with chopped pecans, cover with plastic wrap, and refrigerate at least 4 hours or overnight.

Remove casserole from refrigerator and remove plastic wrap at least 10 minutes prior to baking; allow to come to room temperature.

Preheat oven to 350° F. Bake for 30 to 35 minutes. If casserole begins browning too quickly, cover loosely with aluminum foil for the final 10 minutes. Remove from oven and allow to cool slightly before serving. Dust with powdered sugar, if desired, and serve with maple syrup.

❧

Blueberry Coffee Cake

Contributed by Charity MacLaren Baker
(Shar's sister-in-law)

Ingredients:

For the cake:
3 cups all-purpose flour
1 teaspoon baking powder
1 teaspoon baking soda
1 cup granulated sugar
1 cup (2 sticks) butter or margarine, cold
2 eggs
1 cup buttermilk (for a quick substitution, add 1 tablespoon white vinegar to 1 cup regular milk)
1 teaspoon vanilla extract
1 can blueberry pie filling

For the topping:
¼ cup all-purpose flour
3 tablespoons butter or margarine
¼ cup granulated sugar

Directions:

Preheat oven to 375° F. In a large bowl, sift together flour, baking powder, baking soda, and sugar. Cut in butter or margarine as you would for pie dough. In a separate bowl, beat together eggs, buttermilk, and vanilla; add to flour mixture, blending well. Spread half the batter in a greased 9×13 baking pan. Spoon pie filling evenly over batter. Spread the remaining batter over the blueberry pie filling and sprinkle with topping. Bake for 40 minutes or until lightly browned.

Jumbo Banana Muffins

Contributed by Jamie Baker (Shar's niece)
Makes 16 large muffins or 24 small to medium muffins.

Ingredients:

¾ cup granulated sugar
½ cup packed brown sugar
½ cup (1 stick) butter, softened
2 eggs
1½ teaspoons vanilla extract
½ cup milk
3 ripe bananas, mashed
1 teaspoon baking soda
1½ teaspoons salt
1½ cups all-purpose flour
4½ cups oats
1 cup chopped walnuts
1 cup chocolate chips (optional)
½ cup butterscotch chips (optional)

Directions:

Preheat oven to 400° F.

Cream sugars with butter. Add eggs, vanilla, and milk. Mix well. Combine soda with bananas and add to creamed mixture. Stir in salt, flour, and oatmeal. Mix well. Sprinkle in both types of chips and nuts. Fill greased muffin tins or muffin liners with batter to the top edge. Bake for 15 to 20 minutes.

꽃

Taco Casserole Dip

Contributed by Jamie Baker (Shar's niece)

Ingredients:

2 pounds ground beef
2 envelopes "mild" taco seasoning
1 can (25 ounces) refried beans
2 cups water
2 cups (8 ounces) shredded Monterey Jack cheese
2 cups (8 ounces) shredded cheddar cheese
Tortilla chips, for serving

Directions:

In a skillet, brown beef; drain grease. Mix in taco seasoning packets and allow mixture to sit for a few minutes.

Mix in refried beans and add water; bring to boil, stirring well, then reduce heat to low and simmer 30 minutes.

Meanwhile, preheat oven to 350° F.

Layer meat mixture and cheese in a 9×13 pan and bake for 30 minutes.

Serve with chips.

Vegetable Cheese Soup

Contributed by Charity MacLaren Baker
(Shar's sister-in-law)

Ingredients:

4 cups (32 ounces) chicken broth
2 cans cream of chicken soup
3 carrots, sliced
3 potatoes, cubed
3 stalks celery, thinly sliced
1 onion, chopped
1 package (16 ounces) California blend frozen vegetables
(broccoli, cauliflower, and zucchini)
2 cups milk
1 pound (16 ounces) Velveeta cheese product, cubed

Directions:

In a saucepan over medium-low heat, cook broth, carrots, potatoes, celery, and onion until tender. Add cream of chicken soup and frozen vegetables; reduce heat to low and simmer until the frozen vegetables thaw. Add milk and cheese; continue cooking, stirring occasionally, until cheese has melted completely.

※

Hot Chicken Salad Sandwiches

Contributed by Charity MacLaren Baker
(Shar's sister-in-law)
Serves 6 to 8.

Ingredients:

2 cups diced cooked chicken (about 2 breasts' worth)
2 cups finely diced celery
½ cup chopped cashews
½ teaspoon salt
1 small onion, finely diced
2 tablespoons lemon juice
1 cup salad dressing (mayonnaise or Miracle Whip)
1 cup crushed potato chips
½ cup shredded cheddar cheese
crescent rolls

Directions:

Preheat oven to 400° F.

In a large bowl, combine cooked chicken, celery, cashews, salt, onion, lemon juice, and salad dressing; toss to combine. Place in greased casserole dish; sprinkle with crushed potato chips and shredded cheese. Bake for 20 to 30 minutes, till heated through. Spread on crescent rolls and serve.

Chicken Enchiladas

Contributed by Krista MacLaren Tisdel
(Shar's daughter)
Serves 10.

Ingredients:

10 flour tortillas (burrito size)
2 cups shredded or cubed cooked chicken
1 large jar favorite salsa
1 jar enchilada sauce
2 cups Mexican blend shredded cheese
Optional: Black beans, fresh corn, cooked rice

Directions:

Preheat oven to 375° F.

In a large bowl, mix cooked chicken, 1 cup shredded cheese, 2/3 jar salsa, and any other optional desired ingredients.

Spread a thin layer of salsa in a 9×13 baking dish. Fill each tortilla with a spoonful of the chicken mixture; roll and place in the dish. Drizzle tortillas evenly with enchilada sauce, then sprinkle remaining cheese on top. Bake for 15 to 20 minutes, until cheese melts and edges are slightly crispy. *Tip: For easy reheating, omit bottom layer of salsa and simply spray with nonstick cooking spray.

Lazy Overnight Lasagna

Contributed by Kendra MacLaren Brady
(Shar's daughter)
Serves 12.

Ingredients:

1 pound ground beef
1 jar (32 ounces) spaghetti sauce
1 cup water
2 cups ricotta cheese
2 tablespoons chopped fresh chives
½ teaspoon dried oregano leaves
1 egg
8 ounces lasagna noodles (uncooked)
1 pound (16 ounces) mozzarella cheese, shredded
2 tablespoons grated Parmesan cheese

Directions:

Brown beef in large skillet and drain well. Add spaghetti sauce and water and blend; simmer over low heat for 5 minutes. In medium bowl, combine ricotta, chives, oregano, and egg. Mix well. In the bottom of a 9×13 baking dish or lasagna pan, spread 1½ cups meat sauce. Top with half of the noodles, half of the ricotta cheese mixture, and half of the mozzarella cheese. Repeat with remaining noodles, ricotta cheese mixture, and mozzarella cheese. Top with remaining meat sauce. Sprinkle with Parmesan cheese. Cover and refrigerate overnight.

When ready to bake, remove dish from refrigerator and allow to sit at room temperature while oven preheats to 350° F. Bake, uncovered, 50 to 60 minutes, or until noodles are tender and casserole is bubbly. Cover and let stand for 15 minutes prior to serving.

❧

Wedding Potatoes

Contributed by Chrystal MacLaren
(Shar's mother-in-law)

Ingredients:

For the potatoes:
2 pounds frozen hash browns (diced, not shredded)
1 can (10¾ ounces) cream of chicken soup
1 pint (16 ounces) sour cream
1 cup diced onion
2 cups (8 ounces) shredded cheddar cheese
1/4 teaspoon salt
For the topping:
¼ cup (½ stick) butter, melted
3 to 4 cups cornflake cereal, crushed

Directions:

Preheat oven to 350° F. Mix all ingredients together in a large bowl; pour into a 9×13 baking pan. For the topping, mix enough cereal to absorb all of the melted butter as a light coating. Layer the cereal topping evenly over the potatoes. Bake, uncovered, for 60 to 90 minutes.

Nana's Sweet Potato Casserole

Contributed by Shelly Stokes (Shar's "adopted" niece)

Ingredients:

4 to 6 medium sweet potatoes, peeled, boiled, and mashed, to yield approximately 3 cups
½ cup granulated sugar
1/3 cup (5 tablespoons) butter
½ cup milk
1 teaspoon vanilla extract
2 eggs

Topping:

1 cup brown sugar (If using Splenda brown sugar, use ½ cup)
1 cup all-purpose flour
½ cup (1 stick) butter, softened
½ cup pecans, chopped

Directions:

Preheat oven to 350° F. To pureed potatoes, add sugar, butter, and milk; blend until you reach the consistency of mashed potatoes (this may require more/less milk or butter, depending on the size of the potatoes).

Beat the eggs, then add a bit of the potatoes to the eggs to warm them up before adding them to the entire mixture. Beat until smooth.

Place mixture in a square baking pan or casserole dish.

Place butter in a separate bowl; cut in the brown sugar and flour until no visible chunks of butter remain. Sprinkle liberally over sweet potatoes; top with pecans.

Bake 30 to 35 minutes, or until heated through.

Cherry Salad

*Contributed by Lillian MacLaren Winans
(Shar's sister-in-law)*

Ingredients:

2 cans cherry pie filling
1 can Eagle Brand sweetened condensed milk
1 can pineapple chunks, drained
1 package miniature marshmallows
Chopped walnuts, to taste
½ carton (4 ounces) Cool Whip (or more, to taste)

Directions:

Blend all ingredients and store in refrigerator until ready to serve.

Strawberry Pretzel Dessert

Contributed by Mary MacLaren (Shar's sister-in-law)

Ingredients:

2 cups crushed pretzels
¾ cup (1½ sticks) butter, melted
4 tablespoons granulated sugar
8 ounces cream cheese, softened
1 carton (8 ounces) Cool Whip, softened
¾ cup granulated sugar
1 large box strawberry Jell-O
2 cups boiling water
2 packages (10 ounces each) frozen strawberries, thawed

Directions:

Preheat oven to 400° F.

In a bowl, mix pretzels, butter, and sugar; press into the bottom of a 9×13 baking pan. Bake 6 to 10 minutes, until golden brown.

Set aside and allow to cool completely.

In another bowl, beat cream cheese, Cool Whip, and sugar until creamy; spread mixture evenly over cooled crust.

Dissolve Jell-O powder in 2 cups boiling water. Stir in thawed strawberries and then allow to stand until slightly thickened. (10 to 15 minutes in the freezer speeds up this process.) Spread Jell-O and strawberry mixture evenly over the Cool Whip layer.

Refrigerate at least 4 hours before slicing into squares to serve.

No-Bake Cheesecake

Contributed by Gayle MacLaren Casteel
(Shar's sister-in-law)

Ingredients:

1 ready-made graham cracker crust
8 ounces cream cheese, softened
½ cup granulated sugar
1 carton (8 ounces) Cool Whip, thawed slightly
Canned fruit topping (optional)

Directions:

In a bowl, blend cream cheese and sugar together until smooth. Fold in Cool Whip until smooth. Pour mixture into ready-made crust; top with fruit topping, if desired. Chill at least two hours prior to serving.

Ice Cream Cake

Contributed by Chrystal MacLaren
(Shar's mother-in-law)

Ingredients:

2 cups crushed graham crackers
1/3 cup granulated sugar
¼ cup (½ stick) butter, melted
2 cups 2% milk
3 small boxes of instant pudding (chocolate or vanilla)
½ gallon ice cream (chocolate or vanilla), softened
Cool Whip

Directions:

In a bowl, mix graham cracker crumbs, sugar, and melted butter; press into the bottom of a 9×13 cake pan and set aside. In another bowl, blend milk, pudding mixture, and ice cream; pour mixture over graham cracker crust and top with Cool Whip. Store in refrigerator.

About the Author

Born and raised in west Michigan, Sharlene attended Spring Arbor University. Upon graduating with an education degree in 1971, she taught second grade for two years, then accepted an invitation to travel internationally for a year with a singing ensemble. In 1975, she married her childhood sweetheart. Together they raised two lovely, wonderful daughters, both of whom are now happily married and enjoying their own families. Retired in 2003 after thirty-one years of teaching, "Shar" loves to read, sing, travel, and spend time with her family—in particular, her wonderful, adorable grandchildren!

A Christian for forty-five-plus years and a lover of the English language, Shar has always enjoyed dabbling in writing—poetry, fiction, various essays, and freelancing for periodicals and newspapers. Her favorite genre, however, has always been romance. She remembers well writing short stories in high school and watching them circulate from girl to girl during government class. "Psst," someone would whisper from two rows over, when the teacher had his back to the class, "pass me the next page."

In recent years, Shar felt God's call upon her heart to take her writing pleasures a step further and in 2006 signed a contract for her first faith-based novel, launching her writing career with the contemporary romance *Through Every Storm*. With a dozen of her books now gracing store shelves nationwide, she daily gives God all the praise and glory for her accomplishments.

Through Every Storm was Shar's first novel to be published by Whitaker House, and in 2007, the American Christian Fiction Writers (ACFW) named it a finalist for Book of the Year. The acclaimed Little Hickman Creek series consists of *Loving Liza Jane* (Road to Romance Reviewer's Choice Award); *Sarah, My Beloved* (third place, Inspirational Readers' Choice Award 2008); and *Courting Emma* (third place, Inspirational Reader's Choice Award 2009). Shar's last series, the popular Daughters of Jacob Kane, comprises *Hannah Grace* (second place, Inspirational Reader's Choice Award 2010), *Maggie Rose*, and *Abbie Ann* (third place, Inspirational Reader's Choice Award 2011). *Sofia's Secret* concludes her latest series, River of Hope, which also comprises *Livvie's Song* and *Ellie's Haven*.

Shar has done numerous countrywide book signings, television and radio appearances, and interviews. She loves to speak for women's organizations, libraries, church groups, women's retreats, and banquets. She is involved in Apples of Gold, a mentoring program for young wives and mothers, and is active in her church, as well as two weekly Bible studies. She and her husband, Cecil, live in Spring Lake, Michigan, with their beautiful white collie, Peyton, and their lazy cat, Mocha.